KINGDOM of NYTE

BOOK ONE *of the* **NYTE** SERIES

ALEXANDRIA CAINLOCKE

KINGDOM of NYTE

BOOK ONE *of the* **NYTE** SERIES

Cover Design: Enchanted Ink Publishing
Formatting: Enchanted Ink Publishing

ISBN: 978-1-7352704-1-8

Thank you for your support of the author's rights.

Printed in the United States of America

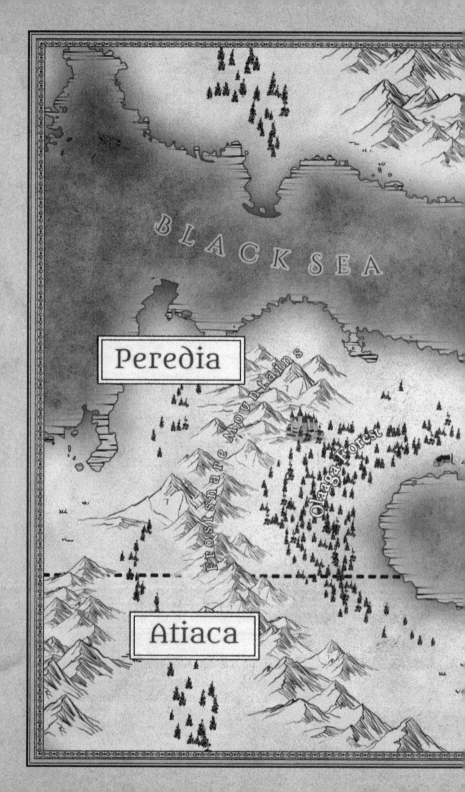

THEY CALLED THEMSELVES NYTES,
BUT SHE LIKED TO THINK THEY WERE NO
MORE THAN SELF-RIGHTEOUS MONSTERS.

PROLOGUE

Peredia, 300 years ago

"Are you sure about this, Anali?"

Evangeline's voice carried over the blare of screeching metal as another train vibrated the rock walls of their underground haven. She hated the desperation and uncertainty in her voice.

"No." Eyes the color of a churning sea, set into a face with equal vastness and depth, met hers. "Not at all."

Anali stepped back and studied her own work. The spot in front of her shimmered, the surrounding air electrified and heavy with unseen power. The portal was far from ready, but he left them no choice. They had to act now or live with the weight of a thousand souls on their shoulders.

Waves crashed and broke through Anali's strong facade. An unfamiliar wetness lingered beneath her dark orbs. "It's time."

Evangeline etched every curve of her face. Every ridge in the obsidian horns that curled around her blackened hair. She'll never forget the woman who pulled her from the brink of hope-lessness. Of death.

"Soon, this will all be a dream," she whispered, but it was a promise.

The facade crumbled, and Anali threw her arms around her. Evangeline returned the embrace with equal fervor. She would not cry. Not when this will have a happy ending.

She felt the presence of the portal like a looming burden. Swirling with a magnetic energy that drew her forward. She squeezed Anali tighter, reluctant to let go when small pebbles on the ground shook. Dust showered the tops of their heads, vibrations shaking the walls of the cavern. This time, it wasn't a train.

They shared a look of dismay.

"He's here! Go!" Anali shoved her toward the portal, a large boulder plummeting down on the spot where she'd been standing.

"Anali!" Evangeline tried to scream, but it was lost in the vacuum of space that engulfed her.

Pain gripped her very being and twisted it. She shouted, but no noise came out, an unbearable pressure crushing her from all sides. She couldn't breathe, she couldn't move. Her skin tightened and loosened. Her long hair grew backwards into her scalp. Bones cracked and mended. She was shrinking into nothing.

Her entire life played out before her. A pair of handsome green eyes was her last memory before it all shattered and dis-appeared. She fought to stay coherent, but it was a losing battle.

A single thought echoed inside the hollow cavern of her mind.

Who am I?

PART I

THE BEAST HIDING BENEATH
A HUMAN MASK

CHAPTER 1

⟶ EVANGELINE ⟵

Peredia, present time

Moonlight grazed through naked branches, spotlighting what she had been searching for all journey. The hole was narrow, the withered tree opening up its carcass, revealing the perfect hiding spot.

Evangeline smiled, even as blood seeped from her chapped lips, snow powdering the top of her fur coat down to her leather boots. *This is it. This will be the one.*

The branches shook in rhythm with her hand, which was more bone than skin, as she reached toward the heart of the tree. The grooves of the wood felt like ice shards through her thin gloves. Next time, she'll remember her fur-lined ones.

Her fingers teased the hollow opening—she prayed no insects crawled out—before delving inside. It should be big enough.

She licked away the blood on her lips and crouched to unstrap her leather bag. A double knot on the sack inside kept

the dried foods and stolen supplies sealed tight, along with a few other survival essentials. Evangeline tucked back a lock of blonde hair and shoved the sack through the gap.

No luck. It was larger than she thought.

She huffed, the wisp of hot breath overtaken by the wind. It was going to fit. She didn't have all night to explore this winter wasteland for another spot.

The wood gave way with a crack as she elbowed the bag into the crevice. It squeezed into the opening, albeit snug. She laughed. Almost giddy. Right before pressing her lips into a grim line. *This trip better be worth it.*

And she wasn't done yet.

Peering over her shoulder, she grimaced against the slap of wind. She felt as if she had walked a thousand steps, and still the massive walls of the kingdom loomed in the distance. Like a creeping stalker, watching her every move. Her nostrils flared and her body quivered. Whether from the cold or the idea of having to return to a home she despised, she couldn't tell. Maybe both.

Beyond the wide stretch of barren winter land she traveled lay her begrudging home and nightmare: the kingdom of Peredia. Humans, like herself, were slaves to the kingdom's citizens—creatures that out-populated humans, taking their spot in the higher ranks of this world. They called themselves Nytes, but self-righteous monsters served as a better title.

To distract herself from her own thoughts, she pulled out a dried stick of meat and shoved it down her throat in an unladylike manner—her friend, Lani, would've scolded her. If she planned to return to the kingdom before sunrise, she'd need the energy, considering she hadn't slept in roughly an entire day. She began this journey with a sense of purpose and apprehension, but now weariness settled in her bones. The snow appeared more like a soft bed and not her own coffin.

Up ahead, the burning lights of the kingdom guided her path, like floating candles flickering in the wind. Evangeline decided she was four-years-old when she first spotted those lights. After all, she didn't know her actual age. Traveling through the gates as a child, the elegant and perfectly cut kingdom, and the powerful Nytes that ruled it—the Aerians—had mesmerized her. It took being beaten, taunted, and forced to work dusk till dawn in her first few years inside its castle for the illusion to dissipate. To see the humanoid winged creatures for what they actually were. Cruel and prideful beings.

And now she was the adopted daughter of one of them. The king's advisor: Ryker Ardonis.

Evangeline lifted her bag, pulling the strap back over and around her waist. She gave the area a quick once-over. A thin cluster of trees encircled her, but she didn't see any hidden figures in the scarce terrain. Though Lord Ryker wouldn't send out guards in search of her this early, let alone notice her absence. They met twice a day. Once at dawn, then again at dusk. The moon still hung high in the sky, giving her just enough time.

She tried to concentrate on avoiding roots or hidden rocks, but her mind strayed back to her supplies hidden in the woods. Was hiding the pack there the right move? What if an animal got to it? Or the winds knocked the tree over and snow buried the gear?

As if summoned, another gust rolled in, and she winced. Stress curved into every crease of her skin. Those supplies were everything. Absolutely vital. It was going to be what kept her and Lani alive when she smuggled them out of the kingdom.

When the next burst of air came, it blew right through her layers. Sunk deep into her bones. Her teeth chattered, and her eyelashes drooped with a gloss of ice. She needed to get out of this blizzard.

A small nook, one she passed earlier in the night, lay ahead. The hillside slumped over like a frozen wave to give a decent-sized cave. Finding her way inside, she plopped down on the stone floor and curled into a fetal position. *A fire would be nice,* she thought. A pack of fire sticks lied somewhere in her bag. Her eyes slid to the cave opening, and she frowned. It could reveal her hiding spot, and she couldn't afford to stay here long.

Exhaustion tugged at her body, and the constant lullaby of air whirling outside her rocky haven coaxed her eyes closed. A comfortable darkness greeted her, and the faint murmurs of scattering rocks took a greater resonance. Sitting there alone, shivering, enclosed by rock, an undeniable sense of déjà vu grasped her. But it wasn't déjà vu, she realized. It was the uncanny parallel between her present plight and a reoccurring dream she'd had since she was a child.

Despite the similarities, the cave from her dream was deeper. She hadn't been able to hear the wind this close. And the darkness—she recalled being completely shrouded in darkness. It drenched her, seeped into her mind where a mix of confusion and anger lingered. She never figured out why. But every time, before she woke up, a bright orb of light blinded her, and the shadow of a hand covered her face. It had taken her awhile to realize that it wasn't a dream, and now, at eighteen, she knew it was her earliest memory of Peredia.

A cluster of pebbles tickled her scalp and clattered off her boots. The howling increased, the strength of it battering her exposed right side.

She groaned and crossed her arms to slump further down the cavern wall. Rumbling erupted in the distance. Vibrations climbed up her from the floor, but she kept her eyes glued shut and her knees folded into her body. As if she could block out the shaking of what she thought was a minor earthquake, or rock shifting overhead. An inconvenience. In fact, the entire cave could collapse, and she'd still be reluctant to move.

A blast of silence deafened her, and her eyes snapped open. No wind. No moving rocks. Nothing.

Energy poured back into her, and she lurched to her feet. She gawked at the opening of the cavern, and every sound rushed her. Like the world had temporarily stopped before stirring back to life in one discordant garble.

What the spitting blazes was that?

Creeping toward the entrance, Evangeline strained to see beyond the flurries whizzing by. At first, she didn't believe it. A whorl of blue light shot across the blanketed mountainside like a shooting star. The woods around it danced, drawing her attention to the rejoining fiery light that blazed, as if the moon had fallen out of the sky and landed on the hill across from her. She waited for it to move, but it grew brighter; erupting the field and bending the trees back. Another quake shuddered the land, prickling her skin.

She didn't know what she had just saw, never having witnessed anything like it. But whatever it was, it wasn't human. And she wasn't staying to find out.

Evangeline snatched up her bag, slinging it over her head, and bolted into the tundra. Sharp whips of wind battered her. Her feet plunged into the snow and she avoided where the explosion had erupted. She'd have to backtrack, taking a longer route around the mountainside versus straight through, but she'd willingly face the cold than whatever was out there. However, after trekking further, avoiding bent saplings and pockets of dark gravel, she realized she may not have a choice. She wasn't getting any warmer, and if she stayed out much longer,

she won't make it back. But if she sought another shelter, she'll run out of time.

She changed course, navigating through the trees.

The tips of her fingers felt numb, despite shoving them into her armpits beneath her coat. She scrunched her face against the furls of frozen rain pecking at her cheeks. It was a task to keep her eyes from closing altogether, and for a moment she caved and kept them closed, pressing into the whirling tundra.

Something snagged her foot, and she plummeted into the white bank and snow flooded her mouth. She started hacking, ice piercing her lungs with every inhale. Gods, blast it all, she *hated* this. The heroes in her books made adventures seem fun and exciting, but nothing about this was fun, or exciting, or life changing.

This trip better be worth it.

Evangeline wiggled her ankle, expecting to have caught it on a root, but it didn't budge. Did she step into a makeshift animal trap? Though, she wouldn't know what that looked like outside her novels. Her survival skills composed of keeping her head down and being as invisible as possible.

Leaning closer, she squinted. The snare on her ankle had four bumps attached to four slender digits. Her eyes traveled along the outline of an arm wrapped in dark leather, up a snow-covered torso, to a frozen nose and blue-tinged lips. Her breath tangled in her throat.

She was staring at a dead man.

A human. At least, she hoped he was, judging by his lack of wings, horns, or tails that would warn her she was dealing with a species of Nyte. Despite that, he still frightened her; reminded her of her own mortality. Though, she should be used to it. Death was a close companion to every human in the kingdom—including herself. Too many of her kind died every day within those walls. Even so, sitting next to a corpse wasn't how she wanted to spend her night.

Fumbling with the flap of her bag, her hands shook as she grasped the small fire sticks. She struck one a few times before it caught fire—only for the wind to snuff it out. She tried again, cupping the dull flame, bringing it closer to the man's face.

Blood stuck to him in dried patches, but she didn't know if it belonged to him or someone else. An animal didn't attack him. The injuries looked like burn marks. Strange. If it'd been bandits (who occasionally roamed these parts) the wounds would be gashes from a sword or a dagger, like the scars she enviously spied on Peredian soldiers and her childhood friend, Ceven. Did he get caught in the crossfire of that explosion? Who was he? A runaway slave from the kingdom? The thought softened her heart. Maybe he tried to escape his fate, like she planned for Lani and herself.

She brought the flame down his length and her toes curled in their boots. The man's hand gripped her ankle. If the Peredian winter hadn't beaten most of the emotion out of her, she might've screamed.

Dead bodies shouldn't be able to move.

Snuffing out the fire stick in the snow, her fingers grazed his neck, searching for a pulse. She blinked in surprise. There, a faint beat. He was alive. At least he wasn't a moving corpse.

Evangeline bit her lip and stared at the man. If she left him, he would die, but if she saved him, she won't make it back to the kingdom in time. If Lord Ryker finds her beyond the walls, punishment would be swift to come. And if he discovers how . . . It will ruin all her plans for them to escape the kingdom and Lani would be as good as dead. She had to leave him.

Peeling his fingers from her ankle, she pushed to her feet when his hand darted out and grabbed her again. She yelped.

His mouth moved, but she couldn't understand what he was saying. It sounded foreign.

She frowned and said matter-of-factly, "I can't help you." She tried to shake his grip, but it was surprisingly strong for an almost-dead man. When she did manage to pry her foot away, he clawed at her coat.

"Help . . . help me . . . please . . ."

Evangeline clenched her hands and cursed this man. She screamed at herself that she needed to leave him and leave him now. But his plea, how he tugged on her coat . . . he wanted to live.

Her eyes flicked to the kingdom's lights, then back at the man. If their positions were reversed, he wouldn't have cast a second glance her way.

As if he could read her thoughts, he let out another cracked whisper, "Please . . ."

She groaned. *It's okay, Eve. You can do this. Both of you can make it back in time.* So why did it feel like she was going to regret this?

Bending down, she tried to lift him, but his weight must have been triple her own—which wasn't hard to manage. She was as thin as the stripped branches swarming them.

"I can't do this by myself," she croaked.

The man grunted, and she wedged her shoulder beneath his armpit, hefting him up. It helped they were the same height.

It took several attempts, and Evangeline gritted her teeth in effort when he got to his feet. She held up most of his weight, but it worked.

"Yep. I'm definitely going to regret this," she muttered.

The man mumbled something in response, but Evangeline couldn't hear. Nor did she care, too focused on dragging him toward the walls of the kingdom in the distance.

CHAPTER 2

~ EVANGELINE ~

E vangeline was panting by the time she reached the kingdom's border. Large, thick stones layered on top of one another formed a wall that shrouded her in its shadow from the soft rays of the rising sun. The heart of the kingdom—the castle—was still a ways beyond the perimeter, perched atop the highest point of the small mountain the kingdom rested upon. Easy to access if you had Aerian wings. Not so much for everyone else.

But the castle wasn't Evangeline's goal. She was aiming for its slave quarters.

Knowing there was a routine set of guards that roamed the periphery, she bent her legs and dug her feet into the ground, trudging toward the far side of the wall that neighbored the Olaaga Forest.

Despite the name stemming from the mythical legend

of Olaaga—a six-legged creature that lived in the woods and haunted every child's nightmare—the forest didn't look scary. It was less dense than it had been in earlier years, most of its woods chopped down for lumber and Peredian trade. But the cluster of tall, thin trees helped shield her from other humans and Nytes that may be nearby.

"'If you don't behave, the Olaaga will come and snatch you away.'" Evangeline recited the words Lani used to chastise her with. "If only she'd snatch *you* away. My shoulder's killing me." She chuckled harder than she should have. The man didn't laugh.

When a large and uneven stone in the wall came into view, Evangeline leaned her heavy load against it with a sigh of relief. She wriggled her hands into the grooves of the rock, her limbs crying in protest, and maneuvered its weight. It exposed the small opening she had used last night. It'd taken her years to find such a structural weakness along the wall's borders and even longer to work up the courage to escape. She'd never had a strong enough reason to.

Until now.

Evangeline managed to smuggle a half-dead man through the kingdom, past the farms and homes on the outskirts, through the cluster of shops and narrow side streets, and across the plaza. If the sun was any higher, crossing the gray and red bricked plaza would've been impossible without being seen. In the afternoon it acted as a bustling market—and sometimes a stage for executions.

A vision of a noose around her neck hovered in her mind. Of Lord Ryker stabbing an accusatory finger at her, right before he kicked out her stool, and she sagged against the rope, strangling to death. She swallowed at the all-too-real image and refused to look at the wooden pole in the center of the empty marketplace.

The kingdom was quiet during this time of year, much to her favor. Most of its citizens kept to their homes, avoiding the storm of flurries and ice that hailed on their tiled roofs. Only a few Nytes and humans were out trudging through snow. Mostly humans forced to work for their Nyte masters, even in the dead of winter.

The slave quarters, where her friend lived, were located beyond the outskirts of the castle grounds. Her quarters were the farthest from the castle. The least desirable place to be, besides the west wing, a chunk of the castle that King Calais condemned years ago.

Normally, Evangeline hated the long distance between Lani's room and the castle. Hated the steep climb and countless steps it took to reach the towering palace at the top. But today, she sent a silent, thankful prayer. She didn't want anyone from the castle seeing her and reporting it back to Lord Ryker.

Up ahead, a small stone building lay waiting for them. A curtain of white flakes shrouded the winding, paved path up the cliff behind it. If it weren't for the oil lamps flickering along the stone frame and up the mountainside, Evangeline would've had trouble finding Lani's window—her personal front door to the slave quarters. It was better than the actual one leading into the communal bathing room, where everyone washed and relieved themselves in the shared, tight space.

She scanned the foundation of the building. *Found it.*

Peeking atop the layer of fresh snow, a tiny window sat. Lani's chamber was underground, helping to keep out the harsher elements.

Evangeline made sure the coast was clear before lugging her baggage to the window. While the quarters were well-guarded, it wasn't as heavily protected as the castle. Not to mention the significant decrease in patrols this time of year. Anyone hoping to escape in the dead of winter was asking for a death wish.

Evangeline was no exception.

She opened the window carefully, as not to startle her friend. The caress of warm air from the fire inside teased her cheeks and encouraged her to quickly squeeze through.

Landing on the concrete floor with ease, she turned and pulled the man's arm. His torso snagged on the frame, but after a few yanks, he slid through—too fast. His body hit the ground with a loud *thump*. She fumbled with the window, the glass squeaking as she closed it.

Evangeline sighed, her bones thawing, the warmth spreading from her fingers to her toes. She dragged the man by the fireplace as a rustle and raspy cough came from the cot in the corner of the small room.

"I'm sorry. I didn't mean to wake you."

Lani's silver-streaked hair was shoved into a messy bun, her eyes a tired, pale gray. Despite her rumpled appearance, her voice was low and curt. "You better not have brought more trouble upon yourself, girl."

Evangeline smothered a snort. Her very existence had caused her nothing but trouble. Unlike other humans that grew up in the kingdom, she couldn't remember where she came from or who her parents were. The only traces of her past were an abandoned cave a Nyte discovered her in years ago and a permanent mark branding the top of her right hand, hidden underneath her glove.

Lani rubbed her eyes before narrowing them at the corpse on the floor. "Who is he?"

"I don't know, I found him injured in the snow. I promise as soon as he is well, I'll see that he doesn't mention this incident."

If he knows what's in his best interest. She recognized Lani's expression. "I'm sorry, I couldn't very well bring him to Lord Ryker."

The man hadn't moved since she'd brought him inside. If it weren't for the slight movement of his chest, she would've thought he'd expired right there on the floor.

Evangeline snagged a cloth hanging near the fireplace and dipped it in the bucket of water next to it. She wiped away the caked dirt and blood from the man's face. A handsome face, Evangeline noted to herself. He looked young, no older than herself. His light complexion complimented his tangled black hair that was currently wet and plastered to his cheeks.

What color are his eyes?

Lani's gaze narrowed on Evangeline's fur coat, leather pants, and bulky bag. "You did it, didn't you? You went beyond the wall." Lani's voice dropped to a whisper. "I told you not to. We'll never escape this place—haven't I taught you that much?"

Evangeline frowned, wishing she had time to change before her friend noticed. As Ryker's adopted daughter, the Aerian court expected her to dress accordingly. The last instance she'd worn anything but a tightly corseted dress during the day was when she was first brought here. Before Lord Ryker set his eyes on her.

"I think it could work, Lani." Her words tumbled out in a rush. "I made it out fine, and now that we have supplies in the woods, we can easily escape." Evangeline didn't know how close the next town was to the kingdom, just that it was far enough that they needed the extra blankets, dried foods and matches she had stored away.

"I can't believe you'd risk your life on a rumor." Lani clicked her tongue in disgust. "We wouldn't survive past these walls. You're wasting your time."

Evangeline shook her head. She knew she was risking everything on mere slave gossip. In a country where most Nytes despised humans, the idea of any Nyte wanting to help slaves get out of Peredia seemed more outrageous than the Olaaga being real. But she had to believe there were Nytes in Helgard who could aid them, because she was more terrified of the alternative:

Lani going missing.

"I'll risk everything if it means protecting you." Evangeline may not have a choice in Ryker being her father, but at least she could choose who her mother was. Lani was the closest thing she had. Even Ryker knew how important Lani was to her, allowing Evangeline to stay with her friend in the unsavory quarters most of the time. The only kindness he'd shown her in the last seven years.

Her friend didn't respond right away, massaging her back before grumbling, "Nobody else as naïve as you would have lived this long."

Evangeline bit her cheek, the cloth swiping back and forth across places she had already cleaned. She heard the words left unspoken between them. Saw it in Lani's upturned mouth, the twitch in her brow, the wrinkle of jealousy in her face she couldn't completely hide.

You selfish girl, you don't realize how good you have it here, and you want to leave?

There was a time when they had been miserable together. Lani had just been shipped to Peredia when Evangeline arrived. Having been separated from her own sister and child, Lani was empty and bitter, whereas Evangeline was parentless and ill-tempered. The two came together like the bricks of the kingdom's walls. Rough around the edges, but sturdy. Together they had worked dawn to dusk, eating scraps for food, and resorting to luck and pure faith of the Gods to make it through another day. But now Evangeline was allowed three course meals, fine clothing, and something more than a thin cot to sleep on in Ryker's suite. She was the only human in the kingdom, and probably the entire country, to receive such treatment, and Lani believed she was a fool for wanting to throw that away. Evangeline would counter that it meant nothing if her best friend one day went missing.

It was an old argument between them. One she *really* didn't want to hash out now.

Evangeline forced a shrug. "Yeah, but you still love me."

Lani rejoined with a grunt, the cot creaking as she shifted. "You both need to get out of those clothes, lest you catch a cold," she said, before getting up.

Evangeline obeyed, rummaging through the wood chest at the foot of the bed where she stored her dresses with Lani's. She changed into a simple green dress, liking how it brought out the same color in her eyes.

On a thin wire, she hung up her coat and wet clothes by the fire. She'd never have to wear them again—if she remained here in the castle.

Turning back to the man, she peeled off his heavy tunic.

Evangeline blinked in surprise at his frame. Lean and muscled, and well-fed, unlike most humans in the castle. Maybe he was a favored slave by a noble? Or worked in the kitchens like Lani?

An unusually studded shirt wrapped around his torso. The small, ornate silver buttons gleamed in the dying fire light. She'd seen nothing like it here in the kingdom. The proper attire worn by all the kingdom's servants was black pressed trousers with a matching long-sleeved blouse and a purple apron to complete it, while most Peredian Nytes draped themselves in open, loose clothing, rich in color. Nothing like the dark leather that encased this man.

Where did he come from? she thought, taking off his shirt. Her eyes caught the dark blue symbols swirling across his lower belly and she gasped, yanking his shirt back down.

Her pulse ratcheted higher. She clenched and unclenched her fists, regretting her decision to bring him here. There's no way.

To confirm her suspicions, she brushed his thick, black hair with her fingers, searching. There. Two small nubs on either side of his temples. Gods *blast* her. This man was a Nyte. A puss-filled Caster.

During one of her regimented tutoring sessions with Lord Ryker, she learned Casters were Nytes with the ability to use language to influence their environment. *Magic*, he called it. And maybe what she experienced on that mountainside was her first taste of it.

She sat back, fixated on the deceptively harmless-looking Nyte. *A Caster. . . I've brought a Caster here . . . to Lani's room . . . Gods help me.*

Her eyes snapped to Lani, worried she may have seen the markings as well. To Evangeline's relief, she faced the fire, scrubbing at her uniform and body.

Face furrowing, Evangeline returned to the man.

She rarely saw Casters in the castle. It was a known fact among Peredians that Casters and Aerians didn't get along. Although only a few visited the castle—for work or the occasional ball—Evangeline always recognized Casters by their long, curved horns adorning the tops of their heads and colorful ink covering their bodies.

But why were his horns so short? Was it a birth defect? Was he a halfling, a Nyte born from two different species? Or was it on purpose? With trembling hands, she removed his shirt. She took the warm cloth and wiped away the clotted blood, revealing fleshy pink skin. Now that she knew he wasn't human, she wondered if this Caster was the victim. Or if he deserved it.

Most of the blood was old, his wounds had stopped bleeding a while ago. Maybe he would've survived without her help, after all.

Lani turned, and Evangeline swiftly threw the blanket over him. Her friend handed her a pillow—a burlap sack stuffed with leftover linen scraps—and she placed it beneath his dark locks. Evangeline pulled off his shoes and socks, massaging his feet to return the feeling to them, all the while scowling. *I'm nursing a Nyte back to health.* Her scowl deepened. She should've left him to die.

He groaned, and she jumped. Could he read her thoughts? From what little she knew of Casters, maybe he could.

Lani placed a cup of water on the floor beside him. "He'll need this when he wakes." She shuffled toward the fire and added a few logs before changing into her uniform. Guilt churned in Evangeline's chest for waking her friend earlier than warranted, knowing the long, arduous hours the Nytes expected her to work.

"I hope you know what you're doing," Lani said, sleep still thick in her voice. "He better be gone by the time I return." The flimsy door slammed shut behind her, leaving Evangeline all alone with an unconscious Nyte.

Beams of sunlight shined through the foggy glass, its rays warm on her cheek even as she broke out in a cool sweat. She was going to be late for her morning meeting with Lord Ryker. She needed to leave now.

"But I have to make sure he doesn't speak of this," she

muttered to herself. If he told anyone that she was beyond the wall, or how she escaped . . .

She tapped his cheek, praying that'd be enough to wake him. No movement.

She tried again, a tad harder, but there was no response. Frowning, she shook him, his head lulling side to side.

He moaned so softly that she wasn't sure if she imagined it or not. Then he began coughing. She grabbed the cup of water, angling his neck forward as she pressed it against his lips. They didn't budge.

"It's water." She hoped he could understand her, or else this whole situation was going to be a lot more difficult.

Fortunately, when she placed the rim to his lips again, he gulped eagerly and his eyes fluttered open. They were blue. Like the color of the sky.

He sat up, and she flung her hands out, as if to stop him. "You shouldn't sit up so soon. Your wounds—"

"My wounds are fine." His voice was deeper than she expected, with the soft lilt of an accent. It was obvious he wasn't Peredian. She wanted to ask him where he was from, but decided against it. The less she knew, the better.

He leaned against the bed for support, and her eyes remained on him, refusing to look anywhere else, lest he try to call the guards. Or worse.

A small smile crept across his face. He probably aimed to put her at ease, but had the opposite effect. "I suppose I should thank you for bringing me . . . here," he said, glancing around the room.

The condescending remark dug beneath her skin. She risked her and Lani's life to save his, and this was what he had to say? This is why she spitting *hated* Nytes. The entitled pricks.

Evangeline responded with, "I don't know you. You don't know me. It would be best if we both pretend this never happened. When I return, I expect you to be gone." She hoped he didn't hear the quiver in her tone.

"Is that a threat?"

Her cheeks warmed, but she met him head on. "If it has to be." She was threatening a Nyte! Gods, save her, she was a fool.

The Caster didn't move, but she couldn't afford to waste any more time. She was afraid Ryker had already sent guards to look for her. She'd have to trust that this Caster would leave before Lani returned tonight.

Leaving him to mull over her words, she exited the room, meeting his eyes as she shut the door behind her.

She sped down the hall, passing a series of crammed chambers occupied with scrawny humans huddling together for warmth. Like Lani's, they allotted each room: one bed, a fireplace, and a box containing the essentials. The king expected every slave to be clean and presentable before work each day. To be anything less was inviting a trip to the whipping post, or worse, the plaza.

Pedaling up the stairs, Evangeline steeled herself for the icy walk to come. The distance between the quarters and the castle.

Her unexpected guest nagged at her brain. What was a Caster doing so close to the walls? They rarely visited the kingdom, let alone left their country. Was he attacked by the Aerians? If so, why? Not that Evangeline cared for politics. She couldn't care less if the whole spitting kingdom burned to the ground. It was best not to get involved either way. She had enough of her own problems to contend with.

The screams hit her first when Evangeline made it to the shared communal, followed by a bombardment of people. She wasn't a fool. She turned to run too, when someone snatched

her arm in a firm, bruising grasp. They whipped her around, her head spinning as she locked eyes on someone far scarier than any Caster—or Nyte.

Vane Jarr, Peredia's most notorious torturer.

CHAPTER 3

⸙ EVANGELINE ⸙

"**J**ust the lovely lady I was looking for!" Vane leaned in, and his garlic breath branded her cheek. His elongated nails dug into her skin, his brown and white bushy tail thumping against her leg.

Vane Jarr was a Rathan. Another species of Nyte that crowded the kingdom.

The emblazoned gold insignia of wings stared at her from the breast pocket of his purple military jacket. She traced its outline with her eyes, trying to control her breathing.

Most Rathans had heightened hearing and agility, like their animal counterparts. It was why most entered into the kingdom's strict military. It was only at night, when whispered rumors sifted through the slave quarters, that she heard how stronger Rathans could morph into feral beasts. Though she'd argue that Vane didn't need to shift into a beast—he already was one.

Lanky with unruly brown hair, Vane wasn't intimidating in appearances if you discounted the short, frayed tail, the tall, pointed ears, and the unnatural amount of hair that gathered down his arms and legs. At first glance, it looked like the slightest breeze could knock him over, the only volume to him being the matted hair covering his beady eyes.

Rather, it was his history that terrified every human in the kingdom.

Out of all the torturers that worked in the kingdom, Vane was particularly fond of human victims, taking sick pleasure in inflicting excess pain and suffering in his punishments against those helpless to prevent it.

His voice was like a vulture's, high-pitched and scratchy. "Lord Ryker has been looking for you. You've been a very bad girl, making him worry like that. You know what happens to those who are disobedient, don't you?"

Evangeline kept her expression blank. Showing fear only enticed him further.

She would never forget the first time she had witnessed Vane in action. The screams of that little girl still pierced her ears as Vane dragged her through the halls of these very slave quarters. Her back had already broken and bloodied from his whip, but he had continued to drag her across the jagged, concrete floor, purposely forgetting where the girl's room was. It wasn't long after the girl caught a fever she never recovered from. She died at nine-years-old because she had stolen a doll from an Aerian child.

"You look tired. Rough night?" Vane smiled, displaying sharp, canine teeth.

Her heart stuttered, and she trained her eyes on his boots.

He couldn't possibly know. She made sure nobody saw them entering the wall. He's bluffing. He must be. She swallowed hard.

"Look at me, human!" He grasped her chin with his clawlike hands and jerked her head up to meet his soulless eyes. His pupils dilated, like a beast right before it pounced. She couldn't control it: a small sound escaped her lips. A slow, malicious grin spread across his face.

He pulled her closer until their faces were barely touching. "We're going to have lots of fun, you and I," he said, yanking her toward the castle.

Two other Rathan guards followed behind them as Vane hauled Evangeline up the mountain path, slick with fresh snow. They passed through the tall, golden gates leading into the castle grounds, crawling up more stairs to reach the double doors. She almost didn't notice when they walked inside the pristine hallways that made up the main hall of the castle, her mind overwhelmed with images of whips and Vane's teeth snapping at her. The toasty heat of the castle didn't penetrate the ice that gripped her core.

Evangeline's upper arm throbbed beneath Vane's grip. He kept a fast pace, and if she fell behind, he wouldn't hesitate to pull her arm out of its socket. Down the hall, slaves scurried back and forth, their black uniforms like puffs of dark clouds trailing along their frail limbs. Nytes strode with purpose. Some in fitted military uniforms, their tails, and ears alert and focused. Others in large skirts, flexing their wings, not caring whose path they blocked. But both slaves and Nytes alike gave them a wide berth, most casting their faces away, not wanting to draw Vane's attention as well.

Her eyes stretched wide. She prayed she hadn't gone too far, that she hadn't pushed Lord Ryker into having Vane punish her. Her skin broke out in slight bumps. She imagined Ryker's enraged face, Vane's slimy smile as he dragged her to some dark crevice of the castle.

Please, no, she thought, sucking on her lower lip.

They stopped in front of a mahogany door. She knew this door well. It was Lord Ryker's suite.

Two male Rathan guards, both garbed in plated silver, stood outside the engraved doors, a small bell hanging above the frame. Their canine-like ears were as sharp as the spears they held on each of their sides. They looked at Vane indifferently.

"State your business," said the one on the right.

"I'm here by request." Vane wrenched her forward as if to prove a point.

The guards nodded. One gave a series of sequenced knocks and opened the door. Evangeline licked away the blood on her lip where she had bitten down too hard. One thing dominated her thoughts: Did Lord Ryker know the truth?

They pressed down the windowless hall, oil lamps casting a dim glow on either side of them. Walking past the fine artwork and extravagant tapestries, they arrived in the sitting chamber— an open room at the center of the suite. Occupied with a black marbled fireplace, a red velvet loveseat and green armchair, the room possessed a quiet elegance.

In the corner, Lord Ryker and another Nyte—a Caster woman—were engaged in serious conversation at the elongated dining table. The Caster managed to look fragile despite the dark, short-curved horns that poked out from her long, black hair. In contrast, Lord Ryker towered over the woman, and that was with his wings fully folded.

Most Aerians already appeared otherworldly to Evangeline, but Ryker Ardonis went beyond that, reminding her of something closer to an apathetic spirit. Devoid of emotion. He wore his light blond hair long, in the typical Aerian fashion. His wings were the color of the sky on a gloomy day: a soft gray with a brush of baby blue. It was unusual to see him in the company of someone other than the king. When he wasn't interrogating Evangeline, he served King Calais as his advisor and personal errand boy.

The couple turned as they entered.

Evangeline prepared herself for Ryker's unfeeling eyes, which would peruse her, judge her. For the barrage of questions that would soon overwhelm her. Questions he asked her every morning and night. *Where have you been? Whom have you spoken to? What were your dreams like last night? How are you feeling?* She straightened her back, hiding the panicked tumble of her thoughts. Would her answers be enough to satisfy him? If he already knew of her excursion, would it matter?

"Officer Jarr," Lord Ryker spoke in way of hello. His eyes traveled to Evangeline, and she immediately turned away, too afraid to meet his gaze.

Vane released her, making a dramatic sweeping gesture with his arm. "I present to you, my lord, the woman you've all been waiting for." The two Nytes didn't seem amused by his show of theatrics.

"Where is this marking you spoke of?" The woman was analytical in grazing every bit of Evangeline's body.

Evangeline frowned. In her youth, she was used to being paraded in front of scholars and scientists, all drawn by the mystery surrounding her marked hand, but when none of them could trace it back to any history concerning the Nytes, they assumed it to be a tribal marking from a lost human village. Unimportant. But that was years ago, so why now?

Vane turned to her, his slitted pupils expanding with excitement. "Well, my dear, if you would be so kind."

She imagined wringing Vane's neck, watching him slowly suffocate to death, as she slid the glove off her right hand.

The pitch-black symbols were stark upon her fair skin, proof that time had no role in lessening its boldness. The symbols mimicked a circle with three smaller triangles inscribed on the inside. Each held a rune no one had been able to decipher. The overall mark was simple yet unexplainable, taking up the top expanse of her hand.

The woman was the first to move. She slid toward Evangeline in one graceful step, her black skirt swishing, showing off the hint of a tattoo curling around her lower thigh—and a smattering of fresh bruises and cuts. Her heels clicked against the marble floor, but Evangeline still stood a finger's length taller than the woman. One slender digit reached out and traced the outline of her mark. Evangeline repressed a shiver at the light touch. When she dared glance down at the Caster, a familiar pair of blue eyes met hers. They eerily reminded her of the mysterious Caster man.

The woman's eyes widened in recognition, fascinated by her mark. Evangeline went rigid. This woman knew something, something no other scholar or scientist had known before her.

Ryker, studying the woman, stated, "What do you know, Avana?"

Avana's hand gripped Evangeline's, her eyes devouring the mark, hungering for more. She didn't respond, and when Evangeline peeked at her mark, then up again, she flinched. Avana stared at her with wild eyes, her mouth peeled open and her breath heavier than it'd been previously.

"What do you know, Avana." It wasn't a question.

In a mere second, Avana's crazed expression morphed into one of feigned mild interest. "I can't be too certain. I would need to bring her back to my country to run some tests."

Ryker wasn't taking the bait. "You can perform your tests here if need be."

"May I at least have a moment alone with the subject?"

"She is my property. Whatever you wish to discuss with her, I have a right to hear," he countered.

Evangeline stayed quiet. It wasn't the first time she'd heard that, but the question remained: Why *did* Ryker choose her? Nytes and humans had passed a rumor around that she resembled his daughter who had died years ago, but he never admitted anything whenever she worked up the courage to ask.

"I will need to think this over. Perhaps we can resume this conversation on another day?"

"Another time," Ryker agreed.

She brushed past Vane without a glance and left the room.

Evangeline let out a breath. She didn't know whether to trust Avana. She seemed different from the other scholars Evangeline had encountered. The way her eyes lit up, the recognition in them, was more than any other scholar had revealed. Or perhaps Evangeline was feeding an old spark of hope. *Not that it matters now. It's not like it'll help me or Lani,* she thought bitterly.

Ryker turned to her, observing her more closely than she liked. "I would like a moment alone, Officer Jarr," he said without tearing his gaze from her.

Vane ducked out of the room, and Evangeline squirmed. Beads of sweat dribbled down the curve of her back, drenching the material of the dress. It was well past dawn, but did he know it was because she went beyond the wall? Did he know about the strange Caster inside their kingdom? *Deep breaths.* She exhaled slowly.

"Do you realize what time it is?"

Her nails dug into the skin of her palm. His voice was low.

So very low. "Yes, Father." He was the furthest thing from an actual father, but he insisted she call him that.

Lord Ryker stepped closer. His gaze moved to where her pulse pumped erratically at her neck. "Where have you been, Evangeline?"

"I have no excuse, Father." She kept her head lowered.

He took a thin strand of her hair, its length gliding through his pale fingers before removing a small, innocuous tree leaf. He touched the ridges of the leaf and brought it to his nose. Evangeline fought to keep her face dispassionate, but her vision was fading and she was having difficulty breathing.

"Did you know that the leaves from trees in the Olaaga Forest all share four distinct ridges along the sides? They also have an unusual scent of bitterness and dew when crushed." He abruptly crushed the leaf in his hand, and she flinched. "And you and I both know that the Olaaga Forest only grows outside the kingdom's walls."

She wanted to respond, to defend herself, but she lost her voice.

Lord Ryker slid back towards the table. He continued to speak, his back facing her. "I have provided you adequate comfort and leisure despite your human nature. I've been quite lenient with you. And now you have betrayed my trust. I've misjudged you, Evangeline. I thought I had raised you better."

"I'm sorry . . ." she whispered, but on the inside, she was screaming, *pleading*, that he wouldn't ask how. That he wouldn't investigate the incident further, that she and Lani still had a chance.

He shuffled through several sheets of paper. A sliver of light slipped through the thick, burgundy drapes in front of him. Evangeline's terrified reflection stared back at her from the speckled floor.

Ryker pulled the lever attached to the wall, and Vane re-entered the room. His mouth was wide, his teeth bared in a twisted smile. It was at that moment Evangeline's heart plummeted to her stomach and she gagged on the air she inhaled. *No, no, no . . .*

"Do what you must, but I don't want any permanent injuries. Are we clear?" Ryker didn't bother to look up. "Have her locked up. She can stay with you tonight."

Evangeline's head shot up, and her eyes widened. Her mouth opened and closed until she got out the word. "Father?"

"Yes, my lord," Vane purred, grabbing her arm.

Evangeline looked at Vane in horror, then at Lord Ryker. "No, no, wait! I can explain!"

Lord Ryker's eyes remained on the sheets of paper. "I will be expecting to see you at dawn tomorrow. Do not be late again, Evangeline."

"*No!*"

Vane yanked her arm, dragging her out of Ryker's private chambers.

"No, please, Father! I'm sorry!" she cried, but the door had already shut behind them.

Vane pulled her down a candlelit corridor. Her limbs dragged against the carpet, lead taking precedence in her muscles. The halls she walked down every day, the ones connecting the main hall to the east wing, had always dragged. But today she wished the long stretches of carpet and stone would last forever.

Purple wallpaper faded into navy blue, the floor a patterned mix of gold-and-blue-speckled tile. They were in the east wing where military operations took place. It also acted as living quarters for the army and high-ranking officers ever since the king announced the west wing unlivable. Vane conducted his business of punishing and interrogating his victims here, as well.

And now she was one of them.

"The infamous Evangeline, finally within my grasp." Vane pulled her down a staircase, descending into what appeared like a dark pit. "You don't know how long I've been waiting for this." He laughed.

She mentally cursed him, screamed profanities in her head, but nothing was going to change the fact that she had messed up.

The smell of must and rust invaded her senses as they reached the front of a thick steel door down a considerably lengthy hallway. He unlocked the door, forcing her into a small room. The one lamp showed a tight space enclosed with solid stone, its walls lined with dark blurs that she couldn't identify. Despite its overall cleanliness, she envisioned everything stained with blood.

The mechanical click of the door locking behind her rang in her ears like a siren. Vane ushered her toward a set of manacles chained to the center of the floor, and she walked numbly toward them. She clenched her hands so hard, her knuckles turned white and her stomach churned. She might vomit.

"Get on your knees, human." Vane spoke as if the procedure came naturally. He walked to the wall. Evangeline's eyes adjusted, and she shivered with dread at the sight of the whips, hammers, and other torture devices arrayed there. His hand paused midway to unhook a whip, one with small spikes. Her mouth went dry.

Vane caught her staring, and his lips curled. Taking out a smoke from his pocket, he lit it with the flick of his lighter and brought it to his lips, all while watching her with half-lidded eyes.

Delaying the inevitable would only make it worse. She should just get on her knees and endure her punishment, but the leer in his eyes made her pause.

He sauntered toward her. Her gaze fell to his feet as they stopped in front of her. Pain exploded in her cheek, and she toppled to the ground.

Her hands flew to her face, cradling her stinging cheek. She wanted to scream. She wanted to fight back. But her body wasn't listening to her. All she could do was stare blankly at the ground. She needed to move. Gods, why couldn't she move? Spitting *move*!

The touch of his hand on her face jerked her back to reality. She refused to blink, to flinch, or do anything to cause him to slap her again.

Vane's rough hand traced the curve of her back, slipping beneath the band of her corset. "Take it off," he said.

Her nostrils flared, and she clenched her eyes, but it didn't prevent the tears from running down her cheeks. *No, no, no . . .*

He inhaled a drag of his smoke and smothered its butt in the side of her neck. She yelped. "Either you take it off, or I'll do it for you."

Her breathing came faster. She was hyperventilating, the corners of her world fading. For her hesitation, Vane rewarded her with a brash kick to her ribs.

He threw his smoke to the ground and crushed it with his boot. He bent down, his face almost touching hers. "You're mine now, Pet." His lips brushed the top of her earlobe.

She snapped.

In a surge of fear-laced adrenaline, her arms slammed against him, and he stumbled backward. Her eyes narrowed on the steel door. She banged, kicked, and clawed at it. She screamed so violently that her throat closed, a burning sensation spreading through her body, spurring her heart to pound faster.

"Get me out of here! Help me! *Help me!*"

Claws dug into her scalp, and Vane wrenched her back, tossing her to the floor. Her temple smacked into concrete. She didn't feel it, numbed to everything else aside from survival. She scrambled to her feet, but he shoved her down and climbed on top of her. The weight of him immobilized her.

She screamed again, throwing her fists at him. He snarled, catching her wrist in one hand. His nails scraped her chest, ripping her dress's collar when the door crashed open. Everything faded into a whirl of motion. One moment Vane was on top of her, then he wasn't. A loud *thud* echoed in her ears as he smacked into the stone wall opposite of her.

Evangeline rolled over and gathered herself on all fours. A wave of dizziness hit her. She tried turning to see who had saved her, but a throbbing pain shot through her head, her vision blurring. Mangled sounds of pain filled the room before a figure leaned over her.

Dark blue wings dipped in gold shrouded her vision.

It can't be . . .

She passed out.

CHAPTER 4

⟁ EVANGELINE ⟁

Evangeline shot up in bed. It took her a moment to remember what had happened, and her heart settled.

Past the large oak columns of the four-post bed, she squinted against the stream of sunlight coming through the glass doors leading to a curved balcony. Emerald-encrusted swords, daggers carved out of amethyst, and uniquely designed bows with handles etched in diamonds, filled the glass shelves. It indicated the room's owner: a collector of rare weapons and gems. Purple wallpaper, garnished with small golden symbols within the print, covered the walls. The only imperfection was a small hole hidden behind a bookshelf; a hole she had created when she accidently shot Ceven's bow, the steel tip narrowly dodging his face, lodging itself into the wall behind him.

Turning, a face she'd wanted to see for the last two years smiled at her. With hazel eyes and chestnut brown hair cropped short, the youngest prince of Peredia leaned casually against the wall, his blue and gold wings tucked close behind him.

Prince Ceven LuRogue. He was here. She wasn't imagining things.

"It's good to see you again, Eve."

Without warning, hot tears spilled over, the events of today crushing down on her.

Ceven darted from the wall and stretched his arms toward her. She shrank away.

His face fell. "Eve, I'm sorry. I'm so sorry."

Evangeline pressed the sleeves of her dress into her eyes and turned away. She had first met the prince when she was eleven, he having just turned twelve. Lord Ryker insisted on her attending the same tutoring lessons as him, much to the royal family's vexation—and her own. She thought the prince to be a conceited tyrant. It wasn't until a couple years later, when Queen Beatrix's dark secret got out, that the two became inseparable.

Nobody expected the youngest prince to be a bastard child.

"What . . . what are you doing here?" she said, trying to keep her voice level. Her eyes flicked to his arms, his dark green sleeves rolled up, exposing hardened muscle. Being on the leaner side, Evangeline had always been envious of Ceven's physique. Years of training with the Royal Guard—an elite group of Aerians who protected the royal family—was notable in his figure. But now, she felt embarrassingly small next to him.

He rubbed his neck. "I got back yesterday. I had planned on surprising you . . . but not like this."

It'd been two years since Evangeline had seen Ceven. King Calais ordered him to ship overseas with his brother, Sehn, and she hadn't heard from him since.

"You didn't even send a letter," she mumbled.

"Eve, it wasn't my . . ." He sighed. "Are you feeling better?"

She brushed the bump on her head from where it had hit the ground. It was sore, along with the burn on the side of her neck. Both would leave marks, but at least that was all she had to worry about. She shrugged. "I'll live. How did you find me?"

"News of Vane's new victim spread like wildfire. Especially considering the victim was the 'infamous Evangeline.'"

Evangeline looked away. She hated the title, given to her because of the drama that followed her. First, it was her mark and bizarre past that gave her the unwanted attention of nearly everyone in the castle, but when Lord Ryker adopted her into the Aerian court, she had collected everyone's attention in the kingdom—maybe the entire country.

Panic gripped her throat. Oh Gods, Lord Ryker. What would he do to her now? She had disobeyed him, not once, but twice.

She clenched her chest and jumped out of bed. "I have to go. I have to find Lord Ryker. I have to explain everything," she started.

Ceven gently touched her shoulder. His cool fingers sent a wave of reassurance through her. "Eve, calm down, it's okay. I talked to Ryker after I brought you here." His eyes shifted away, and his lips set into a scowl. "He's not happy I intervened, but I don't think he intended Vane to be that rough with you. He's dealing with him and expects you back in his suite as usual tomorrow morning." His jaw tightened. "I don't know what he'll do or say, but you won't have to deal with Vane. It's all I could do."

Evangeline closed her eyes and sighed. But her relief was only temporary. She would still have to deal with Lord Ryker tomorrow.

"You didn't have to do that, but . . . thank you." Evangeline rearranged her dress, embarrassed. "I . . . guess I owe it to my popularity that you were able to find me in time."

Ceven's mouth twitched. "First day back and I'm already pulling you out of trouble. You haven't changed much, have you?"

A smile tugged at her lips. "If I remember correctly, it was you who always started it." As a child, he permanently bore an arrogant frown—one that deepened whenever he didn't get his way. She had quickly learned that the young prince had a temper that matched her own.

He chuckled, and the sound was deeper than she remembered. Her pulse hummed a little faster. As if sensing it, he cleared his throat and looked away.

The movement rustled the feathers in his wings. They were a lot thicker now, and wider, the length of them stretching his entire body, with the tips brushing the floor. They looked just as soft and beautiful as she remembered. She reached out and touched his inner left wing, like she had often done when they were children. The individual feathers shifted easily beneath her fingertips, each piece a shade of midnight merging with a rich gold at the tips. Her hand trailed farther up and—

He snatched her wrist, and she jumped.

Her face flamed. "S-sorry, I . . . I didn't mean to, I wasn't thinking . . ." *You're not a child anymore, Eve. He's not the same man you knew.*

He loosened his grip, and she pulled her hand back.

"It's not that." He rustled his hair, color darkening his cheeks. "It's just, your hands are freezing cold."

Liar, she couldn't help but think. Her fingers had been close to the muscle in his left arch. It was a sensitive spot, the muscle never having fully grown. *What's the point in having beautiful wings if they don't work? I'd trade all my beauty to fly,* he admitted to her one rainy afternoon inside this very suite.

"Well, it is the middle of winter," she said, letting the lie slip.

He smiled and opened his mouth, but then closed it.

She fidgeted with her dress as she struggled for the words she'd been yearning to say to him since he had left. He looked different. His skin darker now, a sun-kissed bronze, with a fresh scar peeking out from his open shirt, tucked into loose brown pants. He had always dressed more casually than the rest of his court.

Evangeline had always known he was handsome, but . . . Seeing him again after two years, she'd remembered how devastatingly attractive he was.

Realizing she was staring, her eyes shot up—only to meet his. He'd been staring at her as well. They both turned away.

"Well, I should go . . ." she mumbled. The plush mattress adjusted to its former state as she got up. As if she hadn't been there.

She started for the door, and Ceven put his hand on her shoulder. "Eve, I'm sorry it's been so long. I didn't want to go, but I had no choice."

"I know." It still didn't make it hurt any less. "It's not your fault."

He shuffled his feet, and she couldn't take the pained look in his eyes anymore. She went to rustle his hair, like she'd done when they were kids, but only made it halfway. He was too tall. She awkwardly opted for a light shove instead. "You have a lot to make up for, Prince."

To her surprise, he took her unmarked hand in his. He removed her glove, and her skin was ghostly pale compared to his. He brought her hand to his lips. Her mouth peeled open, a soft breath escaping her.

"Then let me start by giving you this." He pulled out a gold ring from his pocket and slipped it onto her finger. A large sapphire gleamed at her. It was breathtaking the way it absorbed the surrounding light. Immediately, she could tell its worth. "It's handcrafted, one of a kind, made by a famous artisan in Atiaca."

Evangeline stared in awe at the pretty piece. Her heart fluttered at the thought of wearing something Ceven had given her, but also knew it would draw more unwanted attention.

"Ceven, I can't possibly accept this." She tried to take it off, but he closed his fingers around her hand.

"Allow me this. Please." She met his gaze, the fall of his brows. He felt guilty. It didn't fix everything, but he was trying. He smiled, gently tugging her hand. "Come, let's take a walk."

Evangeline trailed behind Ceven through the main halls of the castle. Thick rugs, streaming along black marble, muffled their footsteps as they passed purple textured walls. Sunlight flooded through floor-to-ceiling windows, each one adorned with thick, golden drapes. Voices from distant conversations echoed off the vaulted ceilings, reminding her that no conversation was private inside these stone walls.

Here, in the castle's heart, the rooms were by far the largest and most opulent. When the royal family wasn't engaged in politics and heated debates in the throne room, they hosted festivities in the kingdom's famous 'glass room'. Only favored slaves or bedwarmers served in here. Evangeline had become well acquainted with the main hall. It was where Lord Ryker's suite resided.

She bit her lip, looking over her shoulder. She would've preferred taking a walk in the east wing, farther from Ryker, but she knew she was being paranoid. The castle was enormous. Nearly as tall as the mountain it rested on, with rooms ranging in size from small guest suites to multi-room homes, along with kitchens, washrooms, game rooms and other amenities the

Aerians indulged in. The chances of them accidently stumbling into Ryker were rare—unless he purposefully sought her out.

Sunlight tickled Ceven's ear, reflecting off his small gold hoop. It had been Queen Beatrix's favorite piece of jewelry, the simple gold band, encrusted in rubies so small, one only saw them when they shone in the light. It served as a symbol of the dead queen and a defiant gesture against the king who hated being reminded of her. Evangeline had helped him pierce it, long after the queen was announced dead and her secret exposed. After Ceven's rage had subsided and the two of them started their tentative friendship.

Evangeline smiled. It felt surreal she was now walking side by side with him. Being with him almost made her current situation okay, though she glanced around them nervously, expecting to see Lord Ryker or Vane right behind them. The adrenaline rush she experienced this morning left her exhausted, but if she tried to lay down anytime soon, sleep would evade her. Too many thoughts pressed at her mind.

Ceven's pace slowed. "Evangeline, I wanted to ask you . . . what had you done to upset Ryker that much?"

She opened her mouth and, realizing what she was about to blurt out, snapped it shut. "It's nothing."

He turned his head. The stiffness in his shoulders and spine told her he was upset. It was Ceven's silent tantrum, one she learned to recognize after his visits with the king or when overheard Nytes gossiping about them.

Evangeline focused on the hallway that stretched out before them, trying to ignore the guilt that gnawed at her insides. She wanted to confide in him, but this was different. This was about two humans trying to escape the kingdom.

And no matter how close they had been, Ceven was still a prince. A Nyte.

An uncomfortable silence filled the gap between them, but it felt off. It was unusually quiet. No undertones of soft chatter, footsteps brushing against the carpets, or the clatter of trays in these hallways normally filled with a moderate flow of bodies. "Where is everybody?" she asked.

Ceven's face scrunched in disgust. "Probably off planning the grand welcome ball for me and Sehn. We weren't expected back so soon, and now everyone is rushing to prepare everything, even though it won't be for a few weeks."

Evangeline couldn't help but smile. Ceven always had a distaste for Aerian parties. At least he hadn't changed completely. She wondered if Lani had heard the news of the princes' arrival. If her friend would be back from work later than usual these coming weeks.

"How long are you here for?" *And when will you leave me again?* Evangeline added to herself.

"For as long as it pleases you." He smiled, and her breath caught in her throat.

He led her down a secluded hallway she hadn't been before. She checked over her shoulder occasionally.

Ceven noticed. "Don't worry, I won't let anyone hurt you."

Evangeline relaxed, knowing he spoke the truth. It was when he was no longer there that worried her. "You left so suddenly. I didn't even have a chance to say goodbye. Why?"

He sighed and ran his hand through his hair. "I didn't intend to leave you, Eve. The king wanted to strengthen our relations with the other countries. With no warning, he sent me to Atiaca to reaffirm our relationship with the empress. Sehn had the more laborious task of dealing with an entire council of Casters."

Her eyebrows rose. She wasn't close to the oldest prince,

but the idea of meeting the *entire* Caster council made her stomach flutter for him. "And were you successful?"

"On my end, there was no success to achieve. My presence in Atiaca was a mere formality. The empress has no need to risk losing an alliance with us—she has fair trade and political stability. As for my brother, he was far more successful. The council signed the treaty and has publicly announced their newfound alliance with Peredia." He took in her slackened jaw. "Trust me, I'm just as surprised as you are. Sehn has always been known for his silver tongue, but this is beyond me."

Casters kept to themselves mostly in the small country of Sundise Mouche, north of Peredia, across the Black Sea. But Casters working with other countries was unheard of, let alone Peredia, home to their most hated enemies—Aerians. Some rumored it was because Casters sided with humans against the Aerians in the last war, but she didn't believe it. Like Lord Ryker said, why would any educated Nyte align themselves with such a weak species?

But, since the war, Sundise Mouche's borders have been closed for two hundred years. So why start an alliance now?

They reached a door at the end of the hallway; a part of the castle Evangeline wasn't familiar with. Behind an innocuous wooden door, a small garden in a glass enclosure greeted them.

Evangeline's body softened like a loosened facet, draining all tension from her. It was just like the garden in her favorite book, *Where the Everflowers Bloom*.

Even in the dead of winter, everything continued to grow vibrantly, unaffected. Water trickled from somewhere deeper in the garden. Flowers of all colors thrived here, and a light, floral aroma filled the air. The sun beamed above them. Pockets of rays peeked through gaps of stray vines slithering up the glass cage.

"There's no everflowers here, but I hope it's still just as beautiful," Ceven said.

She turned to him. It *was* beautiful. But it was more than that because . . . "You remembered."

CHAPTER 5

⁓ CEVEN ⁓

Ceven smiled, watching Evangeline bask in the sun. He did remember.

Before he left, he had made a promise to build her a garden that rivaled the one in her favorite book. He didn't build this one, but knew she would appreciate it all the same. He needed to see that bright smile return to her face. A face, he noticed, that looked more worn and tired. Less like the vibrant, stubborn girl he grew up with.

Evangeline bent toward a bush of jasmine, wisps of hair falling over her shoulder. Her hair reminded him of the fields of wheat along the outskirts of the kingdom, strands of it blowing in the breeze. Before he left, it had touched her shoulders. Now, the braided length of it brushed the curve of her back where her corset was bound. Very tightly.

His brows pinched together. Evangeline was always leaner

and taller than other humans, with a graceful frame, but she seemed thinner now. Fragile. Like she could break at any point.

An image of Vane on top of her, his hand tearing at her shirt, flashed in his mind. His nostrils flared, and he crossed his arms to hide his clenched fists. He wanted to kill Vane. And he almost had, but he couldn't risk the king sending him away. Again.

Ceven would never admit the real reason the king sent him overseas. Peredia was never in danger of losing their alliance with the Atiaca Empire. King Calais wasn't a fool. He knew of Ceven's relationship with Evangeline but couldn't touch her, lest he risk losing Ryker's counsel. Or, specifically, Ryker's knowledge on magic and artifacts, which the king obsessively coveted and displayed through charmed necklaces and rings.

So, rather than risk another scandal, King Calais sent Ceven far away. Like a nuisance to be tossed aside at his leisure.

Either bed her and be done with her or face the consequences of your actions. She's a human, with no place in our world. You'd best remember that, the king had said to him.

Lord Ryker finds favor in her.

A flaw in his character that I'm willing to overlook. For now.

And mother? Was she flawed too?

Ceven had tensed for the hard blow to his cheek, but underestimated the king's strength and had tumbled to the ground.

Don't ever speak to me of her again. He had gripped Ceven's chin, forcing him to meet his eyes. *You, of all people, should learn from her mistakes. The same pathetic beings she tried to protect killed her! Her own ignorance cost her her life!*

Ceven hadn't been able to speak, the grip on his jaw too constricting.

Your very presence here disgraces me, and yet I allow you a place by my side. Continue to embarrass me, and I will grant you your wish. You can live with the humans you love so much and be forced to serve and grovel at my feet for the rest of your life.

Ceven hated how he had trembled within his grasp, and the king's responding smile was empty.

If you don't want to act like a prince, then I won't treat you as one.

Ceven's smile disappeared. Seeing King Calais, for the first time in two years, was one of the toughest moments in his life. He thought he'd outgrown his anger for a man who once loved him. A man he had called father. Thought he would no longer cower beneath his stony stare. But as soon as he'd locked eyes with the king, an unsettling mix of nausea and fear swept through him. Ceven had been wrong, he hadn't grown up at all.

His eyes returned to Evangeline's cinched corset. "Have you been eating well?"

She raised her chin. "I'm fine."

He knew she would get defensive. She had always misinterpreted his concern for pity. "Delani, how is she?"

"Lani is fine. We're both fine."

"Eve..."

As kids, Ceven admired Evangeline's courage and strong fortitude, but it also drove him mad with worry. Their backgrounds—him, a bastard prince, and her, the first human adopted into Aerian royalty—put them both in the spotlight. But he was a Nyte, a male Aerian, born with more strength than any other species. More than strong enough to protect himself. Evangeline was a human in a sea of predators, helpless if they attacked.

Just like when they were kids, she didn't realize how vulnerable she was—no, that wasn't it. She refused to see it.

"So, tell me what Atiaca was like," she said, changing the topic.

He stifled a sigh. "It's very different from Peredia. Their winter isn't as harsh as ours, but in the summer . . ." He grimaced. "It's *hot*. The empress is really taken with the sea and had the capital city moved closer to the coastline." He could still hear the crashing of waves outside his window, the endless rhythm often singing him to sleep. "I wish I could've taken you there. I'd never seen the ocean as clear, or as blue."

Her eyes glowed. "What were the people like? Did they have slaves as well?" She leaned in to smell a nearby rose.

"Yes and no. The humans and Nytes there have a different relationship than we do. Humans are still subservient in many places, but most are compensated for their work, or offered their freedom after a certain amount of years." Ceven hoped one day Peredia could adopt the same perspective, moving toward an era where humans and Nytes saw each other as equals. "The inhabitants of Atiaca are more . . . free-spirited than in Peredia."

"Free-spirited?" Her grip tightened, the rose's stem bending unnaturally.

"Well, for one, they wear less clothing. Sometimes none." He smiled at her bewildered expression. "It's only because it gets so hot . . . and nobody cares." He rubbed his jaw. "I guess you could also say they're more . . . generous with their emotions. There are fewer restrictions there, and they can openly embrace their wilder instincts. It was a rewarding experience." And with his title and features, the citizens of Atiaca didn't spare him any in their affections. But he didn't dare say that out loud.

Evangeline looked like she wanted to say something but kept her mouth closed. He pounced on the opportunity. "Has Vane touched you like that before?"

She flinched. Grabbing a strand of her hair, she rubbed it between her fingers, her eyes cast to the side. She opened her mouth—

"Don't lie to me, Eve. I know you well enough to know when you're lying."

Her mouth snapped closed. She forced her hand to her side, turning her back to him. "It doesn't concern you."

He growled in frustration. That she could still get under his skin alarmed him. "Tell me."

She spun around, her cheeks flushed. "I don't have to tell you anything, Ceven. I belong to Lord Ryker, not you."

"Now you're just being unfair."

"You weren't here!"

His chest squeezed, and this time he was the one to look away.

She took a deep breath. When she spoke again, her voice was soft. Quiet. "I haven't seen or spoken to you in two years. I didn't know if I was ever going to see you again. And now you expect me to share such details of my life with you?"

Ceven looked back at her. "You used to."

She didn't meet his eyes. "I . . . I have to go. It was nice seeing you again, Your Highness."

Evangeline turned to leave and paused. She pulled off the ring he'd given her and offered it to him. "Thank you, but I believe it would be better suited for someone else."

Ceven said nothing, knowing she would argue. He took the ring, and she cast him a sad smile before turning away. Without thinking, his arm stretched out, his fingers brushing the tips of her hair. Then he dropped it.

She left the room and didn't look back.

CHAPTER 6

~ EVANGELINE ~

The sun was descending when Evangeline returned to Lani's. She entered the freezing room and didn't see any Casters in the vicinity.

Thank the Gods, I don't have to deal with that Caster man on top of everything else. She sighed.

The bed in the corner was empty. Lani was later than usual today.

She debated whether to see Lord Ryker. That he hadn't sent guards to fetch her, surprised her. But maybe upsetting the prince concerned him more. Or he was confident she wouldn't run away again. He didn't expect her back until tomorrow morning, but her hands clenched at the unknown. What if he sent her to Vane again? What if he hurt Lani instead? She was being selfish, staying here. Pretending it was just another day. Pretending she hadn't escaped the walls yet and still was gathering her supplies and working to convince Lani it was a solid plan. That she hadn't just ruined everything, all because she saved a man. A Nyte.

A loud grumble echoed in the dark room. Hunger clawed at her stomach. Not only did she skip breakfast this morning, but she didn't have her dinner with Ryker.

Wrapping her arms around herself, she shuffled toward the fireplace and threw on a few logs, blowing on the embers. Flames burst to life, and she rummaged through Lani's chest for any extra food she might have stolen away. Shoved at the bottom was a bit of bread and a couple apples that were turning. Sidling over to the fire, she picked away the mold on the stale loaf.

You weren't here!

She squeezed her eyes shut. She didn't mean to yell at him like that. It wasn't Ceven's fault he had to leave. That he hadn't protected her from the Aerian ladies that had cornered her, ripped off her dress and cut her hair. Or stopped the couple of Nyte children from locking her in a small pantry with a feral cat, leaving her there until a human found her the next day with scratches covering her. It wasn't his fault that he wasn't there to step in when Ryker left bruises over her face and arms, blaming her for causing problems. That she dealt with the brunt of the court's cruelty alone for two years.

No, it was hers, for relying on anyone else to save her. Especially an Aerian prince. What she'd done today was for the best. For both of them.

She finished the bread, the dried pieces drawing all the moisture from her mouth. She bit into the apple and grimaced at the sourness, but it kept the hunger at bay. Shadows danced across the floor, and she leaned her head back. If the king sent Ceven to Atiaca for political matters, why did he leave so suddenly?

Without so much as a goodbye? She didn't believe for a second that there wasn't an ulterior motive involved.

King Calais was obvious in his dislike toward her and her relationship with Ceven. Casting her glares that made her skin crawl, discussing potential discipline habits Lord Ryker could adopt at her expense. His cruel smile always left an ominous stench over her for days to follow.

A humorless chuckle escaped her. *And now you've upset the only Nyte who protects you from him.*

The scratching of the wood door jerked Evangeline's attention away from the fire. Before she could react, arms engulfed her, along with the smell of dough mixed with a tang of sweat.

"I thought I lost you . . . I thought I lost you."

When Evangeline's heart calmed down, she returned Lani's embrace, wrapping her arms around her thick torso. Her shirt muffled Lani's wail, and she hugged her friend tighter.

The last time she'd seen Lani like this was when she was a child, before she met Lord Ryker. It had been winter, and after one grueling day of work, Evangeline fell into a fever. For days her body stuck to the bed, waves of heat pounding her. She never told Lani, but at night, when her fever broke, she caught her much in the same way. Crying with her head in her hands, whispering the same sentiment. Lani had been forced to leave behind her sister and child when she was sold to the kingdom. Evangeline was all she had now. And if she were to die. . .

"I'm guessing you heard." Evangeline frowned. "You can't keep anything a secret in this spitting castle."

Lani untangled herself and shook Evangeline's shoulders. "Stupid girl! I told you there was no point in running away. You'll only make matters worse for yourself. For both of us!"

Evangeline gritted her teeth. The memory of Vane's hand brushing her skin was enough to make her hands sweat. But she couldn't admit defeat—not when Lani's life depended on it. "Next time, I won't get caught."

Lani's nose scrunched to meet her eyes. "Then you're the biggest fool I've ever met." Her eyes roamed Evangeline's body. "Are you hurt? What did he do to you? Why are you not with Lord Ryker?"

Sporting the beginnings of an ugly bruise on her cheek and forehead, Evangeline looked worse than she felt. Fortunately, she could cover up the other evidence. The sleeves of her dress covered the bruises from where Vane held her. The burn mark from his smoke, hidden underneath the length of her hair.

"No, I'm fine. Really," she added when Lani narrowed her eyes. "Lord Ryker is busy tonight, thank the Gods."

"The Gods must be on your side if you're still standing. Nobody comes back from Vane feeling fine," she stressed. "I'm glad you're okay."

Lani cradled her face, pressing a long, hard kiss to her forehead. Evangeline swallowed the large lump in her throat.

Evangeline spared her friend the details of her day and changed the topic. "The princes have returned."

Lani didn't look surprised. "And I wish they would've stayed gone." She released her and plopped down on the thin bed. The wood frame gave way to her weight. "Now there's more work to do. I won't be able to spitting move by the end of this month."

Evangeline frowned. She had pleaded with Lord Ryker to have Lani relinquished of her duties, but he repeatedly denied her. Later, when he caught Evangeline in the east wing kitchen helping Lani prepare food for the military, he had taken a stick and beat Evangeline's hands until she couldn't bend them. She shifted uncomfortably, recalling the endless throbbing sensation she had for the next few weeks.

Lani shook her finger. "I know you want to go see him, but it's for the best if you continue to keep your distance."

Her friend knew about her and Ceven, had repeatedly warned her about the consequences of such a bond with an Aerian prince. Bastard or not. Which was why Evangeline mumbled, "I may have already met with him?"

Lani's head whipped toward her. "Blast it, girl. And how long will it be until he breaks your heart again?" She crossed her arms. "Don't even think about it. I have enough trouble as it is, I don't need your moping on top of it."

"I didn't mope," she muttered. But she was lying to herself. The sight of Ceven today had stirred up all those old feelings and memories. Like curling into an old blanket, relishing in its warmth and nostalgic smells of childhood. But that was all it was. Memories. "Don't worry, I know better now. I can handle myself."

Lani lay on the bed, pulling the thin, scratchy blanket around herself. She rolled over, leaving enough space for Evangeline. "It's not you I'm worried about."

She sighed. "Goodnight, Lani."

Tomorrow she'd have to face Lord Ryker. Possibly Vane. She briefly entertained the thought of climbing out Lani's window and trekking through the snow, back toward the movable stone in the kingdom's wall. But this time, she wouldn't come back.

Too anxious to sleep, Evangeline rested her head against the wall. She closed her eyes and allowed the crackling of the fire to sedate her chaotic thoughts.

"Eve, my dear, it's time to wake up."

Evangeline's eyes slipped open. Blue eyes stared at her behind black bangs. An unfamiliar woman leaned over her, her hair tied back between obsidian horns that curled twice on either side of her head.

"Anali?" she said, wondering how she knew this Caster's name.

"Jaden is waiting for you in the tower."

Evangeline sat up in bed, in a room that screamed opulence and regality. She squinted at the sunlight shining through her bedroom window.

Anali went to the closet and pulled out a deep blue satin dress laced with silver lining. Getting out of bed, Evangeline let Anali pull the dress over her head, tying the lace beneath her breasts. The Caster pushed aside her hair from her neck, clasping a silver chain that possessed a sapphire in its claw-like clutches. Stepping into matching high heels, Evangeline looked at herself in the gold-framed mirror. She saw someone else entirely.

A fair haired, elegant woman stared back at her with a stubborn confidence. Dressed like she was going to attend the ball of the century.

She looked like royalty.

"Evangeline. Evangeline, wake up."

Evangeline groaned. She tried opening both eyes but only managed her right, her left cheek too swollen. It took her a moment to realize it was Lani standing next to her, and not a black-haired Caster woman.

"I'm awake," she grumbled.

When she sat up, her back ached, her hips moaning in protest. She'd fallen asleep on the floor last night.

That dream . . .

She licked her lips and grimaced. As expected, she tasted the familiar tangy bitterness of iron in her mouth.

"You're going to catch a cold, sleeping on the ground like that. Get into the bed, at least." Lani was dressed in her black-sleeved uniform, her hair brushed back into a tight bun.

Evangeline rubbed her eyes. "It's that time already?"

"It's not dawn yet, but there's a lot of work, for us slaves, that needs to be done for the ball." Lani didn't bother to hide the irritation in her face.

For us slaves. Evangeline cringed. Whether Lani intended the jab, it didn't change the fact they now lived different lives.

"I'm sorry." She didn't know what to say.

Lani pointed a wrinkled finger at her face. "When you get the chance, get some ice on that cheek of yours. It's looking extra nasty this morning." She yanked the door open. "I'll see you tonight."

Evangeline said goodbye and stood up to stretch, feeling every joint crack.

She glanced at the window. With the sun hidden, she saw her reflection in the fire's glow. Her hair was a disheveled mess, one side of her face bloated, and bags swelled beneath her eyes. The opposite of the beautiful woman she'd seen in her dream.

Putting a hand to her head, she scrambled to recall the details. Details that Ryker would ask her about. She didn't know why he found these occurrences so important or why he wanted to know everything about these "dreams." Or vivid hallucinations, she liked to call them. The difference too drastic. She was more aware of everything. Every smell. Every touch. Every taste. She was fifteen the first time it happened. She'd been invisible and powerless, watching everything play out around here. Feeling everything around her.

And then she would wake up with the taste of blood in her mouth.

The first time, she thought she'd bit her lip in her sleep, but it became too much of a coincidence every time after that. She never told anyone. Not even Ryker. It sounded crazy enough in her head.

Lord Ryker is going to be pleased.

Evangeline couldn't help the hope that bloomed in her chest. Previously, Ryker would reward her with an array of sweets or rebind her favorite book whenever this occurred. This time she hoped it saved her from Vane.

Knowing she wasn't going to fall back asleep, she changed out of her dress into a baby blue one, trimmed in bronze. The material was thin, which was why she donned the white, fur-lined petticoat over it.

Darkness settled across the kingdom. The sun wasn't up, and there was an absence of wind. The land would be calm and easy to travel—if she wanted to go toward the outskirts of the kingdom.

Too risky.

She needed to find out if Ryker had discovered the loose stone in the wall, if he had placed more guards along the kingdom's borders. They couldn't leave until she solved those questions. Evangeline could handle being caught, but not Lani. She wasn't a favored slave, and execution would be her punishment for escaping. They had to make it count.

Evangeline made the bed and wiped down Lani's nightclothes, hanging them by the fire. She also swept, shooing the mice and critters that found sanctuary in the holes of the room,

but the straw broom did little but shove more dirt into the cracks of the floor.

When she finished, it was still dark outside.

She huffed. Usually, she'd grab a book and curl up by the fire, but today she couldn't sit still. She paced the room back and forth like a trapped animal. She needed a distraction.

Evangeline paused in the middle of her pacing, staring at the ground. She held out her palm and clenched her hands, imagining something in their grasp. It's still dark out, there shouldn't be anyone there. It would only be for a bit. She chewed her lip. She was already in enough trouble. If Lord Ryker found out what she planned to do, he'd have her locked away for good.

She glanced back out the window at the inky darkness. Uncertainty and fear haunted her unoccupied mind. If she stayed here, waiting for the inevitable meeting, not knowing if she'd meet Vane again . . . she might go crazy.

Taking the bucket of water, she put out the fire and wrapped her coat tighter around herself before leaving for the castle.

This time of year, a thick layer of snow covered the cobblestone path that connected the slave quarters to the castle gates. Only the tall, metal lamps that lined its perimeter were visible. The dim lighting guided her up the mountain, through the icy darkness.

She stuffed her hands beneath her armpits, her breath coming out in clumps of hot steam as she climbed the steps carved into the side of the mountain. The trail was easier to walk this morning, its path cleared from the humans that'd already left early this morning.

At this hour, the kingdom was quiet. Almost peaceful.

The birds weren't up, and a gentle breeze pricked her hair. Without the thick sheet of snow, the glow of the castle shined bright in the near distance.

It was too dark to see the finer details of the castle, but during the day Evangeline could make out the beautiful designs carved into its walls. The intricate patterns that curled around the thick columns protruded from the rigid structure. And when the sun was at its highest, its rays illuminated the white brick, making the towers of the castle glimmer like fiery beacons.

Her guilty pleasure was watching the Aerians fly to and from the open balconies on them. Gliding through the air, each set of wings different and as magnificent as the last. She despised them, and yet still admired them.

Another stone wall surrounded the castle, built along the uneven lines of the mountain, creating an organic barrier. In the spring, shrubbery and groomed flowers lined the outskirts. The grass cut to perfection. In the middle of winter, however, it looked barren with snow piling atop the once-lush garden beds and bushes. It looked more foreboding than welcoming.

She approached the castle gates out of breath, her legs burning. Thick gold barred her entrance into the castle's courtyard, the metal curled and curved to imitate a pair of wings. The guards lining both sides never turned to greet her, and Evangeline's wave was more mocking than friendly as they opened the gates for her to pass through.

Upon entering the courtyard, a large white marbled fountain greeted her, the water sprouting from the Aerian figurine in the middle, frozen in place.

Its granite smile permanently etched into one of victory. The stretch of its wings—the same ones that flew everyone to the heavens when the world fell to darkness—expanded the length of the fountain. Thick bands of muscle, carved from white rock, were proof of who really ruled this world.

The God of all Gods.

Funny how it looked like the king.

Behind it, three paths branched out. One toward the main hall, the east wing, and the west wing. Though the king had the entire west wing forcibly disconnected from the castle, the massive remaining monument still sat isolated and forgotten in the distance. Its cursed grounds served as the former queen's grave site and a deathly reminder to every human that passed it.

The Red Wash.

It was the day the king had executed over half the human population within the kingdom.

Evangeline's face darkened. She was twelve when it happened, but she remembered the day vividly. The commotion that struck the castle. Sobs and screams rang in her ears as families were ripped apart and innocents were lined up for slaughter. All because of a rumor. That the attack on the west wing had been a group of mutinous slaves.

But there was never any proof. No hints to what really happened inside those walls.

She shrugged away the morbid memories and sneered at both the statue and the cursed west wing as she passed it.

A blast of warm air hit her when she entered the east wing. Sighing, she unbuttoned her coat. The mouth-watering scent of freshly baked sweet rolls wafted from the kitchen, farther down the hall.

Lani worked in the kitchens all day, and Evangeline made it a habit to swing by often. Her friend believed it was to see if she could snag a sweet roll—which she sometimes did if she was lucky—but the real reason was to ease Evangeline's paranoia. To make sure her friend hadn't disappeared when she wasn't looking.

It's still early. I'll check on her later. If Ryker or Vane didn't kill her first.

Humans shuffled past her in a hurried rush, an undercurrent

of chattering and clanking of trays. Aside from the occasional guard, only a few Nytes roamed the halls this early. Most were high-ranking officers, judging by their dark purple uniforms, embroidered in gold. She brushed past them, silently relieved when they ignored her. She wasn't in the mood to be tripped or hurled with insults this morning.

Evangeline came to a stop before a double set of glass doors, leading to the second largest courtyard in the castle. The training grounds for the Peredian military.

Fake figurines and boards for target practice lined the sides. The courtyard spanned long enough that objects and people on the opposite end were mere specks. In the warmer seasons, pockets of dirt sprung up in the yard from where soldiers trained, the grass growing back in patches every year.

Soft flickering lanterns, affixed to the columns, guided her along the outskirts of the field. Barrels and equipment cluttered some of its perimeter, allowing her to lurk behind its shadows, bundling into her coat.

A few soldiers were out practicing; soldiers trained hard, even in winter. But with the return of the princes, most Nytes still laid in bed, too preoccupied with drinking the previous night.

As a kid, she had often visited the training grounds. Initially, it was because she would always find Ceven training here, but soon she became fascinated by the soldiers and the skillful way they fought. She'd sit on the outskirts, waiting for the soldiers to finish, before doing her own rudimentary training. Using a long, sturdy stick, she would mimic the moves of the soldiers, pretending she was a captain, leading her troops into battle. Or one heroine in her books, slaying monsters to save her family. It had been one of her favorite pastimes—until Lord Ryker found out.

She glanced thoughtfully at where her scar would be beneath her sleeve. It ran from her elbow all the way to her wrist. She had many scuffs and scars from where Lord Ryker would beat her if she hadn't studied for her tutoring sessions as a child, or when she would refuse to wear a dress, but this one she remembered well.

It was the day Ceven hurt her for the first time.

Evangeline had pointed her stick at the tall, sack–filled figurine. "Surrender and I may yet spare your life."

She had finished practicing her Atiacan alphabet with Lord Ryker before running to the training grounds as fast as she could. Other Nyte children were playing, but the moment they saw her, they moved elsewhere. It didn't bother her anymore, now that she had a friend to play with—the prince.

"What do you think you're doing?" someone hissed at her from behind.

She jumped and swung her stick, but Ceven caught it right before it hit his face. Her cheeks burned.

"What are you doing here?" she accused to hide her embarrassment.

"I'm training to become captain of the Royal Guard," he announced proudly but glanced around. "If Ryker finds you here, you'll be punished. Ladies of the Aerian court aren't allowed to fight."

She shrugged, knowing her indifference would irritate him. "I'm human, I'll never be a part of the Aerian court, so I don't see the problem with it."

"You need to leave, Eve. Now. Before you get in trouble."

Nobody had caught her yet, and she wasn't leaving just because he told her to. "Careful, or else I might think you really are the Prince of Peredia." To further annoy him, she resumed swinging her stick.

Evangeline jumped when he thrust a real sword in front of her face. She didn't like the smirk he wore.

"Fine. I challenge you to a dual. If I win, you'll leave. If I lose, I'll train you myself."

He knew her too well. They both knew who would win, but Evangeline refused to back down from a challenge. Especially from him.

She snatched the sword, thrilled to test her skill with something other than a stick. "Alright, I bet you're all talk, anyway. There's no way a scrawny Aerian like you could defeat me."

Evangeline straightened her back and lifted her chin. She gave her new weapon a few practice swings, testing its weight. It was built for practice. Thin and light in her hand with the tip severely dulled.

She pointed her sword at her opponent. "Let's see what you got, Prince."

Ceven met her stride for stride, metal clashing. She knew he was only humoring her, but she enjoyed herself, nevertheless.

"You have the confidence of one of the best knights of Peredia, yet lack quite some skill. If I didn't know better, I would've thought you had the strength to take on an army," he teased.

"An army, huh?" She grinned as he parried her attack aimed at his left side.

Sweat built beneath her brow as her blade met his. He successfully blocked every attack, spurring her to be faster and more unpredictable to break his defense, stealing the occasional opening. It wasn't until the blade she was wielding became heavier, her breath coming in haggard gasps, that she realized

they had drawn a crowd. Soldiers looked at them with disapproval. Aerian onlookers sneered at them.

Ceven started hitting harder. He moved a little too fast, his blows becoming more difficult to defend. Exhaustion screamed in her bones, but she wasn't about to give up. Ceven meant only to disarm her but, underestimating his Aerian strength, came down too hard on her forearm, slicing the length of it.

To this day, Evangeline still remembered the pain. She was lucky. If it hadn't been a practice sword, she would've lost her arm completely. When Lord Ryker heard the news about their duel, he was furious. He dragged her to an empty storage room below the castle, gave her the heaviest sword to wield, and forced her to swing it over and over again. Locked in that room for the next three days, he watched her struggle to swing the heavy sword repeatedly. When she collapsed from fatigue on the fourth day, he ended the punishment, but Evangeline lost all desire to pick up a sword ever again.

Until now.

She clung to the sides, avoiding the clutter of crates and other miscellaneous objects she couldn't make out in the low light. She skimmed over the barrels, crates, and dummies tossed to the side, their sack-filled figurines torn to bits, until she found what she was looking for. A rack of weapons.

None of it would be useful in an actual battle, all of them dulled for sparring. She clasped the long, narrow sword. It was made of steel and felt heavier than it looked, the tip rounded.

For a moment, she stood there, sword in hand. In the quiet

morning, the thud of her heart was like a drum pounding in her ears.

Aside from the two Rathans at the other end of the court-yard, no one was close enough to recognize her from this distance. She looked up. Stone columns surrounded the courtyard, supporting the balconies that looked onto it from above. Anyone could look down and see her. She treaded farther into the field, away from the cast of the light until darkness shrouded her.

When she was nothing more than a silhouette, she gripped her practice sword, blade out. Her fingers tingled, and an excited smile broke across her face.

She swung.

The movement brought back a wave of nostalgia, of all those times soaked in sweat, battling alongside the soldiers in secret. She tested out the sword's weight in both hands, re-training herself on how to grip the hilt and swing without losing her footing. It didn't take long before she felt more confident and swung in earnest.

Her blood pumped faster, and she imagined slicing through soldiers, taking them down one by one with her prowess. Then, with no one left standing, she and Lani would walk out the kingdom's front gates and not look back.

But that would never happen, because she wasn't strong enough. Couldn't protect herself. Stand up for herself.

Lord Ryker allowed Vane to drag you off to be punished like some animal.

She gripped the sword tighter and swung.

His sharp claws had been so close . . . his breath, the smell of his smoke as he dug it into your skin.

She swung again.

And all you could do was cry and scream for help.

Evangeline came down too hard, the sword slipping from her hands. She didn't pick it up. Instead, she stood there, panting.

She had been beyond the castle walls. Leaving was possible. She could protect Lani, save her from being the next missing person. But she wasn't careful enough. She had messed up. And if Ryker found out how she left, she might not get another chance to get them out of this kingdom.

Marching over, she snatched the sword and started swinging again. And it was then she realized it wasn't the fighting she missed, but the illusion it gave her. Because, for a moment, she could pretend she was as strong as any soldier. As any Nyte.

"What do you think you're doing?"

Evangeline jumped, losing grip on the handle. She fumbled to catch the sword before it fell to the ground. She wasn't successful.

Heart in her throat, she whirled around. "Ceven?"

Ceven stood, arms crossed, the blue fabric of his coat stretching tight, showcasing the firm muscle beneath. She couldn't help but glance enviously. If she had Ceven's strength, she wouldn't have any trouble fighting her way out.

"You're lucky it was me and not someone else. I thought you would've known better by now. You know, learned your lesson." She could tell by his tone that he wasn't just angry. He was furious.

Her own temper flared, and she cocked her hip. "What's that supposed to mean?"

He narrowed his eyes. The dark brown and green irises appeared almost black in the early morning light. "It means you're looking for trouble." His eyes shifted to her cheek, and his features abruptly softened. "Your face . . . is that from Vane?"

Bending over to pick up the sword, she shielded her cheek from him.

And the terror in her eyes.

Ceven was right. What if someone else had seen her? She hadn't heard him walk up behind her. If she had a Nyte's sense of hearing, she'd never worry about being snuck up on again.

"It looks worse than it is. And no, I wasn't looking for trouble. I was looking for a distraction." He wanted to argue, but she cut him off. "What are you doing here? I didn't think you trained this early." She was trying to avoid him, not the opposite.

"I don't. I wanted to blow off some steam by myself before I entertained the masses today." He sighed. "Sometimes I miss Atiaca."

"Then maybe you should go back." She lashed out with the blade, clenching the handle. A warm hand landed on her back, another cradling her elbow. She sucked in a sharp breath.

"Your form is wrong." He leaned down, and his cheek brushed her ear. "Strike out like this. Keep your elbow up."

She immediately stepped away from him. "I know." And swung incorrectly.

Ceven reached out and caught the tip in his grasp. She tried yanking it away, but it was futile.

"It's obvious you're upset, Eve. Talk to me." When she gave him a sour look, he added, "Please."

Her grip slackened, and he took the sword from her, tossing it aside. She wanted to confide in him. To tell him about her grand plan and how she had royally screwed up. How she hated this place, hated Ryker, and, most of all, hated how spitting useless she felt.

But Ceven was a prince of Peredia. She couldn't risk trusting him. Not when it could cost her Lani's life.

Evangeline gave him an apologetic smile. "You're right, I'm sorry. Yesterday was just . . . hard. I'm fine." It wasn't a total lie.

His lips pressed into a firm line. "I won't let Vane touch you. I won't let anyone hurt you."

Two years ago she would have relished those words. "Thank you, Ceven, but I can fight my own battles." She looked around. Other Nytes had trickled into the courtyard. The sun still wasn't fully up, but the sky had brightened considerably since she had first arrived. She gnawed on her lower lip, her breathing coming fast. It was almost time to see Ryker.

Ceven took in her expression and opened his mouth to speak when something caught his eye. Two Aerians headed their way—Ceven's two shadows.

Tarry and Xilo had been Ceven's personal guards since the day he was born. Both part of the Royal Guard and having served for at least forty years, the youngest prince's safety was their duty. As they walked side by side, the difference in their statures was apparent.

Tarry was bulky, his muscular build intimidating to his enemies before he eliminated them. Two axes hung at his waist, along with a single sword strapped to his back between his blue and gray wings. His skin was dark mahogany, his complexion marred with scars, showing off his time in battle. The few strands of gray marring his black hair were a testament to his age. He was nearing sixty, giving him forty years left to serve in the Guard.

Tarry's strides were blunt. His legs demanded the snow to move out of his way, his body acting like a plow while Xilo's was long and careful. Like he was gliding atop the thick terrain rather than plunging through it.

At fifty-three, Xilo was taller than Tarry, but his frame was vastly smaller. He kept his black hair tied in a ponytail, the length brushing his hip. Like Tarry, a long sword was strapped to his back, but rather than axes, he kept an assortment of blades at his waist. His wings were smaller than his companion's and matched the dark purple uniforms they both wore, the emblem for the Royal Guard plastered across their right breast—a pair of golden wings encircled in a band of stars.

"Your Highness, you know you shouldn't leave without our protection," Xilo said when the two men drew closer.

Tarry said nothing, his arms crossed. He peered up at Ceven with, what seemed like, a disappointed gesture. With his hard-set lips and narrowed eyes, it was hard to tell.

Ceven sighed. "I understand."

Evangeline blinked. Whenever they had run off together as children, Ceven's response to the same admonishment was always an irritated eye roll.

"Good morning, Tarry, Xilo," Evangeline said politely. "It's nice to see you two again." Both had accompanied Ceven to Atiaca.

They looked at her and nodded. Evangeline had become comfortable with Xilo and Tarry, having grown up around them. They had never shown her anything but indifferent politeness, but she didn't take it personally. It was more of a response than any other Nyte gave her. She also knew their priority was to protect the prince. Even from his friends.

"Remember, the king is expecting you this morning. He wants a full report," Tarry's voice rumbled.

"Of course." His lip turned up in distaste. Evangeline didn't envy him. Being in the king's presence was an exercise in mental fortitude.

Ceven turned to her. "We'll talk later." His expression told her they'd talk about this later.

Evangeline nodded and bade the three of them farewell. Pink and orange stained the sky. It would've been beautiful—if it was any other morning.

She swallowed.

It was time to see Lord Ryker.

CHAPTER 7

⌁ EVANGELINE ⌁

Evangeline was in front of Lord Ryker's suite, and any courage she had wavered. How would he react to her disobedience? Would he send her to Vane once more? Could she endure whatever Vane had in store for her?

The strong-jawed Rathan next to her rapped on the door in the familiar pattern, announcing her presence. *Tap, tap, tap-tap-tap, tap.* She crept inside, her teeth nibbling on the inside of her cheek.

Lord Ryker sat, legs crossed, in his favorite green armchair, waiting.

He held a cup of tea in his hand, steam wafting from it. His loose, crimson shirt billowed open in the front, showing a smooth, pale chest, the ends of it tucked into a pair of black trousers. His hair was splayed across the back of the chair, his wings tucked into his sides.

When she entered the room, his eyes slid away from the fire to pin her with his usual cold, intimidating stare. They trailed to the bruise on her cheek. His lips thinned in disapproval, but he didn't comment on it.

Evangeline forced herself to walk closer and look directly at his eyes. "I understand I have been disobedient, and I am prepared to take full responsibility for my actions." Her voice quivered, but she kept her chin up in determination. She had to earn his trust again.

"Sit down, Evangeline."

She immediately sat on the velvet loveseat across from him. He always offered her a beverage and have a plate of food brought to her. Today, silence greeted her. He set down his cup on the wood table beside him, its legs carved with intricate flowers. The same fine artistry wrapped across the elongated dark wood separating the two of them. Her eyes followed his hands as he picked up the plate of food beside him.

Evangeline smelled the savory aroma of poached eggs, steamed beans, and crispy bacon. She resisted the urge to glance at the plate as he scooped up a slice of egg and put it into his mouth. Then she realized: He was doing this on purpose.

"How was your reunion with the prince?" he asked.

"Surprising."

He raised an eyebrow and delicately cut into his egg again. He dangled the piece on the edge of his fork, as if pondering it, before slowly taking the bite. She refused to lick her lips or swallow the saliva that pooled beneath her tongue. It wasn't the first time he'd used food to punish her. *How long will he starve me this time?*

"Oh, I'm sure. It's been . . . what, two years now?" He picked up a slice of bacon, twisting it between his fingers. "I know you two are close." He bit into it, making a small noise of approval.

"Were," she corrected.

His eyes met hers, but he didn't remark on her statement. He finished the slice of bacon and wiped his fingers on the blue cloth next to his plate. "I want to know where you went and what you discussed."

Evangeline didn't hesitate. She told him about the enclosed garden and Ceven's visit in Atiaca. She was as detailed as possible, neglecting to mention she had run into him again this morning. "We didn't talk for long. He had important matters to attend to," she finished.

"You're lying."

She yanked her hand away from her hair and winced in pain, having pulled out the strand wrapped around her finger. "We had a disagreement."

"About what?"

Lord Ryker's meticulous interrogation was a normal occurrence, but it never got easier. She sighed in defeat. "Vane."

He smiled. "Did His Highness have an issue with your punishment?"

You know perfectly well he did. "Yes."

Evangeline hadn't been expecting an apology, but the fact that he glided over how Vane had attacked her left a pit of needles in her stomach. Jabs, insults, and the occasional shove from a Nyte was expected, but anything more and Ryker always intervened. As much as she hated it, he protected her where others of her kind weren't so lucky. Did he not care anymore? Did he only let it slide this time because the prince came? Had he really lost his patience with her? The questions hung on her tongue, but she was too much of a coward to ask him.

A flashback of Vane dragging her down the hall assaulted her. His grip tight on her arm, his hand gliding over her body before climbing on top of her and—

She clenched her eyes shut.

Ryker set aside his food and folded his hands in his lap. "How did you get beyond the kingdom's walls, Evangeline?"

Her eyes flew open, and she flinched at his steely gaze.

Is he testing me? was her first thought. Either he didn't know and was fishing for information, or . . . he wanted her to admit it herself. But what was she supposed to say? What could she say without condemning both of them in the future? She gritted her teeth. *Why didn't I come up with a believable lie sooner?*

Ryker leaned forward, his wings extending. He appeared even bigger. "And what were you doing beyond those walls, Evangeline?"

Her mind raced with excuses. None of them sounded feasible enough for Lord Ryker to believe.

She lowered her head. "I'm sorry. I'll take full responsibility for my actions," she repeated, her eyes wide beneath her curtain of hair. No matter what happened, she couldn't reveal her true intentions.

"Is that your final answer?"

"Yes." She was ready for anything.

He sighed and stood. She didn't raise her head, but she could feel the weight of his eyes on her. "Then I suppose it is best that Prince Ceven will be occupied for most of the day. I wouldn't wish for anyone interfering with your punishment again."

Evangeline was proud of herself for not jolting off the couch. Instead, she lifted her eyes, focusing on the small crack in the soft amber wallpaper right behind Ryker's head. She trailed down its length, estimating its depth. How wide it was. The imperfection was almost beautiful. Real. The slim line breaking up the faulty wallpaper, rebelling against the posh, organized room.

When she felt that her voice wouldn't shake, she met his eyes. "I had another dream last night. Do you wish to hear it?"

Her heart squeezed when his head shot up, his curiosity piqued. His eyes narrowed. "You better not be playing games with me."

She forced her face to remain still.

He stared at her longer before uttering, "Go on."

She told him everything, starting with the Caster woman that she had called Anali, to how she dressed her in a gown made of blue and silver silk. She also remembered being told to meet with someone named Jaden.

"Who is Jaden?" Ryker asked.

She shook her head. "I don't know."

Lord Ryker smiled, and it gave her hope. *Let me go, let me go, let me go.*

"You will tell me the instant you have another dream."

"Yes, Father."

Ryker walked over and pulled the lever on the wall. The sound of the door opening echoed throughout the suite, the chinking of metal getting closer until a guard appeared before them.

"Tell Officer Jarr that I am no longer in need of his services."

Evangeline's eyes stayed on the ground. Her shoulders slumped with overwhelming relief. She wanted to cry and laugh at the same time.

The guard bowed and left. Ryker turned his attention toward her. "You will no longer be allowed to go into town. If I catch you even a step past the slave quarters, there will be consequences, Evangeline." His eyes pierced hers, and her spine straightened. "I mean it." He looked away. "That will be all today. I will see you tonight."

She forgot how to breathe. "I'm . . . dismissed?"

"Don't push it."

She tried not to trip over her own feet as she gave a bow, her hair grazing the floor. She raced out of the room with a speed that matched her beating heart and flung open the door—running nose-first into a hard body.

Rubbing her face, Evangeline looked up and met Vane's slitted glare.

Her nostrils flared, eyes widening as she bit back the instincts telling her to run. Vane was clutching his right side, and underneath his shaggy, untrimmed beard, were yellowish blemishes. Bruises.

He pinned her against the door, the grooves digging into her back. His claws wrapped around her throat. She choked and sputtered for air, her fingernails scratching at his hands when two swords unsheathed on both sides of her.

Ryker's guards pointed their weapons at Vane. "Release her, at once," one said. "Lord Ryker is no longer in need of your services."

Vane dropped her, and she crumpled to the floor, drawing in deep breaths. *Took them long enough to say something.* She grimaced as her hand cradled her neck.

Vane's cackle was loud. "I never thought I'd see the day that the Peredian military would be protecting a *human*. What is this kingdom coming to?" He stared at her, and his lip peeled back into a snarl. "Ryker can't protect you forever. And when that day comes, you better run." He turned on his heel, knocking the guard's sword out of his way before walking off.

The guards didn't offer to help her up as she gathered herself and fixed her dress. She wanted to thank them, but their contemptuous stares had her hurrying away.

Evangeline climbed down the purple carpeted stairs in the main hall. Sunshine rained on her from the glass ceiling above the winding stairwell. She preferred it over the lift. The black wires that churned and raised the wood platform had snapped six years ago, killing two humans. Ever since, she refused to take it.

Her meeting with Ryker left Evangeline more confused. Did he know about the weakness in the wall, or not? She needed to find a way to check it. Sneaking out at night was an option, but what if more guards have been posted? And if she's caught beyond the slave quarters . . . Vane would be waiting for her.

Her fingers glided along the polished chestnut wood railing when the sound of light laughter echoed behind her. She lowered her head and squeezed herself against the railing as two Aerian ladies passed her. Their navy and lavender gowns hung low to accommodate their wings, their breasts piled atop their corsets to give a revealing display of their assets. The olive-skinned brunette sliced Evangeline with a scathing look while her friend admired her nails. Evangeline scrunched her nose, assailed by a gust of perfume.

For a moment, she wondered what it would be like to live as an Aerian girl. To walk freely without being harassed, to travel anywhere she wanted. To be safe from Nytes like Vane.

To be Ceven's equal.

Her foot paused mid-step. Where had that thought come from?

She made it to the ground floor, where the two opposite sets of stairs spilled into the entrance hall. A large, gold-framed painting of the king and queen settled in the space between them.

Her gaze lingered on the painting, her eyes meeting the sharp, green gaze of the queen. She was more than beautiful; she was angelic and bold. Daring and compassionate. Every story and compliment Ceven had ever told Evangeline about his mother came to life in this captured image. From the thick brown waves of hair that rained down her scooped coral gown, to the midnight-colored wings, highlighted with streams of dark blue and a hint of gold.

The only flaw was her smile.

It crawled underneath Evangeline's skin every time she saw it, lingering, raising the hairs on her arms. She was sure Ceven wasn't the queen's only secret. But she would never tell him that.

Her stomach growled, and she frowned. Time to go check on Lani. *And maybe steal a sweet roll.* Her lips curled into a smile.

She left the entrance hall, the queen's eyes following her.

Down the hall, humans with trays of food walked out the revolving double doors of the biggest kitchen in the castle. Evangeline pushed the door open—and went head-first into a slim girl with a tray of boiling food.

"I'm sorry!" She put out her hands to catch the tray, but the girl had already regained her grip and slid past her with a dirty look.

Evangeline kept along the sides of the large kitchen as more slaves strolled past in a flurry of motion. The kitchen contained four large stoves, making the room toasty, almost uncomfortable, as she rolled up the sleeves of her coat. Its ceilings stretched higher than the hallway. Small windows at the top fogged from the steam, since the brick chimneys lacked proper ventilation.

She scanned the swarm of humans working over pots of food, others slicing meat and hanging the slabs on hooks by the blazing fire. To feed the amount of people in the east wing alone was a heavy task, and now even more had returned, along with the princes.

Lani was on the other side, washing dishes in the large porcelain sink. Next to her was Ranson. Evangeline wrinkled her nose in disgust. She recognized Ranson's head by the little hair he had left. He bent over Lani, a permanent curve in his back that became apparent several years ago.

Ranson was one of Lord Ryker's personal servants, and Evangeline saw him often in his suite, but they never had gotten along. He viewed her like the rest of the humans did. A pampered, Aerian pet. She returned the favor by thinking him a grumpy old man whose only expression was a sneer. He lingered around Lani in the mornings, and it was obvious the old man had a crush on her, as much as Lani denied it.

Evangeline squirmed through the crowd, keeping her eyes on Lani's silver-streaked hair, when several Nytes entered the kitchen. Black uniforms stretched across their wide frame, a familiar pair of golden wings sewed over their right breasts.

Overseers. She cursed underneath her breath.

The black-clad Aerians and Rathans watched over the slaves of the castle. They also were the ones who delivered swift and harsh punishment to those that stepped out of line. If she tried to snag a sweet roll now, she'd be lucky just to be escorted out. Worse, the slave in charge of making the rolls would be beaten. It'd happened before.

Turning on her heel, she marched back out of the kitchens empty-handed.

She could go to the storage rooms below the east wing. It was almost noon, and she knew the guards switched shifts around this time, having waited and learned their patterns over the course of a couple months. A pantry of dried fruit and vegetables sat close to the entrance that she could steal. She knew because it was where she'd gotten her supplies for her escape.

I don't need it. I'll have less to eat when I'm out in the woods in the middle of winter with Lani. She swallowed down the saliva at the thought of biting into a hot, soft roll and continued walking.

During the day, Evangeline visited the library or, in recent months, traveled to the kingdom's marketplace with an escort of guards, planning out her escape. Despite the sense of urgency she felt, she needed to stick to her normal routine to avoid more unwanted attention from Ryker. She had been planning this escape for months, had nearly died for it to work. She wasn't about to ruin everything by being impatient. *Library it is, then.*

The doors to the library weren't as gigantic as the main hall's but were far more beautiful. Her fingers brushed the dark, textured wood. The fine, detailed lines and curves in the thick panel shaped the feathers of an Aerian's wing. She grasped the bronzed knob, pulling the door open, the wooden feathers shifting in the lamp light. Like an Aerian in flight.

Sunlight hit her face, and a wave of must and candle wax overwhelmed her. Evangeline's spirits instantly lifted.

Windows swept from the floor and arched up to meet the dome ceiling of the library, casting the rows of tall bookshelves and golden banisters in a warm, decadent light. Her boots pattered across the tiled floor, white with rectangular specks of black and blue, passing tables with other Nytes quietly reading and talking in hushed conversation. A few humans often were scattered about, wiping bookshelves and tables, but never reading. It was against Peredian law for a slave to know how to read and write, making Evangeline the only human in the kingdom to know how to do both.

Climbing the spiral stairs to the third story, she retreated to the back corner, away from the balcony overlooking the main floor.

In a small nook, by one window, was an oversized red lounge chair. The fabric was worn and faded, but she loved it. Behind it, in the distance, were the Frostsnare mountains, separating eastern Peredia from the west. The snowcapped peaks resembled a rumbling sea of green and white, spanned out far beyond the kingdom and its confining walls.

Her fingers skimmed over familiar titles on a nearby bookshelf. One caught her eye, and she pulled out the thick volume. *Oylani's Edition: Atiacan.* She heard children giggling, the faint echoes of a memory teasing her. Two kids pressed together on the large, red chair. A younger Aerian prince and a girl, with blond hair kept short at her ears.

Evangeline's face scrunched in old embarrassment, remembering the horrible haircut. Looking back, she now found it humorous, seeing how everybody thought Ceven was the girl, her the young boy. But twelve-year-old Evangeline had been mortified.

Ceven's long brown hair sat tangled around his and her shoulders as he peered down at the book across both of their laps. He pointed at something, and her mouth opened in a giggle, showing a gap in the set of crooked teeth. Lani had pulled out her last baby tooth that morning. She repeated the Atiacan word, and the two of them shared another bout of giggles.

Evangeline smiled. That day, she and Ceven had learned every curse word in the Atiacan language.

She put the heavy book back on the self, her smile faltering. An emptiness inside her swept in like fog on a sunny morning. She missed those days.

Snagging another book, she climbed into the oversized chair and tucked her feet underneath her. She brushed away the old memories and opened to the first page.

"He's gone!"

Evangeline jerked awake. She sat up, wiping away the drool creeping down her chin, and looked around, disorientated. Her book had fallen off her lap and onto the floor. *How long was I asleep for?* She glanced out the window. It was almost dusk.

In the distance, someone muffled a sob.

"It's okay, I'm sure he's fine. He's probably busy with work and hasn't gotten back yet." It sounded like a woman on the other side of her nook.

"It's been four days, Gardia. *Four days!*"

There was another broken sob. The noise lured her from the chair and she peeked around the corner. There were two women, humans dressed in their black uniforms. She recognized the shorter brunette, hunched and crying. She worked in the kitchens with Lani, but Evangeline didn't know her name. The taller one with short black hair and tanned skin rubbed the brunette's back, consoling her.

"What if he's disappeared like all the rest? Not my boy, not my precious little boy!" The brunette clutched the front of her friend's shirt, her eyes red and puffy. The other woman brought her into a hug, whispering to her. She turned and their eyes met.

Evangeline whipped back around the corner. *Someone else has gone missing.* She frowned, picking up her book and putting it back on the shelf. *What if Lani's next?*

Her friend's time was running out.

By the time Evangeline returned to the slave quarters, it was dark out and the frigid air nestled deep into her bones.

"Thought you wouldn't show." Lani was by the fire, hanging up her uniform.

Evangeline shrugged off her coat and hung it next to Lani's black shirt and pants. "Ryker held me later than usual tonight. I'm surprised he let me leave, to be honest," she said, pulling a night gown from the chest and changing.

She had reported to him what she saw: another slave had gone missing. He said nothing on the matter. Not that she had expected him to. Whenever she brought it up, he was always indifferent on the subject. Most Nytes were. After all, it was only humans disappearing. Not beaten to death, ill, or shipped to other parts of the country, but completely vanishing. For months, now.

Lani reached behind her and pulled out a roll from her apron. Evangeline's eyes lit up. She grabbed the sweet roll and inhaled it in one bite. Ryker had left her with nothing tonight and forced her to watch him eat honeyed slices of ham and roasted potatoes.

"Did he find out? About how you left?"

Evangeline licked the cinnamon off her fingers, savoring the taste. "I don't know. He hasn't mentioned it again." He had pressed her with the usual questions: *Where did you go today? What did you do? Did you talk to Ceven?* But nothing about what she'd been doing outside the walls. Or how she had gotten there. Maybe he was biding his time.

Or worse, he already knew.

"Why do you ask?" she said.

Lani shrugged. "No reason."

Evangeline didn't believe her. "Another slave went missing."

"Who?" Lani sat on the bed and massaged her calves.

"She works in the kitchen with you. I don't know her name, but she was talking about a boy—"

"Shani. Her son." Lani rubbed her face. "Nobody has seen him for a while." She sighed, gazing back into the fire. The lines on her face were more defined in the harsh glow. "He was always attached to her. A clingy mama's boy, but . . . he was a sweet kid."

An image of a small boy crying out for his mother tortured

her thoughts. All alone in a dark room with no one coming to save him. Evangeline shied away from the image, uncomfortable that her imagination may not be far from reality.

"We don't know that for sure. Maybe he's . . ." But Evangeline knew it was pointless. No one would see the boy again. "Tomorrow, I'll figure out what I can about our escape route. If it's still a viable option. As soon as I find out it's safe, we're leaving. For good."

Lani clicked her tongue, rolling onto the bed. "Sometimes I don't know how you can still be so spitting hopeful."

Evangeline didn't bother to fight back a huff. She was sick of arguing this with her. "And I don't understand why you always fight me on this."

Her friend snorted. "You really think we can escape this place? You got caught the first time. What makes you think it won't happen again? What makes you think Vane won't kill us both—"

"We won't get caught."

"But what if we do?" Lani stared at her and Evangeline crossed her arms. When she spoke again, her voice was softer. "It's dangerous. To believe anything good will ever happen to us. Countless humans are beaten and killed for attempting stunts less dangerous than yours. I just . . ." She sighed. A weary, worn sigh. "I just don't want you to get your hopes up."

Evangeline blinked at the fire as it cracked and popped. Lani wasn't arguing with just her, but with herself. "Hope is all we have. I have to believe we'll get us out of here. I love you too much to risk losing you. This *will* work. It has to."

Lani didn't respond and Evangeline stoked the fire before crawling on top of the thin mattress. Silence passed between them for a moment until her friend's wrinkled hand found hers and squeezed it.

"Fine. For your sake, I'll believe in this . . . insane plan." She let go and rolled away, grumbling, "I just pray we both don't freeze to death out there."

Evangeline smiled at Lani's back. As much as the old woman denied it, she had always believed deep down. If she didn't, she never would have told Evangeline about the storage rooms underneath the castle. She would've tried harder to stop her when Evangeline first discussed the outlines of her plan. Of hiding supplies beyond the wall, and testing the area, before making the long trek to the next town by foot.

Because, deep down, Lani was more terrified of disappearing forever.

An icy fear crept up Evangeline's neck. But what if Lani's right? What if they did get caught? Or freeze to death, like that Caster almost had? Her thoughts wandered to the blue-eyed man. Was he even still in the kingdom? And what had attacked him out there in the snow?

It all left a bad feeling in her mouth.

CHAPTER 8

⤳ EVANGELINE ⤶

Avana and Ryker huddled over a table filled with vials of liquids while Evangeline waited on the couch. She hated when Ryker had company, but upon seeing Avana this morning, her irritation turned to excitement. Maybe this time the Caster would tell her about her mark.

The Caster wore a high-collared blue dress that was modest on top and curved around her body. The sleeves were cut short, and the edges of dark tattoos peeked out from under the fabric, forming slithering bands around her upper arms. Thumb to her lips, she focused on the journal in front of her. Ryker hovered over her, his braided blond hair falling over his shoulder. His wings were the color of heavy rain clouds, damp from a morning shower, the tips dripping water onto the back of his emerald shirt.

Evangeline's cheeks felt flushed, but it wasn't from the

crackling fire she sat next to. All morning she had felt dizzy. Lethargic. Her stomach rumbled in pain, and her eyes moved to the empty trays of food on the dining room table. There was no food waiting for her.

"Use this first, then . . ." Avana picked up a small vial filled with a blueish-greenish liquid, shook it, and put it back. "No, this first, then we'll go to that," Avana said. It was more to herself as Ryker stood by, arms crossed, while she fiddled with the contents on the table.

Taking the sharp end of a dinner knife, Avana pricked her finger. A single red drop welled up, and she squeezed it into the vial with clear liquid. The drop slid down the glass before mingling with the clear substance. Red blossomed instantly when it hit the surface. Its contents glowed for a brief second before changing into a yellow color.

Avana's lips moved beneath her breath and the whole process entranced Evangeline, never having witnessed anything like it in her life. Rathan and Aerian scholars had run the previous tests on her.

"Evangeline, come," Ryker said, beckoning her forth.

Wary, she got up. Avana held her hand out, the other one holding the vial. Evangeline tensed. *I hope this doesn't hurt as much as it did last time.* The last scientist had been years ago, but she remembered the unpleasant needles and incisions. Wasted efforts in trying to discover what her mark was.

Avana's hand was smooth when it held her wrist, while Evangeline's was clammy as she removed her glove.

"Don't worry, this won't hurt," Avana murmured, swirling the contents, prepping it over her hand.

Evangeline tried not to flinch when Avana spilled the liquid over her mark. It didn't hurt, to her relief. Just colder than she thought. The yellow liquid gravitated to the bold lines of her tattoo, like a magnet, and sank into her skin. Not a single drop fell to the floor.

Avana rubbed her thumb over the mark, the bold lines stubbornly remaining. Her face lit up. She repeated the step, pouring several more vials over her hand, liquid seeping into the mark. Some made her skin itch, while others made it heat uncomfortably. Evangeline had to admit, she was excited to watch the liquids mold to her mark. Excited to see Caster magic at work. Some part of her didn't believe what Ryker taught in their tutoring sessions. She wondered what it all meant.

After the table turned into a mass of empty bottles, Avana stepped back, shaking her head. "Amazing, simply amazing. I didn't think . . ."

"I was telling the truth?" Ryker finished.

She turned to him, still in awe. "Can you blame me? This isn't something I thought I'd ever find. I've been searching all this time . . . I almost gave up believing that it was real."

Evangeline blurted, "What do you mean?"

Avana opened her mouth, but Ryker interrupted her. "Now that you have the evidence you need, will you reconsider my offer?"

Evangeline observed the two of them: Ryker's calculated expression, Avana's intrigue wiped from her face. Indifference and a blank stare were all that remained.

"I'll think about it," Avana said, gathering her vials and notes.

"Those vials, your magic," Evangeline quickly asked. "How'd you do it? What did it do?"

"You ask too many questions, Evangeline." Ryker flicked his hand, dismissing Avana from answering her.

She recognized the warning in his tone, but she was too excited to heed it. "Think of it as furthering my education on Caster magic," she tried.

Ryker narrowed his eyes. Evangeline's shoulders dropped.

Avana stepped forward, shielding her from Ryker. "It's only fair that you know what's going on." Her gaze slid to Ryker's, seeking permission. He kept his stare on Evangeline but eventually nodded.

She continued, "My magic"—she put a hand on her heart—"comes from me, essentially. From my being. For Caster magic to synthesize and manifest, our blood and will has to be involved. We do this using the Castanian language, either by writing it or speaking it aloud. Depending on the spell, sometimes both are required." Avana gestured toward her mark. "What I did today was see if your mark was real. If it was made through another Caster's magic."

Evangeline took in a deep breath and licked her lips. She stared at her hand as if someone just told her what her life's purpose was. "So, it is Castanian. But . . . how come no one has figured that out?"

Ryker's lips stretched thin, but he didn't interject.

"This symbol is from . . . another time," Avana said, glancing at Ryker. "Only a few Casters would recognize it as Castanian, and even then, they wouldn't be able to decipher it."

"Can you decipher it?" she pressed.

"That will be all today, Avana." Ryker swept up a few sheets from the table, handing them to her. "Please think wisely about my offer. My patience is not endless."

It was clear Avana wanted to say more, but she nodded instead, assembling the rest of her materials into a decent-sized leather duffel.

Evangeline ground her teeth. All her life she had wondered about her mark, where she came from and why. Now that she finally was getting answers, Ryker was refusing her that right. Why? What was he hiding?

A knock at the door signaled Ranson's presence. He breathed heavily, his black uniform hugging his stomach as he bowed. Ryker jerked his chin, and he scurried toward the table to gather the empty silver trays.

Avana slung her duffel over her shoulder, the weight digging into her dress. She bowed and brushed past them. The front door clicked shut.

Ryker didn't move or say anything. Evangeline stared hard at the ground, holding back the fiery rage that licked at her insides. *How dare he try to hide something as important as this from me. It's on my body, I have a right to know!* But she didn't dare say that aloud. She exhaled slowly through her mouth, channeling her rage. It wasn't worth it. Wasn't worth another encounter with Vane.

"We will be having a formal dinner with the king tonight," he said after a moment. "I expect you back early this evening to get ready." He dismissed her.

Nothing about her mark. About what Avana had revealed. Nothing about what he was hiding from her.

She kept her voice calm as she asked, "Why wouldn't you let her say—?"

"Do you want me to call for Officer Jarr?" he snapped.

Evangeline blanched. "N-no, I'm sorry, Father."

"Then I'd advise you keep your mouth shut. Now, leave."

At first, her feet froze to the marble floor, too surprised by his sudden outburst. It was upon seeing his eyes, flecks of gray swirling about maddeningly, that she pedaled out of the suite.

A formal dinner with the king tonight? Evangeline groaned, peeking out the large windows onto the training grounds.

The last time she'd had a formal dinner with the king was

two months ago. And it had been painstakingly long. Something about merchants and trade between the kingdom and the cities along the west coast of Peredia. She didn't remember the details, trying her best to drown out the boring conversations that had ensued for three long, tortuous hours.

The king tolerated her presence, only occasionally sneering at her and making comments like how he didn't appreciate Ryker bringing animals to the table. When accompanying the king, Evangeline had a nasty habit of biting her cheek until it bled. The pain made her eyes well up, but it kept her from saying something she'd regret.

And now she had to endure all of that again tonight.

The wind howled on the other side of the glass, snow flurries whirling. The storm from this morning still going strong. It was probably why she didn't see any soldiers out practicing today—or see a pair of blue and gold wings.

Her face warmed at the treacherous thought. She needed to keep her distance from the prince, not pursue him.

Soldiers and guards passed her in the hall, but she could only pick up on tidbits of their conversations, all useless to her. She had taken this route on purpose, knowing a lot of Peredia's military ventured these halls. Eavesdropping wasn't the most reliable method for getting answers, but it was the safest and quickest.

A group of Nytes headed in her direction. They were all soldiers—except for one. A Rathan, whose outrageously bright yellow pants popped off his charcoal skin.

On top, he wore a short-sleeved black shirt, showing off firm muscle and the thick fur that traveled down his arms. Only his palms—which he moved about excitedly as he talked—and the skin of his forearm were left bare. Pointed black-furred ears poked out of his cropped hair, the top longer than the rest.

The Rathan was explaining how he had single-handedly taken down five bandits by himself to the soldier next to him. But it might as well have been to the entire castle. Every word blared down the hallway. When Evangeline passed them, the Rathan caught her staring. He smiled and winked at her.

Evangeline missed her step and stumbled on her dress. "Stupid, blasted dress," she muttered before whipping around. The Rathan didn't pause, continuing his conversation to the soldier next to him. Did she imagine that?

What a strange man. He can't be from Peredia. Not only did he have a thick accent, but his behavior was too unusual.

When she retraced her steps down the same set of hallways for the tenth time, she gave up on overhearing anything useful and went to the kitchens. Through the blaze of heat and humans, she spied Lani chatting in the corner.

The delicious combination of cinnamon and butter in the air made her stomach cramp in longing. She found her prize sitting on the cooling rack in the back corner. Like an arrow, she shot toward it—and a large Aerian blocked her path.

Evangeline hopped back. Craning her head, a grim face that would have been handsome if not for the two scars that ran down the sides of it, peered at her. It was an Overseer.

His deep brown wings expanded, blocking her. His smile was far from pleasant. She took the hint and backpedaled out of the kitchen.

To her relief, he didn't follow her. *How did I miss an Overseer?* Hunger must be making her careless. Her head felt light, her body sluggish. If Ryker decided not to feed her again tonight, she might pass out somewhere. Other kitchens occupied the castle that she could go to, but Overseers would be there too.

Good thing she knew of another place to go.

Beneath the east wing was an entire labyrinth. The first time she snuck down here, she'd gotten lost in the multitude of rooms and halls that all looked the same. Some doors were labeled—but not all.

Head-sized hunks of stone made up the walls on either side, guiding her down into the damp, cold underground. She turned a corner, and two Rathan guards lurked further down, leaning against the wall and chatting. If it had been the Royal Guard here, Evangeline would've been sniffed out as soon as she entered the basement, with a warning already sent to Ryker. If he found out she snuck food, he'd find another way to punish her, and she *really* didn't want that.

Hovering close to the wall, Evangeline pushed through a wooden side door. The adjoining room was home to shelves of plates, bowls, and other miscellaneous junk. She cut through and opened the door on the other side when voices echoed nearby. Too close. She ducked back into the room, pressing against the wall.

She left the door ajar, a finger's length of light streaming in. The talking got louder and louder. Evangeline bit her lip, urging whoever it was to continue walking. An image of a broad-chested Overseer peeking around the corner, a grin splitting his face, made her break out in a cold sweat. Then it morphed into Vane and her heart drummed painfully.

The talking stopped, but the sliding and tinkering of metal still clattered close by. It was another set of guards. Her heart squeezed as they walked closer. Their shadows brushed the open gap in the door as Evangeline tiptoed back, ready to exit the other way.

The shadow of light moved through the crack, metal grinding. Her hand felt for the knob behind her when the sliver of light vanished. They stood in the open door. Her heart pounded.

They walked away.

Evangeline blew out a long sigh when the door behind her swung open. The wood frame knocked into her back, and she tripped, her knee slamming into the corner of a box.

Pain radiated up her leg, but she whipped around, prepared to face the guards. Instead, it was a short-haired, olive-skinned human. She was dressed head to toe in black with dirt and flour staining her purple apron.

Evangeline's shoulders sagged. *It's just a human.* She rubbed her knee and turned to the woman. Her face was familiar.

The woman fell to her knees, her hands folded above her head in a gesture of forgiveness. "Please, my lady, forgive me. I was careless. I know I don't deserve your mercy, but please spare me and I'll vow to be a better servant. Please, please . . ." Her words were shrill and tumbled out in fast rasps. She sounded hysterical.

Evangeline was dumbstruck. Never had anyone referred to her as a lady, and never, *never,* had they begged her for anything. Did this woman mistake her for a Nyte? With her forehead touching the ground, she probably hadn't realized Evangeline was human.

"I'm not a Nyte. Don't waste your breath, I'm not going to do anything," she said, looking behind her. She strained to hear over the bumbling woman, who hadn't even glanced up. If running into the box hadn't drawn the guards' attention, this woman certainly would. *What was her name . . .?*

"All I ask is that you spare me. I will do whatever you say, I promise to be loyal and devoted, whatever you need of me . . ." the woman continued to babble.

She was in the library with Lani's friend, Shani. What did she call her? Evangeline stared at her until it clicked. "Gardia!"

The woman jerked up with wide and red-rimmed eyes. She said nothing.

"Gardia . . . right?" The woman still didn't respond, but Evangeline continued anyway. "Look, I'm fine, it's nothing." She extended her hand, and the woman flinched. Evangeline curled it into a fist and dropped it back to her side. "I said I'm not going to hurt you, but fine. Don't mention this and we'll go our separate ways, okay?"

Gardia's head bobbed.

Evangeline turned, trying to shrug away the entire experience, when Gardia said, "Please, don't hurt him."

Evangeline stopped in her tracks. Her head turned. "What?"

Gardia's chin rose, her shoulders straightening as she got to her feet. "The boy, he's only nine. He did nothing wrong."

The boy . . . ? Evangeline felt herself blush. Did she mean Shani's son? But that couldn't be right. She'd never even met the kid. "What are you talking about?"

Gardia's face lost all color, and she stepped back. "I-I promise I won't say anything. I mean, I only heard—"

"Heard what?"

She shook her head. "I'm—I'm sorry. I didn't mean to—"

"You think I hurt Shani's son? You think I'm the one who kidnapped him?" Her look confirmed it, and Evangeline's blood boiled. Nasty rumors had been spread about her before. That she was a secret mistress to the Aerian court, seducing even the prince, acquiescing her body to their every whim, and that was the reason they endured her presence. It was how she earned the nickname Pet. But this?

"I had *nothing* to do with that," she growled, taking a step forward. Gardia mirrored it in the opposite direction. "I don't know what's going on or why these people are disappearing, but I'm just as scared as you. So don't you *dare* accuse me of that. I'm not a monster." She ground the last bit out, her temper flaring. "Who told you this? And why?"

Footsteps shuffled nearby. The guards were circling back. Evangeline turned and missed Gardia slipping out of the room. She swore. As much as she wanted to hunt her down and demand answers, she needed to get her food and get out of here.

Evangeline bypassed guards and a few other humans when she came across a room lined with produce, crates, and loaves of bread. The room was tight, the size of a small pantry. Easy to locate what she needed. The last time she'd done this, she'd had a brown bag and had stuffed it to the brim. Now, the same bag hid in the hollow of a tree far beyond the kingdom's wall.

She didn't have a bag, but she planned to only take an apple that she stole from a hanging sack and a bit of bread she tucked into her shirt. She didn't want to eat a lot, just enough to avoid passing out.

Exiting the pantry, Evangeline passed several other rooms. Dried and fresh produce crowded some, others contained junk, but most remained empty. Waste of space. She munched on her apple, her stomach twisting around the bits that slid down her throat. She chucked the core into a nearby empty room and left the basement.

Slaves bustled by with trays in hand. Normally, Evangeline would cast her head down and walk. This time she kept her chin high, observing. Some humans focused on their feet while others gave her a cursory glance, but nothing out of the ordinary—until a young girl with mousy brown hair locked eyes with her.

The tray she'd been holding clattered to the floor, food and drink staining the rug. The girl beside her jumped and cursed until she followed her gaze. They both stared at Evangeline like she was a caged beast.

The brown-haired girl whipped away, shoving the girl

beside her to continue walking. They didn't bother to pick up the tray.

It shouldn't matter what they think, Evangeline told herself. *Who cares if they think you're a monster?*

The thought echoed in her brain, but it didn't dissolve the cold lump in her stomach. Or the questions lingering in her mind.

Who had started the rumor? And why?

CHAPTER 9

⌒ EVANGELINE ⌒

Evangeline arrived at Ryker's huddled over, drawing in gulps of air.

She'd spent the rest of the day lingering around the east wing. Her legs burned from all the walking, but it was worth it to hear news about the wall being breached, though nothing about her loose stone. It also sounded like more guards had been posted around the border, but she needed to find out how many and the frequency of their patrols.

Distracted by this newfound information, she had forgotten all about Gardia and Shani's son—and the dinner she was having with the king tonight.

"Evangeline," Ryker said in greeting. "I feared you had run off again," he purred, his eyes observing her disheveled hair and the fresh sweat beading her skin.

Lord Ryker fitted into a dark navy suit that hugged his

legs and waist. It hung loose on top to display the assembly of chains he adorned for the occasion. His hair was slicked back and braided three times to form a thicker braid, tied with gold bands. It matched the gold plates curving along the arm of his wings, nestled into the muscle like they belonged there.

Two male slaves stood at his sides, no older than Evangeline, brushing out his wings while several female slaves stood against the wall. Ryker snapped his fingers, and the girls descended on her.

They dragged her to the bathing room. They peeled off her dress and scrubbed her skin down with minerals and crushed petals.

She hated this, being polished like some jewel. Dreaded it every time a special event arose. Lord Ryker didn't give her a choice in the matter, so she endured as her skin tingled. Tried not to flinch and jerk away as they unabashedly washed every part of her. Thank the Gods these occasions happened rarely. She doubted she'd have much skin left if that wasn't the case.

They combed out her hair and tied the thin strands into a hefty up-do, entangled with gold pins. Her dress was a dark, thick velvet. The color of fresh blood. Her shoulders and chest were bare, the sleeves hanging down to the middle of her arms. She glanced into the mirror and frowned. The dress would have looked better on someone with curves. On her, it looked like she was playing dress-up. Her only saving grace was the eyeshadow and dark lipstick the girls had put on her face, making her eyes pop and her lips look fuller. She wondered what Ceven would say if he saw her like this. Would he find her beautiful? Would he see a grown woman?

Not that I care, she lied to herself. She scowled at her reflection, and it erased any potential beauty she might've had.

When they left the bathing room, Evangeline met with

Avana. Her black dress was sleek with a high neckline, her hair fashioned back into a neat bun. When she turned to smile at Evangeline, silver and sapphire bands dangled from her ears.

Ryker dismissed the servants. They bowed and left, not saying a word.

"Ready?" Ryker asked, adjusting his cuffs.

Avana and Evangeline nodded, and they all left the suite.

Two Royal Guards escorted them into the heart of the castle. They came across an open archway, big enough to fit an Aerian with their wings stretched. Passing beneath the white marble column, they entered a room Evangeline had learned to dread: the main dining room of the castle, reserved only for royalty and delicate matters with the king.

Their escort left their sides to join the rest of the Royal Guard lining the perimeter of the room—a room that fit Lani's ten times over—their dark silver armor blending into the rich purple walls. In the center, a vase of white lilacs, along with an arrangement of silver cutlery, decorated the long, mahogany table. It stretched the entire room.

A pleasant mix of the lilacs and wood assailed Evangeline's senses as she followed Ryker and Avana to the head of the table. There, both princes, Sehn and Ceven, stood in front of the grand fireplace.

The last time Evangeline had seen Sehn was years ago. Even then, she only ran into him occasionally, but he still looked the same. Like his younger brother, he had chestnut brown hair, but the similarities ended there. Sehn wore his hair long, dark waves ending around the middle of his torso, and had the same unnerving gray eyes as his father. Where he used to be the taller of the two, he now rested a finger's length shorter than Ceven. His complexion was also lighter, courtesy of the colder climate he was in for the past two years.

Both men looked stunning. Ceven filled out his dark pants, highlighting the color of his silk green shirt that laid unbuttoned at the top. One gold chain hung around his neck. Sehn displayed several between the collar of his maroon jacket, which extended beyond his calves. The color matched his enclosed wings, the tips pierced with gold rings. Evangeline couldn't remember if they'd been there before or not.

Ryker stood right of the king's chair, which was so grand it could almost be a replica of his actual throne. Its back curved into a set of expanded wings, and it sat at the head of the table. Evangeline took her usual place beside Ryker, Avana on her left and both princes on the opposite side. Ceven stood across from her.

From beneath her lashes, Evangeline admired the youngest prince. He looked incredibly handsome tonight. More so than usual, if that was possible. He had slicked his hair back, show-casing the strong angles of his face—and the tightness in it. At least she wasn't the only one nervous about tonight.

They all greeted each other and exchanged pleasantries.

Evangeline held a polite smile while Ryker chatted with the princes. Expecting not even a glance from Sehn's direction, she flinched when his eyes slid to hers. They crinkled as he gave her a wide smile.

She looked away.

That was odd, she thought. Ceven had kept his gaze away from hers, and her heart sank.

"I hope adjusting to life in Peredia hasn't been too difficult, Avana." Sehn shifted his attention away from Ryker.

"I've acclimated well, Your Highness. Although, I'll admit, it is quite different from living in the capital city back at home." Avana's voice was smooth. "Thank you again for allowing me to accompany you."

Evangeline's eyebrows rose. *They came here together?* It made sense. Avana arrived at the castle the same time Sehn and Ceven did.

The sound of chatter echoed down the halls, one male voice louder than the rest. Evangeline turned, and her jaw went slack. It was the obnoxious Rathan she met earlier that day, accompanied by two other Rathans.

"I could hear you coming from across the kingdom, Barto. You don't always have to shout, you know." Ceven grinned at the Rathan who came up next to him and clapped him on the shoulder. Evangeline blinked in surprise.

"But at least you always know when I'm coming." His smile showed a row of uneven, sharpened teeth.

His companions trailed behind him. One man and one female. While the man possessed a russet complexion—his face as clean shaven as the top of his head, with furless ears blending into his skin seamlessly—the woman reminded Evangeline of midnight. Her hair was shaven on the side, exposing one black-furred ear. The rest fell in tight braids down her back.

The woman moved to stand next to Barto, the other following suit. Like him, they both wore unusual clothing. Both dressed in brown, short-sleeved tunics with pants that tightly fitted to conditioned legs and tucked into a pair of plated boots. The only thing normal was the swords they carried at their sides. Except for Barto. From where she was standing, he was naked of any weapons.

Barto caught her staring and raised a brow. He went to speak, but the noise of metal clasping against metal interrupted the room. Every Royal Guard member in the room fisted their right hand over their hearts.

The king of Peredia had arrived, with five Royal Guard members moving in sync around him. Everyone bowed.

King Calais's wings were a brighter gold than the jeweled necklaces displayed through his open shirt, the span of them brushing the sides of the white columns as he entered the room. His eyes, the color of dark clouds right before a thunderstorm, pierced every person in the room with a chilling stare. He didn't smile. His face was bereft of any emotion, his features outlined by a sharp jawline and cheekbones. The silver-white hair, that hung loosely down his back, was the only hint to his eighty-two-year reign.

King Calais strutted passed Evangeline. His thick, purple robe dragged on the floor behind him as his steps clicked against the marble floor. A nearby human pulled out his chair and he slid into it. The king waved his hand. Everyone sat down.

"Glad you all could join me this evening." The king's voice was soft with a tinge of curtness to it. "Shall we begin tonight's feast?" He raised a hand, and the walls on either side of the room opened, revealing hidden doors within the paneling. Humans garbed in black came out with pitchers, pouring water and wine into their glasses.

"First and foremost, welcome to our country, Miss Quincara. Liaison Nu'yuen." King Calais nodded toward Avana and Barto. "I hope your stay has been pleasant thus far."

"It has been an honor, Your Majesty. Peredia is more beautiful than I could have imagined," Avana said, her fingers sliding around the glass of wine.

"Likewise." Barto grinned. "Though I've never been too fond of the cold."

"Or the heat," Ceven remarked.

Barto shrugged. "If you had even half the hair on my body, you'd understand why the heat would be bothersome."

During the interplay between the two men, Evangeline snuck a glance at the king. In the past, he would make a small comment to Ryker or sneer at her, but tonight he was on his best behavior. Was it because they had mixed company?

She snorted. Unlikely.

The king leaned forward, twirling the red liquid inside his glass. "I'm glad to see my son was in such good care during his stay in Atiaca. Tell me, Sir Nu'yuen, how is Empress Zelene?"

Barto's smile faded a bit. "The empress is well. She sends her regards."

Evangeline reanalyzed his odd attire, the accent. It made sense now. He was Atiacan. *How did this strange Rathan befriend Ceven?*

The king took a sip of wine, the contents staining his lips. "I am happy to hear that, especially in light of what has been happening recently." The king's gaze remained on Barto.

Barto stiffened. His eyes shifted to Ceven's for a second, then back to the king. He smiled. "I shouldn't be surprised that news has already spread to Peredia."

Avana leaned forward. "News of what, if I may ask?"

Sehn spoke up, his glass untouched. "There has been a string of disappearances within Atiaca."

Evangeline's head perked up. Ryker glanced down at her.

Barto nodded. "The matter is under investigation by our best men and women. I have no doubt they will bring the situation to heel in no time."

Avana rested forward on her forearms, eager for more detail. She wasn't the only one.

Instead of continuing, Barto posed another question. "The empress has decided to move forward in making slavery illegal. Having halted the trade on human cargo a few years back, this may be no surprise to you. So, if I may be so bold, Your Majesty, what are your plans for the future?"

Evangeline clenched against the thick upholstery she sat on.

She sipped her water and avoided eye contact with everyone at the table.

The king raised his eyebrows and took another sip of wine. "In the future, I will continue to do what is best for Peredia. As for your empress, I wish her the best in her endeavors. Changing long-established traditions is no simple task."

"Though not impossible." Ceven locked eyes with the king who didn't respond.

Sehn crossed his legs, a curl to his lips. "On the subject of change, I believe our future relations with Sundise Mouche will prove to be a smart decision for both countries moving forward." He directed the statement at the table but was staring at Avana.

Avana tilted her glass in acknowledgment. "Both of our countries have much to learn from each other. Having our borders closed to the rest of the world would only breed ignorance. I'm glad our Council has changed that." She smiled, but it didn't reach her eyes.

"And we vow to make sure your Council won't regret their decision." The corners of Sehn's mouth grew.

King Calais waved his hand, beckoning the first course of the night. A human filled the glass bowl to Evangeline's left with greens and mixed vegetables, a citrus dressing poured on top. Evangeline fought to keep herself from inhaling the entire bowl and its contents.

Everyone at the table picked at their salads. Light conversation ensued about the recent increase in snowstorms and re-bricking the pathways that had fallen to disrepair. Evangeline remained silent, observing the players at the table.

Unlike their companion, the two Rathans beside Barto remained quiet. Though with how much Barto talked, he made up for their lack of conversation.

Ceven and Barto chatted amiably, the only genuine smiles in the room. Evangeline strained to hear over the others and picked up tidbits of their conversation. How Ceven wrestled a tiger during a camping trip in the jungles of Atiaca, and something about a beverage called *mumba* they imbibed during their visits with the "ladies."

Evangeline stabbed at her salad. The fork clanked against the porcelain.

Everyone else discussed the future trade opportunities between Sundise Mouche and Peredia. Something about exchanging Peredia's highly sought-after mineral, frostlite, for Caster-made equipment. Nothing interesting. The king didn't make any comments or glance her way once.

Don't get your hopes up, Eve. There's still a lot left of the night to go. She inwardly groaned.

The king called forth the next meal. A thin, orange soup, with mixed greens sprinkled on top for garnish. Her mouth watered at the sight, the salad barely satisfying the raging appetite that clawed at her insides.

"Evangeline, is it?"

Evangeline gulped the spoonful of soup that was in her mouth. *No, no, no, don't drag me into the conservation!* She reluctantly looked up and Barto gave her a sideways grin.

"It is, isn't it? We haven't been formally introduced, but Ceven has talked about you quite a bit," he continued.

Ceven coughed, his eyes looking everywhere but at her.

He talked about me? Evangeline quickly squelched the warm sensation that stirred in her gut. *Of course he would, Eve. We spent most of our childhood together.*

"Yes. It's . . . Evangeline, my lord." It took a moment to find her voice. It sounded embarrassingly loud despite the crackling of the fireplace and the casual scraping of silverware. She waited for Ryker or the king to cut her off so she wouldn't have to feel everyone's eyes on hers. No one spoke up, and Barto continued to look at her expectantly.

"And you are the liaison for Atiaca?" She prayed her voice didn't sound as weak as she felt.

Barto shrugged. "You could say that. I am here on the behalf of the empress, and"—he shoved his thumb at his two companions—"Rasha and Quan are here to keep me out of trouble."

The couple remained expressionless, reminding Evangeline of two other bodyguards in particular. *Speaking of Xilo and Tarry . . .* She turned her head and, as expected, the stoic Aerians stood behind Ceven along the wall.

"I am sure it is quite odd for you to find a human dining with us tonight," Ryker spoke up, not having talked much this evening.

"It is odd," Quan said, his eyes meeting Ryker's.

Evangeline wanted to curl up and die.

"At least for a dinner of this sort," Barto quickly added. "Though it isn't uncommon in Atiaca for humans and Nytes to dine together."

"Evangeline is definitely the exception here in Peredia." The king looked at her for the first time tonight. It wasn't disgust or irritation shining in his eyes, but something else.

Something sinister.

A shiver crawled down her spine.

The king called the main course forth. They placed a giant stuffed boar in the center of the table, along with baskets of rolls, potatoes, and other hot foods that swarmed Evangeline's nose. She was already full, but everything smelled so good.

Sehn made a toast about new beginnings and good fortune for all three countries present. Evangeline raised her glass half-heartedly, grateful the night was almost to a close. She took a sip and peered at Ceven over her glass. All of dinner, she'd tried snagging his attention, if just to share a moment of mutual camaraderie. She knew he hated this as much as she did. Or at least he used to. But he didn't look at her once. And, blast it, if it didn't get under her skin.

The final round was a small cake drizzled in chocolate, but Evangeline could only muster a bite. She rubbed her stomach beneath the table. It cramped painfully, bile resting in the back of her throat. She prayed the night would end soon. If not, she might puke all over the table.

Cool fingers grazed Evangeline's elbow, and she found Avana staring at her with concern.

"Are you okay?" the Caster whispered.

Evangeline nodded and her gaze flickered around the table. Everyone had imbibed their wine, their cheeks flushed as Barto told a story about how he had mistaken one of the empress's consorts for a lady at a tavern he frequented. Nobody was paying any attention to them.

"Here, give me your hand." Avana pricked her index finger with the point of her nail and grabbed her wrist. Her bloody finger drew scarlet waves on top of her skin, and Evangeline waited for her to mumble something, but she remained silent. The symbol sank into her hand and disappeared altogether. A wave of relief swept over her, like a cool breeze carrying with it a hint of peppermint. "It won't help for long, but it should at least get you through the rest of tonight," Avana assured her.

Evangeline was eternally grateful. She felt ten times better. If she closed her eyes right then, she would've enjoyed the best sleep of her life.

The night ended. Humans came in and grabbed the empty plates, the king's personal escort surrounding him as everyone bowed their farewells. Evangeline was still feeling the soft breeze from Avana's spell, her eyes half closed. She didn't register that they had already said their goodbyes and were in front of Ryker's rooms.

The guards saluted them as she and Ryker strolled through into the dark suite. Ryker flipped a switch and the lamps slowly built a small fire that lit their way into the sitting chamber.

Still out of it, Evangeline jumped when he took her hand. "What spell did Avana use on you?" he demanded, his cheeks no longer flushed.

"She made me feel better. I was feeling ill at dinner." His eyes bored into hers, as if he didn't believe her. "I haven't eaten in days, and tonight I ate a lot. My stomach couldn't handle it." He held her gaze, then nodded, releasing her.

He started a fire and sat down in his green armchair, leaning his head back. A soft sigh escaped him. Evangeline sat across from him, mimicking his position. The room felt warm, and with a full belly, sleep pulled at her.

"Are you feeling better?" he asked.

Evangeline didn't know if the question came out of genuine concern or not. "Somewhat."

"Hmm . . . Tonight was interesting. Sehn's just as charming as I remembered. I'll even admit Ceven has grown these past couple years. Though, I did find it strange he acted like he didn't know you the whole night."

Evangeline debated responding, knowing he was only saying it to bait her. She used the pull of sleep as an excuse not to reply, letting her eyes close.

They were quiet for a while, the logs in the fireplace snapping and sizzling.

"Do you trust Avana?" Ryker asked awhile later.

Evangeline had almost fallen asleep. Her voice was heavy when she responded, "I don't know, she seems honest enough, but I just met her."

It was quiet again before Ryker replied, "Do you think she knows the truth about your mark?"

The question felt like an injection of adrenaline. It helped push away the abyss of sleep. "Yes."

"If she told you, would you believe her?"

Evangeline frowned. *Why is he asking me this?* "I would like to believe her. She seems to know more than the others." And that was true.

Ryker followed with a soft grunt, and the cool winds from Avana's spell stopped. Her stomach immediately cramped in pain.

Evangeline lurched from the couch with one hand over her mouth. Ryker came alive. He reached for her, but she was already halfway to the bathing room.

She flung open the door and fell to her knees, her hands wrapping around the cold, porcelain bowl. She vomited. Dizzy and hot, she retched again and again, her shaking hands clasping the sides of the toilet as her world spun.

You'll get used to it. I couldn't keep it down the first time, either.

Evangeline spun around, thinking Ryker was behind her. There was no one.

It tastes disgusting. That was her voice . . . but not her voice.

It does . . . but it gets easier. Trust me.

Evangeline clenched her eyes shut. It was a hallucination. She pressed her hands against her closed lids, taking a few deep breaths.

You shouldn't have eaten that much. Her eyes remained closed. *Are you better now?*

She covered her ears.

Evangeline?

"Please, stop . . ." she whispered.

Two hands gripped her from both sides, yanking her hands from her ears. Ryker peered down at her, eyebrows pinched. He was calling her name. She wanted to say something, but she couldn't, staring at him.

He snapped his fingers at her. She blinked and squeezed the words out, "I'm fine . . . I'm fine." He loosened a breath. For a moment she almost believed he cared.

"What happened?" he asked softly.

Evangeline wiped her mouth, grimacing at the wetness she felt there. "A hallucination, I think. I didn't see anything, but I kept hearing a man's voice and . . . a female's." Admitting she had heard her own voice unnerved her more than it being someone else's.

He helped her up off the floor. "What did they say?"

She rinsed her hands and face in the sink. "Nothing important, just about how it tasted bad."

Ryker raised a brow, and she shrugged. She didn't know how else to describe it.

"I think you should stay here tonight."

"But Lani—"

Ryker crossed his arms.

"I understand." She didn't even try.

They bid each other good night. Evangeline snuggled into her bed in the small room next to Ryker's. A tinge of guilt tickled her conscious. The mattress molded to her body, amber wallpaper and a sense of security surrounding her, while Lani slept by herself on her old, worn cot with a door that barely closed.

Lani . . .

She'd never hallucinated before like this. Not when she was

awake and aware of her surroundings. What if this happened while they were trying to escape? What if she attacked Lani, thinking it was someone else?

Would she be able to protect her? Even from herself?

CHAPTER 10

~ CEVEN ~

C even hurried back from the main dining hall to his suite on the top floor of the castle. The paintings he passed—of other royals propped up in formal displays—reflected a similar stiffness in his own posture. A side effect of tonight's dinner.

Being around the king was like a game of chess, unable to see your opponent's pieces. Never knowing when they'd strike.

Thank the Gods it's over with. Barto's companionship was a blessing, and his shield against the king's questions. Ceven hated to be reminded that he was a liability. A body to be used at the king's gain and leisure. It took effort not to argue the finer points of the kingdom's welfare at the table. As if the king would listen to Ceven over Sehn. Telling himself that it would've solved nothing helped ease his growing frustration. He hated feeling helpless.

For most of the night, he'd been doing a halfway decent job of minding his own business. Until Barto had brought Evangeline into the equation.

Avoiding her gaze was like a starving man refusing his next meal, her presence begging to be appreciated. Tonight, she glowed.

The rich fabric highlighted her milky skin. A braided up-do kept her hair off her shoulders, giving him a perfect display of her neck. Vulnerable to a lover's kiss. His jaw tightened at the thought.

Tonight tested his limits. In more ways than one.

Tarry followed behind him, his footsteps quiet. Xilo had left after dinner. Knowing the last time Xilo saw his son was ten years ago, Ceven and Tarry turned a blind eye to the blatant breaking of the Royal Guard's code.

The night was quiet, and the soft glow from the hallway's lamps added to its atmosphere. They passed a couple suites, stopping at the engraved, gold embossed door at the end of the hallway. Ceven couldn't wait to peel off his gaudy clothes and lie down with nothing but his thoughts for the rest of the night.

His fingers barely curled around the golden knob when Tarry's hand flicked out, crinkling the fine fabric of his shirt.

"Powerful magic is in the air."

Ceven's eyes fell to his shoulder, where Tarry's scarred, brown hand rested. The frostlite rings gracing his fingers, whorled with a cloudy mix of blue and black. The sensitive mineral found deep within the Frostsnare mountains had never steered them wrong. Something was amiss.

Tarry jutted his chin at the door, and Ceven nodded. Tarry proceeded into the dark suite with his ax drawn. Ceven followed close behind, pulling the dagger from the side of his boot.

He wished he had his sword. Screw the rules of decorum King Calais forced him to uphold at dinner.

The hallway leading into his sitting chamber was cold, but with it carried a thread of warmth, vanilla and firewood dancing in its wake. The soft lilt of melody swayed in the air, the sound foreign and enchanting. It made him uneasy.

Tarry's muscles flexed, the shifting of the dark metal shimmering in the low light in the distance. A familiar figure greeted them when they entered the chamber.

"Sehn?" Ceven didn't hide his surprise. Or irritation. Tarry kept his ax drawn.

Still in his garb from dinner, Sehn turned around. The red glow from the fire behind him outlined his broad frame. The song that fell from his lips came to an abrupt end.

"I was wondering if you got lost, brother. It hasn't been that long since we've left the castle." The corner of his mouth perked up.

Ceven glanced at Tarry's hand. The gemstones had returned to their usual state—a creamy pearl color.

"I detected strong magic, Your Highness. Is there anyone else in the room with you?" Tarry's voice was an octave deeper than Ceven's and never betrayed his true intentions. The only telltale sign of distrust was how Tarry shifted his weight, the slight movement of his fingers on his ax as he lowered the blade, forcing his muscles to relax. All signs to give the enemy the wrong impression, right before he struck a surprising blow. Ceven knew from experience. Just never thought it'd be directed at his brother.

Sehn's smile didn't waver. He turned, gesturing at the empty bottle on the end table. "I understand your alarm, Tarry, but there is no need to fret. I was simply trying my hand at something I discovered in Sundise Mouche." He looked at the two of them. "I was getting cold waiting and thought a fire would be nice to return home to."

Ceven made sure he wasn't quiet as he put his hand on Tarry's shoulder. One unwarranted move would be all it took to set him off. Tarry's muscles tightened beneath Ceven's fingers, but his bodyguard stepped back, re-hooking his ax to his side.

"What are you doing here?" Ceven asked, brushing past Tarry. He wished it had been an intruder rather than his brother. At least the former would've been dealt with quicker.

"I merely wish for us to catch up. It's been two years, brother, and we've had little time to chat."

The muscle in Ceven's jaw twitched. "You had all dinner, and yet you barely said two words to me."

Sehn shifted his eyes to Tarry. "I was hoping for a more heart-to-heart conversation. Away from prying ears."

Ceven didn't want to have a heart-baring conversation with a man he loosely called brother, but the sooner he found out what Sehn wanted, the sooner he'd leave. He looked over his shoulder. "Tarry, you may go."

Tarry bowed, his eyes lingering on the empty bottle beside Sehn. "I will be outside the door if you need me." He left.

Sehn's fingers traced the back of the off-white sofa before he perched on top of its armrest. He folded his hands in his lap, looking around the room. "Have you settled back in well?"

Ceven unbuttoned his shirt, the silk sliding off his body, and flung it over the back of the couch. Next to Sehn. "I'm your brother, not a guest to be dazzled." He rubbed his eyes. "Cut the small talk and tell me what you want."

Sehn's eyes slid to his bare chest. Ceven knew he was looking at the jagged scar he'd received in Atiaca, the skin still pink. It had been a close call.

When he spoke again, Sehn's voice lacked his usual purr. "I

don't remember you being so . . . ill-tempered."

"And I don't remember you ever giving a damn. So why now?" Ceven crossed his arms, blocking Sehn's view of his chest.

Sehn's eyes flicked back up to his face. "We're older now. Our relationship shouldn't be tethered to our past. Nobody is perfect, Ceven. Not me, and certainly not you."

Ceven's entire body rippled, and he balled his fists into his chest. "If the purpose of this is to make yourself feel better, to make amends for everything you've done, you're wasting your breath. You forget I grew up with you, have seen you lie time and again. I'm not in the mood tonight."

It was quick. Sehn's upper lip curled into a snarl before the false smile returned. "Fair enough, then I won't waste any more of your time. I came here with a proposition."

Ceven waited.

Mahogany hair fell over Sehn's shoulder as he turned to face the fire. "I believe your views on humans haven't changed? Unless I have misunderstood your affections toward Ryker's pet."

Ceven reached Sehn in two strides. His hand came down on the sofa between his shirt and where his brother sat. Sehn blinked.

"Her name is Evangeline, and she is not a part of this conversation." His tone left no room for discussion.

Sehn held up his hands in mock surrender. "Of course, dear brother. But you didn't answer my question."

"You know my answer. Get to the point," he said behind gritted teeth.

Sehn tilted his head, his eyes wandering back to the fire. "You and I both desire a new direction for this kingdom. Too long has the king strangled it under the guise of tradition. I have seen true power, Ceven, and it is not Peredia."

Ceven leaned back, the words dancing around him. Now,

Sehn's reason for being here was starting to make sense. A viper unfurled in the pit of his stomach.

When Sehn turned to face him again, his eyes were alive with a passion Ceven understood too well. "Isn't it time we rescued her? Brought back the beautiful country that once stood at the center of the world and ruled it?"

Ceven stared at him. He watched the light fade from his brother's eyes.

"I think it's time for you to leave." Ceven's eyes never left his.

Akin to moving water, Sehn removed himself from the couch, standing to his full height. Flames flickered. They danced along his high cheekbones, lighting up the dangerous edge that gleamed in his narrowed eyes.

"You forget yourself, Ceven. One day I will be king. I speak now from a place of companionship and mutual gain, but if you wish to soil that, the consequences will be on your shoulders. Not mine." He flicked his robe back. His wings trailed behind him like a corpse, leaving old blood in its path. He paused in the opening to the hallway, not once turning around. "Don't say I didn't try." With a sharp gust of wind, Sehn disappeared along with the fire, which instantly died.

Ceven stared at the now-cold fireplace, then back at the empty hallway.

All his life Sehn and the king had belittled him. They thought him weak, like the queen. Too temperamental. Too emotional. Unfit to lead like a true Aerian male. But he refused to be cowed. To bow his head and bend to their will.

It wasn't the first time Ceven has had this discussion with his brother, and it wouldn't be the last. He knew what Sehn wanted from him, but if he was going to play a part in murdering the king, it was going to be on his terms.

And nobody else's.

CHAPTER 11

⤚ EVANGELINE ⤙

The next morning, Lani was missing from the kitchen.

Evangeline had woken up late, with Ryker nowhere to be found. He left a note saying he would be gone most of the day and a plate of breakfast that was cold to the touch. After last night, she didn't have an appetite anyway.

It wasn't until people were bustling through the halls at lunchtime that she noticed her friend's absence.

She waited outside the kitchens, asking around. Most avoided her, but she snatched a young boy before he could run.

Lani hadn't shown up for work that morning.

Evangeline raced down the slippery steps from the castle to the slave quarters. *I should've gone to her last night. What if something bad happened?*

She rushed into her friend's room. "Lani?"

Lani was lying in bed, her chest moving. She was breathing.

Evangeline ran to her side, propping herself on the cot. Lani's breaths came in rugged, harsh gasps, and Evangeline's hand burned where she pressed a palm to her forehead. It looked like a fever.

She pulled out her thicker dresses from the chest, draping them across Lani. Taking some clean cloths, she dipped them in the bucket of warm water by the fire and placed them across her wrinkled forehead.

Lani didn't move or acknowledge her presence at all.

Evangeline's breath clotted, and her chest swelled. She tucked in Lani's body, covering her from head to toe. She could call a healer, but the likelihood of help was slim to none. Lani wasn't a favored slave. Evangeline could ask Ryker, but she didn't know where he was or when he would be back. What if Lani woke up while she was gone and tried to get out of bed and exhaust herself even more?

Creak!

Evangeline jumped and spun around. The window was open, cold air blowing into the room. And in the opening crouched her blue-eyed Caster man, holding a knife.

She screamed.

He was too fast for her eyes to follow as he slammed her against the wall, covering her mouth. "I don't intend to harm you," he whispered, eyes roaming her body. Searching. Snow clung to his black ringlets, and he had traded his plated leather for a slave's working attire. The cuts and bruises that had marred his face were nonexistent, and beneath his head of hair, his horns were still invisible. He could easily pass as a human.

Evangeline's heart thrashed inside her ribcage. It took every effort to try not to shove him away. He was too close. Deadly calm eyes searing her body.

As if deciding how to kill her.

Her eyes welled up in terror. *Calm down, Eve.* She tried to get her breathing to a normal tempo by inhaling through her nostrils before exhaling slowly. He removed his hand but not his body, his presence still too close for her to feel relaxed. *Gods, why did he have to come back?*

Flattening against the wall as much as possible, she glanced at Lani and then the open window blowing in cold air. She needed to protect her friend. Somehow, she needed to get him out of this room.

"Can . . . can I close the window?" She kept her voice level, hoping he would allow her to do that much. He nodded and gave her room to move, but followed close behind her as she shut the window. Lani hadn't stirred.

Turning, Evangeline met his gaze. She prayed he had one sympathetic bone in his body. "I don't want Lani to see this." *And I don't want you anywhere near her,* she didn't say. He didn't respond, and she gestured toward the door. For a moment she thought he would refuse before he nodded and stretched an arm, indicating her to go first.

She walked into the narrow hallway. The Caster closed the door behind him, shrouding them in darkness. No windows.

Evangeline took a few careful steps back. Slow enough that he wouldn't think she was trying to run away. "Why are you here?" She thought he'd be far away by now.

He ignored her. "You are a human, yes?" The question sounded like an accusation.

"Yes," she said, surprised by how calm her voice sounded. "What else would I be?"

He shrugged and leaned against the wall. "A Nyte in human clothing."

"Like you?" she said before she could stop herself.

He appeared thoughtful for a moment. "Yes."

Evangeline knew she should shut her mouth, should avoid asking too much, but she wanted to know who she was dealing with. "Is that why you cut your horns? So you can hide your identity?" she pressed.

His smile was answer enough.

She bit her lip. If he wasn't a threat to Peredia, he wouldn't need to cover his identity. And that cold, calculated look in his eyes . . . It was clear he was dangerous. Maybe he was an agent, hired to kill? But why was he so far from the kingdom? And how did he get injured?

Her curiosity got the best of her. "What's an assassin doing injured out in the middle of the snow?"

His eyes lit up dangerously. She took another step back.

"I never said I was an assassin."

But you're not denying it, either. She knew she shouldn't get involved, and here she was, her morbid curiosity luring her into what was likely an inevitable death trap. She was dancing with a murderous Nyte.

"I don't want any trouble, my lord." Evangeline used the title to remind him she was just a human. That she wasn't a threat. "I don't know who you are, nor do I want to know. If you leave, we can put this behind us."

All traces of amusement left his face. "I'm sorry, but now that you're aware of my presence here, I'm afraid I can't leave you to your own devices."

Pure panic.

Her mind scrambled for ways to weasel herself out of this predicament. She couldn't run. With his inhuman speed, he would catch her in seconds. Calling for help would be useless and grant her a quick death. That left only one option. She had to convince him with her words. "Are you going to make me regret saving your life?"

He held up his hands in a disarming gesture. "You misinterpret my words. I still stand by what I said. I do not intend to hurt you." It also went without saying that he could've killed her at any point before this. "However, if you betray me, I won't hesitate to kill you. Regardless of whether you saved my life."

She nodded, though she didn't trust him for a second. She didn't know what his motives were or how ruthless he was. "So if you don't intend to kill me, what do you want?"

"I need information, and you're going to help me."

Her fingers bit into her closed palms. The last thing she wanted was to be caught in the middle of Nyte politics. "What kind of information?" she asked.

"What do you know about Prince Sehn?"

Sehn? Why him and not the king? She shrugged. "That he's an Aerian prince, nothing more."

It wasn't a lie. Ceven and his brother had never gotten along, and Sehn, like his father, preferred to pretend she didn't exist. So, Evangeline treated him no differently than the rest of the royal family—by keeping her distance.

But . . . he was acting bizarre at dinner. By her standards, at least. Nothing worth mentioning to an assassin.

The Caster studied her. "Have there been any mysterious disappearances recently? Rumors about dark magic within the castle?"

Evangeline stiffened, and a tingle went down her spine. "People have been going missing for a while now. Only humans." She thought of Shani's son. "They've only been reported missing; their bodies not discovered yet. That's all I know."

In the dark hallway, Evangeline couldn't make out the finer points of the Caster's features, but when he glided toward her, his entire presence blurred. Like a silent shadow.

Before she could yelp, both his hands pinned the wall on

either side of her. Heat emanated from him, and his blue eyes crowded her vision. "Don't play me for a fool, Evangeline. I know you're the advisor's adopted daughter."

It was dead quiet, but there was a loud ringing in her ears. "How . . . how do you know that?"

"I've heard all about you, the infamous Evangeline. You don't have a lot of friends, do you?"

Red flashed in her mind, an instant fire that gnawed at her insides. Before she had time to cool off, it sprouted from her lips. "I answered you honestly. If you didn't get what you were looking for, perhaps you should ask someone else and leave me alone."

He didn't respond right away, and her heart skipped a beat.

"Tell me why Ryker Ardonis is so interested in you."

"I don't know," she said. *How did he gather all this information so quickly?*

A flash of light reflected off something in the darkness— then a cold blade pressed against her neck.

"I'll try this again: what does Ryker want with you?" The sharp blade dug into her flesh.

"I said I don't know!" He plastered her back to the wall, the pulse at her neck pounding against his dagger. "You promised you wouldn't hurt me!"

"I changed my mind."

"You spitting, puss-filled—!" Blood dripped down her neck, and she sputtered words. Whatever she thought of to satisfy him. "I'm not like other humans! They found me in a ruin, with a mark—"

"A mark?" The pressure let up.

"Yes, yes, a mark! I can show you, so please, can you put down the blade?"

When he removed his hold on her throat, she almost collapsed in relief. She held her neck protectively. The bastard.

"Show me."

He was still close enough to attack her again, so she rushed to remove her glove. The thin leather slid off her hand with ease.

Before she could show him, he captured her wrist and traced the outline of her tattoo with a black-gloved finger. His mouth opened in awe, his eyes glued to her hand in disbelief. She wasn't blind to the uncanny similarities between him and Avana as he assessed her mark in the same manner. She didn't think it was a coincidence, but now wasn't the time to ask.

"Where did you get this?" he demanded.

"I was born with it, or at least I've had it for as long as I can remember."

He rubbed the mark, and she flinched when he pinched the skin. He looked up at her again, a bewildered expression on his face. Then his shoulders started to shake. She squinted and realized he was shaking with mirth. Were all Casters this crazy?

"What's so funny?" she couldn't resist asking.

"There's no way. This has to be a mistake," was the only answer he gave.

She looked at her mark, then back at him, and all her previous terror fled as an uncontrollable excitement squeezed her heart. "Wait . . . Do you know what this symbol means?"

Her excitement died at the slow smile that spread across his face. She knew he wouldn't offer her that information for free.

"What will you give me in return?"

She scowled at him. "You said you wanted information. Tell me what you're looking for."

He pondered for a moment before responding, "Find out what Ryker knows about your mark, or at least what he thinks it means."

"He doesn't know anything, I've asked."

"Then you're more naïve than I thought." His look turned grave. "These missing persons . . . What do you know so far?"

She shook her head. "Not much, just that it's been happening for the past couple months. At first it was one person, then a handful . . . Now it feels as if anyone could disappear at any moment."

He rubbed his jaw. "Find out what you can about these people. What they were doing before going missing, if any suspicious persons are involved, or anything tying them all together."

"And in exchange, you will tell me about this mark," she finished for him. "How will I know you're not lying?"

"I could ask the same of you." He stepped back, and Evangeline loosened a breath. "If you give me false information, I will return in favor. Let's not waste both of our time." He grabbed her marked hand again, but instead of looking at it, he placed a vial into her palm.

"What's this?" She squinted at it, but she couldn't see that well in the dark.

"An antidote. It will keep your friend alive tonight but won't cure her completely."

She twisted the vial in her hand. "An antidote? For what?" She paused and looked up, narrowing her eyes. "How do you know this?"

His lips curled into something unpleasant. "I had to ensure you would cooperate with me, Evangeline."

She stared at him. Her hand clenched the vial, almost breaking it. "*You* . . ." She choked on the rest of her words.

"If you decide to waste my time, the poison in Lani's body will stop her heart in three days. Without my antidote, that is," he said with a sigh. "I thought you'd know more, especially once your life was on the line."

If she could incinerate someone with her eyes, he would have burned to ashes.

He raised an eyebrow. "No need to be so upset. Look at it this way, we both get something out of this now. To think you don't know the meaning behind that mark of yours."

"Why did you have to drag her into this?" she snarled. Gone was the fear. Something far more primal gripped her bones. Lani's life was in danger. Because of him.

This is all my fault.

"Don't take this personally. For both of our sakes, I'm sure this will work." He held out his hand.

Knowing what he intended with that gesture, she stared at his hand instead of taking it. She should've left him to die out there in the snow.

He kept his hand up. "I don't think you're in any position to refuse, my dear."

I'm going to kill him.

Left with no choice, she slowly lifted her hand, every muscle in her body yearning to shove a fist into his face instead.

He brought her hand to his mouth, his lips brushing her knuckles. "My name is Raiythlen, and it is a pleasure doing business with you, Evangeline."

PART 2

WHEN LEGENDS
BECOME REALITY

CHAPTER 12

⟶ EVANGELINE ⟵

Raiythlen parted ways with Evangeline shortly after, disappearing to do Gods-knew-what while she stayed by Lani's side.

He told her Lani would need to drink the entire contents of the bottle. Lani still wasn't responding, so Evangeline held her head up, drizzling the liquid down her throat, making sure she wouldn't choke. Her eyes fluttered, but she wasn't responsive to anything else.

"Lani, what have I done?" Evangeline thrust her hands in her hair, wanting to pull the strands out. This is what she got for helping a spitting *Nyte*.

Getting up to add a few more logs to the fire, she calculated where she could go to find clues. It wasn't going to be an easy task. This has been happening for a while, and no one had found any answers yet.

Or really, no one has cared enough, since it's only humans disappearing.

She winced when the flames came up and licked at the logs, the heat brushing her skin.

Ryker had avoided her every time she'd brought it up, and Ceven wouldn't know much; he just got back from Atiaca. Unless . . . She propped her hands on her hips. *I wonder if the missing persons in Atiaca are human too?* She figured it wouldn't hurt to ask, but she still needed more specific clues to what was happening here. She feared bringing Raiythlen anything less with Lani's life on the line.

As much as she wanted to avoid it, she needed to talk to those closest to the victim. Shani and Gardia.

Evangeline sat back down on the cot, relieved to see Lani's breathing back to normal. Color returned to her cheeks, and her previously pinched face seemed relaxed. At least Raiythlen hadn't lied to her about that. To think, saving a man's life would end up costing her so much. It was clear this Caster had no heart, nor cared that she had nursed him back to health. She could have forgiven him for threatening her life, but now . . .

She would never forgive him for what he had done to Lani.

A meaty cough brought her out of her thoughts. Lani was awake.

"How are you feeling?" Evangeline squeezed her hand. Her smile wobbled. This was her fault.

Lani drew in a deep breath, pounding her chest as another hackneyed cough hit her. "Feels as if I've been run over by a horse."

Evangeline winced. She grabbed a glass of water and watched Lani chug the whole cup. She thought about Raiythlen, and if Lani had seen anything. "How did you get sick?"

Lani took another breath, a yawn stretching her mouth.

"I'm old, who knows. Don't worry, this won't be the death of me, though I wish it were."

"Don't say that." She grimaced, the comment not to off the mark. "Did . . . did you see anyone when you came home last night?"

Lani lay back down. "No." Her eyes closed. "You better not be sneaking anymore boys in here. One was enough."

She was glad Lani didn't see her lips tremble.

It wasn't long until Lani's snoring filled the room. It was best for her to rest and conserve her energy.

Evangeline wrapped herself in a coat and pecked Lani on the forehead. She lingered on her face a moment longer before heading out.

It was late afternoon when Evangeline made it to the east wing. She knew Shani worked in the kitchens with Lani and went there first.

Evangeline found her. Her brown hair was in a high bun, apron clean and pressed, with a silver tray in hand, walking down the hall. Evangeline trailed behind her, following her up the stairs to the third floor. Shani glided across the speckled marble despite carrying a full tray of food.

Eventually, she paused in front of a door and knocked. Evangeline assumed they were in the residential part of the east wing; there was an absence of noise. No chatter or people walking back and forth. A few guards stood stationed throughout the hall, but other than that, it was empty.

The door opened, and an overly tan man poked his head out. He was short for an Aerian, only a head taller than Shani, and from where Evangeline huddled—which was a few doors down—he didn't look happy.

"About time," he grumbled. He yanked the tray from her and slammed the door. Shani flinched and walked back toward Evangeline.

Evangeline took a deep breath and stepped out. She was a head taller than Shani—which wasn't surprising as Evangeline towered over most human females. She just hoped her height wouldn't be too intimidating. "Shani . . . I'm sorry to bother you, but I need to talk to you, it's important." She hoped her smile didn't appear too fake. Shani came to a dead stop, surprise flashing across her face before an indescribable expression took hold. Her head dropped too fast for Evangeline to make it out.

"I'm sorry, my lady, I am very busy. . ." She bowed.

Evangeline frowned. There was that title again. No one ever referred to her as "my lady". What was this rumor about her and why?

Before Shani could rush past her, Evangeline reached out and grabbed her arm. "Shani, please, I only need to ask you a few questions, and I won't bother you again." Shani tugged at her arm with more force than Evangeline expected. She gripped tighter.

"Please," she tried again. Shani stopped struggling, but Evangeline didn't release her grip. "I'm sorry to bring this up, but I need to talk to you about your son." Shani yanked away again, but Evangeline's grip was stronger. "I need to know everything that happened, right before he went missing."

Shani's breathing hitched. "He's fine. I know he's fine."

Evangeline's heart broke at the utter hopelessness in those words. She wanted to let her go, she didn't want to do this, but she was more afraid of the consequences if she didn't. "Was he acting strange recently? Was there anything unusual you noticed right before he disappeared?"

Shani shook, holding back silent sobs. "He did nothing wrong, why him?"

Evangeline swallowed. "I'm trying to help. Maybe I can find him." The lie slipped too easily from her tongue. "But I need to know what happened right before he . . . left."

Shani's eyes widened, and she yanked the front of Evangeline's dress. "Why did you take my boy! *Why did you take him!*" she wailed, tears seeping down her face. "Give me back . . . my boy . . ."

"I didn't take your son." Evangeline's voice was firm, but she was shaking on the inside. She wanted to ask her: Why? Why was everyone so afraid of her? But Shani was already hysterical. It was best to gather as much info as she could without upsetting her more. "I'm trying to figure out what's been going on." She grabbed both of Shani's arms, removing her hands from her dress. "Lani is in danger. Please, I need to know."

Shani's breaths slowed, and she looked up at her with blood-shot eyes. "It all started with these marks." Her voice wavered, but a fire sparked in her eyes. "I didn't realize it at first . . . I . . . I'm such a horrible mother." She started crying again.

"Marks? What marks?"

"They were all over his body . . . I didn't know . . ." She muttered something, but it was incoherent.

"Was he hurt? Was somebody hurting him?" Evangeline pressed.

"He must have hurt every day. . . Why didn't he tell me . . .?"

She tried to remain patient. "Shani. Where did you last see him? What was he doing the day he disappeared?"

Shani went still. Evangeline realized she was still squeezing her arms and yanked her hands away.

"I don't know where he went that day." She hugged herself. "He was a stable boy; whenever he wasn't home, he would be there. But he wasn't in either of those places . . . I don't know where he is . . . what happened . . ." She put her head in her hands.

Evangeline stepped back. She wanted to know more. To know if all the victims had these "marks" and what they looked like. But at least she got something. "I'm so sorry, Shani. I really hope he's okay."

She sniffed and wiped her nose on her sleeve before jabbing a finger at her. "I hope Lani is next. I hope you suffer, knowing you will never see her again. Suffer like the rest of us!"

Evangeline blinked. The insult lashed at her skin, deepening a wound that was already there. "Goodbye, Shani." She stepped passed her.

When Evangeline was farther down the hall, Shani's sobs crashed off the stone walls as she relived her worst nightmare. The wound oozed, guilt festering beneath its surface.

Evangeline kept her head high.

Next stop, the stables.

CHAPTER 13

Evangeline

The stables were on the castle grounds, near the front gates. It wasn't far, but far enough where the cold settled into Evangeline's bones again. Her lips were beyond chapped, bleeding where her skin split.

Her encounter with Shani left her feeling like she'd fallen into a deep pile of mud she couldn't wash away. She concentrated on Lani, reasoning that Shani's boy was already gone, but Lani was still alive.

Harsh, but true.

The stables were a cluster of mixed stone. White and gray stuck together to form multiple structures. Snow covered the tin roofs in a thick blanket from the storm the other night, and the whinnying horses bombarded her as she approached.

The doors were open. Two human boys, half a head shorter than her and both with dark hair, carried piles of hay back and forth from a wooden cart. One looked up at her arrival, his face too haggard for a boy his age. He continued working when he realized she wasn't a Nyte.

They ignored her, and she ignored them as she walked inside. It wasn't as warm as the castle, but warmer than being in the open air. She breathed into her hands, peering around the stable. Nothing looked out of the ordinary. Stacks of hay, stalls filled with bins of water and saddle equipment. She didn't know what she expected to find. Blood, maybe? A body hidden in the piles of hay? She snorted.

She walked back out and caught the gaze of the other boy walking in. Upon closer inspection, she realized he had a limp.

"Hey, has anything strange happened around here in the past few days?" she asked.

The boy looked around, scratching his head. "Nothing, aside from the horses, who seem to be more skittish today than usual."

Not what she was looking for. "Have you seen . . ." She cursed, realizing she didn't know Shani's son's name. "A young boy who used to work here? Shani's son?"

The boy shrugged. "Sorry, Ma'am, they just reassigned me and my partner to this side of the castle a few days ago. There was only an older gal working here when we came."

Footsteps thundered behind her. "Why do you want to know?"

Evangeline's stomach clenched. She recognized the voice before she saw his blue-and-gold wings, the tuft of loose brown hair that wasn't slicked back today.

Accompanying Ceven was Barto, with Tarry and Xilo trailing along farther back.

Ceven wore a brown leather tunic and matching riding pants, with a thick fur coat layered on top. Barto opted for a long-sleeved green shirt, tucked into a pair of loose slacks. Not a coat to be found. Tarry and Xilo had traded their thicker plated metal for more form-fitting armor—black rings meshed together that glided over their skins. The one exception being the pair of wings and stars stitched over their right breasts.

Evangeline's heart fluttered, but she squashed the feeling. She didn't want Ceven involved in this. To suspect anything.

They all walked toward her, impervious to the chilled air.

"What are you doing here?" she countered.

He hadn't looked at her once last night, and as much as she didn't want to admit it, it hurt. Had he ignored her for the king's sake? Or had he reconsidered their shaky friendship and decided to keep a safe distance from her?

"Well, it's not to sit and chat over tea." He smirked. Turning, he smiled at the boy with the limp who then bounded back inside the stables.

Yes, because I thought the stables would be an ideal place to partake in hot beverages and light conversation, she almost retorted, but her eyes flicked to the Rathan. "I didn't expect to see you here, Your Highness."

Ceven frowned at the same time Barto leaned on the balls of his feet, slinging an arm over his friend's shoulders. "His Highness is hiding from the gaggle of women his father brought to the castle for him."

The two Aerian ladies Evangeline passed on the stairs the other day came to mind. Sophisticated and beautiful. She thought of them surrounding Ceven, flirting with him and touching him. Her toes curled in her boots. "Is that so?"

Ceven slapped the Rathan in the ribs. He let go of him immediately, complaining that Ceven broke one of them.

"He's trying to marry me off, get rid of me. So, I decided it was a good time to check the borders," he said.

"And avoid your future brides." Barto gripped his side. Evangeline looked to Xilo and Tarry for confirmation, but they stood expressionless. Barto turned his yellow gaze to her. "You look lovely this morning, Evangeline. I hope I didn't scare you too bad last night."

Her first impression of the Rathan was of an obnoxious Nyte with equally poor taste in clothing. "No, of course not, my lord," she lied.

He waved his hand. "Please, call me Barto." He grinned at her hesitant expression. "I won't answer to anything else—well, except maybe for sweetheart, or handsome, or—"

Ceven slapped him again. Barto yelped and stepped a few paces away from him, massaging his other side.

She cocked her head, curious at the exchange between them. "Barto," she said as her cheeks warmed. "Where are your . . . friends?"

Barto glanced warily at Ceven and shrugged. "Rasha's probably hunting me down as we speak. Had to give her the run this morning; she can be terribly dull to bring along with company. Absolute mood killer. Quan . . . he's likely found a small corner of the castle to snooze in."

Evangeline frowned. Were all Atiacans this strange, or was it just Barto and his group?

She wanted to ask more questions, like how the two of them met, and about these "future brides," but she needed to stay focused. And get out of the wind. "Well, you all have fun freezing to death. In the meantime, I'm going somewhere much warmer." She waved and walked past them.

Ceven caught her shoulder.

"Or you could join us." His expression didn't change, but his gaze intensified. In the light, flecks of gold nestled in the deep green and brown crevices of his eyes.

A cold snap of wind rustled through, kicking up the skirt of her dress. She shivered and turned away. "I don't know . . ." She paused. Riding with Ceven sounded a lot more fun than standing around searching for dead ends. But that wasn't why she was thinking of going. "Will I be back in time to see Ryker?" she asked.

"Of course. I only planned on checking the east wall."

The east wall. Perfect.

Evangeline nodded. "Okay, then."

Barto sighed loudly. Ceven glared at him, and Barto appeared disgruntled, an expression Evangeline hadn't thought the Rathan capable of.

The boy with the limp came out with a couple of gray horses, their coats dusted with white dots, and the other boy followed behind him, pulling two brown mares. They saddled them, and Barto, Xilo, and Tarry climbed onto their mounts with practiced ease.

Evangeline ran her hand along the neck of the gray horse, its skin moving beneath her hand. She had never gone horseback riding on her own. She only ever rode with Ceven on the rare times they snuck beyond the castle and into the kingdom.

"Ready?" Ceven asked.

She straightened her back and nodded. He gripped her waist, hoisting her upwards. She flew into the air. Her hands grasped frantically at the saddle to keep from falling, both of her legs hanging over to one side.

Ceven climbed behind her. He leaned to grab the reins, his chest brushing her shoulder. She stiffened and tried not to think about how close he was to her. Or that her pulse hummed like a woodpecker at her neck.

"You're a lot lighter than I expected," he said, waving at the two stable boys before flicking the reins. They started with a gentle trot.

Heat rushed her face. "I figured as much when you nearly threw me *over* the horse, instead of on it."

His chest rumbled with laughter, and her face heated even more.

Ceven flicked the reins again, and they picked up speed. Evangeline tightened her grip on the head of the saddle and turned, her hair flying around her. Barto stayed farther back, keeping pace with Xilo and Tarry.

"Why were you asking about Daniel?" Ceven said after they traveled farther away from the stables.

"Who?"

"The boy who used to work at the stables. Why were you looking for him?"

She huddled into her coat, not daring to lean closer toward Ceven's warmth. "I heard he went missing, so I went to find him."

"That's awfully nice of you."

She peeked up at him. "What's that supposed to mean?"

"You know what I mean, Eve. You don't . . . play well with others."

"Not for lack of trying," she snapped. "And maybe I'm trying to change that."

He raised an eyebrow. She mimicked his earlier gesture and slapped him in the ribs. He chuckled.

They followed the beaten path in the snow, a mix of wagon tracks, footsteps, and other horses traveling through, until they strode to the front gates of the castle. The two guards, stationed at either side of the golden bars, fisted their hands over their right breasts as they passed through.

Evangeline ducked, but it was pointless. Ryker was bound

to find out she had gone into town. She hoped using the prince as an excuse would be enough to save her.

"It's been awhile since we rode together," Ceven said.

"What? Oh, yes . . . It has been awhile." The last time was years before he left for Atiaca. Before she planned on leaving the kingdom with Lani.

"Don't worry, I'm a better rider than I was back then," he teased, a suspicious glow in his eyes.

The last couple times she'd gone riding with him, he didn't have complete control over his steed, and they both had fallen off. More than once.

"So, you're telling me that if I fall off this time, it won't be an accident?"

He leaned forward, a mischievous smirk on his face. "It means you better be really nice to me."

She made the grave error of gazing up at him. This close, she saw the dimple in his left cheek. The sunlight streaming through the loose strands of his hair. She wanted to reach out and brush it back, to feel its softness between her fingers.

His smirk faded and her lips parted. His eyes trailed down her face to rest on her mouth as an excited shiver vibrated through her. She forgot about Barto. About Tarry and Xilo. He leaned closer, and the heat of his body tickled her skin. Closer and closer . . .

Then her eyes widened in panic.

He's going to kiss me!

CHAPTER 14

~☙ CEVEN ❧~

Evangeline's stare captured Ceven's, holding him hostage. They passed underneath a barren oak tree, pockets of sunshine illuminating her eyes. Blue clashing with green. Like the Araji Sea he loved so much from his time in the empire. Her lips were a pale, rosy pink, matching the tip of her nose where the wind teased it. He bowed his head, as if drawn to her warmth, wanting to taste it on his lips.

Evangeline flipped her head away, her hair smacking his neck.

Ceven blinked. *I'd been about to kiss her.* His cheeks burned, and he tightened his grip on the reins, focusing back on the road. He was grateful for the chilly breeze that rolled through, his body uncomfortably warm.

They made their way down the steep mountain path,

traveling passed the castle's farthest slave quarters in silence. Humans were trailing toward the shelter.

Evangeline glanced at the shelter, frowning. *Was she thinking about Lani?* Ceven thought. He hated he didn't know how Lani had been these past two years. How they both fared while he was gone, but he knew better than to ask. He wasn't about to risk spoiling the moment with a fight.

"You looked handsome at dinner last night," she said, breaking the silence. Her voice was quiet, as if embarrassed.

"You looked absolutely beautiful." His thoughts lingered on the low-cut dress she had worn and her bare chest. He imagined pressing light kisses along the cut of it and trailing along her collarbone, up her neck, and to her lips. . . He cleared his throat. "I'm surprised the king invited you. Maybe he's finally having a change of heart."

She kept her eyes on the road. "Well, Ryker can be very persuasive when he wants to be. Though I wish he wasn't so persistent. I could have happily stayed far, far away from the king."

Ceven tilted his head. "The king asked Ryker if you could attend. He said as much while I was with him."

She turned to him. "What?"

He shrugged. "No joke. Maybe he wanted to see your lovely face." *A very lovely face,* he couldn't help but think.

Evangeline rolled her eyes. "Or please his own morbid curiosity. I think it's just another game he's playing." Her eyes flickered to him, then away.

He recognized the look. "What?"

She waved her hand, dismissing it. "It's nothing, not a big deal."

"Eve, just say it."

"No, it's nothing."

Ceven pulled up on the reins, the horse slowing to a crawl. "I will stop this horse until you tell me."

She glared at him. "I swear, you're so . . ." She let out a sharp sigh. "You didn't look at me once. The whole night."

He stared at her, then flicked the reins. The horse resumed its slow trot. "You know why."

"Looking at me wouldn't cause the king to kick us both out of the room."

He bit back a harsh laugh. If she only knew.

"I don't want to give them a reason to punish you," he said.

Evangeline was quiet for a bit. "I wish things were different."

His heart squeezed at the same time he grimaced. Maybe asking her to ride along was a mistake. He hadn't thought of the consequences, just wanting to be with her.

I could turn around now, drop her back off at the stables. Deny any reports of us together and keep my distance from her, he thought.

But he didn't.

The path evened out, the paved trail leading them passed bricked houses, snow pilling on top of the pointed roofs. A few Nytes were out, covered head to toe in heavy petticoats and fur. Some bowed as he passed. Others stared, their mouths open. He relented a nod to a few but kept his pace. Evangeline's head stayed lowered as they passed more people on the street. It got underneath his skin. She shouldn't have to hide.

"So, did Sehn hit his head while in Sundise Mouche?" she said.

"Sehn?" His first thought was of a melancholic lullaby and his brother standing in the fire's glow. The melody crawled over his skin; he never knew his brother could sing. "Why, did he do something odd?"

Her nose wrinkled. "He smiled at me."

Ceven threw back his head and laughed. "Yes, how odd," he got out.

She turned in her saddle. "How is that not weird? Sehn acknowledging me, let alone smiling at me? I don't think I've ever received so much as a small peek from him."

Ceven was still smiling. "Well, I admit he's matured since returning. He's even more of a pompous ass now than before." That was an understatement.

A smile broke across her face as she turned to hide it. "I'm not surprised." She paused for a moment, then looked behind them. "So . . . Barto. He's . . . unusual."

Ceven almost forgot about the rest of his entourage following a few paces behind them. "He definitely grew on me, that's for sure."

"How did the two of you meet?"

He stretched the muscles in his neck. "My first day in Atiaca, the empress assigned him to show me around, learn the culture. He was . . . an eager tour guide. Talked so much, I mean, just rambled about the most random things, and his jokes . . ." Ceven smiled, shaking his head. "They were awful. It got to where I tried to lose him every chance I got."

Evangeline raised an eyebrow. "But . . .?"

He sighed. "But he ended up saving my behind more than once. I didn't know the land as well as I thought I did. Ventured too far into the jungle and almost got sucked into this sandpit. It was the most bizarre thing ever. Like the ground was opening up its jaw, trying to suck me in. If Barto hadn't been there, I might've died."

Evangeline's eyes widened.

"After that, I put up with the incessant chatter, and once I accepted that part about him, I could see all the good traits that were hiding underneath. He really is a nice guy. Someone you can trust to have your back." Ceven looked at the Rathan. A light layer of snow dusted his black fur, his mouth wide and smiling as he laughed at something Tarry said. He looked up and shot Ceven an inappropriate hand gesture.

Well, Barto was nice *most* of the time.

The two of them continued to chat about his time in Atiaca, falling into their old, familiar banter. They traveled farther, the houses becoming closer and closer together until they were clusters. Ceven shifted the reins, waving behind him to signal Barto and the others to follow him down a side alleyway. They traveled down several narrower streets and paths until they were fast approaching the far-left side of the kingdom's wall, neighboring the Olaaga Forest.

Evangeline appeared more tense. Her head swiveled every few paces, scanning the area. There were more guards than usual roaming these parts. Their silver metal armor shone in the late afternoon sun. They saluted Ceven as they passed, giving Evangeline a look that lingered longer than he felt comfortable with. He tapped the reins and picked up their pace.

"There are a lot of guards." Evangeline lifted the collar of her hood.

"There was a question about the security of our borders. I don't know the reason behind it, though." No one had seen any bandits near the wall or heard any reports of runaway slaves.

His gaze traveled to Evangeline, where it stayed for a moment. *Could it be . . .?*

He tore his gaze away.

Ceven slowed their pace, trotting parallel to the wall. It stretched high with stones, the size of his horse, stacked together and pointed, golden arches decorating the top. They passed towers spanning high enough to surpass the top of the wall. Too high for them to see the guard stationed at the top of every one.

Barto's loud chatting echoed behind them and Ceven imagined Tarry and Xilo's stoic faces looking at each other in shared anguish. People gathered where they were patrolling. Nytes, mostly Aerians, came out of their homes. Children flew overhead to see the prince and his entourage. Most cast him dirty glances, whispering to one another. It was only a handful that smiled or gave a bow of respect.

He didn't spare another forced wave or nod and kept his head forward.

Evangeline shifted in her saddle and lifted her coat, hiding her face. Ceven frowned. He moved the reins, unbuttoned his jacket, and pulled her head into the warmth of his chest. She stiffened, then relaxed, tucking her hands into his shirt. He flinched.

"You're freezing, Eve." His arm ensnared her waist, pulling her closer. The cold hardly bothered him, his blood running hotter than a human's. It was only a nuisance when a cold snap of wind blew through. He hadn't thought of how uncomfortable Evangeline must be.

"I-I'm fine," she whispered.

"We should head back."

She gripped his shirt. "No!" Her eyes shifted. "I mean, I don't want you to turn around because of me."

His earlier inkling of suspicion grew, like a seed taking root in the pit of his stomach. He was tempted to ask, but bit his tongue. They hadn't spent time together like this in a while, and he secretly enjoyed her head on his chest too much for the mood to sour.

They continued like that, her body propped up against his, his arm wrapped around her waist as the sun declined, the temperature dropping even more.

Her entire face pressed against his chest, occasionally taking peeks at where they were going. Her shivering got worse. It was time for them to head back.

He motioned to Barto and the others that he was going to return. As much as he didn't want to let go, he moved his arm, gripped both of the reins, and increased their pace.

"Where are you going?" Evangeline's voice cracked.

"The sun's almost set, and you're freezing to death, Eve. We're heading back."

"No, please, just a little more." She peered up at him. She tried to smile, but her lips were too chapped, and she licked the blood away.

This time, he said what was on his mind. "Why?"

Her gaze moved to the snow-covered ground. "I don't want to go home yet."

He wanted to believe her, to trust her.

But he knew it was a blatant lie.

Evangeline looked up at the same time Ceven leaned down, his wings curling around them, blue and gold-tipped feathers dancing in the winter wind. Their faces hovered a breath apart.

"Then why couldn't you look me in the eye when you said that?"

Her mouth opened for a second before she turned. Her hands left his chest to fold underneath her armpits. "Never mind. Let's just go."

Ceven's jaw tightened. Today, he thought he had bridged the gap between them. Rekindled a friendship he had sorely missed for the past two years. But here she was, keeping secrets and lying to him. Burning down that bridge and pushing him away.

What are you hiding from me, Eve?

He gripped the reins a little tighter and dug his feet into the side of his horse, propelling them forward. Evangeline was nearly jostled from her seat, her hands flying to grab onto him and the saddle. She shot him a nasty look.

Ceven bit back a smile, feeling a little better as they returned to the castle.

CHAPTER 15

⁓ EVANGELINE ⁓

Evangeline was grateful to be inside the warm castle. Her butt was sore from the saddle, and her bones were still defrosting when she walked to Ryker's suite. The sun had set on their way back, lampposts coming alive as they galloped to the stables. She had mumbled a farewell to Ceven, waving at Barto and the others. Ceven hadn't responded.

She frowned as she passed gold-trimmed paintings. Frustration bubbled under her skin, but it was more directed at herself than Ceven. They had been so close! Had they gone up a little farther, she would've known if her escape route was still there. Instead, she acted like a fool and possibly revealed her true intentions.

And no matter what, she couldn't tell Ceven.

She touched her cheek, still feeling the heat of his chest. His scent, the dark forest blending with a hint of spice, still lingered on her coat and in her hair from where she had cuddled his body. She missed his closeness, had relished in the intimacy, even if it nagged at the part of her mind that told her it was wrong. It'd been a long time since they'd done anything together, and she'd enjoyed herself. A little too much. Talking with him, being with him . . . he made it so *easy*. Like nothing had changed. But everything had. Soon, the king expected him to marry, to uphold his duties as an Aerian prince, and she'd be a human on the run from the law.

This path they were treading . . . it wouldn't end well.

She came to the front of Ryker's suite and the guards knocked on the door, signaling her arrival. *One thing's certain, there are a lot more guards than when I first left. Next time, it won't be so easy,* she thought, entering the dim hallway.

Ryker sat in his usual chair with two empty teacups on the table in front of him. Someone was just here.

"Good evening, Evangeline," he said. His words were clipped.

Evangeline fisted her hands, her stomach tight. She knew this tone. "Good evening, Father." She sat down and wished he could've stayed gone the whole day. *I wonder where he went?*

"Where were you this evening?"

Evangeline avoided his gaze. "I . . . was with Ceven."

"Doing what?" He gripped the edge of the armchair.

"We went horseback riding," she whispered.

"And where did you go, Evangeline?"

"Into . . . town." There was no point in lying. He already knew.

Ryker stood so fast she flinched and paced in front of her. "Do you enjoy testing me, Evangeline?"

"No, I just—"

"Maybe you need a personal Overseer to watch your every move, since you can't follow orders."

Her tone was desperate. "I was with the prince and his escorts. We didn't go beyond the wall."

He stopped right in front of her, his face tight with anger. "Maybe I should assign Officer Jarr to be your new personal guard."

Fear would have been the healthy reaction. Instead, impatience swelled inside her. "Why do you care so much—!"

He struck her face so hard her head snapped back. Her eyes watered, and her skin stung where her cold gloves brushed it. Anger boiled inside her.

"Go to your room, Evangeline."

Lani. Raiythlen.

Her anger evaporated. "No, I'm sorry, I promise it won't happen again—"

"Now!" he roared.

"*I can't!*"

He stilled, and she cursed herself.

"And why is that?" His voice was as smooth as Atiacan steel.

Her cheek throbbed, and she stroked it. "Lani . . . she's not feeling well," she admitted. "Someone has to make sure she's okay. Please, I need to see her."

Ryker smiled, and Evangeline thought he was going to let her go.

"Then maybe you should have thought of that before disobeying me." He turned, dismissing her.

Heart in her throat, she got up and stormed to her room. She wanted to slam the screen door but let it gently shut behind her. Tears spilled over, and she took the pillow from her bed, drowning her cries of frustration. She should've never gone off with Ceven. She should've known better to push Ryker more than she already had. Her fingers tore into the silken pillowcase, and it ripped.

This is my fault.

Eventually, her shoulders stopped shaking and her breathing calmed. She removed the pillow and sat on the bed, deflated. Through her window, the moon snuck through a thick expanse of clouds. She didn't believe in the Gods like Lani did, but tonight she folded her hands together and prayed to anyone who'd listen.

Please protect and watch over Lani. I beg of you.

She didn't bother pulling back the covers and lay on top of the bed, her eyes staring blankly at the ceiling. Sleep didn't come for a while.

His heart pulsed in her bloody hand. The tirade of screams, a familiar melody in her ears.

Next target.

Turning to the left, her eyes narrowed on the cluster of Aerians and Rathans dragging two Casters, whose faces were bloodied and raw. Dropping the heart to the ground, she focused on her next victims. She pulled two sharp daggers from her belt, and the weapons eased into her palms with a contented sigh.

Before the Aerians and Rathans could blink, her knife entered their throats, blood decorating the front of her face and the dirt below. She wiped the blood from her chin as the bodies dropped to the ground next to others. Puddles of blood oozed into the brown soil. Homes and what was left of a city lay decayed and broken, its destruction brought about by her own doing.

It was war. And she would kill anyone who got in her way. Smiling, she licked the blood on her lips.

Next target.

Evangeline flew from bed, covering her mouth. A wave of nausea gripped her insides as she ran to the bathing room.

Her knees hit the floor, and she heaved into the toilet, spit dribbling down her mouth. She tasted the familiar bitterness of iron in the back of her throat, causing her to hurl again, but nothing came out. Her stomach was empty.

When the worst of it subsided, she undressed and climbed into the bath, the scalding water rinsing away imaginary blood that had coated her other self. Images of scarlet hearts and strewn bodies crept up, but she shoved them from her mind, lest her nausea come back tenfold.

She hopped out and wrapped herself in a silk robe. In the sitting chamber, Ryker set down a silver tray of food. It was early, judging by the darkness outside the windows. He must have fetched the food himself.

"I'm sorry for waking you." Her body was sore, her cheek hurt, and she hardly slept.

Ryker picked up the small pot and poured water into two mugs, steam puffing out from them. "This is the second time you've been sick. Are you ill?"

She sat down, hugging herself. Her hair was damp, and the fire Ryker started hadn't warmed up the room yet. "No, I'm fine." She grabbed a mug, her fingers embracing its heat.

"Clearly." He sat across from her, his own cup in hand.

"I . . . had another dream."

He set down the cup. "I know. I could hear you yelling in your sleep."

And you didn't bother to wake me? But of course not. If he woke her, she wouldn't be able to tell him what she saw.

She recounted the entirety of it to him. Closing her eyes, she swallowed hard, trying not to dwell on the details. On the blood. The guts. *Deep breaths.*

"These . . . dreams, my hallucinations, they're getting more frequent," she finished. "What's wrong with me?"

Ryker stared at his cup.

"You should eat," he said after a while.

Evangeline looked at the sweet rolls and the eggs lying on the plate before her. Usually, the smell of cinnamon and butter would make her mouth water, and considering she went to bed without food last night, she should be ravenous. Instead, her throat closed up. She shook her head.

"Eat," he said again, more adamant.

Evangeline swallowed, looking down at the food. She picked up the roll and nibbled on it.

Ryker drank his tea, and she ate in silence. She forced herself not to breathe while she chewed. It helped the food go down easier. In the end, a roll and some eggs sat uneaten on her plate.

"May I go?" Evangeline asked, peeking at him.

He stared at her unfinished plate but said nothing. He stood, and Evangeline frowned when he disappeared into his bedroom. Rustling and the shuffling of drawers echoed in the quiet suite before he returned to her.

"You wish to see Lani, I'm assuming?" He gestured at her. She held out her palms, and he dropped two small white capsules in them. "This will help ease her pain." He idled on her cheek. "And yours."

Her brows rose, clutching the pills. She met his gaze, and

for a moment she swore she saw something in them. Something she imagined she'd see in a real father's eyes. But this was Lord Ryker. Surely it was wishful thinking.

"Thank you," she whispered.

"I expect you back at our usual time." Her head bobbed, and when she got up to get ready Ryker added, "And, Evangeline, the next time I catch you beyond the castle grounds . . ."

"I understand," she said, but there was no weight to her words.

The wind was calm as Evangeline trekked down the mountain path toward Lani's. The sun was rising, and she passed a few humans along the path, most of their faces bundled into their coats and flimsy shawls. Her fur-lined coat helped keep out most of the cold, but she couldn't shake the tingling feeling in the back of her neck. As if someone was watching her.

She made sure not to slip on parts of the brick path that iced over, sneaking glances around her. It was too dark to see anything far ahead or behind, and aside from the occasional human, she was alone.

You're overreacting, Evangeline. Being paranoid, as usual. But she still picked up her pace. Bumps broke out along her skin, and the slightest brush of wind felt like a warning.

Something grazed her neck. She spun around.

A thin layer of snow blanketed the ground, the icy path reflecting the flames dancing inside the lamps. Nothing unusual. *It was probably just the wind.*

She forced a laugh at her own paranoia when her heart stuttered—a shadow figure slunk amongst the brambles and empty trees. It wasn't in the shape of a human. It looked like an animal.

Every joint in her locked up. She refused to tear her eyes away, as if the longer she stared at it, it would eventually go away.

But it didn't.

Move, you need to move. She took a step back. Then another. The shadow creature followed, shifting into the glow of a lamp. The light illuminated fur the color of dirt mixed with fresh snow. It highlighted its four-legged body and the narrow muzzle of what looked to be a wolf.

Her pulse ricocheted against her throat. *How can there be wolves on this side of the wall? There's no way!*

Evangeline took another step back. Lani's wasn't that far away. She couldn't outrun a wolf, but hopefully she'd have enough time to make it inside. Or die trying.

Inhaling deeply, she took another step back before turning around.

She ran.

The wind blew past her, her arms pumping, propelling her faster as she raced down the slippery slope. The crunching of snow and padded paws on the brick path echoed close behind her. She focused on the building ahead. Closer and closer. So focused that she missed the slick of ice on the ground. Evangeline tumbled headfirst, legs spreading, catching her balance in time. To her relief—and luck—something skidded behind her, claws scrambling to find purchase. She didn't hesitate, taking off once more.

The slave quarters were in plain sight. The wolf behind her had quieted, but she didn't dare turn around to see. She barreled forward until she slammed into the door. Her fingers scratched at the handle until she peeled it open. The wind blew her in, and she turned, shoving it shut. With no lock on the door, she sat down with her back against it, waiting, praying nothing would come banging on it. The room was empty, the smell of soap and mildew heavy in the air.

Air rushed into her lungs, and the sound bounced off the

stone walls. She shut her eyes, trying to control her breathing. She listened for howling, or footsteps. Anything. But all she heard was the wind. She waited a little longer before risking a peek out the door.

Nothing.

She was still on edge, but at least nothing was waiting for her outside somewhere. Then it occurred to her. *Had that been a hallucination?* The thought was more terrifying than it actually being a wolf.

Evangeline had never seen wolves or any other predatory animal on this side of the wall, nor had she heard others talk of them. Not to mention she was the only one who saw it, though others had passed her on the trail.

Please, no. I don't want to be crazy. She rubbed her temples, a headache forming.

Her legs were shaking from leftover adrenaline when she entered Lani's room. The fireplace was burning, the room warmer than the damp, cold chamber above. Her friend was lying on her back, eyes closed. For a moment, the room spun. Then Lani's chest moved. She was breathing.

Reaching into the front of her dress, she pulled out Ryker's pill. She had taken hers earlier, and all her aches and pains vanished. Her cheek was blissfully numb.

The cot squeaked as Evangeline sat beside Lani, pressing a palm to her forehead. It was hot. Evangeline propped her friend's head up and held the pill to her mouth.

"That won't work."

She jerked and the pill almost went flying. Raiythlen propped against the wall with his arms folded. He was still dressed in a slave's working attire, but the look in his eyes screamed of something far more dangerous than a human. *Where the blazes did he come from?*

"You said she would get better," she bit out.

"I said it would be temporary. I still need your continued cooperation."

She pinned him with a glare. "If she's not back to work soon, she'll be as good as dead." Lani's been gone for two days now. If she was out much longer, an Overseer might decide she wasn't useful anymore. She'd seen humans shipped to other parts of Peredia, or the empire. Torn apart from their friends and family, like Lani had been, when they were no longer needed at the castle. The rest . . . didn't live long.

"Where were you last night?" he asked.

"With Lord Ryker. I'm still a human. I can't do whatever I want," she retorted. She knew she needed to be nicer, considering he held Lani's life in his hands, but all she could envision was taking his head and bashing it into the wall.

Or slicing his neck open with a dagger.

Images from her dream assaulted her, and she closed her eyes, blocking the memory and swallowing the vomit creeping up her throat.

"No, but compared to Lani, here, you have quite the life," he drawled.

She bit her tongue, breathing out through her nostrils. "I found out something yesterday. That is what you're here for, right?" She glanced at Lani. "Let's talk in the hallway."

"There are too many witnesses in the hall. She's dead asleep. She won't hear this conversation." He raised an eyebrow. "Did you find something worth my time?"

Her lips pressed into a hard line, but she wasn't in any position to argue. "I talked to the mother of the boy who most recently went missing." *Or tried to, at least.* "She said something about markings."

"Markings?"

"I don't know." She shrugged. "She was hysterical, but said he came home with marks all over him. I don't know what they look like, or who hurt him and why." Or why Shani and Gardia thought it was Evangeline who had kidnapped him, but she wasn't going to tell him that.

"Did she say anything else?"

She shook her head. "Not really, just that he used to work in the stables. I went to search it but didn't get the chance to look around."

"Because you went on a joy ride with the prince."

She gaped at him. "How did you . . .?"

He rolled his eyes. "I'm a professional, Evangeline. I've been doing this for a while."

How long? she wondered. "You don't look much older than me."

He smiled. "My life is very different from yours. And the less you know, the better." He removed himself from the wall, holding out a vial. Evangeline took it. "This will help her for the next two days."

She popped the cork on it and gave Lani the antidote. "How long until she's cured?"

"That all depends on you, my dear."

She really hated this Caster.

Lani's breathing eased and her face became less pallid. Evangeline brushed a hair from her forehead, a crease in her brow. Something poked at her conscience. A deadly curiosity. She shouldn't ask, it was best that she didn't . . .

"Do you have a sister?" she asked.

He stiffened, and the grim set of his lips told her she had said something she should've left dead.

"Why?"

Evangeline cleared her throat. "I-I was just wondering.

There's another Caster here . . . and she looks an awful lot like you."

She thought he wouldn't answer, but he surprised her. "Yes. You have met my sister."

I knew it. There were more questions she wanted to ask: Were they working together? What was Avana's goal? But this time she kept her mouth shut.

He walked closer to her, and she made the mistake of meeting his eyes. It was like encountering the wolf all over again. "If you tell, or even hint about my presence here to her, I'll make sure you and Lani die a very slow and painful death."

Evangeline opened her mouth, but no words came out. She nodded instead. *Well, that answers one of my questions.*

He stepped back and smiled, the expression more intimidating then when he'd been indifferent. "You've done well so far. I'll do some investigating of my own around the stables. Now, I need you to do is ask your lover about Sehn and the king."

"Lover?"

"Don't act coy." He waved his hand. "The prince, of course. Ask him how his father and brother have been, if anything unusual has been happening behind closed doors."

She didn't stress that they were just friends. He was taunting her. She bobbed her head.

"I'll give you some time, so I'll meet with you here the night after tomorrow." He bit his finger, red bubbling from the tip, and smeared something onto his arm. He opened the door and paused. "Oh, and Evangeline?"

"What?"

"Good luck," he said before vanishing into thin air, the door swinging shut.

CHAPTER 16

⤐ EVANGELINE ⤏

Evangeline had forgotten how busy the youngest prince usually was. How was she supposed to ask him questions if he was always in meetings or doing routine inspections with the Peredian soldiers, or off doing other princely things she didn't know about anymore? Now that they didn't have lessons together, it was harder to locate him in the massive castle.

She almost gave up all hope of finding him when something rushed down the hall behind her. Strands of her blond hair kicked up, and she whipped around in time to spy two familiar Rathans racing. She would've been concerned if she hadn't seen Barto laughing—not even hindered by the fast sprint—at his companion, bald Rathan who had been at dinner the other night. Stray Aerians walking down the hall gave the two of them wicked sneers, but they didn't notice. Or care.

Evangeline thought about waving down Barto. With how close the two of them were, he might know where Ceven was.

She called his name, but he had already turned the corner. Clicking her tongue, she picked up her skirts and followed.

What Evangeline expected to be a quick sprint ended with her trailing them all the way to the training grounds. She would catch up only for the two of them to start running again. If it weren't for Barto's loud, distinguishable voice, she never would've been able to follow them. Bent over, using a column for support, she sucked in heaps of brisk air.

The sun shined down on a thin layer of snow covering the training grounds. Patches of dead grass peeked through where a few Nytes currently trained. Barto and the other Rathan were already wielding a pair of swords, fighting one another in only a shirt and tight pants.

They're crazy. Insane, Evangeline thought, catching her breath.

From her peripheral, a tall blue figure came over, leaning on the column next to her. Soft blue feathers rustled in the breeze, threads of gold dancing in the light from the afternoon sun. She didn't have to look to know it was Ceven.

He was geared in a loose, blue jacket tucked into dark pants, a single sword strapped to his side. His hazel eyes were bright with amusement, making him look devilishly charming. Over his shoulder, Tarry and Xilo lurked on the other side of the courtyard, blending in with the stone columns.

"Don't tell me you tried racing Barto and Quan?" Ceven smirked, his arms folded.

"Not on purpose," she wheezed. *Quan, that's his name.* Evangeline remembered him being a lot more formal at dinner.

"What are you doing here?" he asked.

Looking for you, she almost said, but changed it to, "I saw

Barto running and thought he was in trouble." She finally got her breathing under control and straightened. "Is he insane? What Nyte thinks it's okay to run through the castle halls for sport? Especially a supposed emissary?"

Ceven smiled widely. "This is tame compared to how they act back in Atiaca."

"The king's going to kick them out."

He shrugged. "Barto would probably be grateful. I don't think he's fond of Peredia."

She scowled. "That's not my point."

Evangeline asked him if they could speak in private when Barto said, "It's about time you caught up, bird boy."

It was Ceven's turn to scowl.

Barto and Quan walked over and joined them. Quan's smile left his face when he saw her.

"I told you not to call me that," Ceven said in greeting.

Barto shrugged. "Would you prefer princess? Or maybe my little dove, or—"

"Barto."

Barto put up his hands in surrender, but his smile didn't go away. His slitted pupils moved to her. "*Cu holda al aba,*" he said in Atiacan. The sun embraces you.

"And you," Evangeline replied in Peredian. She knew, from her studies, the traditional Atiacan greeting. She also knew how to say it in Atiacan, but was too embarrassed. Her pronunciation was horrible.

"Well, Goddess burn me. It's not often I'm surprised." He mistook her embarrassment for discomfort. "Take that as a compliment, sweetheart." He wiggled his brows suggestively at Ceven. "Careful, I might steal her from you." Her face grew hotter.

Ceven rolled his eyes, but pink dusted his cheeks. "I'm going to train," he muttered, stalking over to one of the sack dummies next to Quan, who'd already left the conversation and was engaged in a mock battle. He held a spear with both hands, moving and fighting with such fluidity that Evangeline frowned. She'd never win against a Nyte.

"Do you practice?" Barto asked, still standing beside her.

"No, my lord," she said instinctively, her eyes fixed on Quan.

His lips curled at the title, but he let it slip. "Really? Ceven said you used to all the time as a kid."

Her eyes widened. Why would Ceven say something like that to another Nyte? Did he want to get her in trouble? "I used to," she relented. "But I realized I was wrong and will never pick up another weapon again." She watched Quan pounce back and strike with the butt of his spear, his movements quick and decisive.

Barto's eyes remained on her. "Somehow, I find that hard to believe."

She blushed and repeated what Lord Ryker had told her. "The Gods created men so women wouldn't have to fight. It's not my place." Not to mention the kingdom forbid humans from picking up a weapon, let alone using one.

Barto's laugh reverberated off the stone columns and balconies. Quan and Ceven glanced their way briefly before resuming. Evangeline wanted to sink into the snow.

He gripped his stomach. "Oh, if only Rasha heard you say that."

She was sure her face was now entirely red. "Well, what about in the empire? Are women allowed to fight there?"

He looked at her as if she had two heads. "Allowed? It's second nature—for everyone. Protecting yourself, knowing your body and its limitations, it's not only vital for survival but instinctual, a concept instilled in every Atiacan. Men and women alike."

Evangeline frowned. The concept was so foreign to her. She believed she was simply unnatural for having a desire to fight. *How different would my life be if I had been born Atiacan? Could I have been a soldier?* She smiled and fantasized about a large sparkling sea, her traveling through thick lush jungles she had seen only in books. A sense of freedom eclipsed her. No king, no castle, no Ryker.

"I wish Peredia was different," she admitted.

Barto was quiet for a moment. "Humor me. I challenge you to a sparring match," he said.

Did he not listen to a single thing I said? Her sigh was short, her breath billowing out in a huff of steam. "I told you, I can't."

"Can't or won't?"

"You don't understand," she pleaded. "If I'm caught with a weapon, I'll be in a lot of trouble." *And who knows what Ryker would do to me if he caught me.*

Barto scratched his chin. "If anyone asks, I'll take the blame."

Evangeline rolled the idea around in her head. Her hand twitched to pick up the set of blades laid out in the center of the courtyard. To feel its weight in her hands again and experience the rush as she cut through the air. Until any Nyte nearby mentioned it to Ryker. Or the king.

"Maybe next time," she said.

"What if you practiced somewhere private? Where no one would catch you?"

By the Gods, this Rathan is insistent. How does Ceven put up with this?

She bit her lip. "Still too risky. If Lord Ryker finds out—"

Evangeline jumped when Barto grabbed her by the shoulders. "Oh, forget about that winged ass." She choked, and her eyes darted around to make sure no one was eavesdropping. "I see the way you look at those blades, how your eyes light up. And to be honest, I'm dying to see how much spark you have." He grinned, giving her a thorough inspection, head to toe.

This man's mouth is going to get us both in trouble! "I don't know, I don't think—"

"What if Ceven taught you?" His smile turned mischievous, a twinkle in his eyes.

Her face was now on fire. "Definitely not!" *But wait . . .* Getting Ceven alone, somewhere private, would be the perfect opportunity to ask him about Sehn and his father. To see if he had any leads on the missing persons, or if he knew what these markings were about, without risking someone overhearing them—or drawing Ceven's suspicions as to why she wanted to talk to him alone.

As if summoned, Ceven joined them, wiping his brow with the back of his hand. "What are you two talking about?"

Barto eagerly recited his idea before Evangeline could stop him.

"Absolutely not." Ceven crossed his arms.

Taken aback by his quick response, Evangeline thrust a hand on her hip. "Why not?"

Ceven took a deep breath and ran a hand through his hair. "I don't want you to get hurt."

Both hands were on her hips now. "I'm not going to face off with the Peredian military, Ceven. I just want to learn some basic techniques, and if no one sees us, what's the harm in it?"

He gave her an incredulous look. "What's the harm in it?" His face turned a few shades darker. "What's the *harm* in it? Oh, I don't know, maybe the king or Ryker *finding out.*"

"They won't," she fired back.

Ceven took a step toward her, but she didn't back away,

meeting his steely gaze head on. "But what if he does? What if he sends Vane after you again?" He took another step. "What if I'm not there?" He peered down at her. "What will you do then, Eve?"

They stood a breath apart, trapped by each other's heated gazes. Despite herself, frustrated tears gathered in her eyes. He was right, but he didn't have to shove it in her face like that.

"You're still a human. No matter how hard you train, you'll never be able to outmatch a Nyte," he said, striking the final blow.

Her gaze withered, and she dropped her head.

"You know that's not true." They both turned to Barto, who had been quiet the entire time. His pupils were dilated, the dark slits glistening. "With the right weapons, and the right tactics, she could hold her own. Everyone has a weakness."

Ceven glowered at him. "It's too much of a risk." But something else hovered in his eyes. Fear.

"That's for her to decide," Barto growled.

Evangeline glanced at Barto and he gave her an encouraging smile. Her own faint smile formed. "Barto, would you be willing to train me?" she asked, an edge to her voice.

Barto gave her a satisfied look. "Why, *of course*, sweetheart."

Ceven pinched his nose, aggravation etched into his features. "And what if you get caught, Eve?"

Her bravado faltered a little. A dark room with whips and manacles flashed in her mind.

Ryker can't protect you forever.

"*We* won't get caught," Barto said, with such conviction that it bolstered her spirits. "Ceven, you said it yourself. She's living in a nest of Aerians. She deserves to know how to defend herself, at least." Ceven gave him a look and Barto's gaze narrowed. "*Even* if it buys her enough time to seek help."

This strange Rathan's concern for Evangeline's well-being touched her. And surprised her. *He's a Nyte, and he doesn't even know me. Why does he care so much?*

"But if it means placing her into harm's way, it wouldn't matter," Ceven argued, but there was no actual weight behind it. He knew he had lost this fight. "There are eyes and ears everywhere in this castle. Where could you guys possibly go?"

Evangeline thought about it. She couldn't go to their suites, too many witnesses and not enough room. She needed space and a place where not many people went . . .

"I think know a place," she said.

The two men stared at her.

"Below the east wing, are some empty storage rooms. Only a few guards patrol there during the day. It would be perfect."

Barto agreed. Ceven's jaw ticked.

Evangeline's heart picked up. "We could go now."

"We're to meet with the king soon," Ceven said. Her excitement flatlined.

"How about tomorrow at this time?" Barto offered.

"That would work." She nodded, explaining how he could disguise himself, accessing the storage rooms from the outside entrance that she often used to be more discreet. She gave him a rough layout and directions.

"I don't like this." Ceven stared at her, and she stared back.

Barto gripped Ceven's shoulder, ignoring his statement. "We'll be there."

Evangeline waved goodbye as the two of them rejoined Quan, who hadn't stopped practicing or bothered to look at her.

CHAPTER 17

⤚❧ EVANGELINE ❧⤙

"**Y**ou shouldn't sleep on the floor. You'll catch a cold."

Evangeline blinked. She was sitting beside Lani, her head resting on the cot while her body was on the floor. *I dozed off.* Red and orange filtered through the window. At least she didn't oversleep and miss her evening meeting with Ryker.

She squeezed Lani's hand. "How are you feeling? Are you hungry?" *She had to be starving.* Evangeline berated herself for not bringing any food.

"I'm fine, I'm fine."

Lani tried to sit up, but Evangeline placed her hand on her. "Your body is still weak. You need to rest."

Lani rolled her eyes. "I feel like I've been resting for as long as the king has been alive. I'm going to perish if I lie here any longer." But she didn't get up again.

"Don't be so dramatic." Evangeline pursed her lips. *How old is he anyway?* Everyone knew the king was at least over a century old, but he had to be at the end of his life. Most Aerians lived for about hundred-and-fifty years and kept their youthful appearance a lot longer than humans, so it was hard to tell.

She must have spoken aloud, because Lani responded, "Old enough to where it won't be too long until Sehn takes over. Though I'll be long dead before that happens."

"Why do you always talk like that?"

Lani looked at her, the laugh lines on her face more defined when she smiled. "If it means never having to work again, I'm happy with that."

"Once we leave here, you won't have to work."

Lani clicked her tongue. "Gods, you're too optimistic." She adjusted her head and grimaced. "If I don't get back to work soon, the Overseers will have my head."

Evangeline wanted to tell her that this was only temporary, that she wasn't completely healed, but guilt tied her mouth shut. She had brought the Caster here, and now Lani was paying the consequences for it.

Evangeline reached for the white pill in one of the hidden side pockets in her dress. She had stored it away before Raiythlen could take it. "Here. Lord Ryker said this will help with the pain."

Lani raised an eyebrow but said nothing. Evangeline helped lean her forward, feeding her the pill before washing it down with water.

"Lani . . . Have you heard any strange rumors surrounding these disappearances?" They had never really talked about it before. Evangeline always avoided the subject, since it always led to an argument.

She shrugged. "Oh, sure. Everyone has their own story to

share. My favorite is of a giant black cat slinking around and snatching people up."

"I'm being serious."

"I am too," she said, her eyes tight. "All of them are ridiculous, and none are going to bring those people back." She coughed again, and Evangeline's face tightened.

"I wish I could do more to make you feel better." Evangeline stared at her folded hands. "I'm sorry."

Lani swatted at her. "I swear, you think everything that happens to me is your fault. I'm getting old, Eve. I work long hours every day. I'm lucky to even last this long."

"You're only fifty-two. Stop acting like you're going to die tomorrow."

"But I might." Lani stared at her, and Evangeline stared back until she couldn't take it anymore, getting up from the bed and crossing her arms.

There was a gentle knock at the door. Ranson entered, carrying a small bag. Evangeline curled her lip at the same time Lani's eyes lightened.

"What are you doing here?" Lani called.

Ranson set down the bag on the bed, pounding his chest as he wheezed. "I . . . I heard you were ill," he said, still trying to catch his breath.

"What's in the bag?" Evangeline peered around his wide frame.

He scowled at her. "None of your business."

"Ranson." One word from Lani had him fumbling like a boy.

He looked at Lani before glancing away, rubbing his neck. "I . . . brought you some food. If you haven't eaten yet . . ." He trailed off.

Lani's face softened, making her look ten years younger. "No, I haven't."

Ranson cleared his throat.

Evangeline didn't like the old man, but, in that moment, she was glad to have him around.

Feeling out of place, she shuffled her feet. "Well, I should be going." The sun was already setting. She couldn't believe she had passed out for most of the day. She must've been more tired than she'd thought.

"Be safe," Lani said, but her eyes never left Ranson's.

Seriously, what does she see in him? Evangeline scoffed.

Evangeline turned for the door. Ranson grabbed her sleeve. "Lord Ryker's having company tonight. He had me set the table for three."

Her stomach sank. "Thanks for warning me," she said, walking out the door.

Evangeline arrived outside of Ryker's suite. She wasn't in the mood for company tonight. But if she were being honest, when was she ever?

Who will it be? she thought. *The king? One of Ryker's scholars?* Her thoughts wandered to Avana, who she now knew was Raiythlen's sister. Her marked hand tingled, remembering her elixirs and the magic she performed. Evangeline didn't know whether to feel excited or wary.

Evangeline wasn't surprised to find Avana sitting on Ryker's loveseat. One leg crossed over the other with her long black hair wrapped into a high ponytail. She regarded Evangeline with slanted eyes painted in a thick, dark liner.

"You're late," Lord Ryker snapped.

Evangeline spun to find him standing behind her. He scrunched his nose, taking in her long-sleeved green dress.

"Wash up and change into something more appropriate. We will dine with our guest tonight," he said.

Evangeline nodded, heading to the bathing room. She took a shower, taking the luxury of wiping her face and other parts of her cold body with scorching water. Guilt sprouted in her gut, imagining Lani and the other humans washing themselves from the spigot in the shared communal. While the kingdom's water came from the pockets of underground streams and run off from nearby mountains, the castle's boiler room filtered there's, allowing hot water to run to all parts of the massive structure. Everyone else resorted to the freezing winter waters.

Stepping out of the shower, Evangeline dried herself before glancing at her reflection. She usually avoided looking at herself, hating how thin she had become. Her cheekbones protruded more than was healthy, and her hips jutted out instead of curving. She kept telling herself that it was only for now. To prepare herself for her and Lani's escape, but honestly, it hadn't been that hard. The past few years, she had steadily lost her appetite. At first, she assumed it was because of stress, but now, with her growing hallucinations, she worried she was becoming ill. And Lord Ryker didn't seem to care at all, although her body resembled a walking skeleton.

Clean and garbed in a purple velvet gown, Evangeline walked to the table nestled on the opposite side of the sitting chamber. It was big enough to seat six around it comfortably. Avana and Ryker had already taken their seats, Ryker at the head of the table and Avana beside him. An array of food was artfully presented in bowls of silver and gold, garnished with crushed herbs and vegetables in front of them.

Ranson stood by Ryker. *How did he get back here so fast?* He brushed what little hair he had over, the thin measly strands sticking out against the weathered skin of his scalp, his lips curved into a natural frown. His eyes were on her as she took the empty seat across from Avana.

Ryker nodded, and Ranson served the food onto all three plates.

Evangeline wasn't as apprehensive about the ensuing dinner as she'd been for the one with the king. Waiting with her hands folded, she expected to hear questions about her past, her mysterious marking. Questions she had answered over and over again to other scholars, doctors, scientists, and even bored royals. But this time was different. This time she felt Avana could actually help her.

"Thank you for joining us, Avana," Ryker started, dismissing Ranson, who bowed and left the room. "Questions you may have, you are at liberty to ask."

"Thank you, my lord."

Avana and Ryker took small bites of their food while Evangeline pushed hers around. The conversation centered on small pleasantries and differences between Sundise Mouche and Peredia. It turned out Ryker hadn't been spinning her stories when he mentioned air ships and long-range communication in Sundise Mouche. Evangeline was curious of their opinion on humans in their country, if slavery was a part of their culture, but she kept her lips sealed and head down.

"So, Evangeline, if I may ask, Ryker says you were found inside a ruin. Do you recall anything before that?" Avana turned to her.

Evangeline gave a scripted reply. "All I remember is waking up in complete darkness, feeling scared. If I try to recall anything before that, I get an unbearable pain."

"Pain? As in it hurts to remember?"

Evangeline shook her head. "The memory itself is of pain. Like . . . like being crushed. I don't know how to describe it."

Avana brought her fingers to her lips, appearing thoughtful. "And you've always had that mark?"

Evangeline wanted to roll her eyes at the mundane question. "Yes, my lady, for as long as I can remember." Evangeline went to take a bite of food when something brushed her leg. She glanced at Avana but shrugged it off. It was probably an accident.

"Ryker tells me you suffer from hallucinations and nightmares?" Avana continued.

It happened again. A tap against her leg, like she was trying to get her attention. Evangeline met Avana's gaze, searching for an explanation, but she betrayed nothing.

"Um . . . yes, well, not often, it's very rare that it happens." Avana brushed her leg again, and this time Evangeline knew it was intentional. Something cold and smooth rubbed against her bare ankle, but she forced herself to remain calm, her face placid.

"What do these hallucinations and nightmares consist of?"

Keeping her face trained on her food, she controlled a flinch as the unknown object tap against her leg again. *Is she trying to give me something?* She bit her lip. *Why keep it a secret from Ryker?*

When the object hit her ankle again, Evangeline got the hint and maneuvered her foot out of her shoe. "People and places I've never seen before but feel like I should know. Sometimes it's a glimpse of a man's face, other times it's of a Caster woman." Evangeline could put a name to one face from her dream the other morning, Anali, but she had no recollection of how she knew her, or if all of it was her imagination.

"Tell her about your dream, Evangeline," Ryker said, and she jumped. She quickly disguised it as if she were shifting to get more comfortable.

"It was . . . about the same Caster woman. She was waking

me up to meet with someone." Evangeline wiggled her foot out when a small circular object slid down her ankle and into her shoe. She put her shoe back on, her toes squeezing around a small, hard object. "She was telling me to go meet with someone named Jaden."

Avana settled her head atop her folded hands. "Interesting. And what did this Caster woman look like?"

Evangeline thought back to the beautiful woman. Long black hair, horns that curved the outline of her face, and blue eyes . . . "Honestly, she looked a lot like you."

"Tell her the Caster's name," Ryker said.

"It was Anali."

Avana's jaw dropped. "Are . . . are you sure?" she whispered.

Evangeline nodded, her brows wrinkling in confusion.

"You knew about this, didn't you?" Avana accused, her eyes narrowing on Ryker's.

Ryker didn't respond.

Evangeline looked at the two of them. Her curiosity gave her the courage to speak up. "I don't understand. Why is she so important?"

Avana's cheeks turned pink, but Evangeline couldn't tell if it was from embarrassment or anger as she took a deep breath. "Anali is my grandmother."

Evangeline's eyebrows furrowed deeper. Why would she be having dreams about Avana's grandmother? How could she dream about someone she'd never met? "But how—"

Ryker interrupted. "It's getting late, and Evangeline and I still have much to discuss."

Avana looked like she was far from done, but she straightened her back, nodding. "It's been a pleasure, Lord Ryker." She turned. "Evangeline." Avana rose from her chair, fixing her skirt, and bowed. "Another time."

"Another time," Ryker agreed.

As soon as Avana left the room, Ranson returned to clear the table. Nobody said a word. Plates and utensils clanging together was the only sound in the suite. Ryker looked at Evangeline's plate of half-eaten food but said nothing.

Evangeline wiggled her foot, the object squeezing her toes together. Their conversation with Avana left a lot of things swirling in her head. Had Ryker really known who Anali was and not say anything to her? Did he know the real reason behind her dreams?

If you really believe Ryker doesn't know anything, you're more naïve than I thought.

Raiythlen was right; Evangeline just didn't want to admit it. Ryker knew more than he let on.

Evangeline broke the silence. "Why didn't you tell me you knew who Anali was?"

"I do not want to have this conversation right now."

Ranson paused in his duties. One glance from Ryker had him swiftly wiping the table.

Evangeline's hand curled so tightly that her nails bit into the flesh of her palm. "You never do. Why are you lying to me? What's so important that I can't know the truth?"

"I said, I do not want to have this conversation right now. Do not make me repeat myself."

She breathed through her nostrils. *Calm down, Eve. It's not worth it.* But she had a right to know. A right to know why could hardly sleep or eat. Why she was seeing and hearing things. She was getting sicker, and he wasn't telling her why.

"Well, I do," she growled. "I have a right to know! This is my—"

Ryker was at the head of the table, siting calmly, when he charged her. She didn't have time to duck when his palm smacked her cheek, knocking her from the chair. No amount of pills could take away the pain that erupted in her face.

"Don't you dare speak to me in that tone."

Tears welled up in her eyes, and she glared at him. Her anger was transparent, her fury boiling over. "I'm so sorry, *Father*."

Her sarcastic response rewarded her with another slap. This one harder than the last. Evangeline yelped, her cheek splintering like sharp needles stretching her skin. Her left eye clenched shut, and her anger dissipated. Her temper was going to get her killed.

"I've protected you, fed you, clothed you. I've given you a life any human would kill to have." Ryker's hair brushed her shoulder as he gripped her chin, forcing her to meet his eyes. "You ungrateful human."

You ungrateful monster!

Evangeline blinked. One moment it was Ryker holding her. Next, it was a man who had replaced Ryker's large wings with a set of long, blue horns. His face hung near hers. His saliva smacking her face when he yelled.

You will do as you are told. Now kill them!

Evangeline swatted the arm away, but it didn't budge. People screamed, and she looked around frantically. She stood in a village. Heat brushed her skin, and flames ate at the surrounding houses. Nytes and humans ran from something she couldn't see in the dark night.

Out of the chaos, a human woman dropped to her knees in front of them. Her hands cradled her neck in an attempt to stop the blood pouring from it. Evangeline reached out to help the woman when her eyes caught on her mark. The naked runes illuminated brightly, and something tugged at her mind.

Take it. Take it. Take it all and leave nothing.

She blinked and looked down. She held the woman's snapped neck in her hands, her throat ripped open.

"*No!*" she screamed.

Evangeline hit the ground and slammed back to reality. Ryker had released his grip on her face. His mouth moved, but all she could hear were screams. Shouts from the soldiers. *Soldier.*

Ryker shook her shoulders. "Evangeline, what's happening?"

"Soldier. Fire. Casters."

"Where are you?"

Evangeline gripped her chest, and her mind tried blocking the horrifying vision. She didn't want to hear it, feel it, *see* it. She wanted it to stop. "I don't know . . ." Her voice wobbled.

Ryker didn't ask her anything else.

"What's wrong with me?" She wrapped her head in her hands.

Crash!

Both of their heads jerked to the table. Ranson coughed and fumbled to clean up the plate he had dropped. Evangeline had completely forgotten he was there. Judging by Ryker's expression, he had too. Ryker walked toward him.

Ranson put his hands up. "I–I'm sorry, Master, I—" In a heartbeat, Ranson's head was between Ryker's hands.

With a loud crack, Ryker snapped his neck.

Ranson fell to the floor in a sagging heap. His eyes stared at her, his head at an unnatural angle. Evangeline's mouth opened in a silent scream. Her eyes fixed to Ranson's blank expression. He wasn't dead. That didn't happen. It was another hallucination.

Ranson wasn't dead.

Ryker didn't even glance at him. Like he had just squashed

a bug and not a living person. "Need I remind you, you will tell no one of these visions. If I find out otherwise, I will kill them."

Her head moved on its own, still transfixed on Ranson. Evangeline had never told anyone. Not Lani or Ceven.

Ranson's lifeless face continued to stare at her. Why couldn't she look away? Then she thought of Lani, and the tears crept over. *Lani. Oh Gods, Lani, I'm so sorry. I didn't mean for this to happen.* Either the Gods didn't exist or they were crueler than she'd thought.

"You will not leave this suite until I say otherwise. Is that understood?" Satisfied with her slow nod of agreement, he dismissed her. Evangeline gathered herself, shuffling into her room.

After sliding the screen shut, she sat on her bed and stared at the wall. Mechanically, she took off her clothes and removed her boots. A small glass jar fell out, clinking against the floor. Avana's gift had slipped her mind. When she picked it up, thick blue liquid sloshed against the glass. Tied around it was a note.

Ryker settled into his room on the other side of the screen, and she shoved the jar beneath her pillow. He didn't enter her room, to her relief. She didn't take the vial back out. She'd deal with it in the morning.

Lying down on the bed, she gazed up, her eyes tracing the faint lines in the textured ceiling.

The lines faded, dripping down the cracks like blood. A woman's face stared back at her, her neck gaping open as her life spilled out. Then it turned into Ranson's soulless eyes glaring at her, accusing her. Their wide mouths screamed into her ears.

She pulled the blankets over her face and cried.

CHAPTER 18

∽ EVANGELINE ∾

"Evangeline."

Evangeline stirred in her sleep. Her lids felt sewn together.

"Evangeline, my love."

She snuggled into the mattress, wrapping the thick comforter tighter. Something brushed her hair, her cheek, then her lips. She must be dreaming.

"We will be together soon," they whispered against her ear.

Evangeline jolted up and surveyed the room. Nothing out of the ordinary. She licked her lips, her expression souring at the taste of blood. Maybe she bit her cheek in her sleep, since she couldn't recall having any vivid dreams. Her fingers grazed her face where Ryker had slapped her. It didn't hurt at all. It didn't even feel swollen.

Her screen door opened, and Ryker walked in. "It's time to eat," he said, still in his black robe, his hair not brushed.

"What?" She blinked.

He arched a brow. "Food, Evangeline. It's time for breakfast."

She looked around the room again. "Did you try waking me up earlier?"

He gave her an odd look. "No. Get dressed and come eat." He left, leaving the screen open.

Her skin crawled, but she ignored it. She spied Avana's vial on the ground when she got out of bed and changed. It must have fallen on the floor in her sleep.

Flicking her eyes to the door, she quickly snatched it up and tucked it into the top of her dress for safekeeping.

Evangeline met Ryker in the chamber, wearing another long-sleeved dress with a dark blue fabric that hung off her body. She smiled as the warmth from the fire snuggled into her skin.

Her smile froze. Ranson was dead.

She glanced at the spot where he'd fallen to the floor. There was nothing but shiny speckled marble. She dug her fingers into her palm, trying to keep the wave of nausea away. What was she going to tell Lani?

Sitting on the loveseat, she picked at the plate of food. They didn't talk about last night, or much of anything.

She asked to excuse herself after forcing down as much food as she could. Ryker glanced up from his tea, looking at her for the first time since she entered the room. He looked dazed, like he was still half asleep. He nodded at her, and she didn't waste any time leaving the suite.

Evangeline tugged and pulled at her bodice, shifting Avana's vial into a more comfortable position. *I wonder what it is.* She crept down a secluded side hallway, looking both ways before

opening the curved wooden door. Sunlight flooded her vision as she entered the same garden Ceven had shown her. The scent of roses and jasmine surrounded her as she ventured deeper, checking she was alone before pulling out the vial. Not even the sun's rays filtered through the dark blue liquid inside the corked vial. She untied the small, folded note wrapped around it. The first line left her shaking.

> *Ryker won't tell you the truth, but I will. Meet me in the game room tomorrow night. Drink this before you leave and make sure no one sees you. If they do, then this all will be for naught.*
>
> *—A*

The note had a small, rudimentary map below of where Evangeline would find her.

It's a trap, was her first thought, trying to douse the flames of hope that sparked inside her. *She wants something and will probably threaten or manipulate me into getting her way.* Raiythlen danced in her mind, the cruel twist of his lips. Why would Avana be any different?

Still, doubt crossed her mind. The sincerity that flashed in her eyes when Evangeline had asked about her mark, about

Caster magic. How she had helped her at dinner. It made her think Avana might not be as evil as her brother. And what if this was her only chance to find out the truth? To find out why she was going crazy?

Evangeline re-read the note, but there were no directions concerning the vial except to drink it. She glanced at the blue liquid again, swirling it around in her fingers. It was disgustingly thick, blue residue leaving streaks on the side of the glass. *What if this is poison? Some elaborate plan to kill me?* Though, she didn't think that was the case. Not with how much Avana coveted her mark.

Considering the timing of the note, Avana wanted to see her tonight.

Evangeline left the garden and slipped the vial into the front of her dress. She'd take the risk. It was her best option to find out what was wrong with her, and Ryker wasn't going to tell her anything soon. She didn't know Avana, but she trusted her to tell her the truth, more so than her brother or Ryker.

Swinging by the kitchens, Evangeline poked her head inside and spotted a head of brown and gray hair bobbing between busy bodies on the other side of the room. Evangeline frowned. Seeing Lani back in the kitchens, instead of in bed, made her worry spike. But she understood why. It would've only been a matter of time before an Overseer dragged her out of the slave quarters.

Her friend looked better, her skin flushed as she hovered over the deep porcelain sink and whisked dishes clean. Evangeline wanted to ask how she felt today but didn't go in any further. Not because of the tall, intimidating Aerians lingering along the sides of the kitchen walls, eyes scanning the crowd for anyone slacking in their work, but because she wasn't ready to confront Lani.

Coward.

But what was she supposed to say? That she saw Lord Ryker snap Ranson's head like a piece of firewood? That she watched him step over his lifeless body like he was a tea stain on his imported Atiacan rug? Ranson didn't even get a proper burial, his body surely thrown in some dark pit with other humans unlucky enough to be found by Nytes first before friends or loved ones.

She covered her mouth. Bile threatened to climb up her throat. No, she wouldn't tell her. She couldn't.

Evangeline asked a few more humans if they knew anything about the disappearances or these "markings." All she got were fearful looks and terrified ramblings begging her to spare them. Her blood boiled. Whatever these rumors were about her, they were getting worse. And she still didn't know who started them and why.

But as the sun snuck farther up the sky, thoughts of different fighting postures outweighed all her worries. To feel a sword in her hand again. She wondered what type of weapon she'd train with today.

Stay focused, Eve. You're doing this to get Ceven alone. To find out if he knows anything. She frowned. *If he shows up.* After their fight, she wasn't sure if he was going to come or not, and honestly, she didn't even know if she wanted him there.

You're still a human. No matter how hard you train, you'll never be able to outmatch a Nyte, Ceven's words rang inside her skull. Her hands curled. "You think I don't know that?" she said to no one.

Her excitement dampened a little, but not entirely as her feet glided across the carpeted castle halls to the east wing's storage rooms.

Traveling down the concrete steps into the damp under-ground hallway, she smelled the must and trapped moisture that had sunk into the walls. She kept her footsteps light and peeked around every corner, watching for guards or other peo-ple who might be lingering.

She turned another corner, following the same directions she'd told Barto, when an Aerian leaning against the wall froze Evangeline in her tracks. Relief washed over her when she rec-ognized the tall, thin frame and purple wings.

Xilo pulled back the brown hood of his coat, covering his armor, and nodded at her. He waved toward the door across from him, and she walked inside.

Barto and Tarry stood inside, but her eyes were drawn to Ceven's. *He actually came.* Ceven towered over the Rathan next to him and stood a fraction taller than Tarry, who dressed in a long coat like Xilo's and leaned against the stone wall behind them. He gave her a tentative smile when she entered, but she looked away.

Aside from a couple of discarded cloaks on the ground, the room was empty. Not just of barrels and crates, but also of any swords, axes, or daggers.

Her confusion must have been clear on her face when Barto responded with, "What? Not happy to see me?"

He and Ceven both wore open, loose shirts tucked into neu-tral breeches and dark boots. Not battle attire. "Where is all the equipment?" she asked.

Ceven propped his hands on his hips. "When's the last time you exercised?"

She avoided his eyes and mumbled, "Does climbing nearly a hundred steps a day count?"

He sighed. "First, I want you to focus on your endurance and stamina." Evangeline didn't miss the once-over he gave her

or the crease in his brow. "But I want you to take it easy. Don't push yourself too hard."

Do I look that weak? Her hands squeezed the cotton of her dress. "I'll be fine," she muttered and looked down at her dress.

"Here, I brought you these just in case." Ceven tossed her a lump of clothes, and she pulled them apart to find a pair of breeches and a shirt. "They were the smallest size I could find, but they should work. We'll leave and give you time to change."

"If you need any help, I'm sure Ceven would gladly assist you," Barto snickered, and Ceven clipped him in the shoulder.

Her face grew hot and she snuck a glance at Ceven. She blinked at the heated look in his eyes. He instantly turned away.

They left, and she changed, keeping Avana's vial tucked in the folds of her dress. The thin cotton shirt was almost a dress on her, but she tucked it into the breeches, using the string in the waistband to tighten it as much as she could. It wasn't ideal, but it was easier to move around in.

They returned. Ceven's eyes flicked down her figure and abruptly away. "Ready?" he said, his jaw tight.

"No," she replied a bit brusquely, but she followed his instructions.

The three of them stretched while Tarry leaned against the wall, observing. Evangeline's body ached and screamed before the real workout even began. At this rate, she was afraid she'd pass out. She didn't think she was that out of shape until they started jumping, jogging in place, and performing other mundane exercises. It was a struggle to just keep her balance.

"My Goddess, girl, have you ever worked out a day in your life?" Barto said to her hunched form. She tried to respond, but it hurt to breathe.

"We haven't even gotten to the hard part yet," Ceven said,

his tone light. Evangeline glared at him as he unsuccessfully held back a smile.

"I thought Barto was going to train me. Maybe he wouldn't have killed me as quickly," she retorted.

Barto and Ceven shared a look and laughed.

"Oh, honey. If you can't manage this, you wouldn't want to know what I had in store for you." Barto glanced at Ceven, and the two took part in some unspoken conversation. "Well, I'm going to go grab us some lunch." Barto nodded behind him. "Tarry, want to keep me company? I got lost the first time coming down here."

Tarry appeared wary, but tilted his head once. The two men left the room, hoods drawn over their faces. Evangeline still crouched in pain, and Ceven stood over her with his arms crossed.

"Ready?" Ceven asked when she caught her breath.

"For what?" she barked at him, expecting a break.

A slow smile spread across his face. "Unless you want to call it quits?"

Her eyes pierced daggers at him, but she stood. He was challenging her, and she wouldn't back down.

CHAPTER 19

⤙ CEVEN ⤚

The room was smaller than Ceven liked, but wide enough for the two of them to run. They'd done quite a few laps. Evangeline's labored breathing started on the fifth lap, while he was only getting warmed up. He kept pace with her the entire time, making a few attempts at conversation, but she was too winded to respond, and soon he stopped trying.

On the fourteenth lap around the room, Evangeline's legs gave out, and she collapsed to the floor, her breathing coming in sharp rasps. Ceven's brow furrowed. He leaned down beside her, his hand on her shoulder. He hated the sound of oxygen being sucked in, as if she hadn't tasted fresh air in ages.

"Take it easy. Breathe," he said, holding her hair, allowing air to brush her nape.

"I feel like I'm going to die," she wheezed. Her entire body oozed sweat with strands of her honey hair plastered to her face and her white top soaked.

He grinned. "You look like it."

Evangeline raised her head, casting him a look. His grin grew. She shook her head, a smile teasing her lips. Then, as if remembering something, it vanished and she turned away.

He knew what was on her mind. What had been on her mind since she came here. "Eve . . . I'm sorry." She didn't look at him. Her lips wavered, and his brows knitted together. "I didn't . . . I didn't mean to be that harsh with you." He ran a hand through his already-messy hair. "I was scared. I'm *still* scared."

She tilted her head back, and he met her green eyes. "But you still meant it," she whispered.

He didn't break away from her gaze. "When I saw Vane on top of you—"

She winced.

"—I lost it. I wanted to *kill* him. I still do." His fists clenched at the thought, and the fiery rage still blazed beneath the surface of his skin. "There's only so much sway I can hold over Ryker, but at the end of the day, he has the final say. And if he punishes you like that again . . . if Vane, or anyone, touches you like that again . . . I may not be able to stop it, and that *scares* me. I just . . ." He struggled for the words. "I think I wanted to scare you as much as it scares me."

She surprised him when her hand grazed his, as if seeking permission. Without a second thought, he tangled his fingers with hers, marveling at how soft her skin was. So smooth compared to his calloused hands from wielding a sword daily.

"Hey, I managed for two years. I must be doing something right." She gave a weak smile.

He knew she meant to console him, but her words only tore at his heart more. "I'm sorry I wasn't here."

Her eyes widened at her mistake. "No! I didn't mean that, I meant . . ." Her fingers tightened around his. "All I meant was that it's okay. You don't have to always look out for me. I know . . ." She swallowed. "I know I've relied on you a lot in the past, and that's my fault—"

"Eve, you didn't—"

"—but I'm not the same girl anymore. I want to fight my own battles. I'm not as helpless as you think, Ceven. And I want you to realize that."

But you're still human, Eve. Alone in a world of Nytes. He didn't say it, but she could read it in his eyes.

Her face shut down. She turned away from him but didn't remove her hand.

They stayed like that, fingers folded together for several tense moments. Her eyes still trained away from him, but he continued to stare at her. A bead of sweat trailed down her forehead to the curve of her neck. His eyes caressed the tender spot, down her body to her sweat-soaked shirt, which clung to her chest. Even when she was mad at him, he was still fiercely attracted to her. He wanted to say something to make everything right, but nothing came to mind that would fix the situation—and still be honest.

"My body is going to feel like hell tomorrow," she said, breaking the silence and pulling her hand away. He already missed her touch.

He flashed a smile, hiding his true thoughts. "Remember, you asked for this."

Evangeline rolled her eyes, but the subtle curve of her lips told him they were at a truce. "I didn't ask to be tortured, only how to fight."

"Aren't they the same?"

She sighed. "You know what I mean."

He leaned down, and she stilled as his thumb grazed her cheek. He wanted more. She gave him a quizzical look.

"You had dirt on your cheek," he lied.

She blinked, frowning. "You could have just told me."

He knew he shouldn't say it, was risking being pushed away, but he felt compelled to admit, "But then I wouldn't have the excuse to touch you."

Her mouth peeled open, and her breathing hitched. "Ceven . . . I . . ." Her eyes softened, but worry shimmered in their depths. He hushed them with a quiet murmur, longing to caress the curve of her neck and draw her close. His eyes trailed down her face, his lips parting. She licked her own, as if in response.

He leaned closer, breathing in the smell of sweat laced with vanilla and something uniquely her he couldn't describe . . . He abruptly reared back.

Pain crossed her face. "What?"

"Food," he said, right as the door opened with Barto holding several brown paper bags.

"Who's hungry?" Barto announced.

Tarry remained outside with Xilo while the three of them sat down, chewing on the fresh sandwiches Barto had brought. Evangeline nibbled at hers and Ceven frowned. Barto asked how the training went in his absence, and the two of them shrugged. Wanting to break the tension, Ceven forced a smile, mentioning they had a lot of work to do—she couldn't outrun the oldest person in the kingdom at this point. Evangeline told him where to stick it, but he was glad things were back to normal between them.

They continued to talk about Peredia, passing small talk around. Evangeline looked like she had something on her mind but kept it to herself.

It wasn't until a pause in the conversation that she spoke up. "What's going on with all the missing humans in the castle?"

Ceven was leaning back, his posture relaxed, when his muscles tightened. Barto's smile vanished as he took another big bite from his second sandwich, bits of lettuce stuck in the black hair at his chin.

Pausing for a moment, Ceven said, "I found out not too long after I got back." He shared a look with Barto. "We've done some investigating, but not much has come up yet."

Evangeline watched the two of them with narrowed eyes. It was obvious she wasn't buying it, but it wasn't something he wanted to tell her right now. Besides, even if they had several culprits in mind, there wasn't any proof.

"We?" she asked.

"Barto and myself, and other Peredian officials. I'm sure we'll have everything resolved soon."

Her face twisted, and he felt a tinge of guilt for not being truthful with her. This entire event had more mystery surrounding it than anything he's ever tackled, and nobody was giving him straight answers.

Evangeline opened her mouth to ask more, but he cut her off. "But, I think we're all done for the day. I don't think Eve can take any more of my torture session." He smiled at her, but she didn't return the favor. He knew it upset her, but he couldn't tell her the truth, especially when he was still trying to figure out the big picture himself. She had enough to deal with.

"Same time tomorrow?" she said instead, grabbing her folded dress off the floor.

"If you can handle it," Barto quipped, sliding him a relieved expression. Ceven's lips twitched. Barto didn't know Evangeline as well as he did. She wouldn't let them off the hook that easily.

"Don't underestimate me," she said, waving to the two of them.

Ceven shook his head, bidding his own goodbye to Barto.

Why did I have to fall for such a troublesome girl?

CHAPTER 20

∽ EVANGELINE ∼

E vangeline tried to ignore the feeling of Avana's vial nestled between her breasts as she came to Ryker's suite. Her
meeting with Avana tonight helped distract her from troubling
thoughts about a particular prince, but not entirely.

She still fumed over Ceven and Barto quickly brushing off
her questions, as if she were a naïve child. And Ceven . . . she
flexed her fingers, remembering how they'd felt twined with
his, and her face warmed. It was clear they still didn't see eye to
eye on some other things as well. *I'm not done with you yet, prince.
I'll find out what you know, even if I have to keep pestering you about
it.* The only issue: she would have to face the growing unease
she felt when around him. Acknowledge the flutter in her chest
and the surge of desire she got when he was near.

The desire to kiss him and blast the consequences.

She wiped her hands on her dress and entered. Would Ryker notice her nervousness? See the suspicious lump in her chest?

He didn't. In fact, he barely acknowledged her presence, giving her an apathetic look as she sat down and ate the food in front of her. She was tempted to ask if he was okay. He wasn't acting like himself. *Was he feeling guilty over what he did to Ranson?* She swallowed the chunk of meat. It slid down her throat uncomfortably.

He didn't ask any questions, didn't even say farewell when she finished and got up to leave. All he did was stare blankly at his empty cup, like he had just realized it was empty this entire time. Ignoring the small piece of her that felt pity at the sight, she left the room.

Avana's hand-sketched map came to mind as Evangeline navigated the main hall. On her way, she passed other Nytes, ones clearly not from this region.

They were mostly Rathans garbed in thin dresses that clung to their skin, the fabric sheer in places that left little to the imagination. Some had long, thick tails, while others had short ones. Large pointed ears sprouted from their heads, with hair that grew thick down their arms and along the sides of their necks, brushing their cheeks. But what made her avoid eye contact as she passed were the slitted pupils that lingered too long. As if they were sizing her up to eat.

A few Aerians turned their heads, gaping at her. She assumed they were from the countryside, not used to seeing humans dressed in anything as fine, even if her dress was a simpler design to others of the Aerian court.

Everyone must be arriving for the ball coming up. It was still two weeks away, but Evangeline already felt the increase in Nytes and their personal servants, as if the very air inside the castle was more condensed. Keeping her head down, she traveled through a less crowded hallway.

The stone wall was cool against her back when she stopped to take a breath, wiping her sweaty palms. She felt for the vial. Avana told her to drink it before the meeting tonight, but she still didn't know what it did, just that she needed privacy.

Evangeline ducked into a small walk-in pantry, swinging open the panel door that blended into the wallpaper.

It was occupied.

The two kissing humans scrambled away from one another in surprise.

Evangeline put up her hands up. "I'm sorry, I didn't mean to interrupt—"

They didn't give her a chance to finish as they covered their faces with their aprons and ran out the door. As if they thought she would to report them. She scowled.

For a moment, she imagined being in Ceven's arms, his lips pressed against hers as the tight closet crammed them close together. Heat stung her cheeks. Having her first kiss in a cleaning closet wasn't her idea of romantic, but with Ceven, would it matter? Her scowl deepened as she yanked the door shut, shoving that fantasy far, far away from her mind.

A single light shined overhead and Evangeline's gut clenched. The closet walls squeezed closer to her, and in a panic, she cracked open the door. The soft breeze cleared her head enough to focus. Taking a deep breath, she pulled out the blue liquid. The cork came off with a pop. *Here goes nothing.* She plugged her nose and chugged the contents. The thick liquid dribbled down her throat, and she struggled not to gag. She didn't feel any different. *At least it wasn't poison.*

The tips of her toes and fingers tingled. Then it spread all over her body. It wasn't painful, but ticklish, as she scratched her skin. She glanced down and gasped.

A beautiful, bronze gown with a wide skirt replaced her simple tailored dress. She blinked a few times and rubbed her eyes. The image didn't change. Her hand reached down to feel the fabric, but it went right through to touch her real dress. *This is amazing!*

She did a quick spin, watching the skirt twirl with her. It looked real. Her skin tone was darker as well, a soft brown that hid the freckles that sprinkled her arms. She pulled forward her loose hair, and though she could feel it in her hand, she couldn't see it. *So, this is what Avana meant.*

Excitement rose within her. If she could get her hands on more of this stuff, she and Lani could easily sneak out of the kingdom. *We can walk right out the front gates!*

With her hopes high, Evangeline left the pantry.

The seventh floor of the main hall appeared the same as the others. Purple carpet decorated with tips of gold swirls along its perimeter. Large, sweeping windows lined the halls, reflecting out onto either the gardens or the castle gates, depending on what side you were on. She twisted and turned, glancing both ways. She hoped she headed in the right direction.

Only a few Nytes sprinkled the halls, since it was a residential area, casting her nods and polite smiles. Some even bowed. Evangeline was lightheaded from the attention. She didn't know how to handle anything other than scorn. Should she smile back? Turn away? Her former self would have lowered her gaze, but now she didn't think that would be appropriate.

I may look like a Nyte, but on the inside I'm still painfully human.

It wasn't long before she stumbled upon an opening leading into a larger room. Several couches were angled in front of the white stone fireplace, a long counter filled with glasses and bottles taking residence on the opposite side. Along the back of the room were large windows, revealing a balcony. Hoping Avana was outside, she made her way to the double doors.

A blast of icy wind slapped her face and sent her reeling. She wrapped her arms around herself and looked both ways. The balcony stretched the entire room, wide-set windows separated at intervals, reminding her that anyone could see her out here at any point. If Avana was going for secrecy, she didn't choose well.

Something scurried across her boot, and she jerked back. It was a small rodent. She clutched her chest, chuckling half-heartedly. *Now I'm jumping at the sight of mice. Calm down, Eve.*

She padded to the far end, where the balcony curved around the corner, and spotted her. Or at least who she hoped was Avana, wearing a disguise similar to hers.

An Aerian woman with plain brown hair was leaning over the iron railing, her figure hidden behind a large potted shrub. The wind brushed the short length of her hair against her bare shoulders, the creamy complexion contrasting against the purple fabric of the low-cut dress. Her wings were a shade darker than her hair.

Evangeline followed her gaze, and her previous concerns seemed less important as she too glanced into the distance. From this height, she could see the tops of the trees dusted with snow, where the castle grounds ended, beyond the stables, and where the steep mountainside began traveling downwards into the rest of the kingdom. Evangeline dreamed of a life beyond these walls. Roaming through the Olaaga forest in the spring with the sun basking down on her, the intense feeling of freedom propelling her to run faster than she ever had before. Taking shelter in all Peredia's beauty. To finally be confident in claiming it as her home. Maybe then, the hatred she harbored toward it would finally go away.

The Aerian woman tapped her shoulder, and Evangeline broke from her reverie.

"I didn't mean to startle you. You looked quite peaceful. I almost didn't want to disturb you."

Evangeline's life was far from peaceful, but for a blissful moment she'd forgotten. "Are you . . .?"

The woman's lips curved. "Yes, it's me. I was worried you wouldn't show up." Avana surveyed Evangeline from head to toe. "I'm glad to see the glamour worked."

"Glamour?" Evangeline didn't think she'd ever get used to Caster magic.

"A powerful illusion spell that's attached to the user. Don't worry, it's only temporary, but be careful about bumping into anyone or anything. It's only an illusion, not a manifestation, so if someone catches your 'wings' going through walls and plants, well, you may run into some problems."

Evangeline frowned. She figured that much out.

Avana turned toward the edge of the balcony. "But, if you don't mind me asking, what were you thinking about?"

At first, she debated telling her, then shrugged. "I imagined what it would be like to live outside the kingdom."

Avana blinked a few times, appearing thoughtful. "If you had the chance, would you leave Peredia?"

Evangeline looked at her. The innocent question held a dangerous meaning behind it, and she knew Avana wasn't that stupid. "I think you know the answer, my lady."

Avana tilted her head. "I understand, you know. To have the freedom to pursue what you truly desire. It is a feeling like no other. You deserve to live your own life, free of other's expectations."

Her response wasn't something Evangeline was expecting. "I don't think Lord Ryker would agree with that statement."

Avana didn't respond right away, her mouth twisting. "The reason I brought you here tonight . . . is because Ryker and I don't always see eye to eye. I wanted a chance to talk to you, alone."

Evangeline nodded. *Though I'm risking a lot more to be here tonight than you are,* she thought, her eyes darting behind her and through the open windows.

Avana followed her gaze. "Don't worry, I picked this spot for a reason. I made sure all the windows would reflect only the environment, not us. And if anyone decides to come out here, well, it's a perfectly reasonable place for two Nytes to be having a casual conversation." She shrugged.

It eased some of Evangeline's fears, but not all. "If I may be bold, my lady, I would like to make this as quick as possible." She lowered her eyes, afraid she was being too forward. "I hope you understand."

Evangeline flinched when Avana grazed her chin and tilted her head up. There was a fierceness in her gaze.

"You can hold your head high with me, Evangeline. As you always should." Her eyes narrowed with intensity. "You shouldn't have to cower to *anyone.*"

The conviction in her tone defied the soft edges of her face, the delicate beauty of her glamour.

Evangeline opened her mouth, but no words came out. She looked away, frightened by the determined gaze in Avana's eyes. *I don't know how it is in Sundise Mouche, but here, things are much different for humans. But of course, you wouldn't know. You're a Nyte.* "Force of habit, my lady," she said instead.

As if sensing her hesitation, Avana sighed. "You want to know the reason I left everything behind and came to Peredia?"

She waited for Evangeline's nod before continuing. "I left for you, and everything you represent."

The sincerity of her words, and the weight of them, struck Evangeline. "What do you mean?"

Avana leaned against the railing, tendrils of her brown hair waving in the breeze. "You . . . your mark . . . my grandmother, Anali, created it. It's a part of our history, the Quincara legacy." She turned toward her. "You are a legend to me, Evangeline. And you deserve to be *respected.* Not wasting away here."

Evangeline blinked and stepped back as if Avana burned her. But that was putting it mildly. A cyclone of excitement and confusion toiled in the pit of her stomach. *Respected? A legend?* A dose of reality quickly squelched the thought.

"I can't be a legend. I'm nothing, a human. I can't even pro-tect—" Evangeline stopped and sighed. "I'm sorry, it's just . . ." She glanced down at where her mark would be through the glamour, tracing its outline in her mind. It was the closest thing she ever had to the truth, but it sounded so . . . unbelievable.

"You need proof?" Avana finished.

Evangeline looked up and nodded.

Avana gave her a knowing smile, and she noted how similar it was to Raiythlen's. "That's the real reason I sought you out tonight."

Evangeline eyed her warily. *I thought she only wanted to dis-cuss my mark.*

Avana's expression hardened. "What I'm about to propose may seem impossible, dangerous, and completely out of the question, but I'm going to ask you anyway: Would you go with me to the cave where you were first discovered?"

Her brows pinched. "You're asking me to go beyond the kingdom's walls?"

The glamour Avana wore couldn't disguise the glimmer in her eyes. "It's not like you haven't done it before."

Evangeline reared back. "No . . . I'm sorry, but no. Besides, no one could find anything, anyway. It'd be a waste of time."

Avana held up a finger. "But that's where you're wrong. This opportunity would be invaluable to both of us. I'm certain we'll find the proof we're both looking for, and—" She swept her arm across the balcony, gesturing at the twinkling lights from houses in the distance. "I know you want to get your friend out of here, to protect her. This would be the perfect moment to survey the land, see the safest path out of here. With a little help, of course."

Evangeline's eyes flew wide. *How does she know?* Terror gripped her. It crept up her neck, settling in her skin. If Avana told Lord Ryker any of this . . .

Avana saw her expression, and her face softened. "You can trust me, Evangeline. I may work with Lord Ryker, but I do *not* answer to him." She held her gaze.

The uneasiness didn't leave her. "That cave has been searched top to bottom, and there was nothing but rock and bits of old metal."

Avana grasped both of her hands before she could step away. "That's where you come in. These . . . dreams, hallucinations—whatever you want to call them—I want to see if, by bringing you to the place you were first discovered, you would remember anything."

"Already tried that," she said, watching Avana's face fall.

Avana released her, staring at the ground. Thinking. "When was this?"

Evangeline thought back to when Ryker brought her to that cave, with the same hopes in mind. She had been twelve, or maybe thirteen, and all she remembered was an empty cave that smelled of limestone. She told Avana as much.

Avana tapped her chin with her index finger. "But you didn't start having your . . . visions until recently, correct?"

Evangeline nodded hesitantly. "They've started to occur more frequently, yes."

Avana's lips curved. "If you weren't having any dreams or hallucinations yet, and you haven't been back there since, who's to say you wouldn't have a 'vision' when we revisit the cave this time around?"

Evangeline thought about it. She was just as curious as Avana, curious to see if the cave from her earlier memories was accurate. If there was some clue or proof to what Avana was saying, even if she found it hard to believe. But what if nothing happened? What if it was just a cave? She would risk Ryker's wrath for nothing. And if he found out she went beyond the kingdom's walls a second time?

"You're mine now, Pet."

She sucked in a sharp breath and rubbed her arms, as if she could wash away the feel of Vane's claws.

Before she could refuse, Avana interrupted. "We won't get caught. Please, Evangeline, this may be our only opportunity to discover what really happened."

What really happened . . . "I don't understand. This mark . . . you said your grandmother made it?" The black-haired woman bubbled to life in her mind. "But how? And why?"

Something flashed across Avana's features, but she quickly shielded it. "That's why I'm here. Why we need to go to that cave, so we can solve this together. I don't have all the answers, only bits of information left behind in my grandmother's journals."

Why do I feel she's not telling me everything? "Where is Anali now?" Evangeline asked, but she suspected she already knew the answer.

Avana gave a sad smile. "She's no longer of this world."

Evangeline waited for the sorrow or grief to hit her for the woman in her dreams, but it never did. Anali was a stranger to her.

A frightening thought occurred to her. "Wait, does Lord Ryker know? About any of this?" Avana's face went blank, and Evangeline's wariness increased tenfold. She prepared for the lies to spew from her mouth.

Avana frowned. "To be honest, I don't know what his true intentions are, but he knows more than he's letting on."

Still doesn't answer my question, Evangeline thought, but she didn't push it. She already feared Ryker knew more than he was telling her. If she was going to figure anything out—her mark, how it related to Anali, and if it was connected to these hallucinations—she would have to do it on her own.

"If I agree to go with you . . ."

Avana's face lit up.

"I need you to promise me we won't get caught, and . . ." *Getting Lani out of the kingdom is going to be harder than ever. More guards have been posted, and now I have a Caster assassin breathing down my back.* "I want you to give me a few vials of this." She gestured at her glamour. It would help her and Lani avoid the guards, but it still didn't solve the problem of how they were going to get over the wall—and avoid Raiythlen and his schemes in the process. But she would figure that out later.

Avana placed her palm over her chest. "I promise, Evangeline. And I promise to supply you with whatever you need to help your friend."

"When do we leave?" She couldn't believe the words coming out of her mouth.

"Soon. I will make the necessary preparations and send you further instructions on when and where to meet." Avana flashed a row of white teeth. "I will forever be grateful that you took this risk for me. For both of us."

Evangeline rubbed her forehead. *I'm not doing this for you. I'm doing it for Lani. For me.* "I still don't believe we'll find anything."

Avana's smile faded, and her gaze snapped behind Evangeline.

Evangeline stiffened. "What?"

Avana returned her attention to Evangeline, but her eyes expanded, her shoulders squared. "I'll contact you soon." Her voice lowered to a whisper. "Be careful, there are eyes and ears everywhere." She brushed past, her fingers squeezing Evangeline's shoulder as the clicking of her heels faded into the winter night.

Evangeline waited a few moments. She scanned the balcony for signs of movement, sure that Avana had heard something. The wind whistled, flirting through the strands of her hair, but there was no other sound. She continued her search of the balcony, but when she didn't see anyone or anything, she decided the danger had passed. Time to return to Lani's for the night.

She rounded the corner and felt a slight breeze behind her.

Right before a hand covered her mouth.

CHAPTER 21

～ EVANGELINE ～

The hand muffled Evangeline's scream.

"That wasn't very nice. Going to my sister for information I promised to give you," a low voice whispered behind her. "It's almost like you don't trust me."

Raiythlen!

Her nostrils flared. She jerked away, but he yanked her back, his arm snaking around her waist. Her chest heaved, and blood rushed in her ears. His hand went through her imaginary dress, grazing the top of her corset down to her naval.

"She was never good at making glamours. Only managing a mere illusion." He clicked his tongue. "At least you didn't totally disappoint me. If you'd told her I was here . . . well, let's just be grateful you didn't."

Evangeline licked his palm, tasting the salty bitterness of it.

He dropped his hand in surprise and she got out, "I'm not going anywhere, so let go of me."

Raiythlen conceded. She pulled away, putting two paces between them.

He wiped his hand on his black leather pants. A matching fabric wrapped his torso, except his chest that was covered in rows of dark metal circles. Each engraved with a symbol. It was similar to what he wore when she'd first found him, before making the big mistake of bringing him inside the kingdom.

"What do you want?" Her eyes stayed on him, watching for any sudden movements. *As if I'd be able to stop him if he decided to throw me over this balcony.* She grimaced. The view didn't seem as beautiful now.

A half smile teased his lips, as if he could read her mind. "To start, I don't want you asking my sister for information."

"I didn't. She volunteered."

He sighed. "You can't trust anything she says, Eve."

She folded her arms. "That's rich, coming from you," she sniped. "And it's Evangeline." She shouldn't let this Nyte get under her skin, but his infuriating attitude, the way he toyed with her and Lani's life, it drove her to see red.

Raiythlen didn't respond. Nor did he move. Not even his chest, like he didn't need to breathe.

She squirmed, and her eyes darted to the door.

"At least I'm honest in my intentions." His words came out clipped. "The last thing Avana wants is for you to be beyond her reach. She promised to help you escape?" He snorted. "She might as well let all her years of searching and research go to waste. You're the only thing keeping her here in this backwards country, and you think she would just let you go? Don't make me laugh, *Evangeline.*"

She ground her teeth. "I'm not a fool. I never said I trusted

her. But that doesn't mean I trust you, either." *You're playing with fire, Eve. Cool it.* She took a shaky breath and reminded herself that this Caster held Lani's life in his hands.

But that enraged her more.

"When the time comes, you may not have a choice." His stare shifted to the kingdom beyond the iron railing. "I know more than you could possibly imagine. More than Avana." The clouds moved overhead, a sliver of moonlight highlighting the blue in his irises, the pitch blackness of his hair curling around his neck. "Everyone lies, my dear, but at least I'm open with you about my indiscretions. Remember that." His eyes met hers. "Did you gather anything useful from your Aerian lover?"

Evangeline blinked for a moment, caught off guard by the swift change in topic. "He's not . . ." She shook her head, sighing. "No, I haven't. Not yet. But if you *know* so much, I still don't see why you need my help."

She managed one step backward before he closed the distance between them. He ensnared her wrist and yanked her forward. His face was sharp, unyielding. "In my line of work, if you're not useful, you're dead." His expression gave way to a familiar smirk. "And believe it or not, my dear, I find you a lot more charming alive." He released her, and she stumbled back. "With that in mind, I hope you'll have something useful for me tomorrow night."

Her heart pounded, the icy night freezing her to the spot. *I hate him. I hate him so much.* "How do you expect me to gather anything useful by then? Nobody seems to know anything!"

He shrugged, and she almost lost it. Almost.

"Fine," he said. "Gather what you can, and I'll come to you. Not tomorrow night, but soon."

"When?" She needed a timeframe, she didn't want any

surprises coming from him. "And what about Lani? Will she be okay?"

He rubbed his jaw, as if debating his reply. "Lani will be fine. The poison should have left her system by now." At her hopeful look, he added, "But if you decide to be unreasonable, I'll rectify that. I'll meet with you soon." He nipped his finger, blood welling up, and pressed it against a symbol on his torso. Evangeline's eyes widened when he disappeared from sight all together. Again.

She clenched her fists. *Soon? What the spitting blazes did that mean?* The idea of him popping up at any time didn't sit well with her.

"Oh, and one more thing."

She gasped, whipping around only to see an empty balcony.

"Go ahead and work with my sister, but when it all blows up in your face, don't say I didn't warn you." The air shifted. He was gone . . . or at least she hoped he was.

"Gods, I'm really starting to hate Casters," she muttered.

CHAPTER 22

❧ EVANGELINE ❧

The sharp pain in her lower back and the numbness in her toes rose Evangeline from her slumber. She groaned. She wanted to fall back asleep, but the fire had gone out, and the room was freezing.

Careful not to wake Lani, she slipped out of bed. Her bare feet brushed the floor, and its coldness seeped into her skin, knifing up her body. The sun was still sleeping. The moon casted a faint light throughout the room.

She ignited a small flame, and Lani rolled over, the cot moaning.

"It's too spitting early," she croaked.

Evangeline hummed in response.

Lani grumbled something to herself before getting up and shuffling toward the chest, pulling clothes out. Evangeline continued to stare at the fire.

"Lani . . ."

"Hmm?"

"Never mind."

Lani grabbed the comb, yanking it through her hair before splashing water on her face from the tin bucket on the floor. Evangeline crawled back into bed, wrapping the blanket around herself. Avana's promise haunted her. And Raiythlen's warning.

"What if I told you we could leave soon? Maybe in the next few days?" Evangeline prodded. If she was to believe Raiythlen, Lani was no longer poisoned, and once Evangeline got ahold of those glamour potions, it gave them a fighting chance at sneaking out. And depending on Avana's plan, maybe they could leave the same way.

"How?"

"I have a new plan."

Lani turned around, her lips set into a permanent pucker where Evangeline was concerned. "And how is this one better than the last?"

Because now we may have help, she almost said when she glimpsed a dark blemish across Lani's cheek. "What is that?"

Her friend turned around. "What?"

Evangeline got up from the bed. "Your face, it's all bruised."

Lani shrugged and continued to get dressed. "It's nothing."

"No, it's not *nothing*. Who did that to you? What happened?" Her voice rose.

"Leave it be."

"Is it because you were gone for several days? Or—"

Lani spun around. "Enough!" She balled her hands, the skin taut. "I said leave it be, Eve."

Evangeline's mouth snapped shut. She crossed her arms and shot Lani a glare.

The two of them refused to speak. Lani finished getting

ready, and Evangeline rolled over in bed to face the wall. It wasn't until the door opened that Lani whispered a goodbye. Evangeline didn't respond.

The day went by fast. Ryker was distant again this morning, and Evangeline nibbled her food in silence. No questions from Ryker, not even a glance in her direction. She wasn't up for conversation, anyway, her thoughts still circling back to the bruise on Lani's cheek and their fight.

Her mood improved by the afternoon, when she met with Barto and Ceven in the storage rooms. Ceven acted like his normal self, and she returned the favor, grateful to fall back into their comfortable banter and teasing. No weapons yet, but she couldn't complain, since she was still struggling with her own body weight.

By the time night rolled around, she was thoroughly sore and sweaty. It was time to see Ryker.

Before she approached the guards at Ryker's door, she sniffed herself. Would Ryker smell the sweat lingering on her? She had discretely discarded the other clothes into the washrooms near his suite. She prepared an excuse in case.

The suite was dark. Empty. She furrowed her brows and crept farther in.

"Father?" Evangeline called out.

No response.

Walking into the sitting chamber, she perused the coffee table and the dining room table, but there was no sign of a note anywhere. *That's strange.*

The fireplace was empty and cold, but the curtains hung open, allowing what little daylight was left to stream through.

Maybe he was running late. It wouldn't be the first time, although it was rare.

Thinking it wouldn't be long until Ryker showed up, Evangeline started a fire and curled up on the small couch. She stared into the flames, tapping her foot.

When the sun descended, the only light flickering from the fireplace, she began to worry. What if something had happened to him? What would that mean for her? She clenched her palms. *Stop it. You're overreacting.*

Deciding to make better use of her time, she took a bath.

She scrubbed all the grime and sweat from training earlier and sat for a while, allowing the steam to sink into her pores. She closed her eyes and leaned back. The strong outline of Ceven's jaw, the softness of his hair falling around his temple, teased her behind her eyelids. An enticing swirl of green and brown looked down at her, luring her closer to his lips.

She wanted to kiss him badly, and a small piece of her hoped to find him alone today so she could do just that. And it scared her senseless. To have her own desire be stronger than her logic. To know nothing could ever happen between them but have her body say otherwise.

You'll be far away soon enough. But this time, the thought left her feeling depressed. And that terrified her more.

Something thumped outside the room.

She sat up, water sloshing over the side of the tub, and waited to hear Ryker, or anyone, call out for her. Nobody did.

Her eyes fixed on the gap beneath the bathing room door, waiting for it to open, or for a small knock. Anything to let her know she wasn't alone with a murderer.

You're being paranoid, Eve, it's probably nothing. But assassination attempts weren't uncommon. Rare, yes, but not impossible.

And it just so happened that she lived with not just any royal member, but the king's personal advisor.

Her mind raced. *Are all the windows locked? Was one left open, and I didn't notice?* Alerting the guards was an option, but if someone was in the suite, they'd kill her before she could leave the room—or scream.

Evangeline focused on the gap beneath the door when an idea came to her. She eased out of the tub, making as little sound as possible. Puddles of water followed her as she turned off the lamps, the flames dwindling until the room was dark. The only light streamed in through the tinted window behind the bathtub and from underneath the door. But it was dark enough for what she wanted.

She analyzed the glow of the lamps coming from the gap, watching for shadows. The light glistened against the wet marble floor. She held her breath. It wavered as a shadow passed by.

Someone was in the room.

Evangeline covered her mouth, silencing her heavy breathing. *It was Ryker, it had to be Ryker. He probably got back late.*

But he would have announced that he was home.

She carefully put out her hands until she felt the soft fabric of her robe hanging by the door and slipped it on. Maybe she could walk out, acting ignorant, and hope whoever it was would hide—giving her the opportunity to warn the guards. If she wasn't killed immediately. Or maybe she could run, but if it was a Nyte, she would be dead first.

Evangeline couldn't see in the dark bathing room, but tried to remember its contents. In the end, aside from a hairbrush or a few towels, she didn't have anything to use to her advantage.

Her gaze returned to the gap of the door. She peered beneath it, but all she could see was the side of Ryker's enormous canopy bed, the thick purple drapes crafted around it, blocking her view of the other side of the room. She listened for any sounds. A rustle. Then another. It was coming from the other side of the bed.

The suite shuddered as the front door swung open, and she jumped.

"Evangeline!" someone bellowed.

She didn't hesitate and thrust open the door, running like her life depended on it. She sprinted past the canopy bed, spotting short, dark hair and the backside of a woman or a young man before they jumped out the window.

Evangeline burst into the sitting chamber and collided with one of Ryker's guards.

"What's going on?" he demanded, his gray-dusted blond hair making him appear almost bald in the dim light.

"I-I . . . T-there was . . ." *Someone was in here! In the same room! I could've died!*

The guard looked down and narrowed his eyes at where she gripped him. She immediately let go.

"Where's Ryker?" she said after drawing a shaky breath.

The guard shoved a white envelope into her hand. "A message from him. And it's Lord Ryker to you, *Pet.*"

She ignored him and took the envelope, peeling it open to find a letter. In his usual elongated handwriting, Ryker stated he wouldn't be home for the evening. *Would have been nice to know earlier.*

The guard did a quick perusal of the suite before shaking his head. "Well, if there's no real problem, I'll take my leave." Turning on his heel, he walked down the hall.

Evangeline thought to call him back, to tell him what happened, but she held her tongue. In her panic, she caught little of the intruder, but she didn't miss the pair of horns curling from their head. A Caster had been in Ryker's bedroom. It hadn't looked like Raiythlen or Avana, but what if it was someone helping them?

The front door clicked shut. Now that she was alone again, Ryker's suite seemed way too big.

Feeling vulnerable in her white robe, Evangeline went back to the bedroom, peeking into the room first, scanning every dark crevice.

Empty.

The room had dropped in temperature from the open window. She closed it, checking the lock was firmly in place. Feeling a little safer now, she slipped on a thick dress, grateful for the extra layer of protection. She wrung out her hair, tied it into a quick braid, and reassessed Ryker's room.

There weren't any damages or signs of theft, except Ryker's desk. Drawers were open, papers shuffled about on its usually pristine surface. Evangeline debated leaving it and alerting Ryker when he returned, but . . .

What were they looking for?

She gathered the papers, scanning uninteresting contents. Letters from nobles, documents on different teas, and the perfect leather for the home. She put them back into the top drawer when a book on the ground, its pages spread open, caught her attention. It was a journal, the cover a plain brown. She picked it up and flipped through it, frowning as page after page had only lists of names, some crossed out, others circled. *What is this?*

Her eyes flitted about each page, confused, until she spotted several familiar names. Shani Thorp, Gardia Madison . . . Delani Adelstein. Her hands froze. *Lani...*

It was a list of all the slaves in the castle.

Skimming further was Shani's son's name, Daniel, but unlike the others, his was crossed out. Evangeline narrowed her eyes, tracing the outline of the black ink. Some faded, some fresh. It was Ryker's handwriting. Was he investigating the disappearances too?

Another possibility, a darker one, emerged from the crevices of her mind, but she didn't want to look at it too closely.

She put the journal back into the drawer, closing it shut. At least now she had something to tell Raiythlen. If he didn't have something to tell her first.

Evangeline's eyebrows puckered together. *Who was that Caster, and what were they looking for?*

She wrapped herself in a thick coat and headed to Lani's quarters. In the dead of night, a wolf howled in the distance.

CHAPTER 23

⊸ EVANGELINE ⊶

Ryker returned the following morning, and Evangeline told him everything, keeping what she'd found in the journal to herself. He hadn't shouted for the guards to come in and search the area. Instead, he went . . . still. So still that Evangeline's skin broke out in bumps, the imminent sense of danger thick enough to taste on the back of her tongue.

He asked her questions, all through gritted teeth. She answered as calmly as she could. "Yes, they had horns. No, I didn't see their face. The only thing they touched was your desk." He asked if she had looked through the documents, and she felt if she lied, he would kill her right on the spot.

"Yes, I glanced at them as I put them back."

"And?" he asked, his fingers thrumming against the armchair.

She swallowed, attempting to smile. "I found it funny that you had papers on leather furniture when you don't own any."

He didn't smile back.

Ryker dismissed her shortly after and she left, feeling his stare dig into her back like a dagger.

The next few days followed the same pattern: wake up at Lani's, meet with Ryker, do some more investigating, train with Ceven and Barto, and meet again with Ryker at night.

One evening, after she returned from her training, Ryker scrunched his nose, remarking that she should bathe more often. It wasn't until the following night that he became more suspicious. She countered, saying she was exercising more, wanting to better her physique. He narrowed his eyes but didn't comment on it.

During her training sessions, Barto became somewhat of a friend to her, even if he talked too much for her liking. She found it odd for a Nyte to so readily accept her, which was why she kept him at arms' length, wary of his true intentions. But his playful banter and easy-going nature made it hard for her to keep her distance. He was also a patient mentor, guiding her and gently chastising when she failed to learn one basic technique in an entire session.

She and Ceven kept exchanging jokes and casual conversation. They never mentioned that day when they were alone together, and she was glad for it. As much as it pained her, deep down she knew keeping their relationship platonic was for the best.

Evangeline also hadn't run into any more Casters, though every day she grew more anxious that Raiythlen would show up, demanding information. Information she was finding increasingly difficult to collect with nothing but dead ends, and Ceven and Barto avoiding all her questions on the subject. She believed Raiythlen's threat wasn't empty, but was relieved to find Lani still in good health. Aside from the bruise she had found on her days before, nothing new had emerged since.

With the ball getting closer, Evangeline only saw Lani after returning from Ryker's for the night, usually with her friend already fast asleep, or when she swung by the kitchens in the morning. Exhaustion wore at her friend, and she rarely chatted with anyone. Evangeline knew Aerian parties meant hell for every human slave for however long they lasted. Outrage surged in her chest. It wasn't fair.

But life was ever fair.

This morning—after Ceven and Barto ended her training session early to meet with Peredian military officials—Evangeline got fed up trying to get answers out of them and demanded answers elsewhere.

She asked around again. As expected, most humans brushed her off or flat-out avoided her. It wasn't until she became aggressive, cornering those unlucky enough to cross her path, that she wriggled out some information.

"T-there have been rumors going around about t-these tattoos," one girl stuttered. "T-they just started s-showing up."

"We thought it was a way for the Nytes to brand us, but then it wouldn't be long before they went missing," another said.

"All I know is if you see someone with a mark on them, avoid them at all costs."

There were other theories, too. The Aerians had developed a taste for human blood and were eating them. Others claimed it was the Gods punishing them for their disobedience, demanding that sacrifices be made to please the skies. Evangeline brushed most of it off as scared bickering, but the idea of Aerians eating humans lingered with her. She'd heard about species of Nytes preying upon humans, but they were far away from Peredia, and not socially accepted by most Nytes. Including Aerians. She hoped that hadn't changed.

Wanting to find out more on these "marks" and the other strange theories surrounding the disappearing persons, she aimed for the library.

Evangeline embraced the familiar overarching bookshelves and the smell of paper and wood as she entered the place she considered to be her second-home. Passing by tables occupied with Nytes reading or whispering amongst one another, she scanned the rows of books.

While searching for any information on old Peredian scripture and old rituals, she pulled out the apple Ceven had given her, insisting she eat to regain some energy. She sank her teeth into the apple—which was still too ripe—and browsed the titles, searching for anything that sounded useful. Most of the titles were familiar from when she had researched her own mark in the past.

Evangeline pulled several volumes off the shelf, collecting the heavy stack into her arms. She quietly placed the books on a nearby table, sitting down. She wasn't keen on lugging her load to the third floor to her usual spot. However, as soon as she sat down, she regretted not trekking up those stairs when a cascade of low murmurs and whispers trailed behind her.

"It's Lord Ryker's pet—"

"Her presence disgusts me—"

"I heard Vane beat some sense into her."

"Serves her right—"

"—learn her place."

She tuned them out. Taking the first book, she opened the large volume, the pages a tinted yellow. She grazed across the text and leafed through the pages. Most displayed old Peredian flags and symbols, but nothing tying them to ancient rituals or a history of missing persons. As if it were going to be that easy. She opened another book on Peredian history and began reading.

> For over five centuries, Peredia has been the governing country of the world. However, it wasn't always ruled by an Aerian king, but by a Council. Present scholars refer to it as the 'Old Council', which consisted of Nytes from every race and settled matters unanimously . . .

Evangeline yawned. Most of this she already knew. Though she'd always been curious as to why the Old Council crumbled, and why Casters had isolated themselves in Sundise Mouche since then. It was a part of history that even Ryker had omitted in his teachings.

Her fingers tapped against the thick wood table, making a low thudding sound. Her mind turned toward Raiythlen and

Avana, and Peredia's newfound treaty with Sundise Mouche. *I wonder...*

She picked out another heavy volume, rubbing her hands across the rough surface before flipping it open on the table. She scanned the pages, hoping to find more information on Peredia's relationship with Sundise Mouche, but most of it, again, was what she already knew.

> Tension always existed between Peredia and Sundise Mouche. The Peredian kingdom was founded upon tradition, upholding rituals that have held strong throughout generations preceding it. By keeping to a patriarchal society, ruled under one king, Peredia handles matters in a regimented way in hopes that history will not repeat itself and that the one and true kingdom will remain consistent and strong.

Evangeline found little information on Sundise Mouche, but she knew from her discussions with Lord Ryker that Casters had reformed the Old Council and lived differently from them.

Evangeline idly slid her fingers over the top of her leather glove, right where her mark was. Did Avana really know about her mark? Or was she leading her down a slippery slope of lies and false hope? For all she knew, maybe Avana could figure out where Evangeline came from, or at least why she was having such vivid dreams and hallucinations. Or . . . confirm that her mark meant nothing, and that she was simply crazy.

Focus, Eve, that's not why you came here. Grabbing another book from the pile, she returned to her original task. She finished skimming the first half of the book when something slammed into her back.

Evangeline jumped, hissing in pain as hot wax grazed her neck. The iron candle holder had toppled over. Holding her neck, she turned to find that the flame hadn't gone out, her eyes watering as the smell of smoke filled her nostrils.

Her chair had caught on fire.

She yanked it from the table, skimming for something to put out the small flame licking at the green fabric. Nothing. She resorted to using the end of her dress, patting it against the fiery tendrils. She winced as heat seared her through her skirt, but the fire died down, leaving behind black, singed fibers at the end of her dress.

A stream of giggles brought her attention to the group of Aerian men and woman gathered close to her. The two woman's rich gowns bumped into each other as they tried to hide their laughter. The men veiled their smirks behind white, gloved hands.

Hiding her fury beneath her curtain of hair, Evangeline brushed off her skirt. She tried rearranging it so that the burns weren't as noticeable, but it was pointless.

She swallowed back tears of humiliation and grabbed the book she was reading. Their laughter followed her as she left the library.

The sun beamed high in the sky outside the castle's main garden. It was larger than the training grounds, taking up the entire length of the main hall. It was something pleasing to look at from the royals' balconies, she guessed.

In the warmer months she would read here, knowing most royals rarely walked through these gardens. It was only when they had imbibed too much at parties that she'd spot couples sneaking off into the thick shrubbery bordering the gardens. It gave them privacy to continue their love affairs in secret—or at least what they thought was in secret.

Vines intertwined the bricked pathways, lined with a variety of winter flowers. Enormous trees loomed over the iron benches with their weeping branches, arranged throughout the corners of the garden. But what drew her attention was the sculpted fountain implanted in the center. Intricate designs of roses slithered along its rock walls, and a large Aerian woman, holding a swaddled winged baby, settled on top of the structure. It was said she gave birth to the God of all Gods and that her beauty was unparalleled. Evangeline believed it, finding the carved face to be the most beautiful thing she'd ever seen, her kind smile comforting her whenever she was feeling troubled.

Evangeline lurked behind the brown, barren bushes before gliding across the ice-slicked walkway toward the fountain. Although the water had frozen over, the view was still breathtaking. Setting her book down, she swept her fingers across the ice, welcoming the calmness that drove away most of her ire.

I hope Ryker doesn't hit me for ruining this dress. She glowered at the frozen surface. *I wish I had the power to go back and make them pay.* She sighed, looking up at the Goddess's granite face.

As much as she hated them, she wished she had been born an Aerian. To be strong and beautiful. To be accepted.

"Marvelous, isn't she?"

Evangeline gasped and spun around, slipping on the slick walkway. A firm hand reached out and caught her before she could fall flat on her back.

"I apologize, I didn't mean to startle you." a familiar voice said. Dread filled her stomach.

Evangeline bowed, more to avoid eye contact than out of respect. "No, it was my fault, I wasn't paying attention. Thank you, Your Highness. I will be more alert next time."

She moved around him when he stepped in front of her. Long, slender fingers grasped her chin, tilting her head. Evangeline slowly trailed up his body, not wanting to meet his gaze. Burgundy wings hung intimidatingly around his figure, the tips gliding against the ground. His body filled out the dark gray coat he wore, and a series of long gold chains shimmered where they nestled in the middle of his unbuttoned chest.

Her gaze dragged across the same high cheekbones and full lips of Ceven, set in an older face, and up to meet Prince Sehn LuRogue's eyes.

CHAPTER 24

⌯ EVANGELINE ⌮

"**N**ot so fast, my dear." Sehn's eyes crinkled, making his features even more exquisite. "Relax, I simply wish to talk. No need to be scared."

Evangeline forced a smile, trying not to appear as confused as she felt. Talking with Ceven's older brother was the last thing she wanted to do, but . . . why was he talking to her? Being *nice* to her? Something wasn't right.

"The garden has always been my favorite spot. You?"

She nodded, not trusting her voice yet. Had he always been this tall? Maybe it was because she'd never been this close to him before. She only ever encountered the heir to the throne in passing—usually with him pretending she didn't exist.

"I see."

He inspected her, pausing at the frayed ends of her dress. He turned and slid toward the flower beds, caressing one of the delicate, white flowers before plucking it. "I am curious. What brings the infamous Evangeline out here today?"

She wriggled her toes inside her soft-soled boots, her spine stiffening. What was his game? "I came out here for some fresh air, Your Highness."

He arched an eyebrow. "Is that so?"

She was itching to run away, but uneasiness settled in her bones like lead.

Sehn walked closer to her. She prepared herself for a nasty comment, some type of jab that would make sense of this odd encounter. Instead, he held the flower to his lips before tucking it behind her ear. His touch lingered along the side of her cheek, a bit too long for her comfort.

"You should be more careful. This castle is a wicked place for humans. Especially infamous ones such as yourself." His face hovered next to her ear, his cheek brushing hers. Her pulse lurched. "There are monsters lurking in every dark corner."

She knew he could hear her heart pounding inside her ribcage, smell the beads of sweat forming on the small of her back. And there it is. The whole point of this conversation. It was all to toy with her. Scare her. And it worked. At least now his feigned consideration made sense. Her hands curled.

Sehn withdrew. "Well, I hope you enjoy the rest of your day. I'm sure we'll meet again soon." His smile was mocking as he strode off.

When he was out of sight, Evangeline withdrew the flower from her hair and crushed it in her palm. She'd make sure there wouldn't be a next time.

Evangeline attempted to read after the older prince left, but she couldn't concentrate. Her anger at Sehn and the puss-filled

Nytes at the library ate away at her. Snapping the book shut—she couldn't find any answers in there anyway—she left for Ryker's.

She entered his suite and shifted her dress to hide the burn, but the stain was too large. She sighed, giving up.

"You look exhausted," Ryker said in greeting, his green-silk-covered legs crossed in his designated chair by the fire. A tray of food sat on the dining room table. She wondered who delivered them, now that Ranson was . . . gone.

Evangeline plopped on the couch, her body wanting to melt into the thick cushions. "I am."

He looked at her dress. "And what were you up to today?" His tone changed. Short and sarcastic, a combination Evangeline was *so* not in the mood to deal with right now.

"I spent most of the day in the library until I knocked over a candle. The dress didn't make it."

Gray eyes bore into her, and Ryker's lips thinned. Evangeline fidgeted on the couch, glancing around the room.

Silence.

A log shifted in the fireplace, and flames eagerly licked up its carcass, spitting out sparks. The winter wind howled outside the window above the dining table, the glass vibrating against the golden lock. His eyes remained on her.

She broke. "And . . . I may have run into Prince Sehn today. He was unusually charming."

"How did you burn your dress?"

Her face scrunched. "I told you—"

Ryker uncrossed his legs. "I've raised you for the past seven years. You still haven't gotten better at lying, Evangeline."

Her mouth snapped close. All her previous fury came rushing back. It boiled inside of her, spreading like wildfire, from

the heat in her cheeks to the clenched skin in her fists. "Someone else knocked over the candle."

"Who?"

"Some nobles, of course," she huffed. "It's fine. It's always been this way, hasn't it? Humans don't like me, most Nytes hate me. It would be better if I just disappeared next." She crossed her arms. *Go ahead, punish me. Strike me. Blame me for causing problems again.*

Ryker didn't reply right away, but his jaw was tight. When he did speak, his voice was deadly quiet. "Describe what they look like."

Evangeline hesitated at the look in his eyes. Like he was ready to kill someone. He had always blamed her, never the ones that actually started it.

"Describe. What. They. Look. Like," he repeated through closed teeth.

Her eyes went round, and she stammered out some basic descriptors: red dresses, pale yellow wings, the men of a darker complexion than most Peredians. Ryker sat back, nodding. "Pull back your hair."

Her stomach twisted, and she wanted to pull her hair closer around her face. "Why?"

"Don't make me ask again."

Evangeline flipped her hair behind her shoulders, some thin strands falling defiantly back over. He sucked in a hiss between his teeth.

The chair nearly fell backward as he stood, and she braced herself for a slap, but he walked past her, into the bedroom. He came out with a glass jar.

"Stand up and hold your hair back."

She did as he said.

He took some pale white cream and rubbed it on her neck.

She winced at first, the burn marks flaring, until it cooled, almost tingled.

"Leave this on. It should heal in a day or two." He handed her the glass jar. "Reapply if it starts to sting again."

Evangeline nodded, a little taken aback.

When she sat down, silence descended once more, Ryker sipping his tea. Staring into the fire, a reoccurring thought bubbled up. She had asked in the past but had gotten nowhere. But maybe now . . .

"Why . . . Why me?" She rephrased her question when Ryker didn't respond. "Why did you pick me? Is it because of my mark?" She swallowed. "Or because I look like your daughter?"

He stiffened, and she swore he was going to yell at her. Then: "Go eat your food, Evangeline. You will stay here tonight."

She sighed, and he walked into his bedroom. This time he didn't come back out. Evangeline mustered a few bites of her dinner before her body forced her to go to bed. She was fast asleep before her head hit the pillow.

CHAPTER 25

⁓ EVANGELINE ⁓

E vangeline gripped the slender, dulled blade, feeling the harsh leather-bound handle in her smooth hands. Barto stood in front of her, his loose-fitting trousers and white shirt reflecting hers. Except hers was drenched in sweat.

"Bend your knees, raise your right arm. You're getting sloppy," Ceven barked from behind, his arms crossed around a tight brown tunic, tucked into baggy pants. The small gold hoop in his right ear shone more vibrantly after the recent haircut he'd had this morning, the sides trimmed short while the top was longer.

"I'm trying my best," Evangeline spat, adjusting her position as Barto swung at her with his dulled blade. She went to block the incoming strike but miscalculated his aim and he struck her lower ribs.

"I told you, read the feet, see where the opponent's weight is being shifted to—"

"I know, I know!" She tried to blow a piece of hair out of her face, but the strand stuck to her cheek. "You don't have to be a jerk about it." She tried to block the next attack Barto threw at her but was, again, unsuccessful.

Ceven scowled. "Do you want our help or not?"

She sighed, not bothering to wipe away the sweat that poured continuously from her scalp. "Yes, sorry. I just thought this would be easier."

Barto shook his head. "No one becomes a master warrior overnight, honey. Though, you aren't the quickest learner, are you?"

Evangeline told him where to shove it, and he laughed.

After two more rounds of practicing defense techniques—which Evangeline failed to master—Xilo came in with bags of food. His long black and gray hair was pulled taut, like his usual facial expression, as he set down the food. Evangeline gratefully took a sandwich and collapsed on the floor.

Xilo joined them, and they all devoured the ham and cheese sandwiches on fresh bread.

"I can't believe the ball is next week already. I barely see Lani anymore," Evangeline said after a while, nibbling at her sandwich.

"An Aerian ball." Barto scratched his furred ear, his tail flicking back and forth. "I'm sure it won't be as fun as our festivals, but it'll be interesting to see Ceven acting as the ever-so-welcoming and princely host."

"And I'll give you a wonderful tour of the ballroom's balcony—right before I throw you off of it." Ceven turned to her. "Lani, how is she? I didn't see her in the kitchens the last few times I checked on her."

He went to see how Lani was doing? Evangeline swallowed too big of a bite and coughed. She guzzled down the canister of water. "She's fine now," she got out. "Just a small fever."

Ceven frowned but didn't respond.

"Something must be going around, because Rasha was complaining about her nose being all stuffed up, and let me tell you, when that women's sick, she can be a real pain." Barto rambled about how the "she-beast" abused him while she was ill, and Evangeline tuned him out. She was getting good at it.

After giving time for their food to settle, they resumed their practice, Barto still being her opponent while Ceven fixed her form.

A soft touch at her elbow, another at the small of her back. Even though they were brief brushes, it felt like his hands were everywhere. Evangeline swallowed a little harder, squaring her shoulders. She knew he was only trying to help, but she couldn't concentrate, feeling the weight of his hands every time he touched her, driving her mind into a mess of nerves. After little to no progress, she gave up and called it quits for the day.

She changed back into her dress, and everyone packed up. A farewell stuck in her throat and she bit her lip, shuffling her feet. She took a breath. "Please, tell me what's going on in this castle. I know you guys have to have some sort of clue." It was blunt, but she needed answers. Not only to keep a murderous Caster off her back, but for herself. For Lani.

Xilo, who had spoken little, surprised her by saying, "For your safety, I'd advise you drop the subject. Permanently." Ceven cast him a look, and Xilo straightened, a pinch in his brow. He turned and exited the room.

Barto shrugged. "As much of a bore as Xilo is, he is right in this case. It's not something you should go digging about."

Ceven nodded. "Don't worry, Eve, we have it under control."

No. She was done with them avoiding her questions, treating her like she was a child. Hands on her hips, Evangeline retorted, "That's not what I asked." She turned her gaze toward Ceven, softening. "Please, I need to protect Lani, but I can't if I don't even know what the threat is."

Ceven ran a hand through his hair, tousling the long chestnut strands. He opened his mouth, but Barto cut him off.

"Don't. We can't have her spreading this about."

Evangeline shot him a surprised look, but Ceven saved her from making a nasty comment.

"No, Eve isn't like that. We can trust her." His hazel eyes met hers, and she felt a pit of guilt well inside her chest.

Barto raised his brows and crossed his arms. Both he and Evangeline looked at Ceven expectantly.

His expression morphed. Evangeline had never seen him look so serious, so . . . determined. "We believe Caster magic is involved."

Evangeline's heart picked up. "These markings seen on people before they go missing—you think they're Castanian?"

The two men shot her an odd look, but Ceven confirmed with a swift nod. "However, we haven't tracked down any of the missing persons, or any bodies, to verify this. We are only going off hearsay."

"What does the king say to all of this?" she asked.

Ceven's lip curled upward, his eyes burning. "He doesn't care in the slightest."

"No one does," Barto added, the worried expression he wore an unsettling look on him.

Evangeline pondered for a moment, thoughts racing. "What about Avana? She might—"

"No," they said at the same time. Evangeline blinked in surprise.

"This stays between us. For now," Ceven said with absolute certainty, and she didn't fight it.

They didn't add more on the matter. They really hadn't figured out as much as Evangeline had thought. Unless . . . they still weren't sharing the whole truth. But at least she had something.

Barto waved goodbye, heading back to his suite in the east wing. Evangeline wasn't too far behind him when Ceven pulled her back.

"Eve . . . I want you to know that no matter what happens, I will make sure that you and Lani are safe. I will get to the bottom of all of this." He gripped her shoulder, his sincere gaze staring into hers.

She smiled. "I know, Ceven, I trust you." And she did, she realized. A small part inside of her still trusted him, even after these years apart. *But if he ever found out I was working with a Caster assassin, would he still trust me?* Her smile vanished.

"You should get cleaned at my suite. We wouldn't want Ryker finding out what you've been up to," he said.

Evangeline shook her head, saying she was fine, that Ryker has said nothing so far.

"Please," he whispered. "I want to talk to you."

Her stomach fluttered, and her first thought was no. That was probably the worst decision for her right now, but she said, "Okay." She hoped she wouldn't regret it later.

Walking back to Ceven's suite reminded Evangeline of old times. In the past, she would sneak into his room after their shared tutoring sessions, where they would complain about Ryker and King Calais. About how hard it was constantly being surrounded by two arrogant and powerful men. It wasn't long after she watched Lani bury a young man after being whipped to death for raising a weapon against an Aerian. He had tried to protect his daughter from being taken by two Aerians who felt entitled to the girl for their own sexual entertainment. Evangeline couldn't summon the energy to complain about her life after that.

She walked to the end of the hallway, the walls farther apart, the purple wallpaper now a reflective gold with swirls of pearl white to give it texture. The floor was of white marble instead of black, and she walked across bronze floor runners that spanned the length of the hallways.

She was on the top floors of the main hall, suites reserved only for the immediate royal family.

Up ahead, Ceven leaned on the wall. The sun outlined the gold in his wings, and his eyes brightened when they met hers. He was still in his casual shirt and trousers. He looked relaxed, with one boot against the posh wallpaper and, in this moment, he looked nothing at all like a prince.

"I thought you might've forgotten the way here," Ceven teased when she got closer.

After leaving the underground rooms, they decided it was best to walk separately to avoid speculation. Ceven went ahead, giving her time to catch her breath and wipe off as much sweat as she could. She hoped she didn't look as gross as she felt.

"It hasn't been that long," she said, following him as they walked to the front door of his suite.

Ceven had dismissed the other guards at his doors, Xilo and Tarry standing post outside instead. They said nothing, and she did the same as she followed Ceven into the large foyer of his suite.

Passing by the same shelves of ancient swords and gems kept safe behind glass, she walked into the sitting chamber. "Do you ever tire of staring at all this purple?" Evangeline said, staring at the purple walls, the purple pillows, and small vases of gold and purple.

Ceven shrugged, sitting down on the off-white loveseat. Peeling off his boots, he tossed them to the side before leaning back on his folded wings and sighing. "I'm not here enough to care."

Evangeline knew Ceven was usually busy. Between attending formal meetings with the king and the military's officials, he also routinely inspected the borders and the kingdom's reserves while still finding time to train with her.

"I'm sure you want to take a shower first." His head rested against the loveseat, his eyes closed.

"Are you saying I smell?" She smiled, taking off her shoes, leaving them by the entrance.

He opened his eyes and looked offended. "No, I meant—"

"I'm teasing, Ceven."

He shook his head as she walked into his bathing room. The layout was like Ryker's, the room slightly larger. A scenic window hung above the tub and stretched the expanse of it. Being on the top floor, she didn't have to worry about anyone looking in, so she left the embroidered curtains open to view the gardens.

She stepped in the tub and let the warm water pelt her body. It felt odd that she was here, in Ceven's shower. She didn't know what he wanted with her, if he planned to question her about her interest in these missing persons, or if something else was on his mind . . .

Evangeline rinsed her body, grateful to smell like soap and not sweat, and bent down to turn off the faucet. The water at the bottom of the tub was red.

She jolted back. Too fast. She slipped and her legs flew, her back slamming into the bottom of the tub. She didn't have time to process the pain when she realized the water dripping down her arms and legs wasn't water at all.

It was blood. She was bathing in blood.

Evangeline screeched, and a wave of nausea hit her stomach like a fist. Crawling out of the shower, she rushed to the toilet, retching.

Three pounds on the door echoed in her ears. "Eve? Are you okay?"

"I-I'm fine."

She looked at her arms and back at the tub. *It's just water.* She sighed.

After getting dressed, she met with a solemn Ceven. He no longer sat on the couch but rested against it, one leg crossed over the other. He gave a small smile, but it didn't touch his eyes.

"I'm fine," she started before he could ask.

"You expect me to believe you make a habit of screaming whenever you take a shower? Because if so, for once I feel sorry for poor old Ryker." His tone was light, but his look said he wasn't having any of it.

"I didn't scream," she said defensively.

He raised a brow at her. "Take a seat. I'll bring you some tea."

"I'm fine—"

"I heard you puking, Eve." His face was tight, and Evangeline knew he was in no mood to argue. "Sit down. I'm going to bring you something that will help." She conceded, resting on the sofa, relishing the heat that came from the white granite fireplace in front of it.

Ceven came back, handing her a porcelain cup of piping hot tea. Her hands nestled around the cup as he sat down beside her, his long legs brushing hers. Over the aroma of peppermint wafting into her face, the smell of him surrounded her. Crushed leaves on the forest floor with the smell of spice.

"Are you sick?" he asked.

She shook her head. "I think I just trained too hard today."
Liar.

He stared at her. "Eve . . . I know you went beyond the wall.
That you're trying to escape again."

She jerked, her tea sloshing. She wasn't expecting that.

Burying her face into the cup, she hid her expression. She
didn't want to lie to him, but what if he tried to stop her? Or
worse, tried to help her, knowing the consequences of aiding a
human trying to escape? The king would denounce him as his
son. They would cast him out. "Ceven, I—"

"Don't deny it. It's why you took up fighting again. Why
Ryker sent you to Vane, and the reason you wanted to travel
farther that day we went horseback riding. It was to see if you
could escape the same way you did the first time, wasn't it?"

The cup in her hand was shaking. She wasn't as calm and
collected as she'd thought she was. "Have you told anybody else
this?"

"Of course not." He let out a breath, running a hand through
his hair. "Why didn't you say anything? Gods, it's the middle of
winter, Eve, you could have frozen to death."

She licked her lips. "I have to, Ceven. So many people have
gone missing. Who's to say Lani isn't next?"

"I thought I was your friend, Eve."

Evangeline frowned and looked at him. Genuine hurt flickered in his eyes. "You are." *You're more than that, actually.* She
took another sip of tea, heat rising in her cheeks.

"Then why haven't you asked me for help? I can send guards,
see if I can make other accommodations for Lani so she's better
watched, taken care of."

"Like you have in the past?" she asked, taking too quick a
drink and burning her lips. "Last time you tried to have Lani

moved out of the slave quarters, your father told you to keep your nose out of human affairs, from what I recall."

"I was a boy then. If I'm old enough to take on more duties as a prince, the least I could do is move Lani, move everyone in those blasted slave quarters, closer to the castle."

Evangeline set her cup on the white coffee table, the peppermint easing some of her nerves. "It doesn't matter. We would still live in fear. She'd still be forced to work, even when she can barely walk. And I'm sure with your help, she'll be scrutinized, made fun of, cast out."

"Like you?" he said.

She looked down at her hands, folded in her lap. "Yes."

His hand closed over hers. Her chest expanded.

"I don't want you leaving here, Evangeline," he whispered. A plea.

Her eyes traced the outline of his face, from his straight, defiant nose down along the rigid lines of his jaw, prickling with a few days of growth. Her gaze fell to his lips, where it lingered. Then, as if realizing it, her eyes jerked back up to meet his.

"I'm not as weak as you think," she said, harsher than she intended.

His hand was warm on top of hers as he squeezed it. "I'm not saying that. What I'm saying is . . . I care about you. A lot."

Her insides twisted, then softened like molten lava, the heat rising up her body to settle into her face. She met his eyes and . . . *Oh, almighty Gods.* Liquid gold blazed at her from within the green and brown orbs. A tender heat and fiery promise lingering there. He meant every word.

Her voice carried below a whisper. "I . . ." *Care about you too, more than you know,* she almost said. But she didn't.

Because nothing good would come of it.

She looked away. "You're a prince, Ceven. A Nyte." *I won't*

take you away from your people. I won't see them ridicule and hate you more because of me. "We have nothing in common." *Soon, you'll find a beautiful Aerian lady, and you'll be accepted among your kind.* "We're only friends out of circumstance." *And I will be far, far away.*

Ceven fell quiet for a moment and Evangeline thought, with growing dread, that he'd agree and take back what he'd said. And although that was what she wanted, a part of her died.

"You're really good at pushing people away," he said, his words sharp. "It hurts me to think, after all these years, you still see me that way."

Her nostrils flared, a lump forming in her throat. *No, that's not true!* But she kept her voice level. "Why do you even care so much?"

"Why do I *care* so much?" he snapped. His words lashed at her heart, and she closed her eyes. She didn't want him to see the truth in them.

When he spoke again, it was soft. "Eve, look at me."

She shook her head, and treacherous tears slid down her cheeks.

"Please," he tried again.

She did and his gaze captivated hers. Honesty and a broken vulnerability she hadn't seen in him since he lost his mother, lingered in his eyes.

His thumb traced a gentle path across her hand. His words were a soft caress. "You are the most beautiful, selfless, and kindest woman I've ever met." She opened her mouth to protest, but he cut her off. "You are, Eve. The way you look after Lani, care for her, and defend her with every part of you, no matter the consequences, is incredibly admirable. And when I lost my mom . . ." He took a deep breath. "When the queen was announced dead, I blamed you, blamed all humans. I was no better than any other Nyte. And I was so cruel to you, Eve, calling you names, getting you in trouble with Ryker. I'll always remember when you would leave his suite covered in bruises. *Because of me.*" His face scrunched in pain at the memory. "But when everyone found out I was a bastard child and scorned me, you were there. You were still willing to be my friend, despite everything."

Evangeline was quiet, remembering those dark times. When the queen's death shook the kingdom, the king claiming she'd been murdered by mutinous slaves. Evangeline had been terrified. For herself and for Lani. The thirst for revenge burned in every Nyte in the kingdom, in the country. And Ceven had been no exception.

But he had it all wrong. She befriended him for her own selfish gain. To find any source of protection she could while living in a pit of predators. He'd been vulnerable, and she used it to her advantage. To save herself.

Take it. Take it. Take it all and leave nothing.

She was far from selfless. And she was definitely not kind.

His hand left hers to cup her face, and she leaned into the warmth of it. "If it wasn't for you, I'd have turned out like the king. Like Sehn." His thumb stroked the curve of her lips. "You made me a better man, Evangeline."

A delicious heat swept through her from where his thumb teased her lips, and for a moment, she closed her eyes and dreamed. Dreamed of them living somewhere else, where they could be together, where Lani didn't have to be a slave, where she wouldn't disappear forever.

But it was just that, a dream.

She pulled away from his touch, and his face tightened. "You are who you are because of you, Ceven. I had nothing to do with that. I'm not the same girl you used to know. A lot has changed."

245

I'm working with a Caster assassin and his sister now, and sometimes I can't tell the difference between reality and what's in my head.

Her eyes slid to his, and she shivered at the intensity in his gaze. She quickly cast her eyes back down at her lap. "All I'm saying is that we've been friends for a long time, and you're just confused on how you feel. I don't think—"

The first thing she felt was the heat of his fingers on her chin, right before his lips captured hers in a fierce yet gentle kiss.

Her surprised gasp melted away as his lips moved with hers. Her body curved toward him, her hands resting on his lap to steady herself as he cradled her face in one hand, the other cupping her neck, dragging her closer. Blue and gold wrapped around them, the soft brush of his wings like passionate caresses all over her body. His lips were soft yet hard, molding to hers. Demanding, yet persuasive, luring her down a path she never been before. The feeling was akin to her body coming to life, like tendrils of fire licking at skin, making her toes curl, her fingers crinkling the fabric of his cotton trousers.

And then he pulled away, breaking the spell.

His eyes were burning, reflecting the fire that still smoldered inside her. "Now tell me, am I still *confused?*"

Evangeline was a muddled mess, her breathing shallow. She kept blinking, the words from her mouth stolen by his lips.

Ceven stood, facing the fire. The hard planes of his face flickered in the light. "It's almost dusk. You should go, Ryker's waiting for you."

She looked at him and opened her mouth, but when her gaze caught on his face, his lips, she jerked her head away, flustered all over again. Instead, she resorted to a nod and picked up her dress, running from the room. She didn't look back.

Evangeline walked the entire way to Ryker's barefoot. In her panic, she'd left her shoes at Ceven's suite. *Better say goodbye to that pair for now. Not like you can show your face in that room anytime soon.*

When she met with Ryker, her face failed to lose its heat, her thoughts curtailing back to Ceven. His lips on hers, how it had felt better than anything she had ever imagined. Better than the chaste, traded kisses in her novels or the sloppy, unwanted kisses Lani had described from previous admirers before she came to the kingdom. And how it may have ruined everything.

Fortunately, Ryker was busy writing at his desk. He left her alone to eat with her thoughts until he dismissed her, not bothering to ask her questions. It seemed he had been avoiding her recently. She shrugged. She was happy to have some distance.

On her way back to Lani's, she noted the nights have been getting warmer and less windy. Or maybe it was in her head, knowing spring was still a few weeks out.

Evangeline found Lani washing her clothes in the tin bucket beside the fire. When she looked up, she didn't bother giving Evangeline a smile, the skin beneath her eyes heavy and weary, her face sagging in exhaustion. Evangeline's ire sparked. How could they work these humans to death? And all for a ball for Nytes to play dress-up and pretend to like one another. It was sickening.

They exchanged a few words, Lani too tired to speak, while Evangeline's head was a flood of chaos. They both went to bed shortly after, a loud ragged snore rumbling out of Lani. Evangeline was wide awake, staring at the ceiling.

Why did he have to do that? She squeezed her eyes shut, embarrassment flooding her cheeks. *Nothing good will come of it.* She rolled over. *I wonder if he'd still want to kiss me if he found out about Raiythlen. About how I'm going insane.* A painful pressure in her temples formed.

Tap, tap, tap.

Evangeline frowned, sitting up and peering into the dark room.

Tap, tap, tap.

It was coming from the window.

She stumbled out of bed and opened it. A flap of wings and the shadow of a bird flying off into the night greeted her along with a small, rolled piece of parchment. Her brows furrowed, and she swiped the paper, closing the window. In the moonlight, it read:

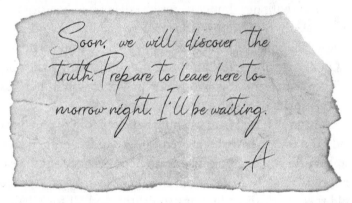

Soon, we will discover the truth. Prepare to leave here tomorrow night. I'll be waiting.

A

Evangeline stared at the cursive writing until it dawned on her. After everything, she had forgotten about her proposal with Avana.

She licked her lips, her limbs itching to jump, run, do anything but stand stagnant. She would finally figure out her past, the reason for her mark, for everything. *Calm down, Eve, you don't know that for certain. The last time you went to that cave, there was nothing there. And that's if you get there. We still don't know how Avana is going to sneak us out.*

But she tampered down the skeptical thoughts and got back into bed. She hardly found sleep that night.

CHAPTER 26

✧ EVANGELINE ✧

A full day had passed, and night had fallen when Evangeline finished her dinner with Ryker and started back toward Lani's. The entire day she had been a distorted mix of exhaustion and anxiousness. How would Avana sneak them out? What if they got caught? What if this all was a trap? Even during her training with Barto—Ceven had been preoccupied with the king, to her relief and disappointment—her mind had been elsewhere, her limbs feeling like they were pushing through mud.

When she made it inside Lani's room, she found her friend was already asleep with long, jagged snores coming from the lump in the corner of the room. Underneath her thick dress and wool coat, Evangeline smuggled a few extra clothes and dry foods in a small bag. She didn't know what Avana's plans were, but she wanted to be prepared.

Changing into more practical clothes, she traded her thick dress for the shirt and pants she wore when she first snuck beyond the wall. So much had changed since then.

For the worse, she thought as a smug-looking male Caster popped into her head. She couldn't believe she'd tasted that bit of freedom only two weeks ago. *But after tonight, I won't be coming back through those walls ever again. I'll scope the area, see what Avana offers, and in a few days' time, Lani and I will be far away from here, with or without Avana's help.* She didn't dare think about Ceven.

Her nerves tingled, and she tapped her foot. Time passed, and with Avana nowhere to be seen, Evangeline sat by the fire, taking everything out of her bag and reorganizing it, debating if she should bring more or less.

She had put everything back for the twentieth time when a faint tap came from the window. Evangeline bounded to her feet so fast she almost tripped over her own bag. Avana waved from behind the glass. Evangeline snatched her bag and added a few more logs to the fireplace before crawling out the window.

"Are you ready?" Avana asked, her hair and face shrouded in a thick fur hood tied tightly around her chin. Multiple layers of clothing and knee-high, fur-lined boots protected the rest of her body.

Evangeline's head bobbed as she tightened her own full-length coat to help batter the winter wind that was blowing harder than previous nights. Much harder.

"It feels like there's a snowstorm coming. Are you sure it's going to be safe to travel?" Evangeline looked around at the flurries of snow flying in the air.

Avana turned and smiled at her. "This is the best time for us to travel." Avana handed her another glamour potion, holding a similar one in her own hand. "Some guards, especially the Royal

Guard, may see through this spell, but it should help to throw any unwanted attention off our trail."

Evangeline raised her brows. "They can see through it? How?"

Avana downed the small potion, wiping her mouth with the back of her hand. "All that jewelry they wear isn't for show. The Aerians have always been wary of Caster magic and do their best to protect themselves against it." A smile danced across her lips, and her body shimmered, the glamour settling on top of her figure. "At least from the spells that they know of."

And here I thought it was because they were vain. The side of her mouth twitched. *Well, that's still true.*

Imbibing her own potion, a familiar tickling sensation trickled down her throat and stomach. From her peripheral, dark blue wings sprouted from her own back, a shade lighter than the ones Avana grew along with a rounder face and a stranger's green eyes that stared at her. Evangeline trailed behind Avana until they reached a withered tree close to Lani's. Avana raised her hand, her lips moving as she unveiled a single gray-and-white speckled horse tied to the trunk of the tree.

Evangeline's brows rose. "We're going to escape on a horse?" She frowned. "Won't that draw too much attention? How would we get out?"

Avana tightened the saddle straps, making sure the thick brown bags on either side didn't jostle out of place. "Through the front gates, of course." She put one foot through the hoop in the saddle before swinging her body onto the mount in one fluid motion.

Avana held out her hand, and Evangeline took it, making sure her foot was in the hoop before thrusting herself up—and landing with her stomach on the saddle, the other half of her body dangling off.

She made it look so spitting easy, too. Evangeline scowled as Avana helped her wiggle her way into the saddle.

Once she got on the horse, they plowed through the half-foot of snow, down the steep mountain path and into the rest of the kingdom. The moon wasn't as bright tonight, its presence covered by puffs of dark clouds. The wind whipped around them, billowing their coats, and she huddled closer into Avana's back, trying to shield herself from the wind. Avana was insane for traveling in this kind of weather.

The hooves of their horse tapped against the cobblestone of the city streets as they passed by multiple-story houses and storefronts crammed together. Some windows illuminated a soft glow from their lanterns. Others reflected their giant shadow passing by.

It wasn't until they passed the town's center, the red-and-gray bricked plaza encircled with stores and small stands that were occupied and filled with merchandise in the daytime, that Evangeline grew more anxious. It started with her chest aching, her heart beating too fast inside its own ribcage. Her bottom lip had chapped, and she nibbled on it, the skin splitting open, requiring her to lick the blood away every few houses they passed.

"And you're sure about this?" Evangeline asked for the third time.

"If you don't trust me, this won't work," Avana said through the howling of the wind.

Evangeline hid her sigh beneath her cloak as the tall, looming gates to the kingdom came closer and closer. Two large wooden doors embedded with metal took precedence within the gray stone wall. The wall itself stretched excessively tall. Even with her neck arched back, she couldn't make out the gold spikes that lined the top of it. The large doors weren't too far from that mark.

As the horse trotted closer, through the gusts of white wind, an outline of what Evangeline assumed were Peredia's castle guards, stood in formation by the gates. Although she couldn't see them from this distance, with the thick wind batting her face, she felt every guard's eyes from the watchtowers above. Evangeline bit down on her cheek, relishing the pain. It distracted her from what they were about to do.

They trounced up, and several guards approached them as Evangeline's hands dug into the hardened leather saddle.

"We're sorry, but no one is allowed past the castle gates at this time," one square-jawed guard said in a disarmingly casual tone. Evangeline, however, kept her eyes on the three other guards, who circled and dissected them with their eyes, the grips on their spears and swords tightening. Or maybe that was in her head.

"I believe you can make an exception for me." Avana reached into her cloak and pulled out a sheet of paper.

Evangeline watched closely as the guard unrolled the paper, her heart hammering away. The guard looked blank, like he wasn't sure what he was reading, then shook his head as if an unseen force had struck him. He returned the paper to Avana, a smile on his lips.

"My apologies, my lady, I did not realize who you were. My men and I can escort you to wherever you need to be. The roads aren't safe this time of night, especially for two young women such as yourselves."

Avana bowed her head. "I appreciate your concern, sir, but we are more than capable of defending ourselves." The guard frowned and opened his mouth, probably to argue, but Avana continued. "If that is all, may you please open the gate, sir?"

The guard gave one firm nod. "Of course, my lady. Please wait here."

The guards left their side as the two large doors shuddered, the weight of them roaring as they opened outward, the force shoving against the snow, creating a flattened path ahead. Once opened, the cool, dark night beckoned them, an endless forest waiting ahead.

Evangeline stared at Avana in disbelief, then back at the guards.

Avana waved, elbowing her to do the same as they passed through the open gates, traveling beyond the kingdom's walls. Evangeline's jaw was still slack.

They traversed the snowy bank of forest right outside, traveling in silence for a few moments before Evangeline felt it safe to speak.

"How did you do that?" She had expected more obstacles, more questions.

"Sehn gave me an identification form when I first came here. As a guest of the castle, I'm not allowed to leave until my permit has ended, but with some tweaking and a spell or two, I thought there was a good chance the guard wouldn't notice the faded drops of blood or the way the words may have been changed around," Avana said, as if it were no big deal.

Evangeline shook her head in disbelief. "So, you weren't sure this would work? You risked my safety on a maybe?"

Avana glanced back and gave her a serious look. "It worked, Evangeline. That's all that matters."

Evangeline wasn't happy, having put her life at risk, but there was no point in fretting over it now. They were outside the kingdom, and she wasn't about to waste this opportunity.

The horse kept a brisk pace, and Evangeline leaned closer to Avana as the wind whistled through the trees. Darkness loomed all around them. Anything could be hiding in the night.

Evangeline's smile was grim. "Well, if the guards don't catch us, maybe the Olaaga will."

Avana's snort was out of character. "That's just a tale to deter bandits and other Nytes away from the kingdom. The king is going to have to be more creative when a real army comes knocking at his door."

Evangeline frowned at her back. *What army?*

Avana let out a low whistle. A flap of wings came from above before a black bird settled on Avana's outstretched arm. Evangeline watched in amazement as the Caster connected her nose to the bird's beak, and then it took off again, flying in the direction they were traveling.

"What was that all about?" Evangeline feared she knew nothing about this woman, and here she was, traveling alone with her to some forgotten cave far from the kingdom. Lani was right. She really was a naïve fool.

"My familiar," Avana said. "It's a creature that some Casters have. Kind of like a .. . . pet of sorts."

Evangeline scrunched her nose. "Why do I feel like there's more to it than that?"

"It's my eyes and ears. It will tell us if there is danger ahead."

Evangeline left it at that, hoping that this strange Caster woman wouldn't kill her on this trip.

The night dragged, and as more time passed, Evangeline's bottom went numb, her limbs stiff. The wind picked up, forcing her to dig her feet into the sides of the saddle, ducking her head to prevent from being knocked off the horse. Avana remained still, her hands on the reins, prodding them through the thick layer of white fog. Evangeline didn't know how the Caster saw anything, or how the horse still kept a steady pace.

"A storm's coming. We shouldn't be out here, we need to find shelter!" Evangeline yelled when another gust of wind almost knocked her off the horse.

Avana turned and put a finger to her lips. Or at least Evangeline thought she did. Her eyes watered too much to see anything.

"Stay quiet. We're being followed." Avana's whisper carried over the harsh flaps of wind.

Evangeline froze.

Avana shook the reins and kept looking over her shoulder, the wind howling all around them. The trees of the Olaaga forest shifted and creaked with each breeze, its barren arms looking like it wanted to reach out and grab them. Tufts of snow eclipsed the small light from the moon and smacked at their faces. If anyone was following them, Evangeline wouldn't be able to tell with all her senses thrown into chaos.

"Evangeline, I need you to hold on to me as tight as you can, and no matter what, don't speak and don't move. Understand?"

All Evangeline could do was nod, wishing they were out of this wind.

Avana released the reins and Evangeline wanted to yell at her to not let go, that they both would fall off and lose the horse, but Avana already had her hands raised to the sky. Evangeline swore she heard whispering on the winds surrounding both of them.

"Hang on, we're going to run." Avana retook the reins, propelling the horse forward at a speed faster than Evangeline had ever experienced on horseback.

Trees flew by them at a rate Evangeline thought impossible. She was as good as deaf, given the amount of air pressing at the sides of her body. Her hood had blown off, her hair stretching against its braid.

Something tugged at Evangeline's waist, loosening her grip on Avana's torso. She looked around and saw nothing, but the next pull on her body was unmistakable. It was when she looked behind her that her heart plummeted to the pit of her stomach. Large, dark shadows traveled behind them, and they were picking up speed.

Her eyes widened. She spun around, holding on for dear life, but her hands were too numb, and she couldn't feel herself losing her grip. The weight around her waist gave another sudden pull, and she was yanked off the horse.

Evangeline slammed into the ground and it knocked out all the air from her lungs. She gasped, her body flailing, struggling to get up as she watched Avana continue to ride into the distance.

No! Wait, come back! she tried to yell, but it came out as a distorted intake of breath. Clawing at the ground, she wobbled to her feet. In a half-daze, she looked around, trying to figure out the direction Avana had gone in—and with a growing horror realized she wasn't alone.

The shadows had caught up to her.

And they had her completely surrounded.

CHAPTER 27

⟿ EVANGELINE ⟾

E vangeline turned in circles, her panic steadily rising as the shadows creeped in around her. There were four, no five, maybe more . . .?

She focused on one silhouette in particular. They broke from the trees, sliding closer to her, when something grabbed her from behind and pressed a gloved hand to her mouth. Instinctively, Evangeline jerked and rammed her elbow into the ribs of her attacker. A low feminine grunt echoed in Evangeline's ear—but it wasn't Avana.

A black mask covered half of the woman's face, matching the armor that fitted her body with silver circles beading the front of it—like Raiythlen's when Evangeline first found him. Two small horns curled away from her head, and the only thing strikingly feminine about the Caster were the narrow, slanted eyes staring at her.

A branch snapped to Evangeline's left. Two other figures stepped out, all dressed in black with their faces covered.

"Do it now," the woman next to her said. Chanting rose from the three Casters, who were now closing in on Evangeline from all sides.

"What do you want?" Evangeline yelled.

Branches, wood, roots, or maybe a combination of all three, erupted from the ground. The land itself screamed, opening its jaw at Evangeline. The chanting got louder, surrounding her, and she didn't see the other two Casters slip away, leaving her alone with the remaining trio. She didn't have time to think, to talk. So, she did the only thing she could.

She ran.

The ground became her enemy as roots attacked her ankles. She jumped, knocking away slithering branches, but there were too many. One grabbed her ankle, constricting itself around it like an iron shackle. *No! No! No!* Her hands tore at the roots, yanking on what felt like solid metal and not bendable branches. The chanting came closer. Its melody sliced her ears, sharper than Raiythlen's knife at her throat.

"What do you want!" Evangeline screamed.

The surrounding grass sank, and she fell backwards as roots climbed up her arms, ensnaring her wrists. "*Let me go!*" Her ears rang, but this time it was the sound of her own panic consuming her.

The Casters didn't respond, their voices lulling together as the roots twisted tight, cutting off her circulation.

I'm going to die. This is it.

She thrashed against her restraints as she lost feeling in both her hands and feet. She gave up using her words, focusing her strength on a battle she knew she wouldn't win. Ceven was right. No matter how much she trained, she'd never be as powerful as a Nyte. And now she would die because she wasn't strong enough to stop them. To do anything. Her nostrils flared, a frustrated muffle bubbling from her when her skin rippled from an invisible force.

Snow erupted and engulfed her, as if every tree in the forest collapsed at the same time. White chunks flew, the ground trembled, and the chanting halted. Evangeline lifted her head but couldn't see anything through the buzz of snow.

Then the screaming started.

Piercing shrills of terror pounded at her from both sides as shadows sifted through the white haze. The sharp whip of air indicated something moving through the sheet of snow. Evangeline jerked against her restrains with renewed strength as people shouted, flashes of light blinding her. Something growled in the distance, and Evangeline seized, her eyes stretched wide.

The sound rumbled loud and deep, coming from something ten times her size. It scraped across her throat, threatening to sink its teeth into her flesh. Her limbs locked up, refusing to make the slightest movement, petrified of luring the beast her way. To have it eat her alive while roots strapped her to the forest floor.

Hands—or claws—landed on her. Everywhere. Her scream was lost in the beast's thundering roar. Like every nightmare became personified, penetrating the pocket of air around her and crushing down on her chest.

I can't breathe, I can't breathe, I'm going to die, I'm going to die!

Something shook her. "Help me get these off!" It was Avana.

The creature roared again, and another flash of light sliced through the snow, creating an empty path in its wake. Like a curtain being drawn, the haze of snow dispersed, revealing the other side of the clearing.

And all Evangeline could do was stare.

In disbelief.

In horror.

Words couldn't describe the depraved *thing* she was looking at. It was as if every dead tree in the forest twined together to create the spindly, six-legged mass that peered into the woods with black and yellow eyes. Then those eyes shifted, fixating on her.

It can't be . . .

"We have to get these off *now,* Evangeline!" Avana screamed. Evangeline ripped her gaze away and helped Avana tear at her bindings. Splinters of wood sliced through the thread of her gloves, digging into her skin. She wiggled out of the slippery branches that had died along with their masters' song, her wrists and torso springing free. They made quick work of her ankles when a blast of air rustled their hair, the tree toppling down right behind them. *"Move!"* Avana yanked her out of the way as the trunk crashed into the ground, kicking up another chaos of white flurries.

Avana shoved something small and hard into her hands. "Hang on to this as if your life depends on it!" Evangeline didn't have time to figure out what it was when Avana wrenched her forward.

Evangeline ran faster than she thought possible. Faster, and far longer than any of her training sessions.

Shouts and screams boomed behind them, and a sizzling wave of heat whizzed past her cheek. Red and orange blossomed in front of their eyes, and another tree crashed next to them. Avana cursed and jerked Evangeline to the left, sprinting in the opposite direction.

Evangeline's body cried in protest with every snap and crunch beneath her boots, and when she caught sight of a gray horse in the distance, she couldn't even muster a sigh of relief.

When they got closer, Avana held out her hand, and Evangeline hopped onto the horse, clinging to the saddle.

"Hold on to the reins, and whatever you do, don't let go of that charm. I'll meet with you later," Avana said in a flurry of words.

What?

She didn't have a chance to respond when Avana bucked the horse forward, Evangeline scrambling for the reins as she darted into the night.

I don't know how to ride! I don't even know where I'm going! Evangeline's mind screamed, her hands white-knuckled around the reins, her fingers entangled in the cold string that Avana had given her, the ends tied to a small piece of thick metal.

The night air rushed around her, the horse guiding them through the maze of the forest. Her face and coat snagged on branches, the bits of wood like lashes from a whip. She winced, staying as close to the horse as possible.

It wasn't until she stopped feeling the sting of branches on her back that she peeked up, her eyes blurry against the icy wind. They had exited the forest.

Ahead were small blinking lights of a town. Unsure of what direction she'd been going in for most of the night, Evangeline didn't know if it was the rumored town that helped runaway slaves or if it was another neighboring one to the kingdom. Avana was still nowhere in sight, but at least she was no longer being chased. The horse came to a slow trot, heading closer to the town.

"Ouch!" Evangeline yelped.

The charm she clutched burned up, the metal scalding her palm. Before her eyes, she watched the metal piece—which had a marking engraved into it—melt. Avana had told her not to let go, but it was searing into her skin, forcing her to drop it into the snow, where it sank with a puff of steam. She brought her hand to her lips, nursing it as the horse led her closer to the twinkling lights.

Evangeline entered the small town. The first thing that bombarded her was the overwhelming silence. In the kingdom, even in late hours of night, there was always someone walking around, or carts being hauled through the streets, the low mumblings of guards walking and monitoring the city, but here . . . only the rustle of trees and the occasional whisper of wind rolled through the empty streets.

The hooves of her horse clicked against the paved ground, a mix of stones, no one alike in color or size. Unlike the regimented streets in the kingdom which were filled with tightly woven gray and red rock. She was used to tall buildings spanning several stories high, each one packed next to each other. Here, the space felt open and beautiful, with buildings large in width, each one designed with a colorful uniqueness to it. There was an unfamiliar sense of peace Evangeline didn't know could exist in such a cruel country.

In the distance, a shadow stepped out in front of her path. Evangeline's heart jolted. She gripped the reins, jerking the horse away when the shadow waved. It was Avana, the outline of her glamour still in place. How did she get so far ahead without a horse?

When Evangeline got close enough, Avana climbed the saddle and joined her, this time sitting behind her.

"You want to tell me what spitting *happened* back there? Where did you go? How could you leave me? How did you get here so fast?" The words tumbled from Evangeline's mouth, the horse resuming a steady trot.

The wind died down enough to where Avana kept her hood

back. "I am just as perplexed as you are. I wasn't expecting that, I'm sorry. I didn't mean to put you in danger."

"Those weren't ordinary bandits. Those were Casters." *And that creature . . .* She shuddered and turned her head enough to look at Avana. "You mean to tell me you have no idea why your kind, which rarely sets foot in Peredia, were waiting to ambush us outside the walls?" Evangeline shook her head. She didn't believe in coincidences.

Avana looked up, and Evangeline followed suit. A black bird hovered above them.

"The ruins aren't too far from here. We should be there soon," Avana said. "And I'm being honest when I say that I do not know why they're here or why they attacked us. As far as I am aware, I should be the only Caster in the area."

Aside from your brother, Evangeline thought with a tinge of guilt. It still didn't explain how Avana got here so fast.

The town wasn't as big as the kingdom, closer to the size of the castle grounds alone. They passed through quickly, the tall metal sign reading "Helgard" as they exited. Evangeline knew the name well, not because it was the name of Peredia's second king, but because it was common amongst the wagging tongues of humans. If she were to leave, this was where she and Lani would have to go. Her hopes soared. The town wasn't as far off as she'd originally thought. She and Lani may actually have a chance.

The farther they got from town, the more barren the land looked. Nothing but a thin layer of snow covered the ground, with clusters of dark trees in the distance.

Evangeline shifted, her entire body sore and tired from spent adrenaline and sitting in a saddle all night. Her limbs felt numb, but at least she couldn't feel the stinging in her palm anymore. "What was that charm you gave me?" she asked.

Avana surveyed the land in front of them as she spoke. "It was a spell that casts an illusionary blanket over its target and immediate surroundings. I don't have the ability or the time to cast a full-blown invisibility spell, so that was the best I could do. If I hadn't created a distraction, they would have eventually seen through the spell due to its reflective nature." Evangeline frowned, and Avana took notice. "Think of it as a mirror. From afar you blended in with the forest, but anyone close enough and talented enough could identify the slight shimmer and the distortion in the air around you. Hence, why we needed to separate so I could lead them away from you."

The more Evangeline thought about it, Avana had gone up against at least five Casters. And that was just from what she had seen. Her spine tingled at the thought that whoever Avana was, she was a lot more powerful and dangerous than Evangeline initially thought. Or at least good at escaping her captors.

"You're very . . . adept at what you do," Evangeline admitted.

Avana was silent, nothing but the wind rushing past them.

"I used to work for the Council back home," she finally said.

Evangeline kept her eyes ahead, but they bulged. She yearned to ask about Raiythlen, if he really was an assassin. If he worked for the Council as well. "But not anymore?" she asked instead.

"No." There was a growl behind her response. "We're here."

A lump of snow appeared in the middle of nowhere. Evangeline didn't remember the entrance to the ruins being so small, but it'd been years since she was last here.

They got off the horse. Avana tied the steed to a rusted iron sign with the words "no longer in service" written on it in old Peredian.

"I never knew what these ruins were used for," Evangeline thought aloud.

Avana tightened the strap and took the lead, entering the

curved stone entryway with steps carved out of rock, diving into inky blackness. "They're old subway tunnels. They used to transport people back and forth to places all over Peredia." Avana's voice echoed as darkness encompassed them. "Now, from my understanding, they're only used to ship goods in and out of the kingdom, but this one hasn't been occupied for quite some time."

Evangeline hugged close to Avana's back, watching her step down the ice-slicked path. It felt colder the deeper they went, and the old lighting used to illuminate the path, no longer worked. Focusing on not falling to her death, she only heard part of what Avana said. Subway tunnels? She'd never heard of such things being used in the kingdom.

Before Evangeline could question how they would see anything, Avana pulled out a necklace from beneath her coat with a small vial attached to it. She shook it, and a soft turquoise glow highlighted the faint outline of their surroundings.

The built-in stairs were uneven, sharp rock jutting out instead of a flat, even surface. The ceiling had collapsed in a few spots, forcing them to crawl and squeeze through several openings between layers of rock. Eventually, they made it to the bottom, their footsteps bouncing off the walls of what sounded like a large room.

"So, correct me if I'm wrong," Avana said, "but you were found here about fourteen years ago. The Aerian who found you claimed you had been wrapped up in a gown, one too large for a small child and finer than anything a normal human would be found wearing. Along with your strange marking, he assumed you belonged to someone in the castle which is when you began your life in the kingdom, right?"

Evangeline nodded. "I don't really remember that time, but that is what I've been told, yes."

Avana lifted her makeshift light and glanced around the cave. She gasped, and the soft glow around them darted off into the thick darkness. Evangeline squealed and immediately followed Avana, scared of anything else that could be lurking down here in the thick blackness.

"What is it?" she asked.

"I knew I could sense it, but it felt so different, unlike any of the others . . ." Avana mumbled to herself.

Evangeline was confused and said as much.

Avana turned, a wide smile on her lips. "You asked how I had gotten so far ahead of you. Well, you're looking at it." She waved her hand. "Not this particular one, but another like it."

Evangeline raised a brow.

"I don't expect you to understand, or anyone outside a small handful of people in the world. But essentially what's here is a portal."

Evangeline was skeptical. "A portal? To what? What do you mean?"

Avana beckoned her forward, and she walked closer when an immense pressure erupted out of nowhere, crushing her chest. The feeling was so uncomfortable that she stepped back from the safety of Avana's light until she could breathe easily again.

"Anali referred to these portals as Shadow Doors. Hundreds of years ago, based on what little she had written, these Shadow Doors were used as regular transportation. When entering one, your very being is condensed and transported to a connecting Door."

Evangeline would never have believed what she was hearing if she hadn't felt the odd pressure for herself. She didn't know if she believed it could transport her anywhere, but she did believe that it could condense someone. And by that, she meant kill them.

Avana wrung her hands. "This is amazing . . . Oh, Evangeline, you don't understand!"

Evangeline frowned. No, she really didn't.

"Shadow Doors . . . they have a distinct energy about them, but this one . . . This one isn't just absorbing the energy around it, but it's as if it's producing its own as well."

"Uh huh," Evangeline said.

Avana cleared her throat. "I'm sorry, I know none of this makes sense to you. Here, let me shine more light and see if you can recall anything."

Avana pricked her finger, drawing Castanian runes on several flat surfaces. Some walls, some on the ground, some in the far distance Evangeline couldn't see, and when Avana whispered beneath her breath, Evangeline recognized the Castanian word for "moon."

The marks glowed softly at first, then brightened to a dull gray, revealing the massive area around them. Equipment, built before Evangeline's time, lined the walls. She remembered seeing scraps of metal as a child, but now she recognized them as large pieces of machinery, though she didn't know what they'd been used for.

Avana continued to circle the area, and something tugged at Evangeline, pulling her toward the large sweeping hole at the back of the cave. It was a large intersecting tunnel, big enough to fit four horses inside and traveled pretty far on both ends. But what interested her was what laid across the drafty hole.

It was just a wall, but something picked at her conscience. A room was on the other side. She didn't know why she thought that, and it could be her mind imagining things, but something told her there was more to this cave than just rock.

Her mind buzzed, a low vibration in her ears, and a headache formed on both sides of her skull. Her face crumpled in pain, but she walked closer to the wall, her boots crunching against rocks as she bridged the gap of the tunnel. The humming got louder. The walls were shaking, rocks were tumbling. Someone was yelling at her.

Evangeline reached out, her hand touching the rigid surface. Static noise filtered through her ears, as the wall before her crumbled and bright lights blinded her, like she'd just walked outside into the unbarred sun.

"Are you sure about this, Anali?" Evangeline asked.

"No."

Anali stepped back and studied her own work. The spot in front of her shimmered, the surrounding air electrified and heavy with unseen power. The portal was far from ready, but Jaden left them no choice. They had to act now or live with the weight of a thousand souls on their shoulders.

Anali wiped her tears into the sleeve of her coat. "It's time."

"Soon, this will all be a dream." Evangeline embraced her, holding on tight, knowing this would be the last time.

Stepping back, Evangeline prepared herself for what was to become her destiny. She had fought for her place in this world, and consequently now ruled it. Cherished it. She would do everything in her power to protect it from Jaden, who wished to destroy it.

The presence of the portal swirled with a magnetic energy, like a looming burden, drawing her closer. She squeezed Anali's

hands, reluctant to let go when the small pebbles on the ground began to shake.

The two women shared a look of dismay when the ground beneath their feet trembled more violently. Anali blinked several times as dust showered the tops of their heads, the vibrations becoming louder, shaking the walls of the cavern.

"He's here! Go!" Anali shoved her toward the portal as a large boulder crashed between them.

"Anali!" She tried to scream, but it was lost in the vacuum of space that engulfed her.

A searing pain brought Evangeline back to reality, and it enveloped her, her body caving in. Her eyes were open, but she couldn't see anything, couldn't breathe. She clawed at her throat, as if something was wrapped around it. She tried to draw in a breath. But she couldn't. There was no air here. No oxygen.

Oh, Gods, her mind screamed, *I'm going to die!*

CHAPTER 28

ᴇ EVANGELINE ᴇ

"**E**vangeline! Evangeline!"

The voice was distant. So far away. Then something slammed into her back, and she gasped, drawing air back into her lungs.

"Evangeline, can you hear me?" Avana said next to her. Evangeline winced and nodded before coughing, cold air needling down her throat.

"I . . . I saw it. What happened here . . . Oh Gods, it's as if it just happened." Evangeline fisted her chest, looking around. She felt everything. Felt Anali's embrace, tasted the magic that covered her skin when she'd entered the portal, felt the fear and pain of something she couldn't remember. All she knew was that she couldn't fail. *Fail what?*

Evangeline repeated what she'd seen, claiming there was more beyond this wall. Avana trembled with excitement. At

least one of them was. Evangeline kept staring at the wall, then at her hands, and around the cave, as if expecting it all to disappear at any point.

"Step back," Avana said.

Drawing a large symbol on the wall in blood, Avana stepped away, turning both herself and Evangeline before whispering an incantation. A small explosion shook the cave. They covered their eyes as dust and debris rained down. Coughing, Evangeline wiped her eyes. A small opening appeared on the other side.

Avana didn't waste any time, stepping over jagged rock and ducking inside the tiny entrance. Evangeline stared at the hole for a fraction longer, shook her head, and followed her.

Darkness greeted them before Avana drew more symbols along the walls. Machinery lay scattered about, frozen in time. Avana brushed off as much dust as she could, but a lot of the equipment was rusted and inoperable.

Evangeline remembered the same pieces of machinery in her vision, not yet tarnished by time and abandonment. Anali had hovered over the large rectangular metal blocks, her fingers dancing across the buttons until words entered onto the black screen above it. Now, the same screen was cracked and frosted over, and if it hadn't been for her "vision," she never would have thought anything was there.

Her teeth chattered, and when she took a step, she swayed to the side, losing her balance. A part of her wasn't sure if she wasn't just imagining all of this. *None of this is making sense.*

"Is this a separate lab used by the Old Council?" Avana asked, but judging how she maneuvered around the room, analyzing every machine, Evangeline didn't think she was talking to her at all. "No, that doesn't make sense. It's too small, too well hidden."

Evangeline perused every crevice of the lab until she came across a desk in the far corner. She brushed through old papers that still lay on top, probably soaked in Caster magic to prevent them from falling to time. The ink was barely visible, and she could only make out formulas and equations.

Our desk, Evangeline said to herself, her fingers brushing the surface. Her focus then fell to the silver box on the floor beside it. "Avana, I think I found something that might be useful."

Avana ran to her side, her breathing heavy, expression as eager as a child with a new toy. She followed Evangeline's gaze, and she bent down to examine the small silver box.

"It requires a blood sample to unlock," Avana said, an edge of disappointment in her tone. "There's no way we'll be able to open it, unless we use the original owner's blood to unlock it."

Evangeline shook her head. "I think we can." Her heart pounded faster, and sticking out her index finger, she pressed it into the finger-sized hole. Something sharp pricked the tip, and with a mechanical turn and click, the door opened.

For a frozen moment, Avana stared at her. Evangeline's eyes remained on the safe. Inside it were a set of books and journals.

Avana was a blur beside her, almost pushing her over, as she reached for them with shaking hands.

Evangeline snarled, something primal and protective washing over her. *Those are mine!* She went to snatch them away when Avana choked on a sob. Evangeline's hands fell to her sides, and Avana began to cry.

"You don't know how much this means, what we found . . ." Avana stopped, her voice catching. "Oh, Evangeline, you don't know how much this means to me."

Evangeline still itched to snatch those journals. She *knew* they were connected to her, but staring at Avana's tear-soaked face, she was content to let her have this moment. She could always look at them later.

Avana wiped away her tears, smiling in embarrassment

before tucking the journals into her coat. She said it was in Castanian, that Evangeline wouldn't have been able to understand it anyway, and she would read and translate what she found when they returned to the castle. Evangeline nodded.

Scouring the rest of the cavern, Evangeline didn't experience another relapse or find anything else of value, so the two decided it best to leave while it was still dark. Evangeline dreaded going back into the Olaaga forest, but Avana reassured her that this time she was expecting company, and they would be fine. But Evangeline wasn't just afraid of the Casters, and she sensed Avana wasn't either.

Rather, it was the other thing that prowled in those trees.

They migrated the forest with ease, taking a different path than the first time. Although Evangeline was on edge, expecting to encounter more Casters or a six-legged monster, all she found were trees and other small rodents crawling through the forest.

When they returned to the kingdom's front gates, two guards came over, their weapons drawn, while another asked for identification. Avana pulled out her form with ease, a smile on her lips. The two guards kept their swords and spears out while their companion observed the document. They walked around the horse, searching through their bags, asking them to lift their arms. Tired and sore from riding, Evangeline scowled when the metal plated Aerian jabbed a finger into her ribs, checking to see if she had anything underneath her coat. Soon after, he gave them a nod and opened the gates, allowing them to pass through.

The streets were unusually quiet, even more so than when they'd left. The storm had died down, leaving behind a fresh layer of snow, and in the distance, was Lani's slave quarters, the underground windows almost fully covered by snow.

Avana stopped far enough away from Lani's window, which had a dull light flickering out from the frosted glass.

"This is where we part," she said, giving Evangeline a hand and helping her off the saddle. "As soon as I read through and decipher these journals, you will be the first to know what I find."

Evangeline nodded. "I still don't know if I believe in all this. I've always wanted to find out the truth, it's just . . ."

"This all seems crazy," Avana finished.

Evangeline rubbed her arms. "I'm sorry, it's just easier to believe that I'm insane. That all of this is in my head. That I'm sick."

Avana's eyes narrowed, a familiar intensity in them. "You're *not* sick, and you're most certainly *not* crazy." Her face softened. "A lot has happened today, a lot that both of us don't understand. If I wasn't raised with this information all my life, hadn't researched it and dedicated my life's purpose to it, I would have thought it was all a made-up fantasy, too. A bedtime story." She looked down, and the wind blew between them, shaking their coats. "Evangeline . . . thank you, for this. Truly. What we discovered tonight . . . I never could have done it on my own."

Evangeline shook her head. "No, I should thank you. I've been searching for answers all my life, and tonight, I learned a lot more than I thought I ever would." She still didn't know how everything was connected, but she was eager to find out what was in those journals, feeling that the truth lay within them.

Avana smiled and pulled something from her bag. "Here, as promised, four glamour potions." Evangeline took the vials. "They expire within six to seven days, so I would make them count."

Her chest swelled. "Thank you."

Avana nodded. "Get some rest. You deserve it." She lifted the reins, and the horse snickered. "Oh, and Evangeline?"

Evangeline turned.

"If you ever feel you're all alone in this world, come and find me. I will always be on your side."

Before Evangeline could find a proper response, Avana had flicked the reins, riding off into the cold night.

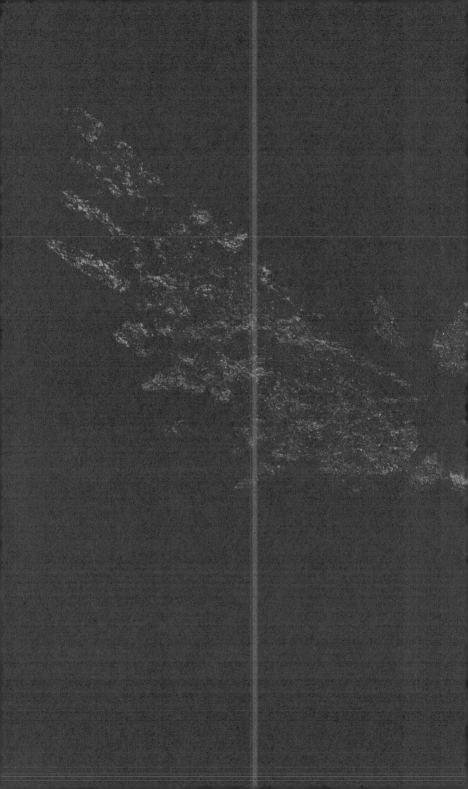

PART 3

To Cage A Beast

CHAPTER 29

❧ EVANGELINE ❧

Evangeline trailed through the castle, seeking the tower Anali told her Jaden would be in. She was still getting accustomed to living inside these stone and marble halls. It was too big; too vulnerable. She always thought she'd want all this, that she deserved it, but the sacrifices it took to get here . . . It wasn't worth it.

Evangeline paused in front of the tower, knocking before opening the door. "Jaden? Anali said you needed me?" Books and papers cluttered the room, and a chaise draped in clothes was thrown in the corner. It was the first part of the castle Jaden remodeled, fashioning it into his private study.

Evangeline walked a few steps when the door shut behind her and large arms found her waist.

"I always need you," Jaden whispered into her ear.

She laughed and turned around. Brushing the long, black

strands of hair, she stood up on her toes to peck his cheek, but he had other plans. He captured her mouth, his tongue delving into hers in a slow, sensuous assault, wreaking havoc on her train of thought. She sighed into his embrace and gave herself over to his pleasurable onslaught.

"Jaden," she scolded playfully when she broke away from his kiss.

He didn't let her go, dragging her over to the chaise instead, and sitting her down beside him.

"Eve." He caressed her face, his skin calloused from years of war.

Bright green eyes stared at her with such adoration and love that it made her heart melt. Before she knew what he was doing, he pulled a ring from the pocket of his trousers. Her eyes widened.

It was made of pure gold, but a wide spectrum of color shone brightly in the light, intertwined in the slender band. "Will you be my queen?" was etched on the inside of it.

Time passed slower than usual, prolonging. Her lips moved, but she was speechless. Those words were the equivalent to a lifetime bonded together as inseparable partners, ruling this world together, sharing each other's body and soul, powers and secrets. He was asking not only for her love, but her trust.

And it broke her heart.

"Of course." Evangeline smiled, but tears flowed from her face. Jaden kissed them away, mistaking them for tears of joy, unaware that she was crying for herself.

Not knowing that she would one day have to betray him.

Evangeline woke with a start, looking around frantically.

The fire had gone out, Lani's room cast in a faint glow from the morning sun. Her friend had already left, leaving the entire cot to Evangeline. Despite the lumpiness to it, she didn't want to get out of it. Her face mashed into the burlap pillow and she squeezed her eyes as another bout of pain struck her temple. Letting out a frustrated sigh, she sat up, holding her head.

Stray tears found their way down her cheeks, and she touched her lips.

Jaden.

Closing her eyes, she was back in his arms, feeling the weight of his kiss. The arms then became fingers, caressing her jawline, the heat of another's lips on hers as the black-haired man morphed into an Aerian prince with blue wings dipped in gold.

Evangeline's eyes flew open, and she swallowed.

The castle in her dream had looked nothing like the halls she walked through every day. *Asked to be queen by a beautiful man in a strange castle?* She scoffed. It had to have been a dream, but still . . . She licked her lips, but didn't taste iron. Then again . . . she didn't remember tasting blood in the ruins with Avana either.

The pain in her head grew, and her fingers massaged her temples.

After lying in bed awhile longer, Evangeline decided she couldn't procrastinate any longer. It was time to meet with Ryker. She was oddly calm about meeting him, as if everything that had happened last night was one foggy dream.

Still in her clothes from the trip, she changed into a simple blue dress, the sleeves cut long. She had slipped the glamour potions Avana gave her into the bottom of Lani's chest, tucking them between the folds of the clothes for safekeeping. Her hair was a mess of tangles, and she tried brushing through it but

gave up halfway, throwing it into a braid. *Presentable enough*, she thought as she tossed the brush back into the chest.

The castle was more alive than it had been the past two weeks. More slaves rushed back and forth, though it was past breakfast. There were also more Nytes.

Groups of Rathans and Aerians had gathered, dressing more provocatively than most Peredians. The women wore necklines that dipped to their navel, the skirts billowing outward but not as large as some other dresses Evangeline had seen. While most Peredian men displayed a healthy amount of their bare chests, these Nytes were practically naked. Wearing only a tunic fastened with one button and loose pants, hanging low on the hips. *Aren't they freezing?*

As Evangeline passed them, she recognized their Atiacan tongue. She understood most of it, but they spoke too fast for her to catch the entirety.

I hate balls. She grimaced. *It gets too blasted crowded.* The castle was going to be crazy for the next several days.

Before she headed to Ryker's, she swung toward the kitchens. Excitement pricked the back of her neck and heels. She had to tell Lani what she'd discovered. That the next town wasn't far from here and they could leave by the end of this week.

We could sneak out during the ball while most Nytes are distracted, she thought. *The guards will be more focused on what's happening inside the castle, not the borders. And it wouldn't be unusual to see two Nytes waltzing through the kingdom with the influx of guests. Even Raiythlen should be distracted enough by the surplus of Nytes not to notice us in the crowds. It'll be perfect.*

Today, steam billowed out the constantly swinging kitchen door, an influx of slaves hustling in and out with trays of food.

Hoots and hollers echoed as they all yelled over the clatter of plates and the clinking of utensils. Evangeline waited before slipping amongst the flow of humans into the hot, stagnant room.

Even though the kitchen was quite large, sweaty human bodies, colliding with one another, overcrowded it. It helped she stood a head taller than most humans. She peered over the sea of heads, but she couldn't find the one she was looking for.

"Have you seen Lani?" Evangeline asked, grabbing one woman who walked past her.

The woman gave her a wide-eyed look and shook her head furiously before scrambling away. Evangeline asked a few more people, but they shook their heads, all too eager to keep their space from her. Deflated, she assumed Lani was out on an errand of sorts.

Evangeline faced the door when an older woman with silver hair grabbed her arm.

At first, the woman didn't speak, just kept a tight grip on Evangeline's wrist. Her eyes looked glossy, her face tired from decades of constant labor.

"What?" Evangeline finally said, pulling on her arm.

The silver-haired woman turned, and although her expression hadn't changed, her eyes seemed sad, pitiful. "She's next."

Evangeline gave the woman a sideways glance. "What?"

The woman shook her head. "Delani . . . it's too late."

This time, Evangeline grasped what the woman was saying. Yanking her arm away, she retorted, "And how would you know? I saw her yesterday, she was fine." There was no way Lani could have gone missing in the night. She'd been there when Evangeline had gotten back and she slept beside her until morning.

The woman gave her a toothy smile, all three that remained. Evangeline turned on her heel and left the kitchen.

There's no way Lani was taken. She was fine yesterday. No markings. But it didn't stop Evangeline from pedaling through the halls, calling Lani's name, humans and Nytes scowling at her when she accidently bumped into them.

The sun streamed in through the windows as she raced down the hall, worry pinching at her face and dread pooling in her core. Maybe Lani was sick again and had returned to her room?

Evangeline changed direction when someone rammed into her shoulder.

"Hey!" she called, rubbing her side. She turned and glimpsed a black uniformed man stalking away. She would have brushed it off, but something about the human made her pause. He was far taller than most slaves, and his uniform fitted tightly to an athletic body. Not only was he well-fed but looked like a trained solider, a feat she found difficult to believe for any slave.

When he looked back at her, the blue eyes and condescending smirk immediately gave him away. Evangeline gritted her teeth. Of course, Raiythlen had to show up at the most inconvenient of times.

He beckoned her with one finger and turned the corner. Following him was the last thing she wanted to do right now, but he would find another way to corner her if she didn't.

Evangeline found Raiythlen leaning against the wall. His entire demeanor showed an aloofness Evangeline found envious. Lani often told her growing up that her face looked like it was set into a permanent scowl. She wondered where she got it from.

"I don't have a lot of information yet," Evangeline whispered.

He glanced around before taking her arm. Her first reaction was to jerk away, but his grip was gentle, his hands surprisingly smooth as he rolled the sleeve of her dress up. He took out a small blade and cut the tip of his finger before drawing on her forearm with his blood.

"What are you doing?" This time she yanked her arm away, but he snatched it back and held it firmly, smearing his blood into the shape of a circle with half a star drawn inside. He whispered in Castanian under his breath, and her skin tickled as the blood sank into her arm in the symbol's outline.

When he released her, she immediately rubbed and scratched at the small black Castanian tattoo, but it was branded on her skin. "What did you do to me?" she yelled, but he closed her mouth with his hand.

Stop yelling. It's not permanent. His voice echoed inside her mind, and she gripped her head, looking at him with wide eyes. *I didn't want anyone listening in on our conversation, but if you move too far from me, we will lose our connection.* He started walking away, waving for her to follow. *Stay close behind me, but not too close. I don't want to draw any suspicions.*

She didn't move.

He then said, *I know where Lani is.*

Evangeline cursed. Of course he knew. He knew everything. She followed a few paces behind him, and to anyone else, it looked like two complete strangers heading in the same direction.

Testing out this bizarre connection, she spoke inside her mind. *Where is Lani? And what did you do to me?*

It must have worked, because he responded with, *I opened a connection between our energies—or, as you Peredians call it, your soul, or spirit.* He took a sharp left, and she followed. *That symbol won't keep our connection open for long, so let me cut straight to the point—we have a very bad situation on our hands.*

You said you knew where Lani is, she said.

This has to do with Lani.

Evangeline froze in the middle of the hallway, staring at his moving back. When she started walking again, her pace became as frantic as her thoughts. *Tell me.*

The markings that you said were on the missing persons . . . well, I think I know what they are now.

Her pulse increased. *What do you mean? What does this have to do with Lani?* She wanted to run up and force him to take her to Lani now, to confirm that she was here, that she hadn't been taken.

That she was still safe.

You will see for yourself soon enough. Turn right into this storage room. I will be right behind you.

Evangeline huffed and turned down the slender hallway. She slid into a small room on the side, the air a pungent mix of dust and cleaning supplies as she squeezed next to the brooms and buckets.

When Raiythlen entered the space, Evangeline pressed flat against the wall, the room far too cramped for two people. One lamp above them lit the area as he closed the door behind him.

Are you okay? he asked, staring at her.

She took a deep breath, drawing in as much air as she could. *Some Nyte children locked me in a closet a couple years ago. I'll be fine.*

He looked like he didn't believe her but asked, *When will you see Ryker again?*

Her stomach clenched. She was supposed to be on her way to see him now. *Soon, why?*

Raiythlen slid his hand into the side of his shirt and pulled out a small vial. Inside the glass jar was a clear liquid. *You'll need this.*

She took it, shaking it before observing the contents. It looked like water.

You want to save Lani?

Evangeline narrowed her eyes at him, but she nodded.

Then you need to get Ryker to drink this, he said.

Her suspicions grew, and she re-evaluated the vial. *What is this?*

It's poison.

She almost dropped it in her surprise and shoved it back at him. *No, no way, I can't do that. I won't.* She despised Lord Ryker, but she didn't want to kill him. Not to mention she would be lucky to receive a quick, painless death if anyone ever found out.

It's not a lethal dose. It will only sedate him, make him unaware of his surroundings. He may even fall asleep. Raiythlen pushed the vial back at her. *We need this. I can't get close enough to do this, but you can. And when he's vulnerable, I can find out what they're planning. This is our best option.*

She gave him a stunned look. *What they're planning? You think Ryker is behind all this? The kidnappings, the disappearances?*

Not just Ryker, he continued, *but he is one of the big players in this.*

Ryker was a controlling, manipulative Aerian, but he was also logical, calculating, and reasonable. Orchestrating the potential murder of hundreds of innocent humans . . . it was unfathomable. Unreasonable.

Ranson's face flashed in her mind, his neck bent at an unnatural angle. The journal she had seen in Ryker's room with the list of names. The strange behavior and the increase in nights where he'd been absent from his suite. Her throat closed. All the evidence stared at her in the face. And yet she still didn't want to believe it. Didn't want to believe that the most obvious threat to Lani had been in front of her all along.

Evangeline shook her head. *How do you know this for certain?*

His eyes went unfocused for a moment, the pupils expanding. *You'll find out soon enough.* She went to ask how when he interrupted her. *We need to stop this, whatever he's planning. You don't understand . . .* He stopped and glanced at her mark.

What?

This is dark magic we are dealing with, magic that isn't supposed to exist. His eyes met hers, and she swore it was fear she saw in them. *It shouldn't be in Peredia's hands, or anyone's,* he continued. *It's why I need you to do this, Evangeline. I would do it on my own if I could, but . . . you have to do this.*

Dark magic?

Raiythlen nodded slowly but didn't indulge her further.

What does this have to with Lani? What's going on? The room was getting smaller and smaller, her panic getting higher and higher.

He looked at the vial in her hand. *Will you do it?*

She didn't even know if he was telling the truth, and he expected her to poison the only Aerian who was protecting her from the wrath of the entire kingdom? The wrath of the king? Of Vane?

No.

Raiythlen's lips pressed into a hard line, his jaw hard and clenched, but Evangeline didn't care if she disappointed him with her answer. If she followed through with his plan and it failed, he wouldn't have to face the consequences.

She tried to hand him the vial, but he kept his arms crossed, so she made it a point to place it on the floor between them. He didn't have to take it back, but she wouldn't carry it around.

Raiythlen's eyes narrowed. He didn't look happy. *Don't believe me?* he practically growled inside her head. *Fine. But before you write all this off as me playing another trick on you, go see Lani. Maybe that will convince you otherwise.*

Her stomach churned uncomfortably. And not from a lack of food. *Where is she?*

She's back in her room.

Squaring her shoulders, Evangeline brushed past him. Raiythlen reached out and touched her arm. An instant image of him holding a knife to her throat caused her to flinch, her hands flying to her neck. He frowned at the defensive gesture and dropped his arm.

I'm sorry, was all he said.

She didn't look at him as she left the small pantry.

CHAPTER 30

❧ EVANGELINE ❧

Raiythlen hadn't lied, to Evangeline's relief. The mark on her arm disappeared after she left him in a hurry.

She made it to the slave quarters where she bursted into her friend's room, her legs aching from running all the way from the castle. "Lani?"

Her friend was lying on the bed—she didn't move or respond. Fear tore at Evangeline's throat. She fell to her knees by the bed, shaking her shoulders. "Lani!"

Lani screamed.

Evangeline snapped her hand back. "What happened?" she whispered, not daring to touch her again.

"Leave," her friend croaked.

"Are you okay?"

Lani's entire body shook as she coughed, the hackneyed

sound turning into fits of anguished cries. "I'm not okay. Nothing is okay," she bit out.

Evangeline reached to console her, but Lani flinched away from her touch, and it hurt more than anything Ryker had ever done to her. "Please, tell me what's wrong?"

Her friend sat up, pain etched into her every movement. Her fingers shook violently as she struggled to unbutton her shirt. The fabric slid down her shoulders to reveal ripped, raw skin painted in black ink mixed with pools of fresh, seeping blood. Evangeline's hands flew to her mouth. A vicious sound tore from her at the horror of what she was seeing.

Lani's shoulders and entire torso were a labyrinth of language dipped in blood. The markings looked akin to something of Castanian origins, dark, rich symbols embedded into her skin, perverting her into a book made of flesh. There was one repeated symbol written within the lines of text that grabbed Evangeline's attention, like a knife thrusted into her gut with fate twisting the hilt of it deeper. It was the same symbol she'd grown up with all her life.

Her own mark.

It can't be...

No wonder everyone was terrified of her. Her brand had been seared into those who had disappeared without a trace, and now . . . now her worst fears had come to life.

Evangeline blinked, and the increasing pool of red around her friend snapped her out of the hazy panic. Lani was dying.

Springing into action, Evangeline ripped off her dress, shredding the expensive silk with her teeth. Lani didn't bother to push her away as she wrapped the pieces around her torso, the fabric soaking up the blood like a dirty rag. She hissed in pain when Evangeline double-knotted the ends to staunch the blood flow.

"Who did this to you?" Evangeline balled her hands to keep them from trembling. Trembling with rage. "I will kill them, I swear it."

Her laugh was hollow. Empty. Like she'd given up. "You can't kill your own father, Eve."

Evangeline shook her head. "What?"

Her friend stared at the concrete wall ahead of her. Her eyes were dead. She said nothing.

You'll find out soon enough, Raiythlen's words echoed in Evangeline's head. This was what he meant. "Ryker . . ." Her voice caught on the name. "Did Ryker do this to you?" She already knew the answer. She believed Raiythlen now, but she needed to hear it aloud. To make it real, because she desperately wanted to believe this was all a dream.

No, it was her worst nightmare.

"Yes."

The life slipped out of Evangeline at that single word, her eyes mirroring Lani's blank stare. Her arms fell to her side as she slumped to her knees, not caring about the small bits of rock that bit into her skin.

They both sat like that for a while. Not saying anything, not moving, just staring at nothing. As if they both could pretend none of this was happening, if only for a little.

"I need you to leave, Evangeline," Lani eventually said, her voice low and exhausted.

"No . . . I . . . I can fix this. I can help you. You need help."

"You want to know what he said to me?" she snapped. "He said that this was all *my* fault. That if I had just stayed away from you . . ." Evangeline flinched as Lani covered her face with her hands. "I've always loved you, but––" She choked on a sob. "But I wish I never met you. I . . . I need you to leave. . ."

Evangeline's nostrils flared. The ground blurred as her heart screamed, the pain of it overflowing.

I wish I never met you.

She couldn't form words. All her insecurities, her guilt weighed down her chest, like bricks, as she tried to breathe. *First Raiythlen and now Lord Ryker ... Lani has always been a target. Her pain, her suffering, all because of me.*

She sat in stunned silence as Lani's cries shattered off the walls of the small room. The sizzling of wood snapping from the fire was the only constant sound as the sun crept higher. The ray of light that touched Evangeline's cheek seemed fake and insincere. What she deserved was total darkness. To embrace oblivion.

When Evangeline closed her eyes, silent tears fell. "I needed you. I couldn't stand to be alone." She opened her eyes and fixed her gaze on Lani. "I know I've been selfish. I've put you in danger, and now I ..."

I can't fix this.

Evangeline wished her friend would look at her, would meet her eyes for just one moment, to tell her how much she meant that. Lani kept her face in her hands.

She clenched her fists, the skin tight across her knuckles. *I won't let it end like this. I won't let you disappear.* "I told you I'll get you out of here, and that's what I'll do. I won't leave you to die like this. To disappear and never come back."

Her friend responded with a whimper.

Evangeline stood. Lani was gravely injured, there was no way they could leave the kingdom now, even with them disguised in glamours. She couldn't ask Ceven, not with the risk of getting him involved in all of this. There was Avana, but she didn't know when she would see her again, and it would most likely be in Ryker's presence.

As much as she hated it, Raiythlen's offer was looking more reasonable. He needed her to drug Lord Ryker, and she considered it, not because of the pure satisfaction she would get from seeing Ryker helpless, but because at this rate, she was running out of time, and it was her best option.

The sun shined high in the sky now. It was surprising Ryker hadn't sent anyone to fetch her. Maybe he already had. Something that could only be described as a half snarl, half smile touched her lips. *I don't care if he sends Vane to come and get me,* she fumed. *I'm ready for it.*

Ready for a fight.

CHAPTER 31

ᴥ EVANGELINE ᴥ

Evangeline wiped the blood from her face and hands, changing from the torn and ruined dress into a rich crimson gown. The sleeves were long and tight, the fabric thick enough for her to wear a lighter cloak.

She turned to say something, but Lani rocked back and forth, exposed skin peeking out from under the blood-soaked fabric, and she lost the confidence. The best thing right now was for her to leave.

It took only two steps outside the slave quarters before Evangeline sank to her knees in the thick snow, letting the cold seep through the threads of her coat and dress. Snow pellets whirled around her, much like the swirl of disbelief and rage that danced in her mind. She knew she needed to get up, to confront Ryker . . . but the cold snow felt so nice. Like it could freeze everything that was happening in place.

Those markings . . . my marking . . . Lani is next . . . she's going to disappear . . . I couldn't save her . . . Her eyes were a blank slate as she stared at her shaking hands. They weren't shaking in shock, but more at the dark thoughts that lingered underneath.

I wonder how it would feel to sink a knife into Ryker's heart.

The sound of clicking hooves echoed in the distance. Across the white expanse, two mounted Peredian guards galloped toward her. Evangeline knew they were here for her. *I'm ready,* she told herself, not bothering to brush off the snow as she got to her feet.

"Lord Ryker sent us to fetch you, human," the male guard, with gray-and-white wings, said when they got closer. They got off their horses and approached her at a brisk pace.

The other, a Rathan who sported a thick white tail, reached for her. Without thinking, she backed away. He growled, and his hand flashed too fast for her to see and latched onto her upper arm. His nails ripped into her sleeve, cutting through the fabric to pierce her skin.

She hissed in pain and tried to shrug herself out of his grasp. "I can walk there myself."

"It's your bloody fault we're sent out in this Gods-forsaken weather to retrieve you like we're some lowly errand boys." His nails sank in harder, and she yelped. "So shut up and do as you're told."

He shoved her toward the horse. Evangeline didn't fall on her face, but saving herself that bit of dignity meant little when they tied her hands together. She jerked away, shouting in protest as they knotted the thick rope around her wrists, the cord cutting into her skin. She tested the tightness of it by stretching her hands and yanking, but it didn't budge. When they tied the rope to the back of the horse, her nostrils flared, and she tugged against her bindings.

"I told you I can walk myself!" she shouted, but they ignored her, climbing onto their horses. Fire unfurled in her veins. "You call yourselves guards. Nytes. But you're no better than us humans. In fact, you're less than that, you're absolute scum! Taking pleasure in belittling those you see below your station. I wonder how long you would last if you had to endure the life these people have. You probably wouldn't even last one day—"

Evangeline was jerked off her feet when the guards flicked the reins, the horses starting a steady trot. Like a leashed animal, they forced her to jog to keep from being dragged along the ground.

Her anger and frustrations rose as she climbed ever higher up the mountain path to the castle. Her throat was hoarse from screaming profanities at her two keepers, stopping only to save her breath and keep from fainting. The sharp rocks she passed would tear her body up if she slowed down or gave up altogether.

The guards dragged her through the main halls of the castle before shoving her onto the floor of Ryker's suite, hands still bound. Her face was brighter than the flames that churned in her stomach. Her teeth had scraped the inside of her cheek from all the slaps the two blasted guards had given her after she bit their fingers, spat on them and shouted more than a few protests.

Ryker loomed above her, waving the two guards away. He stared at her dispassionately, and she stared back, envisioning those pale, gray eyes widening in pain as she carved the same markings on Lani into his own skin. Something shifted out of the corner of her eye. Avana stood in the corner, her eyes fixed on Ryker's.

Evangeline maneuvered her bound hands and tried to get to her feet.

"Don't you dare move." Ryker's voice sliced through the silence.

Evangeline bit back all the nasty retorts she wanted to make. Instead, she kept her tone dull. Apathetic. "I know I'm late, I—"

"Don't speak to me, human."

Evangeline clenched her teeth so hard her jaw locked up. She must have really upset him this time. Good, because she was too.

Ryker leaned forward, his gray irises expanding. "Did you really think I wouldn't find out?"

Evangeline couldn't see past the sheen of red covering her vision, or hear beyond the sound of Lani's sobs.

"Avana told me everything. How you willingly went beyond the walls, about how you planned to escape again," Ryker continued. "You have deliberately disobeyed me for the last time."

Evangeline looked up, his words penetrating the red fog. *This isn't about me being late?* She narrowed in on Avana, and then it clicked. Her world spun. Black dots danced in her vision. The Caster didn't have the courage to look her in the eyes.

I'll always be on your side.

Liar. Liar. *Liar!*

"*I'm going to kill you!*" she screamed.

Red. Red. All she could see was red and flames, licking her all over, burning her. *Take it. Take it. Take it all and leave nothing,* her mind chanted over and over, something unfurling inside her.

"*I'm going to kill all of you! For what you've done to Lani! I'm going to—*"

Ryker struck her, knocking her to the floor. He towered over her, his voice dangerously low. "I think it's time you remember your place."

He went to grab her, but she jerked away from his

outstretched hand, getting on her feet. Her heart was racing, her joints ached and burned, but her mind disconnected from her body. All she felt was deep-seated hatred, the injustice of it all. No. She wouldn't let him take her to Gods-knew-where. Not when Lani's life was hanging by a thread, every moment closer and closer to it snapping. She needed to find Raiythlen, Ceven, anyone.

Evangeline turned and ran.

Behind her, wings flapped and rustled before a hand grasped her upper arm. The cage of his fingers ensnared her, and she thrust herself away. "Let me go!" She fisted her hands, swinging them at her captor.

Ryker captured her fists and held her in place as she continued to twist and turn. "You will stop this, Evangeline. You are acting like a child!"

Evangeline wasn't listening as she kicked her legs and threw her arms. *I have to escape. I can't let him trap me.* She bucked, and her knee slammed into his face. Ryker cursed, holding his bloody nose.

Avana's frame loomed behind Ryker, one hand out, her eyes wide. "Please, stop this, there has to be another way."

Ryker snarled at her, and Avana stepped back.

"I've had enough of this," he said.

He whipped Evangeline off her feet, and slapped her temple. She lost focus. Her legs tangled over one another as she collapsed to the floor. Ryker gripped her arm, dragging her down the hall while she struggled to get her balance, still fighting against his hold.

"Let me go," she slurred. "You can't do this. I have to go . . ."

"The only place you're going is a cage, like the beast you are." Ryker bared his teeth, his hand raised to strike when Avana held it back.

"Please, let me handle this," she said softly. Ryker stared at her for a moment before releasing his grip.

Evangeline's head slumped back, but her eyes burned at Avana. And yet, some small part of her prayed. Prayed that this was all a nightmare. That Avana would deny everything, tell Ryker she'd never left.

That Lani was going to be okay.

Instead, Avana popped open the vial in her hand, pouring sparkling bits of powdered dust into her palm. Without a hint of remorse, she blew the speckled stardust straight into Evangeline's face.

Evangeline's mouth closed around the word "stop" as blissful darkness consumed her.

CHAPTER 32

⚜ EVANGELINE ⚜

E vangeline woke up in darkness. The air smelled of mildew, and a pungent, foulness came and went.

She sat up and winced. Her back felt sore from lying on what had to be concrete or stone. Her eyes wavered frantically around, trying to find something in the blackness to help her identify where she was.

Nothing. Not even the tiniest fraction of light.

She threw out her hands, her fingers crawling across the floor, and came to a solid wall. Then another. And another. The air turned thick and breathing became a labored exercise. Gods, she was going to pass out.

"Hello?" she called. "Anyone?" Her voice bounced back at her, telling her how utterly alone she was. In the dark, surrounded by four walls.

Then metal screeched and a door slammed shut from farther

away, followed by footsteps. Evangeline tripped over her dress, scrambling in the sound's direction. She almost called for help when a familiar scratchy, high-pitched voice made the words clump together in her throat.

"Wakey, wakey, Evangeline. It's time for your dinner!"

Before she could crawl backwards, a small slit opened in front of her, blinding her with its sudden brightness. Her eyes adjusted, and she stared at a pair of brown eyes, the whites tinged with yellow, through the small opening.

"Oh, so glad to see that you're awake!"

Every muscle in her body locked up.

The slit closed, darkness taking over for an instant before the entire wall opened, revealing a hidden cell door. Light illuminated the surrounding space. The room was smaller than she'd thought, the floor and walls made of solid stone. There wasn't a bed, or any windows, just a small bucket in the corner and groove marks in the walls from whoever or whatever had been down here before her.

And in the light from the doorway stood Vane.

Dressed in a loose, blue top, tucked into a pair of black matte trousers, he looked like he had come from a party. His greasy and usually tangled brown mane was combed and slicked back, showcasing the uneven hair prickling his lower jawline and sideburns. But what really grabbed her attention was his belt. Light glinted off the sharp knives and daggers that hung there, promising Evangeline the pain to come.

"Did you miss me? Because I sure have missed you." His smile displayed his sharp teeth. "Didn't I tell you your luck would run out?"

Evangeline's throat closed, and sweat formed behind her nape, the curve of her back. She didn't respond.

Vane stepped into the room, and Evangeline fell into a

defensive gesture, one she had done repeatedly during her training. She bent her knees and planted her feet farther apart. Her arms were loose and close to her body, to help her navigate around her enemy. *It won't matter. He's far stronger than me and faster. I won't stand a chance.* Her bent knees trembled, her arms freezing up.

Vane's eyes slid down her, then snapped back up. "You think you can go against me?" he said, taking the time to crack every knuckle in both of his hands.

Evangeline still hadn't found her voice, but she kept her stance, though it felt like chains had been placed over her legs.

"You're just one little human girl who's had the extreme luck of being favored by our esteemed king's advisor—but let me show you something."

At one point, Vane was standing in front of her. Next, he became a blur of brown and blue rushing at her. He gripped her loose, knotted hair and yanked it. Tears sprang to her eyes, and she let out a pained yell, her hands fumbling to pull back her hair. Her legs swung at him, but he dodged her kicks. Her fingers pried at his in a losing battle as he pulled her up to where she rested on her tiptoes.

Hot breath smacked against her ear. "You are nothing in this world ruled by Nytes. A pathetic human like you has only dreamed of being something more. You have tasted greatness but will never achieve it."

He twisted her hair, and her leg kicked out again, this time her foot landing below his gut. He instantly released her and doubled over.

Evangeline didn't waste any time. Her limbs were liberated from her mental chains, and her freedom shined from the open cell door. White light cascaded on her face as she came into a narrow, concrete hall—right before her face met a metal-plated chest.

She bounced off the familiar black armor of a Royal Guard, his yellow wings branching out so fast that the wind whipped her hair back, the length of him trapping her. Her eyes met a stranger with rustic hair tied down his back.

Sharp nails bit into her shoulder, and Evangeline gasped as Vane came up behind her, his face red and splotchy. "You *little*—"

"Officer Jarr, her food," the Royal Guard said.

Evangeline hadn't noticed the small bag of food in the guard's hand until he handed it to Vane. He snatched it with one hand, sinking his fingers deeper into her shoulder, forcing her backward.

"No, wait!" she yelled, gaining her voice. She turned her desperate eyes on the Royal Guard. "Please, you have to let me go, there's been a big misunderstanding."

His expression remained placid as she fought against Vane, gripping onto the sides of the cell door with both of her arms and legs as he pulled her backward.

"Please! My friend's in danger, I have to help her!" But Vane cut her plea short when he dropped the bag and used both hands to yank her back into the cell. She fell and landed on her tailbone, pain vibrating up her spine.

Evangeline struggled to get back up when Vane punched her, the blow of his fist ramming into the side of her face. Her jaw made a *pop* before the nerves in her face splintered and caught fire. Her hands rose to protect her face as tears welled in her eyes.

"That'll teach you to stay quiet, you puss-filled human."

"Lord Ryker said no permanent damage," the Aerian spoke from the doorway.

He rolled his eyes. "I am well aware, Troy." He grabbed the

bag off the ground, shaking out the contents. Only a loaf of bread and a canister fell out. "Eat up, my dear, and I will see you again very soon," he said, licking his front tooth. "And next time I'll make sure we won't have company." He whispered the last bit to himself.

Evangeline cradled her face and shuddered.

Vane left and she was alone in the dark with a constant ache in her jaw. She slowly removed her hand from her face, reaching for the loaf. Her fingers dug into the bread, and a rush of rage surged in her. She tore it in half. Then tore it again. And again. Each time more aggressively, until only crumbs surrounded her. Still not satisfied, she picked up the canister and aimed it at the wall when something grabbed her wrist. Evangeline screamed until it turned into a pained yowl, her jaw thundering in pain.

"Shh, it's me," a deep, accented voice whispered beside her.

"Ra—" She winced. *What was Raiythlen doing here? How did he get inside?*

"Don't talk, it looks like your jaw is broken. Also, your Aerian guard is still outside the door."

She flinched when he rolled the sleeve of her dress up. His smooth fingers brushed her skin, leaving behind a tickling sensation she now associated with Caster magic.

Can you hear me? he said inside her mind.

Not this again. But she was more than grateful to have someone there with her, even if it was Raiythlen.

Would you rather try to speak with a broken jaw?

She exhaled through her nose. *No. How did you get in here? And how are you able to see? I thought only Rathans can see in the dark.*

He rustled against the ground, material sliding against concrete before the heat of his body pricked her skin. He was far closer than she felt comfortable with.

Close your eyes and stay still.

She did as she was told, which made little difference in terms of visibility. Something warm brushed against her eyelids, the soft whisper of a Castanian word.

There, he said.

Evangeline blinked a few times, just to believe what she was seeing was real. The room had turned into hushed tones of blue and light gray. She couldn't see the finer details of Raiythlen's face or clothes, but she saw the smile that twitched upon his lips.

I'll never get over how amazing Caster magic is, she said.

It comes at a cost.

She frowned and flinched at the shift in her face. His eyes softened, an expression she wasn't used to seeing on him.

I can take the pain away, he said.

No thanks, I don't need your pity. But as soon as she said it, she regretted it, feeling her face pulse with every heartbeat.

It's called empathy, not pity. It wasn't long ago that I stood where you are, and believe me, my situation was much, much worse.

Evangeline expected him to continue, but he didn't. She went to ask, but he interrupted her with, *you want my help or not?*

Her eyes strayed away from his, and she gave a small nod, knowing she was even more indebted to this infuriating Caster.

He pricked his finger, blood oozing from the tip before he brought it to her face. His finger brushed her tender jaw. Her skin vibrated where he touched her, and when he whispered a low incantation, her jaw became cold, almost numb.

It'll take a day or so, but it should heal, he said.

What did you whisper in Castanian just now?

Cold, soothe, hot, mend, heal.

She'd expected a beautiful flow of words, not a bunch of practical words strung together. She said as much.

He raised an eyebrow. *It's what I associate with healing. Most Casters proficient in healing would have used more biologically correct terms to better direct their magic, but I am only familiar with the basics.*

She was about to thank him but bit her tongue. *What do you want in return?*

He held up his hands in mock surrender. *Am I not allowed to be nice for once?*

Although her face felt a lot better, she knew any help from him would cost her. She crossed her arms, waiting.

He shrugged, leaning back on his arms, his outstretched legs encased in a dark material Evangeline guessed was leather.

Fine, I came here to offer you a proposition, he said.

There was a bite to her tone. *Oh, really?*

If you promise me your full cooperation and loyalty, I will personally make it my goal to get you and Lani out of this country.

Avana's betrayal was fresh in her mind. *You seriously expect me to believe you?*

He sat up, his expression serious. Evangeline didn't mock him any further.

Let me see your mark.

She tilted her head but slipped off the brown glove and placed her hand in his open one. He leaned over, a loose black curl dancing over his blue eyes. His touch was gentle as his thumb smoothed over her skin, the bold circle of her mark standing indignantly on her creamy flesh.

Lani has these same marks now.

The thought of Lani, alone and in pain, of her disappearing at any moment, made her claw at her throat. *I know.*

His eyes met hers. *You know what that means, right?*

Evangeline gritted her teeth. *I am well aware of how grave the situation is, okay? I know that means she's the next target, the next . . . victim. But I'm going to prevent that, I'm going to save her.*

He raised an eyebrow. *And how are you going to do that, locked up in here? Do you have an escape route? Even if you got around the first two things, Lani is far too weak and injured to do any traveling, let alone in the freezing tundra that is Peredia right now. You have no power, no resources, no—*

She tried to shout "shut up," but with her limp jaw it came out as, "Ahhh!"

A shuffle of feet had both of their heads turning toward the cell door, and Evangeline clamped her mouth shut.

The slit in the door opened, showing her the brown-and-red-haired Aerian peeking through the opening. Evangeline raised her hand at the sudden flood of light, and in a panic, she looked and found Raiythlen had disappeared.

The Aerian's eyes surveyed the room before giving her an unusual look. He closed the slit, and the room fell into dark gray and blue tones again.

Are you done having a fit now? Raiythlen said.

She jumped and spun. He sat behind her. *How do you always do that?*

He reached into the collar of his tunic and pulled out a silver chain necklace. A rune was carved into the small piece attached to it. *It's a small camouflage spell, allowing me to blend in with my environment. It's how I snuck in when Vane opened the door to your cell.*

Her eyes fixed on it, thinking of all the things she could do with that if she got her hands on it.

He saw the look in her eyes and shoved the necklace back into his shirt. *Don't get your hopes up. It's only activated through my blood.*

Her temporary fantasies dispersed. *Well, since you obviously know so much, what do you propose I do, then?*

When he pulled out a small vial containing the clear liquid, she knew exactly what he was about to ask of her.

Are you willing to try this again? He swirled the vial back and forth.

I still don't understand. Why me? she said. *Why would you bother saving Lani and me?* He could've threatened her to do his bidding. Again.

He leaned down, his hand sliding against her cheek. She jerked away from him.

Trust me, it's more for my benefit than yours.

She really didn't like the sound of that.

He straightened. *I told you before that dark magic is involved . . . but I didn't tell you the full story. Or why it's so important I have you on my side for this.*

She arched away from him and furrowed her brows.

Those markings . . . your mark . . . He paused for a moment, as if debating his words. *I know what they mean, why these people are being taken.*

Evangeline thought about Lani, the blood symbols. *Go on.*

Your mark . . . it's a brand, a form of dark magic created by my grandmother to control another individual.

She tossed his words around in her head. Avana told her that Anali had created her mark, but for it to control someone else . . .

It's a part of my family history, he continued. *One that I'm ashamed of, that no one should ever know. Especially not Avana. It's why I burned our grandmother's journals, why I didn't tell you until now.* His cold eyes met hers. *If you ever tell another soul about what I'm about to tell you, there would be no hesitation, no second chances. I would kill you.*

She smirked, the threat rolling off her shoulders. At this point, death would be a blessing. *My, I'm tickled that you trust me so much.*

Raiythlen's expression didn't change. *I don't. But I need you on my side, and for that you need to understand how bad the situation is.*

She sobered at that.

The symbol on your hand is another word for life. It forces a connection between you and another person, or multiple persons, but it's one-sided. He took a deep breath. *It was used to enslave people.*

Evangeline didn't move at first. Then she leaned back, staring at the gray wall behind his head. *I hate to break it to you, but we're all slaves already.*

Raiythlen scowled at her. *If you don't take me seriously and listen to what I'm saying, you won't be able to save Lani.*

Evangeline returned his expression. *I am listening.* But she wasn't taking him seriously. For all she knew he could be weaving her a tale. *Why would Anali create something like that? And why is it on me?*

Raiythlen sighed. *That . . . I don't know.*

Don't know or won't tell?

He didn't appear upset, almost thoughtful. *Choose what you want to believe, but the power behind your mark is very much real. And Ryker and whoever else is involved have found a way to pervert it.*

How?

His eyes slid down to her marked hand. *They are using it to drain people of their energy, their beings. For what purpose, I don't know, but I intend to find out.*

Evangeline didn't know if she believed him. Draining people's energy? Her mark was a glorified slave symbol? *Whether you're telling the truth, I couldn't care less. All I want is to get Lani out of here.*

I understand that, but this is bigger than Lani. If they can somehow channel that much energy . . . He paused and rubbed his chin. *If we use Lani as bait, we could track down where these people are being taken and stop this.*

She snarled. *You're a bastard.*

Raiythlen gave her a blank stare. *No, I am being practical.* He handed her the vial. *I'm going to assume that you now believe that Ryker is involved. All you need to do is give him this, and I will take care of the rest.*

Evangeline stared at the vial, thinking. She had no other evidence to go on, or any other current means to help Lani. But she did believe Ryker was involved, and if this got Lani and herself out of the kingdom, she would do it.

She tried to grab the vial, but he lifted it out of her reach. *But you have to do this right before the ball and not a second earlier, are we clear?*

Her eyebrows furrowed. *Why?*

Your full cooperation is required, and that doesn't include room for questions, Evangeline.

This man could irritate even the most patient of people. He handed her the vial, and she tucked it into the top of her bodice. *And then what? How would we escape?*

I will make arrangements for you to attend the ball after the deed is done. Once you're there, only then will I tell you the plan. He appeared torn, as if there was more he wanted to say.

What? she asked.

He looked at her. *I need you to be careful. There's been some suspicious activity in the castle this past week.*

More so than usual? Sarcasm laced her tone.

The kingdom of Peredia is known for having the largest population of human slaves, but based on my research, there hasn't been a recent shipping or influx of new humans in almost two months, and yet the number of slaves I have seen has doubled.

Evangeline did find that odd, but not overly unusual. It wasn't humans she feared. *So?*

So, I believe there are other spies amongst us, hiding in plain sight. And I am positive that one of them, if not more, are following you.

That made her skin crawl. She thought back to the Caster inside Ryker's suite, to the ambush outside of the castle. Maybe the two were connected? But if they weren't working for Raiythlen or Avana, then who? *What makes you think they're following me?*

There have been footsteps outside Lani's window, fresh prints, nearly every night. But every time I try to catch them, they are just out of my grasp, as if they know I am watching you as well.

The idea of someone staring at her in the middle of the night through Lani's window, while she slept, while she changed . . . It didn't sit well with her. *How do you know all of this?* He always seemed to have a wealth of impossible knowledge.

He clicked his tongue, and tiny feet scratched against the concrete floor. She turned her head and a small mouse skittered past her. She shied away from the rodent, her toes curling as the mouse found its way into Raiythlen's open palm on the ground.

I have my ways, was all he said.

Evangeline thought to Avana and her raven. She didn't think Raiythlen's fondness for mice was a coincidence.

Now, I think it's best you get some sleep. And tomorrow, try to eat your food instead of destroying it. You're going to need your energy.

She wanted to argue, but he sidled next to her, his hand brushing hers, stunning her into silence.

Sleep, Evangeline. I'll be here with you, don't worry. He raised his hand and puckered his lips.

She knew what would happen, but turned her head too late. The blast of dust pegged her face, drawing her eyes closed. The last thing she felt was Raiythlen's arms around her as she sagged backward into a deep sleep.

CHAPTER 33

⟨⟩ EVANGELINE ⟨⟩

Evangeline's cheek rested against a pillow that was both hard and soft, but warm like a bonfire on a snowy night. Then someone shook her shoulder.

"What?" she groaned, temporarily forgetting where she was and what had happened. Wiping away the drool on her mouth, she blinked and noticed that her "pillow" had been Raiythlen's chest. Color rose in her cheeks, and she sat up, putting space between the two of them.

"Vane's coming," he said. "I have to leave now."

Evangeline took in a shaky breath but nodded, trying to swallow the fear that crawled up her throat.

Raiythlen looked at her. "I'll see what I can do to help you, but I can't promise anything. You need to stay strong."

"I know," she bit out, rubbing her jaw. The pain was a dull throb, but at least she could now speak normally.

"Focus on your anger. Don't give him what he wants."

Footsteps stopped outside the door. *Oh Gods, help me.* She clenched her hands, and the door opened. Vane wore a high-collared purple military uniform, the golden insignia blazing like a beacon in the bright light.

"I'm back, darling!" Vane looked at the floor, the crumbs of bread scattered about, and his nose scrunched. "Look at you, you've made such a mess!"

He walked toward her, the hard-shriveled pieces crunching beneath the weight of his boots. They paused in front of her face, and before her eyes could trail up to meet his, he grabbed her head, shoving it to the floor. The pressure against her jaw made tears well up, but she squeezed her eyes shut to prevent them from spilling.

"I wouldn't want to waste such food." He pressed down harder, and she squirmed. "I expect you to eat every single crumb off this floor."

He released her and kicked a larger piece of bread toward her.

"Eat it."

Wanting to shove it down his throat, she inhaled a deep breath through her nose. She had to pick her battles. She reached to grab it when Vane's boot stomped on her hand. Her fingers pulsed in pain as she sucked in a sharp breath.

"Animals don't eat with their hands, silly!" Vane crouched beside her, his murky, disgusting eyes peering down at her. "Now, eat it."

I'm going to kill him. She imagined slamming into him, taking one of the shiny daggers at his belt and shoving the tip deep into his throat.

She focused on the piece of bread a foot away from her. It looked as hard as a rock, but still relatively clean, at least. Biting

her tongue hard enough to taste blood, she forced herself to lean down and pick up the piece with her teeth, barely chewing it before swallowing.

Vane leaned back and laughed. "By the Gods, I didn't think you'd do it! To think Ryker's pet would turn out to be such a good pet indeed!"

Watching the spit fly from his mouth, his lip bent back in a permanent snarl, Evangeline almost pitied him. *His sense of humor must be horrible at parties.*

She didn't have time to smirk at her own joke when he yanked her hair up, forcing her eyes to meet his. Something in the way he looked at her made her twitch. Want to do something, anything besides sit there, staring back at him.

Focus on your anger. Don't give him what he wants.

Vane wanted her to cower, to cry for help. She wouldn't give him the satisfaction. But when his lips curled into a sadistic smile, his hands catching the hilt of a dagger at his belt, she realized just how hard that was going to be.

He bent down, the cold, sharp edge of his blade touching her cheek. His expression was one of distorted adoration. A twisted sense of happiness that hinged on the pain she would have to endure. She closed her eyes and inhaled, her nostrils flaring. *Focus on your anger.*

"I wonder how you will scream." The blade pressed down harder. Her next breath came in a little faster. "Will you break quickly? Or will you give me a show of courage, right before you realize it's useless?" He leaned in closer, his head even with his blade at her cheek. "Will you be the silent type? Or will you let the whole world hear your pain?"

His hand twitched, and the blade nicked her skin. She hissed through clenched teeth, blood welling up from the cut.

He sighed. "I hope you're one of the loud ones. It's the best music in the world." His irises faded, leaving only black holes. "So raw, and beautiful."

His throat was so close. Her eyes flicked to the blade. and something primal shifted beneath her skin.

Take it. Take it. Take it all and leave nothing.

"I wonder if you'd think the same if it was your own pain and suffering you were hearing," she spat, almost feeling the way his skin would open up like soft butter as she turned his knife back at him.

The blade slid down her cheek, the razor tip of it tugging at her exposed skin as he brought it down to her neck and across her collarbone. "But we're not talking about me," he said, flicking his wrist.

She hissed again when the tip grazed her, the cut so fine that it looked like red thread dancing across her chest. She took another deep breath. *Stay calm.*

His hand, still ensnared in her hair, jerked her head up by her roots. She winced and tried to untangle herself from his grasp. His blade came down on her hand, the steel shredding the tender skin between her pointer and middle finger, down the length to her thumb. She yelped, yanking her hand back, blood slicking it and her dress where she nestled it.

"Tsk, tsk, you need to learn to keep your hands to yourself. If you want to keep them, that is," he purred.

The familiar haze of red washed over her. "You *bastard!*" she snarled.

"Oh my, such language!"

He shoved the blade into her mouth.

The thin edge lacerated her tongue, which instinctually tried to push the blade out, the inside wall of her cheek taking the brunt of it. She choked on the gush of blood, gargling on her yowl of pain. He pulled the dagger back out, slicing the corner of her mouth, and licked his lips, as if he could taste her suffering.

Blood dripped down her chin, and she convulsed, lashing her legs out at him. He readjusted his grip, ripping out strands of her hair before digging his fingers into her scalp.

Stay calm, stay calm, stay calm. But she wasn't calm. She was scared. So scared.

His nails dug further, and scarlet dribbled down her chin, fire licking her lips as she tried to say, "Stop!"

"What was that? I couldn't hear you. You're going to have to speak louder!" His eyes were wide, his mouth turned up into a sharpened smile. He looked crazy. Insane.

His blade came down again, cutting through the fabric of her dress, imbedding itself into the inner curve of her elbow. She jerked, the cut stinging more as she tried to escape, but his hand was like melted steel to her head, pulling her closer to her demise. It wasn't until she swiped at his face that she gave him what he wanted.

The blade came down on her hand again, digging further into the pre-made incision between her fingers.

She screamed.

Vane roared in laughter, bringing her head along when he leaned back, his body shaking from the force of it. An agonized half-cry, half-scream left her again as blood splattered in uneven circles on the stone ground below her, her hand making prints alongside it where she held herself up against his grip. Her vision blurred with tears and spit flew from his mouth as he laughed. This time she couldn't muster a single ounce of humor.

Vane's gaze turned back to her. Her eyes slid closed.

I'm sorry, Raiythlen. I'm not that strong.

She could almost feel his shadow brush her skin as he reached for her once more, when Troy called out, "Officer Jarr, they need you in the circle room." Her eyes flew open, and she looked at the Aerian guard. He cast a quick glance her way, frowning. "Something has come up."

A soft bubble of laughter came from her. She clung to his voice, like an offered hand amid a raging sea.

"*Something* has come up?" Vane released her, throwing up his hands. The room spun. "There's always *something!*"

Vane stood and shot her a glare. Still on the ground, not bothering to wipe away the blood and drool that slid down her chin, she gave him a small, triumphant smile.

His eyes narrowed. "You look awfully smitten for someone who's just had a taste of their own hell." He bared his teeth into a half-hearted smile. "I'll have to rectify that when I get back."

The smile vanished from her face.

"Give her the blasted food. I'll be back," Vane said before storming out.

Evangeline cried in relief, and the Royal Guard set down another bag of food. He inspected her ripped dress, the red smears that graced her face, her body.

"I'm sorry," was what he left her with as he closed the door behind him.

She stared at the bag. Raiythlen's magic allowed her to see its outline, but the spell was fading. Blues and light grays were now closer to dark gray and black. Using her uninjured hand, she crawled toward the paper bag. She didn't realize how much she was shaking until she reached out and grabbed it. Her hand throbbed in rhythm with her face, her jaw, her arm. It was an effort to keep her lips from trembling as a hysterical sob tickled the back of her throat.

Feeling around in the bag, she pulled out an apple along with another canister. The other canister rested by the door and she grabbed that as well. Raiythlen was right, she needed to conserve her energy.

She hiccupped, a small cry hitting her in the chest, as her mind flashed with a scene of Vane returning. Did it matter if she ate? Maybe it would be better if she starved herself to death. Maybe it'd be more painless than being another one of Vane's victims. Who knew how long Ryker would keep her down here at his expense . . . if he would ever let her out.

Her good hand grabbed weakly at the canister, her cheek stinging where her tears mixed with the cut. *I can't think like that. I have to focus on staying alive. For Lani.*

Refusing to think any more morbid thoughts, she took a swig from the canister. A blast of citrus had her coughing, spitting some liquid back out. Her tongue roved over the inside of her cheeks, wincing at the loose skin there. Her mouth burned. The flavor hadn't been bad, but she'd expected water. What had they put in this?

She licked her lips, absorbing the citrus liquid on them. A sharp hunger in her overrode all other thoughts. The sweet, tangy drink made her stomach gurgle in anticipation and she took another sip. It was good. So good, she drank the entire canister.

Craving more, her fingers curled around the top of the other one, not feeling the bite of the wound on her hand. Her fingers slipped on her own blood until she pried it open, polishing off that canister as well.

Evangeline shook both canisters to make sure they were empty. She was thirstier than she'd thought. Her hands slid back against the solid ground, feeling full and comfortably warm. Her eyes glided halfway shut, her breaths coming in slow and deep. She could've still been bleeding, but she felt no pain, almost a blissful sense of peace. Almost.

A loud, disturbing gurgling came from her stomach, and she gripped it. "Oh no," she said, her insides bubbling. Had she drunk too fast?

Suddenly, her stomach—no, her entire body—cramped up, spasming and contracting. The pores of her skin expanded, oozing sweat that dripped down her body. In a matter of seconds, it soaked her dress, and the cold and damp room was too hot. Her hands tore at her dress, ripping the fabric.

Don't take them!

Evangeline felt something move inside her, her bones shifting. Her vocals stretched, and she tried to scream, but nothing came out.

Please! They're just children!

They're killers, Anali.

Stop. Stop. Somebody make this stop. Please. Stop.

You're going to regret this, all of you!

Evangeline's eyes stretched wide. Red veins slithered beneath her eyeballs. Itching. Demanding. Seeing ghosts, images that she knew weren't there. But they were. They had to be real, right? Because if they weren't, that meant she was . . .

Insane.

You and I are the same. We belong together, and together we will create a place we can call home. But sacrifices have to be made.

"Stop! Stop! Stop!" Her fingers dug into her neck, trying to relieve the invisible pressure there, but it wasn't going away. Nothing was going away. Why wouldn't it stop?

The door to the cell opened, but Evangeline barely noticed, her body shaking, convulsing, vibrating faster than she could keep up with. Her Aerian guard shouted at her, but the words were a muddled mess, quiet compared to the blood rushing and pounding against the inner walls of her skull.

Then hands were on her, and the very touch seared her skin.

She screamed. *"Stop! Stop!"* Her throat was raw, her entire body was raw.

Darkness swallowed her.

CHAPTER 34

✣ EVANGELINE ✣

"Evangeline? Can you hear me?"

Evangeline stirred, and her eyelids peeled open. An Aerian stood before her, hair long and so fair that it looked translucent. Powder-blue and gray wings hung behind him, the muscles tense. Ready to attack.

A soft crunch echoed to her left, like small stones crumbling beneath the sole of a boot. Her pupils expanded. Somebody else was in the room.

Keeping her eyes on the Aerian, she moved every muscle in her body with a languid precision until she peered over the white man's wings. She whipped her head and pinned her gaze on the other Nyte in the room. A purr of satisfaction ran through her when the Caster woman flinched, the pulse at her neck pounding beneath her black curtain of hair.

"Evangeline . . .?" the Aerian said.

With her head facing the Caster woman, Evangeline's eyes slid to the man. Her mouth watered, and her stomach clenched in preparation.

Take it. Take it. Take it all and leave nothing.

Her senses expanded, taking him in. The smell of silk mixed with lilac and vanilla with the soft undertone of something sour.

Fear.

Her lips stretched over her teeth into a prolonged smile.

The man took a step back. "Evangeline, it's me, Ryker."

She stared at him. He blurred out of focus, and a shooting pain sliced through her. She hissed, clutching her head. "Ry . . . ker?" Everything spun and her limbs felt like they were treading water. "What's going on?" Avana stood across the room, her eyes reflecting Evangeline's own confusion. "What happened?"

Neither Avana nor Ryker said anything.

Evangeline remembered the pain, the fire she'd experienced, as if it had tried to incinerate her entire being. Her eyes widened. "What happened to me?"

Ryker's back straightened, his voice coiling around her. Commanding. "Get up."

Evangeline didn't bother refusing, though she had a hard time getting her legs to cooperate. Her whole body was sore. Sleeping on the ground shouldn't have been that rough on her.

Avana reached out to help, but Evangeline ignored her, using the wall as leverage. The Caster frowned but said nothing and Evangeline followed her and Ryker out of her cell.

The bright overhead light of the hallway blinded Evangeline. Squinting, she turned, and her stomach twisted. Vane was lying on the ground, still. Purple and blue hues decorated his face, his nose a bloodied mess.

She looked down at herself, at her ripped dress, the smears of blood on the front of it—but not a single cut or bruise on her body. Her tongue licked the inside of her mouth. Nothing. *But how . . .?*

Ryker walked past Vane without batting an eye. She wanted to ask what happened to him but didn't dare speak.

They walked down the long, narrow hallway, concrete surrounding them on all sides. When they reached the winding stone staircase, climbing upwards, Evangeline learned she was far below the east wing, farther than when Vane had first dragged her down here.

Trekking up the flights of stairs to the surface, Evangeline felt like a prisoner being herded off to her execution. It didn't help that it was silent the entire walk back to Ryker's suite, an ominous tension permeating the air.

When they entered Ryker's suite, he slipped out of his coat, curtly telling Evangeline to wash up and change. Grateful to wipe the dirt and grime from herself, she walked toward the bathing room, hiding Raiythlen's vial—which she was glad to find still intact—in her clothing folds until she could sneak it into the bodice of her new dress.

Once Evangeline was clean, Ryker ordered her to stand by the table. A familiar collection of tonics, potions, and shiny needles filled its surface. Evangeline dragged her feet, not bothering to say anything. There wasn't any point.

She was done begging.

She was done fighting.

She had no choice but to bide her time. Wait and see her options.

"Your arm, please, Eve," Avana said, gloves on, with a vial in hand.

My name's Evangeline, she didn't bother saying. It was petty, but she wanted nothing more than to wring Avana's neck. She should've known she'd turn out like her brother. In the end, all Nytes were the same.

Evangeline put out her arm, keeping her eyes down on the marble. She remained indifferent, which wasn't too hard. At this point she was just . . . tired.

Rather than pouring liquids over her mark, Avana withdrew her blood, poking her with the needles neatly lined up on the red cloth. Evangeline didn't flinch when Avana stabbed the needle into her skin, the blood thick and vivid as it whirled into the translucent tube. Avana wiped Evangeline's arm. She performed this task several more times, all the while trying to make eye contact, but Evangeline was having none of it.

Ryker left and the click of the front door broke the tension in the quiet room. Avana's hand tightened on Evangeline's arm, and her voice was a rushed, excited whisper.

"I read the journal. I think I know what happened, with Anali, with you."

Evangeline didn't look away from the ground. She didn't smile or give the Caster the tiniest bit of acknowledgement.

Avana's face fell. "Eve, I'm so sorry this all happened. He already *knew*. About everything. He had planned all of this from the start . . . please, you have to believe me."

You're wasting your breath, Evangeline mulled, trying not to wipe the Caster's hand away from her arm. She wished Avana would stop touching her and leave her alone.

Another click of the front door rang throughout the suite. Ryker had returned with what sounded like an entourage of guards, judging by the sheer clattering of metal.

Panic rushed Avana's words. "The ball is in four days. Meet me there and I'll tell you everything you should rightfully know."

"Avana."

The Caster flipped her head toward Ryker, hiding her irritation under a placid smile.

"I hope you have gotten the samples you need?" he said.

"Yes, my lord."

Ryker nodded and gestured the guards toward Evangeline. They encircled her. Her heart squeezed, her body screaming to run, to fight, but she forced herself to keep calm, even as Ryker told them to return her to the cell. She would wait this out, wait for an opportunity. Raiythlen could end up betraying her like Avana, but it was a better alternative than her, an untrained, uncoordinated human, going against Lord Ryker and the Peredian military alone.

So, when she was once again face-to-face with her dark, small, damp cell, she embraced the fear, the rage, and the impatience, knowing it was a necessary evil. A stepping stone to getting out of there once and for all.

And to save Lani from being the next missing person.

CHAPTER 35

⚺ CEVEN ⚺

"**A**re you sure she's down here?" Barto asked, his leather-soled boots gliding across the stairs leading down into the prison cells below the east wing.

Ceven clenched his jaw. "Yes." He focused on the concrete hall ahead, his body coiled tight. He sensed Barto's gaze and knew what he was thinking: they're getting involved in something that will have serious consequences. But Ceven didn't care. Ryker had gone too far.

As they slipped down the first flight of stairs, Ceven's skin prickled, his ears twitching at the sound of rats skittering across the ground, the smell of water that had been still for far too long. He imagined Evangeline down here alone, sitting in one of these cells, and he growled low. He'd make Lord Ryker pay for this.

"Xilo said a Royal Guard member was assigned to block 18

on the sixth floor below. She should be there," he said, trailing down the circular stone steps.

"It'd be nice if he could've led the way." Barto's tail twitched, a bit of snark in his tone.

"I told you, I don't want to involve them." Ceven admired Barto's views, his almost naïve perspective on the world. But this was Peredia, where law and honor were held above all else. What he was about to do would defy an integral part of what made a guard a Royal Guard. Going directly against the king's orders.

"They've been serving you all your life, have kept your secrets, more than I even know about you, and you still don't trust them? By Goddess, Ceven, I thought I had issues."

Ceven hissed at him. "They serve me, but they first serve the king."

"So, you're assuming they feel the same way instead of asking them?"

Ceven shook his head. "I don't have to assume. It's how it is here. The Royal Guard is about loyalty and honor—to the king and queen of Peredia. I'm just a prince, and a bastard at that."

"Well, we could've at least brought Rasha or Quan," he mumbled.

They both knew he was only pouting. Ceven hadn't even wanted Barto there, knowing that involving him, an Atiacan emissary, in breaking Peredian law would only end badly for both of them. But Ceven was selfish. He knew he wouldn't be able to take on two guards by himself, let alone Royal Guards. He may be strong, but he wasn't invincible.

They made it to the sixth floor, greeted with a long stretch of hallway, a faint light creeping from farther down. They were far beneath the castle. All signs of life, absent. And Evangeline was down here, behind one of these cells. He bared his teeth.

"You could be king, you know. One day," Barto said, breaking him from his thoughts.

Ceven paused and looked at him. Barto's eyes drifted up to meet his before they darted away.

"I'll never be king, and I am perfectly okay with that."

"Even if Sehn turns out to be worse than your father?" Barto said.

Ceven didn't have time to respond when muffled crying drifted down the hall. He whipped his head toward Barto.

"Evangeline," they both said, and sprinted.

With his pupils dilated, Ceven skimmed the outline of a Royal Guard with yellow wings in the distance as his legs bounded forward with ease. The guard had his sword drawn before they were close to the metal cell door.

"Stand down," Ceven said. The Aerian didn't drop his blade.

"That's your prince you're aiming your weapon at," Barto snarled.

The guard reluctantly sheathed his blade, but his hand remained on the hilt, a shielded look of disgust in his eyes. "No one is supposed to be down here, Your Highness."

"Well, I am. Open that door."

The Royal Guard shook his head. "I have orders from the king that nobody is allowed past this door. Including you."

Barto let out a low whistle, stretching his fingers. "Well, ain't that a shame."

Ceven reached for the hilt of his own blade.

"Please, Your Highness, I don't want to fight you, but I would fail my duty to the crown if I allow you two to pass."

A loud wail came from behind the cell door, and Ceven reacted immediately. He drew his blade, the tip aimed at the guard's throat. "Open. The. Door."

The guard remained still, Ceven's blade brushing his throat.

It wasn't until Barto's ear flicked backward that Ceven glanced down the hall. Something was going on here.

The air shifted when Barto shouted, "Duck!" A small dart, the size of his pinkie, whizzed past him, bouncing off the wall.

The yellow-winged guard pulled out—not his blade—but a fistful of something that wouldn't bode well for them. Before Ceven could move, Barto leaped on the guard's back, his fingers morphing into claws, his nails sinking into the thin rings of metal along the sides of the Aerian's armor. The guard roared and shoved himself backward, slamming Barto into the concrete wall. He wheezed but held on as the guard reached behind to pull him off. Ceven leaned down, his sword prepped to sweep the Aerian off his feet, when two other figures emerged from the darkness. There hadn't been one Royal Guard, but three.

Ryker knew this would happen. This is an ambush. He cursed.

A Royal Guard with a dark creamy complexion landed behind Ceven before he could turn around, shoving a cloth sack over his head, while the yellow-winged guard slammed his back against the wall again, knocking Barto's skull into stone. His friend's grip loosened, and the guard flipped him over his shoulder, launching him to the ground with his right arm trapped in a death grip.

Ceven struggled to see through the threads of the sack cloth as the guard wrapped a string around his neck, cutting off his oxygen. He clawed at the string, gasping in a ball of air before slamming his elbow into the man behind him. *Crack!* The tightness around his neck disappeared. He whipped off the sack and whirled around, planting a firm kick in the guard's torso. The Aerian's neck snapped to his chest as he flew backward.

Something whistled, and Ceven jumped back when another dart flew past him. His eyes found the other Royal Guard, slinking back, metal pipe in his hand. Ceven drew his sword, his eyes focused on him when the yellow-winged guard said, "Don't move."

He aimed a blade at his friend's throat.

"Drop your weapon." The guard's blade was inches from skewering Barto, but his eyes fixated on Ceven's.

Ceven didn't move. He looked at Barto, then back at the guard, and sensed the other two guards stalking closer behind him. Barto met his eyes, and a smile brushed his lips. Ceven knew it took more than that to keep his feline friend down, but before Barto made his move, the Aerian dropped to the ground with a loud clash of metal.

Ceven spun as the guard behind him fell too, the heavily muscled flesh smacking the ground.

"I'm disappointed you believe Tarry and I are that ignorant." Xilo walked closer into their line of sight, his long black-and-gray hair braided, his hands also holding a small, slender pipe. He stopped by the guards' bodies, pulling out the darts that had lodged themselves into the sides of their necks.

Tarry wasn't too far behind him, like Xilo, dressed in a black undershirt and trousers. In his hand was a crumpled piece of paper, which he threw at Ceven. "'Out for a midnight stroll, be back soon,'" Tarry mocked. "Honestly, you may be skilled with a sword, but you're not very creative in the head, are you?"

Ceven crossed his arms. "And you expect me to believe that you'd just willingly come to help me go against the king's direct orders?"

Xilo flicked back his hair, giving him a look. "We're here now, aren't we?"

"We don't have to agree with everything you do, Your Highness, but our job is to protect you. For our sake, allow us to do that much," Tarry said.

Barto couldn't resist giving Ceven the "I told you so" look. Maybe he'd been the naïve one. Ceven returned the favor with an inappropriate gesture and checked the guard's bodies for the keys. Low whimpers came from behind the door, and his stomach clenched. It sounded like Eve was in a lot of pain.

He unlocked the door and shoved it open. The light from the hallway flooded the tiny space, no bigger than his walk-in closet. Canisters and food lay waste around the room, smelling of stale bread and blood, and in the middle of the room was Evangeline. Curled up in a ball, her body quivering.

"Eve!" Ceven dropped the keys, his hands swooping to hold her. "Can you hear me?"

She blinked. For a split second, Ceven swore her irises reflected back at him, a kaleidoscope of color before a normal shade of green and blue stared at him.

"Jaden?" she whispered, her hand brushing his arm.

Ceven's brows scrunched, but he held her close, picking her up in both arms with ease. "We're getting you out of here."

"No," the faint sound escaped her lips. "They'll catch us. They always catch us and drag us back."

Ceven looked at Barto. "What's wrong with her?"

Barto's brows furrowed, his lips pressed into a thin line. "I don't think you'd want to hear my opinion."

Evangeline's eyes were wide but unfocused as she gripped the front of Ceven's shirt. "Please, don't kill them, it's not their fault. I can fix this. I can protect you. I can protect everyone. No one else has to die anymore."

"Hush, it's okay now. You're safe," Ceven whispered, holding her tighter against his body. He looked at the rest of them. "We need to get her to my suite. Now."

They all nodded. Xilo led the way while Tarry stayed behind

to clean up their mess, tying the Royal Guard members up before tossing them into the cell.

Barto stayed behind them, watching Ceven's back. His gaze drifted to Evangeline, where it remained for the rest of the way back to his suite.

CHAPTER 36

～ EVANGELINE ～

Blood was all around Evangeline. In her. Circling her. Bodies lay scattered on the ground.

"No, no, I never wanted any of this!" she cried, falling to her knees.

Their hollow faces stared back at her. Blank, mocking smiles searing into her brain.

This was all her fault.

Evangeline's eyes flew open, but instead of seeing the pitch-black darkness of her cell, familiar purple wallpaper surrounded her. Jewel encrusted swords and bows behind glass. *I'm in Ceven's room?* She tried to move her hands, but a thick rope bound them to the bed on either side of her.

"Eve?"

Evangeline turned, and Ceven hesitantly approached the edge of the bed. He must've seen something in her expression as he visibly relaxed and wrapped her in a tight embrace. She went to return the hug, but only succeeded in pulling on her restraints. *How did I get into his room? Why am I tied up? And what happened to the guards?* she thought before her face blanched. What would Ryker do once he found out?

"Why am I here?" An edge of hysteria stained her tone. Ceven's arms retreated and his eyes looked pinched. She tugged against the rope. "And why am I tied up?"

A black figure moved behind Ceven, a long sleek tail flicking back and forth. "We figured you'd much prefer a nice bed over the hard ground. You're welcome, by the way," Barto said, leaning against the tacky wallpaper.

"No, no, I can't be here, this isn't right—"

Ceven brushed a loose strand of hair behind her ear. "Do you remember anything?"

She frowned. "What do you mean?" She remembered going back to the cell after visiting Ryker, how Troy had given her a piece of bread and another canister. Not wanting to repeat what happened last time, she refused to eat it. The guards came in, forcing her mouth open as they stuffed the food and drink down her throat.

"Eve, you've been crying, nearly hysterical for the past few hours. Talking nonsense, going out of your mind. We had to tie you up because you kept trying to hurt yourself."

"And others," Xilo added, standing in the far corner of the room. His eyes lingered on Ceven.

Evangeline's mouth gaped open. "I . . . I don't know . . ." Her eyes slid to the window. The moon was out, the room lit by lamps. How long had she been out of it? How many days had it been?

"Eve, tell me what's going on. Ryker has never done anything like this to you before. What did you do?" Ceven stared into her eyes, the tenderness there melting away at her heart. She was so tired, exhausted, and . . . she didn't care anymore.

"Ceven . . ." She twisted her wrists, the rope rubbing against what felt like fresh wounds. "I'll tell you everything, but can you untie me first?"

Ceven obliged, snapping the rope with his hands. She rubbed her wrists, raw red lines wrapping around the skin, like she'd been tugging at it for hours.

"I . . .I messed up. Pretty big this time." She stared down at her hands, which were wrinkling the thick, white comforter. "I pushed too far, but I wanted to save Lani, and . . ." *Selfishly find answers for myself.* Her nostrils flared, and she squeezed her eyes shut.

Warm hands enclosed hers. "What did you do, Eve?" he whispered.

"I left the kingdom," she admitted. "I went with a Caster back to the cave where I was first found."

Ceven jerked in surprise.

"You went with Avana," Xilo said, his eyes delving into hers.

Evangeline frowned but nodded. "I went with her, thinking that I would be okay, safe from Ryker finding out. I was wrong to trust her."

Barto growled. "You can never trust a Caster. They're all conniving little—"

"Barto," Ceven bit out, his eyes returning to hers. "Why would you do that, Eve? Why wouldn't you ask me to help you?"

Because I don't want to get you in trouble. I don't want to give the king anymore reason to hate you, she didn't say, knowing he'd

339

argue. She sighed. "I need to go back. I don't want to get anyone involved in this."

His lips became a firm line. "You're not going back to that cell. I won't allow it."

Evangeline didn't want to go back either, especially if she hadn't been herself. What had she been doing? What have they been feeding her to make her that delusional? But it was the only way to get back to Ryker, to ensure she followed through with Raiythlen's plan.

You'd trust another Caster over your own friend? A hideous thought whispered, and a sliver of doubt crept into her mind.

"Ceven, you may be the prince of Peredia, but you're not immune to the king's wrath. If he finds out you did this, against Lord Ryker's wishes, you may be in as much trouble as me, if not more."

His jaw clenched, his eyes more heated than any flame in the room. Evangeline knew what his reply would be before he said it.

"You are not going back to that cell, Evangeline."

She looked at Xilo and Barto. "Is it possible that I speak to Ceven alone?"

Barto raised his hands as if to say "good luck" and lingered in the doorway, his eyes on Ceven's, before exiting. Xilo didn't move. Ceven reassured him, forcing him to leave the two of them alone.

"If I don't go back, there will only be more trouble," she tried again.

"And how do you think I'd feel if I sent the only girl I've ever cared about back to a dark dungeon cell to be tortured and assaulted?"

Her face softened. *The only girl I've ever cared about.* A pleasant warmth blossomed inside her, pushing away the horror of her situation. Wanting to feel his skin slide over hers, she cupped his cheeks in both of her hands. "I can handle this, Ceven. I know you want to protect me, but let me prove to you how strong I've become."

He looked at her, but his expression didn't waver. "But Eve . . . you're not."

She yanked her hands away. The tender hold he had on her heart curled around it like a fist. He instantly looked regretful and tried to intertwine his fingers with hers, but she shoved them under the covers.

"Look, I'm sorry, I didn't mean it like that—" he started.

"But you did."

"I meant no matter how strong you think you are, you're no match against Ryker and the king. If they decide to break your bones, hang you, or burn you alive, there would be absolutely nothing you could do about it." He opened his mouth and closed it a few times. "Eve, I don't want to lose you. I *can't* lose you."

She swallowed hard. She understood where he was coming from, it made sense, but he didn't have to make her feel so pathetically . . . human.

"We'll run away together. Right now," he said, and Evangeline knew he meant it.

She smiled, her eyes tearing up. How she had been waiting to hear those words from him her entire life. But not anymore. Not now. "I won't leave Lani behind, Ceven."

"We'll take Lani too. We'll all go to this small little town in Atiaca, far away from Peredia."

It sounded delightful, too good to be true. "Lani's too injured. There's no way she'll be able to get out of the kingdom." Not unless she had an invisibility spell, like one a Caster could cast.

Ceven shook his head. "There are tunnels beneath the castle. We'd have safe passage through them."

She was about to respond when she paused, staring at him. Ceven realized his mistake, and he glanced away from her. *The missing slaves . . .* "What do you mean, tunnels beneath the castle? Who else knows about this?"

He shook his head. "It's nothing, just old tunnels used back in time of war."

She clenched her fists. "Who else knows about this?"

He growled, running a hand through his hair. "Only the royal family. And yes, we think it's connected to the missing humans, before you ask." He put his hands up. "I didn't say anything because I don't want to make you a target, Eve. You already have such a big one on your back all the time."

"You think I don't need to know this? Lani's next. She's going to be the next person to disappear—"

"You don't know that."

"She was *covered* in bloody markings, Ceven!" The comforter stretched taut beneath her fists.

Silence.

"I'm . . . I'm so sorry, Eve," he whispered.

Tears spilled over, sliding down her cheeks. No, not again, not in front of Ceven. But she couldn't help it. It was like a dam had been released, everything washing over in waves she couldn't control, didn't want to control. Gods, it would feel so good to let it all out.

And she did.

Ceven sat next to her in bed, holding her. Her face nestled into his shoulder, and she wept, her shoulders shaking.

"I'll fix this," he whispered. "I'll make sure no one touches her. I'll go to her tonight, make sure she's taken care of, and I'll make sure all three of us will never have to look at this castle *ever again*." He gritted the last part out.

She believed him and wanted to put all her faith and hopes into him, but at the end of it all, it wasn't guaranteed to work. Wasn't guaranteed that Ryker or the king wouldn't find out what they were up to. That they could sneak out, two humans and an Aerian prince.

But there's also no guarantee Raiythlen isn't lying to you, so why are you making excuses? She felt the vial nestled between her breasts, the heat of it against her skin, making its presence known. Would she be able to follow through with Raiythlen's plan, or should she place her trust in Ceven? *Ryker, he hurt Lani. Tortured an old, helpless woman and left her to bleed out. To die. He tried to rip away the one person he knew I cared about more than anything in this world.* She wanted to hurt him, make him pay. Make him feel as helpless. At this point, it wasn't just about leaving the kingdom.

It was about revenge.

"Lani said that it was Ryker. He's a part of all this," she said.

Ceven rubbed her back, his palm sliding down its curve before gliding back up. It did wonders on her nerves. "I . . . always had my suspicions," he admitted. "But there's not much we can do, Eve. At least not on such short notice. The only way is to leave this place far behind."

"You may be right." She wiped her nose on the sleeve of her dress. "But first, can you please make sure Lani's okay? And . . . tell her I'll get her out of this mess? That everything will be okay?"

Ceven tilted her chin, his thumb wiping away the wetness on her cheek. "Of course, Eve." He turned serious. "When I get back, we'll make the plans to leave. The ball is in two days. We'll need to be well away from here before the entire country finds out we've skipped town. I'll check on Lani. Stay here, and we'll solve this when I get back."

She nodded, and he smiled at her, pressing a kiss upon her forehead.

"I'll be back soon, I promise." He gave her one last look before leaving the room.

Evangeline waited, listening to the whispers outside the room and, soon after, the click of the front door until it was quiet once again. She clutched at the vial beneath her dress. Knowing Ceven was checking on Lani eased her rattled heart, but she wasn't out of trouble yet. *I'm so sorry, Ceven, but I can't drag you into this either. I won't risk turning the kingdom on you too. It's better this way.* She stared at the closed door. She knew what she had to do.

Evangeline lay in bed with her eyes closed, steadily breathing for what felt like ample time before she got up. Un-tucking her feet, her toes grazed the cold marble as she grabbed the thick coat lying on the chest at the foot of the bed and paused. She didn't have a coat in the cell and wouldn't be needing one on her return.

She crept toward the door to Ceven's bedroom. The moon shone brightly behind her, through open curtains. She still had time. She reached for the handle when murmured whispers from Barto and Tarry made her pause.

"I thought our country had its issues, but Peredia is one giant mess," Barto said from next to the door.

Tarry's low grunt was farther away. "Peredia is strong. Solid. It's just had some misdirection in recent years."

Barto snorted. "That's an understatement."

Her head pressed tightly against the door when someone knocked on it. Evangeline flinched, heart pounding.

"You can come out, Eve, we know you're there," Barto said.

Color pricked her cheeks, and she opened the door. Tarry leaned against the two-pane window above the small circular table, while Barto was sitting in the black iron chair he'd dragged from said table to be next to the bedroom door.

Barto's boots were propped up, resting on top of a nearby end table. He grinned at her. "I'd say morning, sunshine, but we still have some time before dawn."

She frowned, stepping farther into the sitting chamber and closer to the blazing fire—the only source of light in the room.

"His Highness has gone to check on Miss Delani," Tarry said, his entire figure a shadow in the faint light from the window.

"Don't worry, we'll protect you in the meantime. No big baddies coming in here tonight," Barto added.

Evangeline took the blue silk blanket off the white couch, wrapping it around herself as she stood by the fire. "If I end up staying here, it's Ceven that's going to need protecting. Prince or no prince."

Tarry raised an eyebrow, his bulky arms crossed over a silver mesh torso. "We have orders to keep you safe. So, until the prince returns, you aren't going anywhere."

Barto glanced at the two of them before nodding in agreement.

Evangeline kept her eyes on Tarry, walking closer toward him. "Tarry, I understand that Prince Ceven comes first. That means to protect him, even from himself. We both know if I stay here, nothing good will come out of it."

Barto stood up. "Ceven can take care of himself. Trust me, he knows what he's getting himself into, what he's *been* getting himself into."

Evangeline pointed a finger at her chest. "I can also take care of myself, and I also know what I'm getting myself into. I can deal with this on my own, without dragging anyone else down with me."

Barto looked doubtful as he scratched the back of his partially shaven head. "Look, I'm sure—"

"I agree," Tarry said.

Barto's eyes narrowed. "What?"

Tarry kept his gaze on hers. "I agree that you being here isn't a good idea. Prince Ceven has never been level-headed around you."

Evangeline didn't take the dig personally. She went into this knowing Tarry would take her side, that Ceven would always come first for him and Xilo. "Which is why you need to return me to my cell, before any more damage is done."

Tarry nodded, and Barto looked at the two of them, his mouth a twisted line. He threw up his hands. "Fine, since I clearly won't be able to fight the two of you on this." He looked at her. "Evangeline . . . please be careful, and you know if you ever change your mind and realize how crazy this all is, just remember that you'll always have a place to stay in Atiaca."

Barto's words touched her, and she gave him a warm smile.

Tarry got up from his perch. "Let's go, then."

CHAPTER 37

⤝ EVANGELINE ⤞

Evangeline returned to her own personal hell. It was harder than she thought, forcing herself to walk back into the small, lightless cell.

Tarry had guided her through the castle halls and down the stairs into the levels of underground cells. She had been tempted to ask how many were occupied, having only heard silence from the other cells. But some things were better left not knowing.

Tarry had tied up her Aerian guards, leaving them in the cell. To say they weren't happy to see him when he opened the door was an understatement. The yellow-winged Aerian, Troy, almost ran his blade through him, but Tarry dodged at the last second.

Go on and tell the king what happened here tonight. I'm sure he'll understand how you were bested by mere mercenaries, Tarry had said.

Evangeline gave him a sideways glance, not understanding what he meant by that. The Royal Guards didn't respond but lowered their blades, granting Tarry a single, curt nod. Taking a deep breath, Evangeline thanked him. Tarry nodded, and something close to sadness reflected in his expression. Or maybe that was what she hoped for.

Walking past them, she stood in the middle of the room, watching the light fade as the cell door shut behind her.

Time passed. For how long, Evangeline had no idea. It all blended together. She didn't know if it was day or night, or if time drifted slowly or too quickly. But when her cell door opened, it felt like she was waking up for the first time after sleeping for centuries.

She was lying on the floor, her head lolled to the side, when a tall, ghostly figure reached for her.

"Evangeline," Ryker said. "It's time to go home."

He held his hand out, and she took it.

The walk back to Ryker's suite was a daze. Her hand remained in his as he led her down the purple carpeted halls with the same paintings, watching her as they passed. She couldn't feel his hand's warmth, still cold and numb. Like the cell had buried itself into her soul, chilling her to the bone.

Ryker's hand finally left hers when they walked into his sitting chamber, the fireplace's heat warming her skin. The familiar scent of lilac and vanilla sprinkled the air. She had never realized how much she missed this, the smells, the familiar appeal of everything. As much as she hated this suite, she spent most of her time here.

It was her home.

Ryker faced the fire, his long red robe brushing the floor, his hair tied back in a golden tie. Evangeline crept closer, her boots sliding as she meandered toward the center of the chamber. He didn't speak another word to her, didn't offer her a seat or give her any warning of what was to come next.

When he turned, she kept her head lowered, staring at the ground. She didn't allow herself to feel comfortable, to feel anything. She kept herself sane by walking through the steps of what she would have to do. Obey, follow his every order—and gain some leverage for her to strike. The vial warmed in response.

He walked toward her, his arms outstretched, and she closed her eyes, bracing herself. But he didn't hit or grab her. His arms wrapped around her thin frame and pulled her into a hug. Her eyes widened. *Has he lost his mind?*

"I'm so sorry, my child," he whispered, his hold tightening. "I'm so, so sorry. I couldn't bear to leave you in there any longer. Please forgive me."

Evangeline froze. Had she heard him right? Lord Ryker never hugged her, never showed her any form of affection outside his unusual bouts of telling her to sleep well and travel safely. The vial felt heavier now.

He released her and coerced her to sit on the sofa. She did, and an array of sweets and small candies lined the knee-high table in front of her.

Ryker walked past his usual seat and sat beside her, his weight shifting the couch. He grabbed her hand. "Please, allow me to atone for the atrocities I committed against you. If there's anything you want, that you desire, I will give it to you. Just tell me, Evangeline."

Her mouth opened, but she didn't know what to say. "What .

.. what are you doing?" she asked, unsure if this was real, or another delusion. Yes, it had to be another delusion. She was still in her cell, and this was all a lovely fantasy created by her mind.

"I won't send you back. I refuse." He shook his head. "I didn't ... I wish things didn't have to happen this way. I was ... so worried, so scared."

"Scared of what?" She found her words easily. After all, this was another illusion inside her head. She could ask whatever she wanted. Right?

Ryker was quiet for a moment. "I was scared I would lose you forever."

Did he think I was going to die? "You said you would grant me anything?" she asked, and Ryker smiled, nodding. "Then, I want answers."

His smile disappeared. "What is it you want to know?"

"Are you the one who hurt Lani? Are you behind the missing humans inside the castle?"

He didn't respond. As if the Ryker inside her head would give her the answers she sought. Real or not real, he would never give her the truth.

"I can give you anything, Evangeline. Sweets, new books, a new dress. Just not that."

She almost laughed. How those things would have made her happy, *had* made her happy in the past. Now it paled compared to the reality she was living. "The only thing I want is the truth."

His lips twitched into a half smile. "You sound like Avana."

Evangeline gritted her teeth. She didn't want to be associated with that woman.

Ryker sighed. "I know you hate me, Eve. That you find me despicable, the heart of every evil and misdeed that has ever happened to you here in Peredia." He paused long enough she didn't think he would continue. "I ... no, *we* are only tools.

Pawns in a game bigger and far grander than you or even I can imagine." His face twisted, as if warring with something inside him. "Things have been set into motion far beyond my control. The rest is in the king's hands."

Evangeline burst from the couch so fast her knees almost buckled. Her breathing came hard, and her eyes glared at Ryker's. He might as well admit he played a hand in implementing Lani's demise. *But . . . this is all a dream, right? None of this is happening, right?*

Ryker gave her a defeated smile. "Do you want to kill me now, Evangeline?"

Her chest caved in and out. She wanted to do more than that. She wanted to skin him, burn him, torture him, and every person who had tormented every innocent soul like Lani's. She wanted them trapped down in that cell with the key thrown away. Their bodies left to rot, knowing there would be no one to save them.

"Why?" she bit out. "Why are you doing this? Why Lani? Why did it have to be *Lani?*"

Ryker didn't meet her eyes. "I didn't have a choice."

Evangeline sank back down to the couch, her hands in her hair. "You're playing tricks on me. This is all in my head, isn't it? Another hallucination, illusion. I've gone completely insane now, haven't I?" A manic chuckle rumbled through her.

Ryker petted the back of her head. "No, my dear, you're just now waking up." His face fell flat. "I'm losing you faster than I expected."

She looked at him, not seeing him. *Lies. It's not real, nothing's real. You can't trust anything you see or hear.*

"Why . . . why me?" She had asked multiple times before, and she asked again, not expecting an answer. It was more to make what was happening feel real, to believe she was grounded in reality and not inside her head. "Why won't you tell me any-thing? About my mark, about these dreams? Why I'm seeing things? I know you know." Her eyes locked onto his. "Why are you keeping these secrets from me? *What am I to you?*"

His hand on her head stopped and fell to his side. She never noticed the bags beneath his eyes before, or how his skin appeared more dull and tired. For the first time, she was seeing the real man underneath. The real Ryker who wasn't a lord or a king's advisor, but a sad and lonely old man.

"You used to be the means to an end. Now . . . I'm not sure." He closed his eyes. "I didn't want to hurt you anymore . . . but you kept coming back." When he opened his eyes to look at her, they were glassy. "Why did you come back to me, Eve? I gave you so many opportunities to leave this place, but you kept coming back . . . and now . . ." He shook his head, his expression pained.

Evangeline stared at him. Avana's words rang somewhere in the back of her mind.

He already knew. About everything.

"Now it's too late," he finished.

Evangeline started to speak, but Ryker raised his hand. "Enough." He softened the blow by resting his palm on her leg. "Enough . . . of this. For now. The ball is tomorrow night, and it'll be a busy day. Get some rest. Allow your mind and body to . . . heal from these last few days."

Heal. As if she wasn't trying to hold the pieces of herself together as additional parts of her kept falling off. She needed more than a warm bed again to heal what was happening inside of her. "I need to go see Lani."

Ryker shook his head. "Don't worry, Lani is fine. Will be fine."

She saw red, her anger erupting inside her again. "I was covered in her blood, she wasn't fine—"

"She will live."

"What if she doesn't?"

Ryker stood, his shadow eclipsing her body. "You will see her again. I can promise you that, but it will not be tonight. I have given you more information than I should have, more than I have been allowed. You don't need to believe in anything I have said, but believe me when I say that Lani will be fine."

"You're right. I don't believe in anything you have said, especially now."

He rubbed his eyes. "You don't have a choice in this, Evangeline. Neither of us do, anymore."

Her teeth clamped together. She didn't reply.

"I'll see you tomorrow morning." He put out the fire, leaving a few lamps to light the dark room. "Good night."

Numb, Evangeline walked to her room. Once she shut the door, she slid down it, legs crumpling to the floor. She was left with nothing but her thoughts. Her loud, screaming thoughts.

Kill him. Kill him now!

No, run away, run back to Lani, run as fast as your legs can carry you.

No, we have to poison him, to get more answers, we can't do this on our own, we need that Caster.

What about Ceven? We can leave with him. You trust him, don't you, Evangeline?

Or . . . you can open up that window. Step out on to that ledge.

And make this all stop.

She clenched her eyes shut, hugging herself.

Tomorrow, she told herself. Tomorrow she would come to a decision. One that would shape the outcome of her and Lani's future.

PART 4

Dancing With Legends
and Beasts

CHAPTER 38

⮺ EVANGELINE ⮞

Morning came quicker than Evangeline expected. For the first time in a long time, she watched the sun rise, savoring its warm glow as it peeked over the frost-capped mountains in the distance. She felt like she hadn't seen the sun in so long, though it'd only been a few days.

Ryker was nowhere to be found when she walked into the sitting chamber, still in her gown from the night before.

"Lord Ryker?" she called half-heartedly. When no response came, she trailed around the room, her fingers sliding against the back of the sofa, the dining room table, and the window behind it. She gazed out at those same frosty hills. If only she had wings to fly herself there. Away from here.

Evangeline drew a steaming hot bath, sinking herself into the water. She sighed as the water rose, washing away all her worries.

What's it going to be, Evangeline?

Her brows pinched together. Her eyes flicked toward the vial in the folds of her burgundy dress on the counter. Was she really going to do this? *Well, first things first, I need to make sure he has a drink.* Good thing she knew Ryker loved his tea.

Her fist balled tight. Lani's blood, her marred back. All alone and confused. And Ryker had played a part in it . . . She wished she could do more than drug his drink.

Her face was halfway submerged in the water when a slamming door echoed throughout the suite. She frowned and got out of the tub. Throwing on a robe, she creaked open the door. When she didn't see Ryker, she tiptoed farther, sneaking a glance into the sitting chamber—only to find a familiar, determined face pacing the room.

"Ceven?" She hadn't thought he'd be mad enough to storm into Ryker's suite himself.

Ceven's face looked flushed, his eyes wide. When he caught her standing there, he stormed to her side. "Why did you go back, Eve? How could you? You promised me . . ."

"I didn't promise you anything. How did you get in here?"

Ceven drew back, and Evangeline realized her words had come out rather harshly.

"When I found out you went back . . ." He swallowed for a moment. "I made a meeting to see Ryker this morning, knowing I would find you here." He tugged at her shoulders. "But don't worry, he has business with the king first. If we're going to escape, we have to go now."

Evangeline stepped away from him. "How's Lani?"

He blinked. "She's fine."

"Fine?" Had he looked scared, or was she being paranoid?

"You can see for yourself, if you leave with me. Now."

Evangeline ignored the bad feeling in the pit of her stomach and forced herself to stand firm. The ball was tonight. If she was going to do this, it would be now or never. "No, you need to go. I'll be fine, but I'm not leaving."

He looked ready to argue but thought better of it. "Then I guess I must convince Ryker otherwise."

That got a rise from her. "Don't you dare. Stay out of this. Please," she said, softening her words. "Trust me. I got this."

"Why are you always so . . ." He ran his hands through his hair, sighing. "You are one of the most infuriating women I have ever met, you know that? And that's saying a lot, if you've ever met any of Barto's sisters."

"And yet, you still stick around," she teased, but sobered when she thought back to his kiss, his confession. Maybe all he'd ever wanted from her was her trust, and she kept letting him down.

"I don't want to see you get hurt anymore, Eve."

I didn't want to hurt you.

She pushed Ryker's words far from her mind.

Evangeline sighed. The first thing she wanted to do when she saw Ceven was run into his arms. For him to hold her and tell her everything would be okay, to lose herself in his lips and pretend none of this was happening . . .

Ceven looked at her, his brows together, looking torn. He went to say something, but a click and a shuffle of footsteps made him pause. Ryker.

She thought about the vial, still between the folds of her clothes, in the bathing room. Turning, she went to leave when she glanced at Ceven. "Please don't convince him to let me leave. It'll be a losing battle."

Before Ceven replied, Evangeline into the bathing room and shut the door. She threw her dress on as Ryker gave a hushed greeting. After that was a mumble of voices while she put her damp hair into a braid.

Why wasn't he leaving? She bit her lip and opened the door.

Ceven's voice trailed toward the bedroom. "You didn't answer my question. What do you and the king want with Evangeline?"

Her teeth mashed together. *I told him not to get involved!*

"Our king wants nothing more than for his country to prosper. We all want the same thing, Your Highness. Do not act as if we're not on the same side."

The voices of the two Aerians got closer. Instead of stepping out, she hid behind the door of the bathing room, turning off the light to shroud her in darkness. As much as she hated Ceven's interference, she wanted to hear the rest of this conversation.

"Lately, I can't be too sure of that," Ceven said.

"Your Highness, I am gratified to hear of your concern regarding my pupil, but I fear it's misplaced. No one cares more about her well-being than I do."

"You have a funny way of showing it." There was an edge to his words.

For a second, Evangeline thought they had found her out as silence stretched between the two, nothing but the pounding of her heart echoing in her ears. Then Ryker said, his voice low, "No one understands her more than me. That includes you, Your Highness." Glass tapped against something and shoes padded across marble. "Now, I must excuse myself, as I have prior engagements."

"Of course." Ceven's voice was smooth. "However, before I go, would you show me your personal library? I am very interested in what you have on Peredian history. Old markings and brands in particular."

Evangeline shook her head. *And he called me infuriating. Hypocrite.*

"As you wish, Your Highness." Ryker's tone was like dragging a carcass over gravel.

The two left the room, and she walked out, feeling only a little guilty for eavesdropping. Curious to find out how long Ceven was going to keep up this charade, Evangeline walked into the sitting chamber and froze mid-step.

There, on the edge of Ryker's desk, sat a white teacup.

She could tell it was freshly brewed from the steam and the powerful scent of cinnamon wafting from it. The weight between her breasts increased tenfold, as the vial lay there like a heavy burden to be lifted. Raiythlen said to do it right before the ball, not a second earlier. But staring at the innocent white cup, the moment was too convenient. Too perfect.

Her hand was wet with sweat as she gripped the vial through her dress. Her blood rushed through her ears. *I should wait until it's closer to dusk.* But what if there wasn't another opportunity like this?

No, if she was going to act, she had to act now.

Evangeline emptied her mind and walked closer to the desk. Reaching down the front of her dress, she pulled out the vial with shaking hands. She peered over her shoulder, but Ryker and Ceven's voices were distant. Turning back to the cup, she stared at the contents and pulled off the cork. The sound was like an explosion to her ears.

She prepped the vial over the cup.

Do it.

She squeezed her eyes shut.

Do it.

Taking a deep breath, she dumped the entire thing into the cup.

When she opened her eyes and looked down at the contents, nothing had changed. It looked like an ordinary cup of tea. Evangeline loosened a breath. She did it. It was done. But her gaze remained on the white porcelain. She could accidently knock it over. Undo everything.

Her fingers brushed the tip of the saucer.

It's not too late . . .

"Did you find what you were looking for, Evangeline?"

She gasped and her hands flew to her chest. Ryker stood in the doorway with his arms crossed.

"I-I—" she stammered.

"Feel free to continue your search." He walked toward her, and she stepped back, her hip bumping into the desk. His hand whipped out, and she flinched, closing her eyes.

"That would have been unpleasant," he murmured.

She opened her eyes to see him holding the cup of tea that had fallen off the desk.

He turned, saucer perched in one hand, the cup in the other. "When you are finished, if you would join me in the sitting room."

Evangeline didn't know what to make of Ryker's reaction. He didn't sound angry, almost disappointed.

He took the cup.

She bit her lip but followed Ryker out into the sitting chamber. He sat in his chair near the fireplace, his tea in hand. She forced herself not to stare as she sat across from him. Glancing around the suite. Ceven had left.

"What you want to know, you won't find here." Ryker glanced at his tea, and Evangeline's stomach squeezed. He blew on it but made no move to take a sip. "If there's something you'd wish to know, all you have to do is ask."

Like I did last night? Like I've been doing for years? Evangeline held back the eye roll.

He sensed it. "I only want what's best for you, Evangeline. I know I haven't always been truthful, but . . . it was to protect you."

"Protect me from what?" she snapped.

Ryker smiled at her, and Evangeline wanted to squirm at the foreign expression on his face. "I know I've mistreated you, but I've also protected you from many who would've hurt you. I know you don't believe me, but I've done everything in my power to give you a life better than the station you were born into."

A small sliver of guilt pricked at her, and she scratched her arms, wanting to rub it away. *You have nothing to be guilty over. Try to remember all the pain he has caused you and Lani, all the suffering.* But if it hadn't been for Ryker, she may not be alive today. *Remember the scarred flesh of Lani's back, the raw, mutilated skin. He tortured an innocent woman. He has no right to your guilt.*

"When I took you in, you were only eleven years old. Already this world had proven too cruel to you. Rags for clothes, forced to eat food that wasn't even suitable for animals. I remember it took several days before all the dirt and grime could be fully washed away. Hate me if you want, Evangeline, but I saved you."

And at the same time, he condemned Lani and every human in the castle to live exactly like that. So why her? Why take her in, isolate her from everyone?

Lani's words haunted her.

I wish I never met you.

He may have saved her from a life of hardship, but he also helped in alienating her from her people. "You don't really care about me. If you did, you wouldn't have . . ." Beaten her,

controlled her, tortured her, and terrorized the one woman who mattered more to her than anything in this world.

Ryker was silent for a moment. "I've never told you this, but . . . you look like my daughter." Ryker gazed into his cup, a smile she had never seen on him touching his lips. "Like you, she was a bundle of fire as a child, hair the color of honey." The smile disappeared. "She also never listened . . . and they killed her because of it."

Evangeline was too stunned for words. *So the rumors were true? He had a family?* She took him in, the lost look in his eyes, like he was wrapped up in a distant memory. She wanted to ask what happened, but didn't.

In the end, it still didn't change anything.

His eyes snapped up. "You are very special to me, Evangeline. But I know that one day, I will lose you too."

She tightened her grip, crinkling her dress. *Why is he telling me all of this now? Does he expect me to forgive him? To forget everything he's done?* But honestly, she didn't know what to feel. Angry? Grateful? She certainly was confused on top of all of it.

A sharp intake of breath and shattering glass interrupted her train of thought. Ryker clawed at his throat, and shards of white glass and dark liquid littered the ground.

He drank the poison.

Evangeline lurched from the couch. She pounded on his back, applying pressure on his stomach, hoping he would regurgitate it. His face turned a shade of blue. She thought she could handle this, had convinced herself this was the only way, but the sole thought running through her mind was how much she regretted everything.

No, no, no! Why is this happening? Raiythlen said it would make him sleep! Ryker took another ragged breath, the sound like sandpaper on wood. His wings flapped back and forth, knocking everything around him, including her.

A startling revelation struck her. Raiythlen had planned to use her to kill Ryker from the very beginning.

Ryker grabbed her by the hair and pulled her down. "You . . . poisoned . . . me!"

Evangeline couldn't form a coherent sentence. Raiythlen had tricked her into committing murder.

But isn't this what you wanted?

Ryker's grip loosened, his eyebrows strung together, his mouth open. His eyes seared her with a look of such hatred. He let go of her, falling to the floor.

"Father?" She shook him, but his eyes stared blankly back at her. "Lord Ryker?" She placed her finger beneath his nose. He wasn't breathing. She crawled back so fast that she ran into the end table, knocking it over. "Oh Gods, what have I done? What have I done!" She covered her mouth, her limbs tangled together on the floor. She couldn't move, couldn't speak, couldn't do anything.

Ryker Ardonis, the king's advisor, was dead. Murdered by her hands.

"Father, get up," she said, watching his body for the smallest of movements. "Please, please, please, just get up." She covered her eyes, a soft wail escaping her. She needed to move, to leave, to do anything but sit there. *This is why he said to do it right before the ball* . . . because now the clock was ticking. It would only be a matter of time before the king found out. She swore she would never trust another Caster for as long as she lived.

"Okay, Evangeline, you're fine, you can do this." She made the mistake of looking at Ryker again and jerked away, a muffled, panicked sob creeping up her throat. "Don't look, it's going to be okay." But she knew it wasn't.

Her best option was to remove his body from the main living space in the suite. The bathing room? No. His bed? Maybe they would assume he was sleeping? Surely it would buy her some time before her inevitable demise.

Nit, nit, nit.

Something crawled across her foot, and she squealed, spotting the mouse beneath her dress. Tied to its body was a rolled-up piece of paper and a vial. Teeth clenched, she picked up the mouse, almost suffocating it, and untied the note and vial. *I'll see you at the ball,* was all it read. She immediately crumpled the note and tossed it into the fireplace.

I already killed one Nyte tonight. Another would be nothing, she thought, a bit hysterically, as she envisioned wringing Raiythlen's neck.

Tucking the new vial—which she hoped was a glamour potion or an invisibility spell of sorts—into the bust of her dress, she turned, bracing herself. Ryker's limp body lay strewn on the floor. One hand on top of his chest from where he had clawed at it, the other limply above him. She wanted to vomit.

He had knocked the table over, and black tea splattered across the marble floor and rug. She needed to clean this up, hide as much evidence as possible—because the only man who would have protected her, she had killed.

Pushing away the panic-inducing thoughts, she dragged him into his bedroom, the sound of his body sliding against the slick marble like knives down her back. She tried to lift him on to the bed several times, but he was too heavy.

"I can't . . . Why is this happening?" An uncontrollable sob bubbled up as she stood there, her whole body quivering.

Focusing on her imminent death, she tried again and successfully got him in bed. She pulled the thick blanket over him and forced his eyes closed. If anyone came in, their first thought would be that he was asleep. Until they got closer and realized he wasn't breathing.

I'm going to die.

She grabbed some towels and wiped the puddle of tea where Ryker had fallen. As she scrubbed at the marble and the edge of the rug, tears burst from her chest and slid down her face. She pulled the rug over the stained spot, hiding any leftover residue, and fixed the table. She even bothered to fold the blanket on the back of the couch.

They're going to torture me, burn me, drown me. Kill me in the worst way possible.

Light from the rising sun illuminated the sweat and tears dribbling down her face. It was still morning. There was no way they'd believe Ryker would be asleep in bed all day, and considering she was the last person to see him, she would be the first suspect. She needed to leave now.

Blast Raiythlen and his spitting games. She would do what she had set out to do weeks ago. She'd get Lani, injured or not, and the two of them would leave this kingdom. At this point, she had to risk it all.

Because if she didn't, both of them would be doomed to die here anyway.

CHAPTER 39

⟋⟍ EVANGELINE ⟋⟍

"No . . . No . . . Where is she?" Evangeline stared at the blood-stained cot where Lani should have been.

After cleaning the evidence and grabbing a bag of clothes and some fruit that had been on the dining room table, Evangeline had headed straight for Lani's slave quarters. She'd walked past the two guards with ease. Neither one remarked on the sweat that dribbled along the back of her neck, or her elevated breathing. Maybe they had mistaken her nervousness for something Ryker said to her, but it wouldn't be long before they found out the truth.

Before the whole blasted castle found out the truth.

A scream rumbled up her throat as her eyes bore holes into the empty cot. Ceven told her she was fine. *So why wasn't she here!* Could she have gone back to work? Evangeline shook her head. No, Lani was in far too much pain for that. She chewed on her bottom lip. *She's alive, she must be . . . She has to be. Ryker said she would be fine . . .*

Lani had to be somewhere. She couldn't be out of her reach. Not yet. Turning, Evangeline raced to the castle.

Her friend wasn't in the kitchens. Or in the cellar, in any of the hallways, pantries, or floors Evangeline ran through. She thought about finding Ceven to help her, but decided the less he knew about her current situation, the better. If he found out she had murdered Ryker, he may be forced to tell the king. Or worse, be charged as an accomplice if he didn't.

It wasn't until she checked the last dry food storage in the basement that Evangeline stopped, her breath ragged.

"She's gone, isn't she?"

Evangeline turned to find Shani standing in the doorway. "Leave me alone."

Shani stepped toward her. "You didn't take my boy."

Evangeline pressed her hands into her face, trying to push the tears back into her eyes. A warm hand fell on her shoulder, but Evangeline ignored the comforting gesture as her own mind consumed her. Like a mirror inside her had cracked, and the shattered remains reflected a fragmented, broken girl.

"It'll get easier," Shani said before her footsteps receded, leaving Evangeline alone again. But Evangeline refused to believe her friend was gone for good. She was angry—no, she was beyond that. She was hanging onto her sanity by a thin thread, one that hinged on the hope that Lani was still alive somewhere. Alone and hurting, but alive.

Shooting to her feet, Evangeline picked up the closest thing to her, a bag of beans, and threw it as hard as she could, the weight of it smacking against the wall. She wasn't satisfied. She picked up a crate of fruit, tipping the contents, before knocking down the bags of apples, kicking the rice until it spilled over the floor. Digging her fingers into the loaves of bread, she tore them apart, tossing them everywhere.

Once she had thoroughly destroyed the room, she closed her eyes.

Lani was alive, and she was going to find her. But not on her own. She killed a man this morning for Raiythlen. He owed her. Big time.

And if he refuses? Then I'll personally tell the king there is an assassin within our midst. She didn't care anymore. It wasn't as if she had anything else to lose. Looks like she's going to that puss-filled ball after all.

Evangeline made it past a row of guards rotating along the castle hallways, monitoring the streams of Nytes entering. She ground her teeth to keep herself from running, scared that one of them would reach out and grab her.

Stay calm, act natural. You still have time. But did she, though? Dusk was already approaching. The entire day had gone by without so much as a breath of panic in the air. How had they not discovered her dark little secret?

As she entered the main hall, the sound of conversation and idle movement rushed her along with a wave of perfume and cologne. Pressing her shoulder as close to the wall as possible, she trailed past Nytes dressed in evening gowns and suits. She swallowed.

It's time.

She swerved left, going down a less crowded hallway. Ducking into the crevice behind a thick drape and the potted plant of lilacs, she pulled the vial from her dress. She looked both ways to make sure the hallway was empty before swallowing the blue liquid. Little bubbles trickled down the back of her throat, spreading throughout her body to her hands and toes, but this time it felt thicker. Like she was putting on a coat.

Her dress was now encased in gold with swirls of purple meshing with silver. She reached out, and her eyes widened when her skin brushed the silken fabric instead of passing through it. She fingered strands of her hair that turned into vibrant red curls falling past her shoulders. There weren't any wings, but she was sure if she looked in a mirror, she'd see the curve of horns that she could make out in her peripheral. With her transformation complete, it was time for the hard part. Getting into the ball.

Evangeline knew there would be a guest list of those allowed to enter, but she couldn't announce her own name, and without Ryker, she wouldn't have been able to enter regardless. She hoped Raiythlen had a plan, considering she met him this far. Whether she had the patience not to throttle him when she saw him was another story.

The layer of glamour helped to boost her confidence as Evangeline blended back into the crowd of Nytes, but it didn't eradicate her nervousness. *Focus. First find Raiythlen, then find Lani.*

She followed the crowd until she entered a small opening. Nytes gathered in pairs and lined up outside a set of ornate doors made from wood and clasped in iron. A short Rathan with black hair, dark red trousers, and a matching coat stood in front of the door. He held a long sheet of paper within his stubby hands and granted a slight nod, allowing the next in line to enter the ballroom.

Evangeline frowned, lingering along the edges of the line. It wasn't long before she drew a few eyes, and soon a familiar figure emerged from the crowd—but it wasn't the one she hoped to find.

Avana's hair was tied up into a braided bun, her ears lit with long silver bands on each. Her simple, skin-tight dress curved around her slight frame, flaring out at the knee, and when she turned to squeeze between a couple, swirls of dark tattoos graced her pale back between the deep cut of her dress.

Evangeline turned around, hoping to lose her in the crowd, but an influx of Nytes entered the room and barred her from sneaking away.

"My, I certainly did not expect to see another Caster here besides myself."

Evangeline cursed under her breath. She kept her back turned, pretending not to notice her, but Avana was insistent. When the Caster tapped her on the shoulder, Evangeline held back a sneer and reluctantly turned to face her.

"Allow me to introduce myself. My name is Avana."

It took everything in Evangeline to force a smile before glancing away. She wanted to put as much distance between them as possible, but there wasn't anywhere else to go unless she wanted to delve farther back into the line.

Avana leaned forward, whispering, "Evangeline, please, I need to talk to you."

Evangeline whipped back around, her curls hitting her face. She should've known. Avana probably saw through her glamour from across the room. "Sorry, I'm busy," she said, admiring her cuticles.

"I'm sorry if I offended you, my lady. It just gets lonely being the only Caster at these Aerian festivities, but I promise my company does not disappoint. If I may be so bold, would you care to accompany me to the ball?" Avana offered her arm.

Evangeline's nostrils flared. Did she expect her to follow along willingly? To trust her and make the same mistake twice?

"If you want to get in, which I assume is your plan judging by your . . . outfit, I can help you." Avana lowered her voice, her arm still outstretched.

"Just like you did last time?" she snapped back, still tracing the outline of her nails with her eyes. Avana had watched Ryker drag her to that cell. Had stood beside him while he left her to sit in darkness and be tortured by a deranged Rathan. Avana had proven where her loyalties lay. "If you want to help me, it'd be by never speaking to me again."

Avana sighed, ignoring her comment. "I read the journals we found. I think . . . I think I know what's happening to you."

Evangeline didn't move, but her heart squeezed. Avana could be lying, saying anything to get her to go with her, but . . . what would be the harm in it? Ryker was dead, and she needed to get inside that ball and find Raiythlen. Preferably before her glamour faded, and the guards escorted her to her death.

With that, Evangeline turned and gave the biggest, fakest smile. She took the Caster's offered arm, linking them together.

Avana led them to the front of the line, which earned them a few nasty comments, but no one made any move to remove them. Evangeline didn't realize how respected Avana's presence was in the castle.

The Rathan at the door assessed them with bored eyes. "Your names, please."

"Avana Quincara, and this here is my guest."

The Rathan flipped a few pages before scribbling something on the parchment. "Miss Quincara, you may enter. However, you are not permitted to bring guests."

Avana blew the guard a kiss. If she wasn't standing so close, Evangeline wouldn't have noticed the dust that flitted from her hand into the Rathan's face. "Darling, is that any way to treat an old friend?" Avana brushed the Rathan's arm with a seductive prowess. "Please, we won't cause any trouble."

The Rathan's eyes glazed over, and he smiled. "Of course, anything for you." He bowed and allowed them to enter. "Please, enjoy." Evangeline squirmed. She had almost forgotten how powerful Avana was.

The two of them walked past the Rathan and into the ballroom. The castle was an enormous structure with architecture and décor to stir even the most stubborn of people's admiration, but the one room that stole the breath away from everyone who entered was the ballroom. Although Evangeline had been in what was popularly known as "the glass room" multiple times, it was still as amazing as the first.

No, it was surreal.

White tile, fashioned with a small black cross design on each segment, lined the floors. They shone so brightly that the entire floor appeared aglow. The roof was structured in a dome shape, built out of thick, sheer glass. An array of colors slashed at the sky from the setting sun as clearly as if she stood right outside. In the distance, no building obstructed the enormous expanse of white ground. Tall, lengthy trees whirled in the winter breeze behind the frozen park, segregated by bricked pathways and lampposts that lined its perimeter.

They passed series of small tables, enshrouded with purple embroidered cloths and small white candles. A few Nytes already gathered around them, others collecting themselves outside, on the balcony, to get a better glimpse at the scenery. Evangeline decided if she was going to speak to Raiythlen privately, the balcony would be her best bet.

"Glorious, isn't it? The Aerians certainly know how to put on a show," Avana said, guiding her to a table before handing her a small glass. "I can't tell you how relieved I am to see you here. I wasn't sure if you would come, or if you would be able to."

"That makes two of us," Evangeline said.

"Judging by your glamour, I'm assuming Lord Ryker doesn't know you're here."

Evangeline bit back the bile that came up her throat. "No. I'm certain."

The two rings on Avana's fingers clinked against her glass as she brought it to her lips. She took a sip before gently placing it back down on the table. "So, when did you start working for my brother?"

Evangeline reached for her own glass and paused. "I don't know what you're talking about." She then tilted her head back and took a hearty swig of her drink.

"Well, I'm certainly not inclined to believe Peredians are willingly handing out glamour potions now."

Evangeline waved her hand dismissively.

Avana curved a loose black tendril behind her ear, the silver earring dangling where she brushed it. "Caster magic can be useful and powerful. It can also be dangerous and flawed." She turned to look at her. "And if you know what to look for, professionals like myself can always identify the scent of a lingering spell. Like the subtle breeze of something familiar but intangible."

Evangeline's grip tightened on the stem of her glass. "Your point?"

"The first time we brought you back from that cell, I could smell him on you like a thick, disgusting coat." Her nose scrunched. "I can still smell it. Whatever magic he used on you still remains."

Evangeline tipped back the glass and drank the rest of its

contents. A blissful lightheadedness crept upon her. "What are you talking about?" she said, looking around to see if she could steal another drink.

Avana shrugged. "I'm assuming he marked you. It usually carries a very strong, distinctive scent, one I'm familiar with. It was how Raiythlen found me here in Peredia—before I realized he was tracking me." She peered down at her glass. "He regretted it, however, when I left him for dead outside the kingdom. Where he *should* have remained."

Evangeline mulled over her words, thinking back to the bursts of light she had seen on that mountainside. Her brows rose in realization. That had been Raiythlen and Avana fighting. *But why did Raiythlen's own sister leave him to die like that? Did they hate each other that much?* Avana's words sank into her skin, making it crawl. She felt the urge to itch at it, like she could peel off whatever was on her. "How do I get rid of it? This mark?"

"Finding the Caster's symbol and rubbing a little salt on it should do the trick. The mark could be anywhere, but it would most likely be in a place you wouldn't think to look or would be unable to see without the help of another."

Evangeline wanted to growl, to rip out that puss-filled Caster's throat. She hated how Ryker monitored her every move, and she certainly wasn't willing to trade one controlling Nyte for another.

She jumped when Avana gently touched her hands. "I understand my actions have not been wholly truthful, but it has all been for your sake. Remember, you are the reason I am here." Avana looked at where her mark would be through her disguise. "I find you invaluable, Evangeline. I would do everything to protect you. Raiythlen only sees you as a pawn in his game. You can't trust him."

Evangeline yanked her hands away. "I don't trust either of

you." She turned away, peering through the crowd. Now would be a beautiful time for said Caster to appear. She had a few words to say to him.

"That's fair. And you don't have to. All I ask is that you listen to what I have to say, to what I have to show you. You are connected to Anali, to my family, and you have every right to know your own history. I simply want to help you."

And help yourself, Evangeline thought.

Avana glanced over her shoulder. Several Aerians were walking their way. "I hate to leave you so soon, but I must endure a few pleasantries before I can sneak away again. If you want to hear what I have to say, meet me on the balcony as soon as the music begins." She didn't wait for Evangeline's response as she walked away.

Alone, Evangeline shrank away from the table to the outskirts of the ballroom. Now that she was by herself—a human with a potential price on her head, in the middle of a pit of Nytes—her previous fears and worries came back with a vengeance. She hugged the wall as much as possible to avoid any unwanted attention. Her eyes scanned the crowd, but she still didn't see Raiythlen.

Nytes continued to trickle into the ballroom by the time twilight had arrived, the light from the sun replaced by glass chandeliers hanging on chains so thin they looked to be floating in midair. Humans scattered around, offering food and drink on silver platters.

Not wanting to deny herself all the pleasures an Aerian ball offered, Evangeline obliged herself to a few more bubbly drinks and little bite-sized sensations. She hid her uneasiness by taking gulps from her glass, her mind a war of thoughts. *What if Raiythlen doesn't show up? What if he knew about Avana and was avoiding me?* Another drink. *Should I try to approach Ceven? Would I be able* to, surrounded by so many Nytes? And another. *What if he decides it's too dangerous and forces us to leave without Lani? Or worse, what if he found out the truth? Would he turn me in?*

Evangeline took another swallow of her drink, and her worries seemed less and less. Soon, a smile grazed her lips, and she swayed to an unheard melody, gazing out into the crowd, a strange sense of nostalgia taking hold of her. She couldn't define it, but it was there. Reminding her of things she hadn't known existed. Her dancing in decadent gowns, being greeted by hundreds of people, all of whom had come for her alone.

She glanced down at her empty glass. Maybe she had drunk too much.

"Another drink, my lady?"

Someone put a silver tray in her line of sight, but she declined. When said tray almost collided into her skull, Evangeline turned to scowl and came face-to-face with Raiythlen. Granted, she hadn't recognized him at first—he had brown hair and sported a beard now—but he couldn't hide those crystal-blue eyes. Eyes that peered at her with a predatory stare no human possessed.

Dressed in a slave's uniform, his horns hidden beneath his hair, he appeared human. "Raiythlen?" she whispered.

"Sorry, my lady, have we met?" But his smirk told her all she needed to know.

She snarled, and he winked at her. It took every ounce of control to not slam a fist into his face. He was the reason her entire world was now upside down. That she not only risked punishment, but a fate worse than death if the king caught her. And she had stupidly believed him.

"You *tricked* me!" Evangeline hissed.

"I would never do such a thing. Care for another drink?"

Evangeline saw red. She reached out and took a fistful of his shirt.

Raiythlen lifted his tray higher, offering its contents to other Nytes in the area, drawing attention to them. "I'm surprised Lord Ryker hasn't made an appearance yet." He raised his voice. "You wouldn't have anything to do with that, would you, my lady?"

Evangeline immediately released his shirt and balled her hands at her sides. She tried to calm herself with thoughts of throwing him through the glass wall.

More Nytes encroached upon their small area, and Evangeline stepped away to gain some space when Raiythlen placed his foot in her path. She lost her balance and grabbed his shoulders for support at the same time he leaned in to catch her. The position put their faces close to one another, their noses touching. Evangeline was dumbfounded when she met his gaze, surprised by the seriousness in it. Her earlier rage returned tenfold, but before she could shove him away, he leaned closer.

"We still have a deal," he whispered, his lips brushing hers before stepping back.

She snatched a glass from his tray. "Thank you for the drink," she spat before turning on her heel and walking as far away from the Caster as she could manage.

If Evangeline thought she had been on edge before, now she leaped from it into deep, dark waters. She knew she needed to go back and demand he help her find Lani, but she was worried if she stuck around any longer, she would try to kill him instead. Taking another swig from her new glass, she returned to the outskirts of the ball. She had already lost track of Raiythlen, but she was sure he'd return. And next time she would try to control her emotions.

The room looked uneven by the time she finished her third drink. She leaned against the wall to hold herself up. *Okay, I need to stop. I can't do anything if I'm drunk.* The ballroom felt too hot, too loud, and she eyed the door to the balcony when the entire room dropped in volume. Nytes naturally cleared a pathway leading to the door. She couldn't see over the crowd, but judging by the wave of bows and soft murmurs, she knew that the ball's hosts had arrived.

Evangeline squeezed herself as close to the front as possible. She recognized the pair of beautiful blue wings, the tips painted gold.

Ceven was here, but he wasn't alone.

The woman at his arm flashed a dazzling smile at the star-struck audience around them. Ceven wore a dark gray coat, his hair slicked back, while the female Aerian's gold gown spanned out fashionably, her pale blond hair in a semi up-do.

"Who is this puss-filled Aerian?" Evangeline growled, then covered her mouth and looked around. No one paid her any attention, too caught up in whispering amongst themselves.

Gods, I need to get out of here before I get myself killed.

But she couldn't tear her eyes away from them. She shouldn't be surprised. One day Ceven would have to start courting women, at the king's behest. Still, it didn't stop the pain she felt at the image before her. The girl's hand in his, her body pressed close, Ceven's responding smile as he beamed down at her. This was where he belonged. With his people, with someone who was his equal.

With me, he would only get more ridicule, she thought.

And now, possibly, a death sentence.

Her heart hardened as she dragged her eyes away to find Xilo and Tarry trailing close behind them, dressed in their usual dark, steel armor with gold wings engraved on their breasts.

Farther behind, with his own set of Royal Guards, was Prince Sehn.

He kept his mahogany hair loose tonight, the tip of it brushing his elbows. The smile he wore was elegant and methodical, similar to his fashion statement—a deep red robe, buttoned to the top, rather than brazenly exposed. His burgundy wings stretched back, the muscle taut, the tips brushing the floor as he walked past her and joined Ceven and the Aerian woman toward the back of the ball room.

King Calais was last to arrive, accompanied by the Royal Guard. His presence demanded attention, demanded the crowd's fear and respect. As much as the king terrified Evangeline, she could only stare in awe as he elongated his wings in an arrogant display of dominance. Nytes subtly tried to catch the stray feathers that freed themselves from his wings. She had heard rumors that no other Aerian had ever possessed golden wings. She was sure a single feather would sell for a hefty price. *Maybe I should try catching one.* She giggled and frowned at the sound.

Long white hair was woven into several braids down the king's back, the gold strands matching the golden lining of his deep purple coat, the collar protruding out, gold fans outlining the sides of his rigid face. Casting a faint smile, if it could even be called one, the king rescinded his wings, the strength of them once more tucking into the curve of his back. It was then she noticed the man trailing behind him.

No . . .

Evangeline stared, open-mouthed.

It was Lord Ryker.

CHAPTER 40

⁓ CEVEN ⁓

C even tried to match his brother's demeanor, but he wasn't cut out to be a diplomat. He hated crowds, hated the attention, and didn't care for the endless stream of questions and proposals, just for them to go behind his back and whisper, "Why would the king allow the queen's love child to stay in the royal family?" or "The poor king has to live with his wife's betrayal every day." As if Ceven didn't have ears.

King Calais, Ryker, Sehn and himself walked to the hidden set of stairs that led to a second floor balcony overlooking the ballroom. His brother eloquently disengaged from the lingering group of Nytes while Ceven shot them a smile, sliding past without so much as a backward glance. The woman beside him loosened her grip on his arm when they approached the stairs. He still couldn't remember her name. Rose? Roseanne?

"I hope to see you later this evening for a dance, Your

Highness." The Aerian woman gave a sultry smile before lifting her skirt, curtsying, and backing away into the crowd.

Ceven managed a nod. The girl was beautiful, he could admit, and everything the king wanted, considering he had been the one to suggest Ceven escort the lady. He hoped she would forget about the dance and walked up the stairs.

On the landing, a narrow table sat, along with several purple chairs facing the ballroom. Ceven took a spot at the end, while Sehn, Ryker, and the king followed suit. When the Royal Guard finished shuffling behind them, silence descended upon the room as the king stood.

His voice sliced through the air. "I humbly thank all of you for joining us here tonight. I couldn't be prouder of my two sons, your princes. Let us partake in this celebration on behalf of what they have accomplished for Peredia and what they will accomplish in the future. Be merry!" The cheers from the Nytes were almost deafening in the glass room. Ceven raised his glass in a mock toast.

Streams of Nytes pressed up the stairs to bear their greetings. Hands folded, Ceven kept his lips into a permanent smile, his cheeks straining. A lady here, blessing them for their safe travels, while another, older gentleman offered his daughter's hand in marriage. Ceven's skin crawled, his leg shaking. Sea watery hells, he wanted this night to end.

An older Aerian woman came toward them, babbling about how lovely the two princes were, though her gaze remained on Sehn while Ceven glared at Lord Ryker. *I swear, if he put her back in that cell . . .* Ceven's hand dug into the silk of his trousers. After he'd left Ryker's suite, he had Barto keep watch, in case any harm came to Evangeline. In the meantime, the king had summoned his presence and forced him to bow on the cold floor of his study. Calais's gray eyes cast down on him as if he was a criminal and not a man he used to call son.

Tonight, you will be respectable, presentable, and will follow my every command. Is that clear? the king had said.

Ceven had kept his eyes lowered as he nodded at the king.

I have been relenting, and generous in your freedom, but your time is up. Now, you need to accept your role, accept my authority completely. Or die a traitor's death.

Ceven had quivered with rage, but he bit his tongue. Waiting.

I have several ladies in mind, all of whom would prosper our kingdom tremendously. I will make the final decision, and a marriage will be arranged. The king had leaned forward, his lip upturned in a sneer. *It isn't custom, but since your presence here disgusts me so, I will send you to live with her family. Refuse this, you refuse your king. I will leave you this last and final decision*

As if I ever had a choice.

The king's smile had been without a single shred of kindness. Calais then schooled him on his potential marriage candidates, like Ceven was a trophy to be sold off. Every second that passed, his rage grew, while his worry for Evangeline rose in parallel. *We should've left while we had the chance. Now we're both prisoners here.* Ceven chuckled without mirth. No, they had been prisoners since the day fate placed them in this kingdom, under a tyrant's rule.

After what felt like ages, a brief respite was granted them. Ceven, without waiting for Xilo or Tarry to catch up, stormed from his chair before he acted upon the violent thoughts that he harbored toward the king and his pet—Ryker.

Ceven pushed his way through the crowd, refusing to make eye contact. He was done playing nice. Done playing the king's game. But first he needed to find Barto. Then Evangeline.

"Where did you pick up a lady like that?" Barto's voice

boomed over the crowd behind him. Ceven turned and his friend clapped him on the shoulder as Xilo and Tarry warded off potential visitors. From the corner of Ceven's eye, Rasha's figure approached them. Quan was nowhere to be seen.

"She looked as if she had a death grip on your arm, like you were ready to run away any minute." Barto's pupils were dilated, a relaxed expression on his face. With gold pants and a matching tunic over a deep green blouse, he certainly made a statement. His only saving grace was his brushed-back hair and the handsome smile he wore.

Ceven didn't reply or smile.

Barto frowned. "You're not still mad at me, are you? I told you it was two against one. Evangeline wanted to go back to that cell and Tarry wasn't helping the situation."

Ceven knew his friend was telling the truth, and where his loyalties lay. It wasn't his fault. Ceven should've stayed, but it was too late to worry about that now.

Finally, he cracked a small smile. "Maybe I should have escorted you instead."

"I would've made for a more pretty arm-piece, for sure." Barto winked.

Rasha caught up to them. Her braids were clasped back with several gold bands to match the small hoops that graced her one furred ear that twitched at the sight of Barto. Ceven didn't miss how she curled herself to stand behind his friend, giving herself a full view of the ballroom. Her maroon dress swayed before clinging to the strong curves of her body.

"I told you to stop running off," she snapped.

"Rasha! Didn't expect to see you so soon!" Barto's left ear flicked back before he turned around to snatch a drink off a nearby platter. He took the boy's hand and dropped a gold piece in it. "Good job, boy, keep them coming!"

The human holding the tray almost dropped it in surprise. He bowed, more than once, before scampering off.

"Still don't understand why Peredia doesn't compensate their slaves. I'm surprised another rebellion hasn't broken out," Barto said.

"Keep your mouth shut, lest you want the king to put your head on a pike," Rasha whispered, focused on the surrounding crowd.

Ceven pinched his nose and shook his head. One day Barto's bluntness was going to get him killed. "Where's Evangeline?"

Barto's expression turned serious. "Last I saw, she was headed to that one girl's place. Lani, I think you called her. Then . . ." He shuffled his feet. "I got distracted."

Ceven's heart dropped. He knew Evangeline wouldn't find Lani there. Or anywhere. She had been missing since the night he'd gone to check on her, but he didn't have the heart to tell her that. "*Distracted?*" His jaw tightened. "What do you mean?"

"I received a message from the empress."

Ceven paused at that, and Rasha shot Barto a brief glance before she resumed scanning the room.

His brows furrowed. "Do you have to go back?"

Barto licked his lips, his fingers readjusting his tunic. "No, it's . . . well . . . you're not going to like what she has to say."

Ceven didn't like the worried expression on his friend's face, which was usually so carefree. "What do you mean?"

"Not here," he said, gesturing for him to follow.

Ceven obliged, and Barto led them on to the balcony, Tarry, Xilo, and Rasha not far behind them.

The blast of cold air was far more pleasant than the hot ballroom of pressed bodies. Ceven stretched his arms, leaning against the railing, a few stray feathers blowing in the soft breeze. Barto mirrored him, and Rasha stood beside him.

His friend's eyes shifted to Tarry and Xilo standing behind Ceven, and he gave a small cough. "This matter . . . It's a little private."

Ceven nodded toward the two guards, and Xilo bowed his head, stepping away. Tarry kept his eyes trained on Barto and bent his knees. His dark purple wings spanned out before he propelled upward, blending into the darkened sky. A shot of envy sparked through Ceven, but he ignored it.

With more space, Barto sighed, a tumble of hot air escaping his mouth. "You know about the missing persons, the similarities in these cases between both of our countries?"

Ceven nodded.

"Well . . . it's worse than we'd have you believe." Barto took out a cigar from his pocket and lit it with a match. "Ceven . . . in this past year alone, we've had the highest record of missing people that Atiaca has ever seen. And the worst part is, you would think, with over hundreds of reports, there would be some clue, a body, a witness, *something*, but there is absolutely no trace of them. Just like here."

"So, it's pretty bad. This is nothing new, Barto. That's what we're trying to figure out." Ceven narrowed his eyes. "What did the empress say?"

Barto took an inhale from his cigar. "They tracked down a body. The rumors about the markings, everything, it's true. Apparently a few scouts found a poor Rathan covered in Castanian symbols."

"So, there's a group of Casters behind this."

Barto shrugged. "Maybe, but that's not the part you won't like."

He crossed his arms. "Spit it out, Barto."

Rasha's face remained stoic, but she shifted, her hand brushing her back. Reaching for something.

His friend sighed. He looked . . . nervous? "One marking stood out in particular, one I'm obligated to tell my empress about." He shoved the butt of his cigar into the railing. "It's the same one as Evangeline's."

Ceven didn't move, staring at him. "And?"

Barto looked at Rasha, whose hand clearly rested on a weapon hidden beneath her dress.

"And the empress wants us to take Evangeline into custody."

CHAPTER 41

⸰ EVANGELINE ⸰

Lord Ryker . . . It's Lord Ryker!
Evangeline stared as the man, she thought she'd murdered, walked past her. Only when their entourage gathered up the stairs did she break from her stupor.

"No . . ." she whispered to herself. "That can't be . . ."

Evangeline's jaw still hung ajar, and she snapped it shut. She didn't know how he was alive, or why she had heard nothing about her treason. But for now, she was glad she no longer had blood on her hands. That she wasn't a murderer.

Nytes immediately swarmed the landing, and Royal Guard members stood in their path until a line formed. When the king started speaking, the crowd of Nytes thinned around her and gathered closer to where the royals sat. Evangeline took the opportunity to look for a slave with brown hair and blue eyes.

Raiythlen couldn't have gone far. I still need to find Lani and get us out of here. She squirmed through Aerians and Rathans, all standing in clusters, whispering and gawking at the new arrivals. She passed a few human slaves, but one had been a woman, the other an older man. *Could he have changed disguises already?* She hoped not. She wasn't trying to stay for the entire ball.

Sweat trickled down the curve of her back as she stormed from one side of the ballroom to the other, but she wasn't any closer to finding him. She took a break and propped against the wall, fanning herself with her hand. She was getting nowhere. At this point, she was willing to even go find Avana or Ceven.

Evangeline glanced up at Ceven, perched beside the king. From this distance, she couldn't see his expression, but it had to be unpleasant. She didn't know when he would escape, if he ever would, but if Raiythlen didn't make an appearance, she'd have to ask Ceven for help. *But that'll be my last option.*

She perked up when music began to play, the soft melody luring Nytes out, turning the middle of the room into a dance floor. Avana's words rang in her head, and her stomach twisted. She'd sooner shove that Caster over the balcony then listen to what she had to say.

But what if she really knows what's happening to me? Maybe she can help me get rid of these hallucinations, these dreams? Not that Evangeline trusted anything coming from a Quincara, but standing here, doing nothing, wouldn't get her anywhere.

Evangeline removed herself from the wall, keeping her eyes peeled for Avana as she approached the glass doors to the balcony. Frigid air slapped at her face, the sweat along her back and neck like icy fire against her skin. The balcony stretched along the entire back length of the ballroom, the concrete landing separated into three parts by large shrubbery and iron benches at each interval. An Aerian couple gave her a passing glance as she searched for a black-haired female.

A flap of wings brought her attention to the sky as a dark winged raven soared overhead, toward the end of the balcony. Avana was here.

Her red curls blew as another gust of wind swept over the balcony. Wrapping her arms around herself, Evangeline followed the bird until she spotted the Caster. She was leaning against the iron railing, most of her figure hidden behind the thick bush. She didn't have a coat, but she didn't look bothered by the cold at all.

Avana peeked over her shoulder, and her face lit up. "I'm so glad you came."

Evangeline kept a reasonable amount of distance between them. "And I'm starting to regret it."

The bird flew down, and Avana held out her arm for it to land. Her eyes gazed into its black depths. She nodded. The raven lifted its wings and took off. "You may want to sit down for this." Avana gestured to the bench between them.

"I'll stand."

Avana shrugged, taking a seat for herself, legs crossed. "I won't waste your time, and I won't embellish the truth. What I'm about to tell you is exactly from Anali's journal, and you may choose to believe me or not."

Evangeline nodded, and another breeze of cold air rolled through. Her crossed arms tightened.

Avana opened her mouth, then closed it. She tilted her head as if pondering the words she was about to say. "Anali . . . she mentioned knowing a woman named Evangeline, with characteristics similar to you. And the fact that you've seen Anali in your dreams, found that hidden lab in that cave . . . I don't think this is all a coincidence." She inhaled. "Your dreams . . . and your visions, they're not hallucinations or a product of an over-active imagination. They're memories." She let out a breath and looked up at Evangeline, her blue eyes swirling with excitement and apprehension.

Evangeline stared back but kept her face dispassionate.

The Caster sighed. "I told you about the Shadow Doors, how they were used to teleport people and things. Well, I think Anali found a way to teleport someone through time."

Evangeline's eyes narrowed, but she remained quiet.

"Remember the Shadow Door we found in that ruin? I think . . . I think you were sent forward in time somehow." Avana took in Evangeline's expression and put up a hand. "I know it sounds crazy, and I didn't believe it at first either. But I was there . . . *We* were there. You felt the energy in that ruin, the immense pressure. It was unlike any other Shadow Door. Unlike anything I have ever experienced."

Evangeline couldn't help it. She started to giggle, then laughed, unable to control the surfacing hysteria. "You're crazy."

Avana's face darkened and her thumb flicked the nail of her ring finger with a loud click. "You don't have to believe me, but *don't you dare call me crazy.*" Her voice sharpened, like the unsheathing of an invisible blade.

Evangeline stopped laughing, the smile wiped from her face. "Fine. Then explain how I was only a child when I was found. You said Anali knew Evangeline as a woman."

"I don't know, but there is a correlation here. This is unknown magic. Perhaps it had an effect on you. A negative one."

Evangeline shook her head. Memories? She had been sent through time? She didn't know what else to make of what was happening to her, and these hallucinations . . . They felt real. Anali was real. But . . . it was too much right now. "I think it's time for me to go."

Avana stood and Evangeline stepped back. "I am not crazy." Her eyes widened. "One day I will unleash the truth on this world, and then you will believe me. *They will all* believe me."

Evangeline took another step back. Was this who Avana really was? A delusional, crazy Caster? She didn't want to stick around and find out.

Avana shook as her eyes focused on nothing. Evangeline kept the Caster in her line of sight, scared she would pounce on her at any moment, and crept backwards. Other Nytes gathered nearby. Feeling safer with mixed company, she tore her eyes away from the Caster woman and picked up her skirts.

And ran right into Ceven.

CHAPTER 42

~ CEVEN ~

"**A**re you alright, my lady?"

Ceven felt Rasha and Barto's eyes digging into his back as he steadied the Caster woman in front of him. Her curls wrapped around her face, her eyes wide and her skin cold to the touch.

"Y-yes, thank you," she got out. "Your Highness."

"If I didn't know better, I'd say you were running from someone." He cocked his brow.

She shifted her shoulders, pressing her body together as she shivered. "Just eager to get out of the cold."

Ceven didn't move or respond, his eyes snapping to the flare of her skirt where it collided with his leg. His eyes narrowed, trailing up and down her person.

"I-I need a drink, would you like to accompany me?" She

glanced over his shoulder and back to him. It was clear she wanted him alone.

Ceven didn't move. Barto's words still haunted him, and he was far from done with their conversation, but this Caster . . .

She lowered her voice. "Please, Your Highness, I think someone is following me." Her manicured fingers gently tugged on his arm.

He stared at her, debating how to proceed. Her expression wavered for a moment until he gave her a disarming smile and offered his arm. She hesitated, but then took it. Ceven glanced back at Barto and Rasha, and they all exchanged a knowing look. When he finished dealing with this woman, they would resume their conversation. Ceven opened the door and ushered them both back into the ballroom.

The noisy crowd overwhelmed him and he immediately missed the balcony's serenity. Once inside, all eyes were on them. Nytes turned their heads, whispering to their partners, and Ceven wished he could've stayed on the balcony the rest of the night. The Caster turned to him, but he ignored her and scanned the room. He needed to get them alone and in a position where she couldn't leave.

Where she was trapped with him.

He knew the best solution to his problem, taking her arm and pulling her toward the center of the room. Coupled Nytes danced to the combined lullaby of a harp and several string instruments, performed by the group of Rathans along the side of the glass room. Her expression became panicked, and something satisfactory welled inside him.

Got you now.

"Care to dance?" Ceven raised his eyebrows at her, his palm open and inviting.

Her smile thinned as she placed her palm into his. "I would be honored."

Like the Nytes surrounding them, he placed one hand upon her waist, the other twining with her fingers. They swayed. The woman's movements were uneven, and she moved her feet carelessly. Ceven's smile turned wicked. This was no lady.

He drifted his hand until it rested on her wrist and captured its slim girth in his grasp. "You can drop the act now."

She blinked at him. "Excuse me?"

"I know you're wearing a glamour." Ceven pulled her closer, seeing the terror in her eyes. Good. If this woman was dangerous, he needed the upper hand.

"A glamour?"

Ceven's hand traveled down her waist, and they both watched his hand disappear as it slipped past where her bodice should have ended and her gown fanned out. Her eyes widened. She was a good actress, but careless.

"I noticed when you ran into me," he said. "I know you're not a Caster. A Caster wouldn't have made such a grievous error."

To further rattle her, his hand grazed farther down and caressed her thigh before cupping her derriere. She jerked and yanked his hand back up to her waist. Her eyes shot daggers at him. "Please keep your hands where they belong, *Prince.*"

Something familiar rang in those words, but he ignored it as he tried to figure out who she was. Was she an assassin sent here to kill him or his brother? The king? Or was it information she desired? "Tell me who you are, or I will expose you in front of everyone. Right here. Right now." It was a bluff. He needed to keep this contained, in case others hid in their midst. But she didn't know that.

She swallowed. "It's me, Evangeline."

At the mention of Evangeline, his grip tightened. He didn't

like how this woman knew his connection to Evangeline, or that she was trying to impersonate her. "Don't play games with me. This is your last chance. Who. Are. You?"

"I just told you!"

Ceven turned away, making a show of opening his mouth, when she squeezed out the words, "Ask me anything! I'll prove it to you!"

He turned back to her with a callous smirk. This woman wasn't Evangeline, but he'd play along. "Very well. If you really are Evangeline, do you love me?"

The women went silent, and he raised a brow, expecting her to falsely declare her love for him. It wasn't until her face matched the fiery color of her hair that an inkling of doubt gathered in his mind.

"L-love you? What kind of blasted question is that?" she snapped, her face a model display of outrage. "You could ask me anything, and you ask me that?"

His brows knitted together, taken aback by her response. A response he expected from the real Evangeline, not this stranger. *There's no way.* Evangeline couldn't be here, and with a glamour, no less. Then again . . . Barto had lost sight of her, and she had admitted to working with Avana before. Maybe now was no different.

Ceven's smirk faded. "Eve?"

"That's what I said!" she growled.

Please keep your hands where they belong, Prince.

His cheeks got hot. This really was Evangeline.

Amazement, immediately followed by frustration, swept over him. "Where have you been? Where did you get that glamour? I swear—"

Evangeline stepped on his foot and twirled away, but he

kept her hand tight in his grasp. He pulled her back to him, her fake gown spinning as she braced herself against his chest.

"Stop yelling," Evangeline whispered through her teeth.

"Then you better start explaining yourself, *my lady*."

Now that he knew it was Evangeline in his arms, too many eyes and ears lingered around them. His hand snaked around her waist, molding her body to him as his wings wrapped around both of them. This close, he got a wisp of her scent: lilac and vanilla kissed with something else. Something new and . . . different.

"I . . . I messed up," she bit out.

Why didn't you leave with me? Why do you keep leaving me in the dark? Why don't you trust me anymore? Am I just the means to an end for you? "That doesn't answer my question," he said. Her leg collided with his, and he winced. "And stop stepping on my feet. You're a horrible dancer, you know?"

"Ceven, Lani's missing, and we need to leave the kingdom now before . . ." She narrowed her eyes at him.

He forced himself to remain calm at the mention of Lani. He had wanted to find out where she had gone before Evangeline got involved, but now . . . it was too late. He continued in a steady tone, "Before what?"

Her lips thinned. "It's nothing. I'm simply overreacting."

She was shutting him out. Again.

There was a cue in the song, and Ceven moved his hand, forcing her to spin. Evangeline stumbled and tried to regain her footing.

She flashed him a hot look. "You did that on purpose."

"You know I hate it when you lie to me, Eve. Tell me the truth."

"That's rich, coming from you."

His face flamed for the second time that evening. Yes, he

had lied to her, but couldn't she see it was to keep her safe? That it was up to him to protect her, since she had no idea of self-preservation?

He grimaced, but before he could respond, another arm took her by the wrist and spun her away from him. Evangeline squealed, and he tried grabbing her when she disappeared into the dancing crowd—but not before he saw the familiar gray eyes and hardened face of Lord Ryker.

CHAPTER 43

～☞ EVANGELINE ☜～

Evangeline felt her body shut down. A coldness, number than Peredia's winter breeze, chilled every bone, every muscle, and every nerve.

Ryker looked over her shoulder and gave Ceven a smirk. Evangeline didn't have time to witness Ceven's response as he forced them deeper into the swarm of Nytes.

"You've been a bad girl, Evangeline." His long hair swayed as he forced them into a gentle shuffle, back and forth. "If you'd told him the truth, I would've had to kill him."

"I-I-I—" she stammered.

His lips titled up at one corner. "My, look how frightened you are. As much fun as it would be to continue this charade, it'd be a shame if you soiled yourself right here on the dance floor."

She heard him but couldn't register what he was saying over the pounding in her head. *Run, run, run!* her legs screamed.

His hand moved to her lower back, pulling her closer. "I told you, we had a deal."

It took a moment before his words penetrated the fog of panic clouding her mind. Her eyebrows came together. "What?"

Lord Ryker smiled, but there was something devilishly familiar in his features. Then he winked at her.

No...

"It can't be..." Evangeline gave up the pretense of trying to dance. "You... are you...?"

He chuckled. "The king is getting arrogant. It was embarrassingly easy to pretend to be his right-hand man. Though, I think this is my proudest work yet."

An immense pressure lifted off her shoulders so suddenly she thought she might pass out. It wasn't really Lord Ryker. He wasn't there to drag her off to be killed, but that meant... "Raiythlen? But how...?"

"I've been in the business for a while now, my dear. It'd be wise not to underestimate me. Or ask questions you really don't want to know the answers to."

She shook. "I want to kill you."

"Like you did your poor father?"

Her teeth ground together. "You lied to me."

"And you went behind my back and worked with my sister."

"Worked with your sister? The last thing—"

Raiythlen dipped her back in sync with the tune, forcing her to wrap her hands around his neck to keep from falling.

"I'm not here to fight," he murmured into her ear as he pulled her back up. "I found a letter in Lani's room. It's addressed to you."

All the fight left her at the mention of Lani. "A letter? From who?" She knew Lani couldn't read or write. Unless she had help. "Where did you find it? I was just in her room." And she had seen no letter.

"I may have come across it earlier and taken it for insurance purposes." His eyes twinkled. "I had to make sure you would come to the ball, after all."

She reached to choke him when he said, "Lift up your dress."

"Excuse me?"

"Your real one, not the glamour's. Don't worry, no one will see under the illusion. Except me, of course." He grinned.

Gods, she hated this man. "And why would I do that?"

"Do you want the letter or not?"

She didn't spare him any in her agitation, huffing as she dragged up the front of her actual dress, grateful for the long undergarment stockings she had worn this morning. She hoped the glamour also hid the redness in her cheeks.

Raiythlen maneuvered them until Evangeline's back was to the crowd. She watched as his hands disappeared into her once-solid dress. Icy fingers probed her bare stomach. She gasped, instinct driving her away.

"This isn't going to work if you look like you're trying to run from me, my dear," he whispered through a smile.

Evangeline bit her lip and focused on glaring at him as his hand slipped beneath the waistband of her stocking. She concentrated on controlling her breathing and the slight swaying to the music's beat as Raiythlen touched her more intimately than anyone had ever done before. She felt a slip of paper slide into the front of her waistband, but his hand lingered, gliding slowly back up to pause right beneath her belly button.

"That's enough," she barked. He removed his hand, and she dropped her dress, grateful for the extra barrier.

The song came to an end and Raiythlen spun her around

one last time. Evangeline managed to keep her balance. "Your prince can't save you, but I can." He squeezed her hand. "Meet me back at Lani's quarters as soon as you leave here. You kept your end of the deal. Allow me to do my part."

She replied by curling her upper lip and turning on her heel, her fake curls spinning. She tore through the crowd, bumping shoulders and elbowing Nytes in passing. Some hurled her curses, other sharp stares, but she ignored them. The only thing she cared about was the letter that brushed her stomach. She was going to figure out what happened to Lani and hopefully survive the rest of the night.

Evangeline reached the large double doors, not feeling the heat of Sehn's gaze on her back as she left the ballroom.

CHAPTER 44

～ EVANGELINE ～

Evangeline tightened her coat as she trekked through a
new layer of snow. She approached the slave quarters, her
glamour almost transparent.

Getting on her hands and knees, she propped open Lani's
window when a wolf howled nearby. Her head snapped up. The
vast white field was empty and shrouded in shadow aside from
the lamps and the lights of the castle twinkling in the distance.

Another howl. This one closer.

Evangeline yanked at the edge of the window until it
squeaked open and tumbled in. She landed on her side with
a wince; the sound breaking the room's unsettling quietness.
Without Lani filling the space, the room felt colder. Empty.

And painfully lonely.

She closed the window and fumbled around in the dark
toward the fireplace, rekindling it. When sparks flew up, she

pulled out the letter from her waistband, squinting at the parchment. The paper had been creased multiple times, dark stains gathered around the edges. *Is this . . . blood?*

She held her breath and opened the letter.

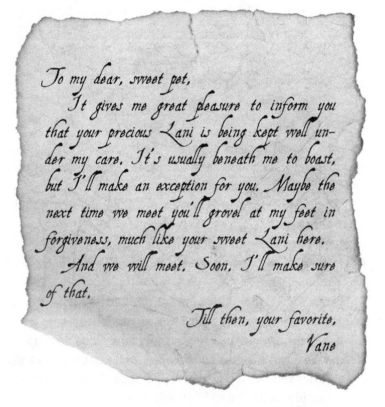

To my dear, sweet pet,

It gives me great pleasure to inform you that your precious Lani is being kept well under my care. It's usually beneath me to boast, but I'll make an exception for you. Maybe the next time we meet you'll grovel at my feet in forgiveness, much like your sweet Lani here.

And we will meet. Soon, I'll make sure of that.

Till then, your favorite,
Vane

Her eyes finished reading the last sentence when she crumpled the paper into a ball. She wanted to scream and cry, but all she did was stare at the crinkled sphere in her hand.

Vane had taken Lani.

The room shifted, and Evangeline leaned against the wall,

the letter rolling out of her hands. *Vane has Lani . . . He's taken her . . . No, no . . .*

No, Anali! Don't let them take us! A child screamed in her ear.

Evangeline put her head in her hands. Not again. Not now. The walls of her skull pulsated. Her legs shook, but before she could make it to the bed, she collapsed. Darkness folded over her.

"No! Please don't take them! I beg of you!"

Three armed humans stormed the house. Terror gripped Evangeline as Anali shoved her and Jaden behind her, but they both peeked out from around Anali's waist.

Anali held out her arms. "I can control them! You can't take them to that place. They're just children!"

"They're not kids, Anali. They're weapons. And they belong to the military along with the rest of their kind." The man raised his gun at her. "Move."

She refused. "These children are not our way out of this war. They have every right to live as you and I."

"They're monsters. You did your job, now let us do ours."

The man fired his gun and struck Anali's hand before she could cast her spell. Another man came behind Evangeline and Jaden, gripping their arms. Evangeline snarled and sunk her teeth into her attacker's hand. The man howled, and the others wrestled her to the floor, holding her immobile. Jaden growled, trying to get out of the man's grasp, but the human slammed the butt of his gun into Jaden's temple and he crumpled to the floor.

"Let me go!" Evangeline cried. "Anali!"

Two humans shoved Anali's face into their kitchen floor

and clasped metal to her wrists. Evangeline met her gaze and cried, struggling as the other soldiers dragged her and Jaden from the house. Their only chance at a normal life ripped away from them.

Evangeline's eyes fluttered open, and a headache pierced her temple. She massaged her head and sat up. Coats covered her and her head rested on a makeshift pillow made of clothes. Raiythlen slept next to her, his back to the wall and chin to his chest.

Evangeline recalled the dream, and her tongue snaked out, licking her lip. No blood.

They're not dreams or hallucinations. They're memories . . . She frowned. Even if she believed Avana, it didn't explain why she was here. Why she had been sent forward in time—if that was the case—or what her real identity was.

And it still didn't fix the fact that she had failed. That Lani was taken.

Horns no longer hovered in her peripheral, and her red hair was blond again. She tried to stand, but her head hummed in pain. It was black outside, but she knew her time was running out.

Using the wall for support, she found her feet and glanced at the sleeping Caster. His black hair fell across his face, the shadow of a beard grazing his jaw. He looked harmless, almost inviting, but she knew the truth. *This Caster better have a plan.*

She shook his shoulder. "It's me!" she exclaimed when his knife almost sliced a hole in her neck.

"Evangeline." Raiythlen looked apologetic and lowered his blade. "How was your little nap?"

"I didn't sleep, I passed out."

"And took a nasty fall." Raiythlen pressed his palm to her forehead. "Are you feeling better?"

Evangeline knocked his hand away. "I'm fine." First, he threatened to kill her, then tricked her into murder, and now he was acting concerned?

His brows rose. "You were screaming in your sleep. I almost had to gag you."

"I don't have time to waste. Vane has Lani. We need to find him before . . ." She choked on the last bit of her words.

He frowned. "I know where they are." His icy gaze locked with hers. "But you're not going to like it."

"Tell me."

He took a moment to ponder his words, his eyes grazing her marked hand. "In Ryker's suite, after you . . . took care of him . . . I found a journal. A list of names of every slave in the castle, showing who's next and who's already been taken."

"And?" This wasn't news to her.

Raiythlen's eyes narrowed, but he continued, "There are a lot more people involved than I had initially thought. Evangeline . . . hundreds of people have already been taken, and a lot more are to follow. This hasn't been happening just in the castle, but all over Peredia."

Evangeline swallowed. She hadn't known that. "I'm aware this is bad, but I don't see how this is going to tell me where she is."

His voice remained calm. "With that amount of people and a lack of evidence, wherever they're being taken, it would have to be in a nearby place no one ever goes to, cut off from the rest of the castle." He looked up at her. "After some investigating, I found out they have been using the abandoned west wing as their base of operations."

Evangeline blinked. "The west wing? That place is cursed, there's no way anyone would go near there." Especially not the king who wanted nothing more than to forget his dead wife. "There's been countless people who've gone there and never come out."

"Exactly."

Evangeline crossed her arms. "I mean both humans *and* Nytes. Whoever's involved in this would have disappeared too, like the rest of the guards that have gone in there over the years to investigate."

"Maybe something has changed."

Evangeline sucked in a sharp breath. "Do you really think Lani is there?"

He nodded.

If Raiythlen was right . . . "And how are we supposed to save her?" There was no way she could do this on her own, and he knew it. "Let me guess: you want to make another deal?"

"No. I'm giving you a choice."

She uncrossed her arms and tilted her head.

He stood and stretched. "If we don't save your friend now, she may not live to see tomorrow. On the other hand, if you do this, you may not live to see tomorrow, as well." He pierced her with a stony stare. "Saving her won't be easy. I don't know what's inside the west wing, but it'll be dangerous. For both of us."

"That's not much of choice."

He put a hand on her shoulder. It was warm, comforting, and the look in his eyes kept her from jerking away.

"Or we could leave Peredia tonight. We would go back to Sundise Mouche and you would be far from here, far from the king's wrath. You would be safe, and free to make your own decisions."

She stared at him. He was serious. *To be my own person, to choose what I want to do, to go where I want to go. I wouldn't be hunted or tried for murder.* She laughed to herself. It had always been a fantasy of hers—and would remain that way.

"So, are you willing to die for your friend? Or live a life you've only dreamed of?" The curve of his lips proved he knew the moment he asked her.

Her eyes slid from the cocky tilt of his lips to his blue irises. She almost snorted. She still regretted saving the Caster's life, but now, in this moment, she regretted it a little less. But only a little.

Her own lips quirked, the corner curving up in a mocking salute to his own. *I never had a choice. Not really.*

"You already know my answer."

EPILOGUE

In the shadows of a cave, a man held the remains of a human heart. It was warm, red flesh drenching his hand. A sinister smile on his lips, he bit into the tender organ, its livelihood dripping down his chin.

Two Nytes, locked in the cage beside him, whimpered.

He dropped the heart on the ground, next to the human with a gaping hole in her chest, her arms and legs scarred with symbols. Wiping his chin, the man turned his green gaze on his next two victims.

"Who's next?" he said.

The Aerian woman wailed. Dirt covered her short brown hair, the black liner around her eyes smudged from crying. The Caster didn't respond, his hands holding the sides of his head where his horns should have been, his eyes staring blankly ahead.

The man tilted his head before reaching for the Aerian woman.

She jerked back, screaming. A tumble of words fell from her, pleading for her life, as he dragged her to the metal table in the center of the cave.

He tied her to the table, muffling her protest with a cloth. Picking up a needle, he licked his finger before flipping through the pages of the old, forgotten journal next to him. The outline of three triangles enclosed in a circle of runes on his right hand illuminated in the dim flicker from the candle beside him. He began to carve into her skin.

The woman yelled into the cloth, shaking and jerking her body.

"Ryker is late today," he murmured to himself and dipped the needle into the pool of ink, returning to where he'd left off.

GLOSSARY

Aerian(s)- A humanoid winged creature with extraordinary strength.

Rathan(s)- A humanoid creature that shares a likeness with a specific type of animal. Possess a greater agility and sense of smell.

Caster(s)- A humanoid creature with horns and the ability to perform magic through their blood.

Halfling(s)- creature born from two different species.

Nyte(s)- Umbrella term for all superhuman species: Aerians, Rathans, Casters, and Wretched.

Castanian- Primary language spoke in Sundise Mouche and by most Casters.

Atiacan(s)- Primary language spoke in Atiaca. Also refers to a citizen of Atiaca, or anything of Atiacan decent.

Peredian(s)- Primary language spoke in Peredia. Also refers to a citizen of Peredia, or anything of Peredian decent.

Frostlite- A mineral found in the Frostsnare mountains. Reacts to Caster magic.

Book Two of the Nyte Series

Coming Soon!

ACKNOWLEDGEMENTS

Boy, was getting this book published a decade long project. Despite the years of writing, revising, then revising some more, I couldn't have done it without the amazing, awesome, spectacular friends and family that have put up with my story ramblings on more than one occasion.

To my incredible, always motivated friend, Tiffany, for seeing the potential my book had and sludging through my horrendous, long-winded first draft, thank you so much for your help and being a dear friend to me for all these years. Your insight made my book into what it is today.

Thank you to my amazing writing buddy and number one cheerleader, Brooke. Your words of encouragement have made this whole process that much better. Thank you so much for your help in both the early revision stages and pre-publication. Glad to have met you and excited to see where your writing journey takes you.

Katarina, thank you for lending me your shoulder to cry on and for being a patient listener in everything. I'm happy to have someone like you to talk to when the road gets bumpy.

Amanda, I appreciate you taking the time to give me some much needed feedback, and answering the gazillion questions I had for this manuscript. You're the best! Thank you, Victoria, for your honest words in the early chapters and support.

To WriteMentor, and its amazing founder Stuart White, thank you for creating a platform to help authors, like myself, find the confidence and skill to really make their stories shine. I am so incredibly grateful to have worked with the talented author Amber R. Duell. What I learned from working with you was invaluable and I can't express how appreciative I am for your mentorship. That summer my manuscript leveled up tremendously, thanks to you.

Alexandra Ott, you're an amazing editor and I learned so much through your feedback. You really helped me iron out all the wrinkles and make this novel come together beautifully.

I never would have made it this far in life if it wasn't for the constant love and support from Sharron, Debra, Shannon, Cindy, Tarry, Jeff, Missy, Justin, and Patty. So happy to call you guys family. To my younger sister and brother, Micaela and Evan, I love you guys bunches.

And to my small community of friends: Kaitlyn, Amainaa, Catherine, Josh, Brandon, Erick, Callen, Mikey, Travis, David, and Anthony, thanks for putting up with my awful accents and even worse dancing skills. You guys are an awesome group of people that I can count on to have my back.

To my longtime friend, Briana, and kick ass cousin, Makenzie, who put up with all my weird shenanigans as a kid, I love you guys so much and can't wait for you two to read the finished product of what used to be a childhood dream all those years ago.

ALEXANDRIA CAINLOCKE is a toss-up between artist, musician, writer, and avid gamer. Coffee is her number one life source and second love to her amazing friends and family. The sunshine state of Florida is where she was born and still resides. Kingdom of Nyte is her first novel.